Game of Twins –
The Special Agent

By
Tom Ranseen

Table of Contents

A note from the author v

Part I 1

Chapter 1 – The Yacht 2

Chapter 2 – New Caanan 3

Chapter 3 – Special Agent Hinke 9

Chapter 4 – J Edgar Hoover 14

Chapter 5 – The Pool Table 18

Chapter 6 - The Polaroids 23

Chapter 7 – Marilyn Monroe 29

Chapter 8 – Miss Gandy 37

Chapter 9 – The Chalkboard 44

Chapter 10 – The Sheriff of New Canaan 48

Chapter 11 – The Guesthouse 55

Chapter 12 – Tommy Muldoon 58

Chapter 13 - Greenwich 62

Chapter 14 – The Gossip 68

Chapter 15 – Dinner with Priscilla 73

Chapter 16 – Witches? 80

Chapter 17 – Get Out of My Town 82

Chapter 18 – Helen and Derby 84

Chapter 19 – Hoover, Hinke & Helen 91

Chapter 20 – Card Tricks 105

Part 2 109

Chapter 21 - Post Hoover 110

Chapter 22 – Twins Murders Redux 118

Chapter 23 – Anniston, Alabama..................................124

Chapter 24 – The Pool Ball.......................................133

Chapter 25 – APD Detective Hollis Delacroix.........................140

Chapter 26 – Dinner in Atlanta....................................146

Chapter 27 - The Rules...152

Chapter 28 – More Breadcrumbs....................................154

Chapter 29 – The Victorian 165

Part 3 171

Chapter 30 – The Invitation......................................172

Chapter 31 – Twins Murders in Georgia 174

Chapter 32 – Mareissa & Matilde.................................178

Chapter 33 - The Granite Crime Scene.............................183

Chapter 34 - Orville Johnston.....................................194

Chapter 35 - Hinke & Giles Make a Deal...........................200

Chapter 36 – Barron Brevard's Edict 208

Chapter 37 – Ted Davies 212

Chapter 38 – The Money 214

Chapter 39 - Orville, Matilde and Mareissa 219

Chapter 40 – The Killers...231

Chapter 41 - Prison 239

Chapter 42 – Asheville 241

Chapter 43 – The Conspiracy 252

Chapter 44 – The Godfather 263

Chapter 45 – The Apology..267

Chapter 46 – Delacroix, Giles, and Hinke 271

Part 4 282

Chapter 47 – The Game is On Again................................283

Chapter 48 – The Wiz 291

Chapter 49 – Black Double Crosses 295

Chapter 50 – The Enlargements..303

Chapter 51 – Caroline 306

Chapter 52 - The Stonemason Search 309

Chapter 53 – Connecticut Witchery..320

Chapter 54 - Priscilla 328

Chapter 55 – The Granite Floor 332

Chapter 56 – The Families 338

Chapter 57 – Helen 341

Chapter 58 – Dinner with Hollis...351

Chapter 59 – The Funeral 355

Chapter 60 – Louis Giles 357

Epilogue 361

Another Note from the Author..367

Author bio 368

A note from the author

Game of Twins - The Special Agent is the historical noire fiction prequel in the Game of Twins series and takes place in the time of J. Edgar Hoover (and yes, he is a character). The other three books take place chronologically in the present day: *Game of Twins, Game of Twins – Kidnapped*, and *Golden Frog Poison – Game of Twins*. Read the prequel first or in any order you choose. I'll leave that up to you, but I hope you enjoy this book and the other three crime/mystery thrillers.

This book is a work of fiction. Names, characters, businesses, locales, events, and incidents are either the products of the author's imagination or used in a fictitious manner. Any resemblance to actual persons, living or dead, or actual events or locales is entirely coincidental.

For more information, please go to www.gameoftwins.com

Game of Twins – The Special Agent © Copyright by Tom Ranseen

V2 July 2024; original publication July 2021

Part I

Chapter 1 – The Yacht

June 1911

Coast of New England

The wharf, home to dozens of oyster fishermen, was quiet even though it was a beautiful, late summer Sunday afternoon. The three girls were going on an adventure that they'd not told their parents about. They were too excited to simply drape their legs off the dock. Instead, they stood fidgeting and watching in anticipation.

"Look, there it is!" said one. "This will be so much fun!"

Seeing the large mahogany yacht with dual sails two stories high sail toward the dock on the inland river, the girls squealed with delight. The majestic boat glided expertly into a slip near the girls. More squealing as the gangplank was lowered to the dock.

A woman of incredible beauty with long auburn hair falling out from under her sun hat, a comely figure, alabaster skin, a hint of freckles, and sparkling green eyes strolled down the gangplank in the latest summer outdoor fashion.

Instead of shaking hands, she hugged each of them. "Are you girls ready for the time of your lives? We're going out in the Atlantic. I have new sailing outfits for each of you. Come on, girls, get on board!"

Within minutes, the yacht was pushing off and heading toward the bay. The yacht's name, in case anyone was watching, was *TWINS*— in old-fashioned letters that were flanked by two large black anchors.

Chapter 2 – New Caanan

April 1950

New Canaan, Connecticut

In his 1940 Chevy, Tommy Muldoon drove down the well-kept two-lane road on the edge of upscale New Canaan, Connecticut. Armed with the directions he'd be given, he turned into an estate with a ten-foot, wrought iron fence and shut off his headlights.

Wanting to make a good impression, the handsome, freckled redhead wore tan khakis, a pressed white shirt, a blue blazer, and penny loafers—the epitome of preppy. He was nervous as hell. Out of his pocket, he pulled the note and read it for the tenth time. In disbelief, he shook his head and asked himself out loud:

"Tommy, are you really doing this? Do you have any idea how much trouble you could get into? It's not too late to back out." But then there was that other voice from his crotch. "Tommy, come on, buddy—it's twins. You'll never get a chance like this ever again. Don't be a pussy."

A mobile sheet of gray was smothering the pitch-black sky. Wind whistled through the nearby pines. No moon to be seen. With the car running, he hopped out and checked both ways down the dark, quiet road. No cars. He pulled the big gate door open—relieved that it wasn't locked. He got back into his car, drove through, hopped out again, and pulled the considerable gate door shut.

He could barely see lights at the Haverford mansion—straight ahead, at least a couple hundred yards away. Headlights off, he inched up the driveway until he saw one bright light to the right. He drove around to the back of the sprawling, one-story guesthouse. It was spitting rain as he exited his car and walked up to the side door, the only door with a light on. He saw no lights on in the house. He pushed the doorbell and heard it ring. He waited a minute, then rang it again.

Nothing. He looked at his watch; a few minutes before midnight. He was right on time. He banged his knuckles on the door.

Nothing from the inside. He rapped again. Now thinking this was total bullshit, he turned and started to walk away but stepped back and tried the doorknob. It wasn't locked. The door opened as thunder boomed in the distance.

Tommy entered and fumbled to find a light switch. Not a sound except for his wooden heels on the lacquered parquet floor. He flipped a light on and walked down the hallway. A cat meowed ahead of him. He stopped. His heart galloped. The hair on the back of his neck twinged. There were red footprints on the floor.

"Nellie, Natalie? Okay, girls, you got me. You win. I know you're hiding. Come on out."

Nothing but another feline cry. He took a few more steps down the hallway and flipped on the light outside a large room off the main hallway.

The gaming room was worse mayhem than any horror movie.

"Oh, dear God. Lord Jesus, please NO! NO!" he yelled.

An enormous green and gold-trimmed, round Tiffany lamp, now lit, hung from the ceiling. The Haverford twins were laid out, naked, parallel, on their backs on the pool table in the middle of the room. He was standing in a pool of blood in front of the girls' feet, which dangled off the table. The girls and the green felt were spattered with blood. The twins had been mutilated and were dead.

The most disturbing part: the black crosses impaled in each.

Tommy stood in shock; for how long, he didn't know. Then his brain kicked into survival mode from his time in Army Intelligence. *I've got to get out of here now.*

The black cat reappeared, meowed, and scampered in front of him down the hallway. Trying to retrace his steps, he walked back through the room and into the hallway. His shoes added to several other footprints. He pulled a handkerchief from his pocket and wiped the two light switches. On his way out, he wiped the doorknob.

He told himself, *"Good as I can do."*

The storm had closed in as Tommy ran to his car. Now, with his headlights on, he drove back out to the gate, opened it, then gunned it back through—not bothering to close it behind him. He shook his head. *God, I am so screwed.*

Thunder, lightning, and rain escalated, and he was driving way too fast. Trying to navigate a sharp turn, his Chevy spun out, barely missing the guardrail. But the shock of the near crash jolted him to high alert.

Driving more slowly now—with one hand on the wheel—he ripped the note from the twins into several pieces and balled them up. He opened his window and tossed the wad out over the hood of his car into a ditch on the right side. He then worked off his left shoe and winged it over the hood. He put his left foot on the gas, took his right shoe off, and flung it.

Tommy breathed a huge sigh of relief and tried to steady himself. *I'll be fine. I didn't murder them; no one knew I was there.* But ten minutes later, he entered his apartment unconvinced. He pulled off his coat and wet socks. His hands were shaking as he poured a generous Scotch. He sat down in his oversized lounger and threw down the liquor in a few gulps. His mind raced. *Who killed the girls? Why? Who set me up? Why me? Did I leave any evidence? Did the girls mention me in their diaries? The note would be a wad of wet gunk. My shoes. Hopefully, the blood would be washed off the bottoms. Who would find them in a ditch anyway? What alibi should I have? How could this happen to me? Beautiful Nellie and Natalie—who will find them? This is so fucked up.*

He got a refill and pounded that down in a couple of minutes. He got up again, now a little wobbly. He saw the corner of his bed through the open door. It was calling him. He took off the rest of his clothes and let them drop on the floor. Then he collapsed in bed.

Dead asleep, he felt a tap on his shoulder once, then a few more times. His bedroom light was on. Groggy as hell, he rolled over on his back. His boss, Priscilla Loncart, headmistress of the Greenwich Academy, stood over him. The auburn-haired woman was as gorgeous as ever and dressed in jet-black. Then he saw a couple guys standing at the other side of the bed; also, in black. He managed to pull the bedsheet over him.

Before he could open his mouth, she cooed, "Hi, Tommy."

He slurred, "Mrs. Loncart...what are you doing here? Am I dreaming?"

"No, I assure you you're not dreaming. Here, I'll prove it to you."

She pulled off her long-sleeved black sweater. No brassiere. She sat on the bed and took his left hand, and placed it on one lovely breast, then the other. She pulled the sheet off him and watched him harden.

"See. They are quite real."

She stroked him for a minute, then said, "Tommy, were you a naughty boy tonight? Fun and games with the Haverford twins— before you murdered them?"

In an alcohol fog, he exclaimed, "No, no. I didn't do anything, I swear. They were already dead. I didn't kill them. I swear I didn't."

Priscilla held the typed note in her hand. Then, read from it. "Here's how it ends: 'See you Easter midnight in the Big Cottage. N & N.'"

"No, no...I threw that away."

"Yet here it is. It's going to be tough for the coppers to think you didn't kill the twins."

Tommy whined, "No, I didn't. Swear to God, I didn't do anything. They were dead when I got there."

"Tommy, it's okay. I'm here to help and take care of all your problems." She and the two men huddled away from his bed and whispered. On his back in bed, he watched Priscilla take off the rest of her clothes. Naked, she sat next to him on the bed and stroked him more vigorously.

"I know you've always wanted to fuck me, Tommy, like you wanted to fuck the Haverford twins. You see, I can hear your thoughts—and much more. I know what you did with them in the tutoring room at school, but who could blame you? They were beautiful. A pity..."

Wasting no time, she planted herself on top of him. Her long, auburn locks waved and perfect breasts bounced as she rode him.

He yelled, "No, no. This can't be happening. I gotta be dreaming."

"But Tommy, it is happening. I'm your consolation prize in our game. You played your part well."

She looked back at both men. "They already had their fun; now it's my turn. Besides, I always wanted to see how big you were. I'm impressed."

Tommy Muldoon was more confused as Priscilla rode him. For Tommy, it was all surreal as she bucked like a wild filly on top of him. Reggie took a handgun with a long barrel from inside his black coat and kneeled at the edge of the bed. She nodded. He put the gun in Tommy's right hand and firmly, with both hands, pressed the end of the barrel against his temple.

Tommy exploded into her. Then, one pop of silenced gunfire. It all went dark for Tommy Muldoon.

Straddling the dead man still, Priscilla grinned. "Heckuva way to go out, Tommy Muldoon. And your dick's still hard after you're dead!"

Driving the five minutes back home from the passenger seat, Priscilla grinned at the two men. "That should keep the coppers chasing their tails for now. Don't you think, boys?"

They chuckled in agreement.

"I need a bath and a drink, and then maybe both of you could join me in the master suite."

Tonight, she knew her position in the Game annals was assured for eternity.

Chapter 3 – Special Agent Hinke

Two weeks later

Washington, DC

Early that morning, in her small, tidy apartment near the zoo, Derbert Hinke was on top inside of Marjorie Gale, banging away. Hinke was a big man and fifteen years older than the lovely, waif-like blonde beneath him. But the prim and proper Marjorie was a screamer, and when he came inside her, she wailed like a banshee as he continued, and she climaxed. Hinke had to admit that he looked forward to Marjorie's primordial proclamations, no question, the best part of their sex. But with Marjorie, sex had its parameters: only in one position (missionary), in one place (a bed), and excluded anything other than a tongue in her mouth or a cock in her pussy. He wondered what her apartment neighbors thought about her coital outcries and, frankly, was amazed no one had ever beaten on the door and complained. Maybe a turn-on for them, too?

Hinke pinched off the rubber he wore and rolled off her onto his back. He put an imaginary cigarette between his fingers. He lusted for one, but Marjorie didn't like the smoke, and it was her place. She cozied up close to him.

"You know that I love you."

Hinke turned his head toward her and smiled but said nothing.

"You know, if you ask, I'll say yes."

Hinke nodded and got out of bed. With FBI-like efficiency, he was showered and dressed in six minutes.

Sitting on the bed with the sheet around her, she said, "Please, Derbert, can we please talk about it?"

He bent down and kissed her on the top of her head. "I promise, but I must get to work."

He'd heard this all before and couldn't get out of his girlfriend's place fast enough.

FBI Special Agent Derbert Hinke's dinky, spartan office was in the basement of the Department of Justice. No windows. Had the feel of a tomb. He hated it.

Hinke had the sturdy, athletic build of guys a lot younger: six feet one-inch tall, square jaw, short blond hair, and scar above his left eye. He was dressed in the FBI uniform: dark suit, dark tie, white shirt, dark shoes, and dark socks. He was bored to tears, thumbing through one of the files on his gunmetal gray desk.

"God, I'd love a cigarette," he said out loud. He opened his top drawer. None there, but Hinke knew the smoke made the walls close in on him more. Instead, he daydreamed about a babe he'd recently met in Hollywood on his last trip there.

The phone startled him. He picked up.

A female voice said, "Special Agent Hinke, the Director would like to see you in ten minutes."

Stunned, he could only manage, "Yes, ma'am."

Before he could say anything else, she'd already hung up. He hoped he'd heard her right. He jumped up too fast and banged his knee underneath his cramped desk.

"Damn!"

He grabbed his suit coat and flew out the door. He ran to the elevator, which was at the far end of the hallway. He arrived at the elevator and pushed 5, the top floor. The top floor—he assumed that was where the Director's office was. He looked nervously at his Timex, then at the elevator floor arrow which seemed to be taking an eternity.

"Come on. Come on," he said anxiously.

Finally, he jumped on the elevator. New people got on and off each floor. He glared at his Timex again. After the elevator finally opened at 5, he realized the coffee was talking. Where was the john? He looked up and down the floor. A secretary popped out of an office. He ran up to her and asked, "Could you please tell me where the men's room is?"

She smiled and pointed down the hallway. Hinke rushed to a urinal and peed like a racehorse. In his haste to finish, he flipped his dick and managed to drizzle all the way down his suit pants to his Johnston & Murphy's. No paper towels. Of course.

He rubbed his suit pants and dried his shoes with his handkerchief. He then shoved it back into his lapel coat pocket. He looked up and down the hallway. He had no idea where the Director's office was. He guessed and turned right, jogging, trying to read the doorplates. He looked at his watch. Less than a minute left. Near the end of the hallway, he saw the sign for "Director of the Federal Bureau of Investigation—J. Edgar Hoover."

Hinke started to knock but then turned the doorknob and cautiously peeked in. He was breathing hard from his hurrying and from his anxiety about meeting Hoover. Sitting at her desk, Helen Gandy rose and greeted him with an amiable smile and handshake.

"Come in. Are you okay, Special Agent Hinke?"

Getting his wind, he said, "Yes, ma'am. Sorry, I ran down the hall. Thought I might be late."

"Special Agent Hinke, the Director, will be with you shortly. Please have a seat. Could I get you a cup of coffee?"

Not wanting to spill on himself or need to pee during his meeting, he politely declined. "Thank you, ma'am. No, I'm fine."

Hoover's longtime secretary (now with the title of Executive Assistant), Helen Gandy, wasn't beautiful—but was captivating in a mature way with few wrinkles and lively brown eyes. At five feet, four inches, she wore a matronly, yet tasteful, tan dress that did nothing to accentuate her figure, which she thought was quite suitable for her age. She didn't like the dress—or how she was. She was expected to wear her brown hair, plastered to her head in the acceptable style for working women. And her low heels—she despised them. But it was the dress code for an FBI female.

"Please call me Miss Gandy. Everyone else does."

Hinke sat on the chair, directly across from her. The Director's Cerberus, who controlled all phone calls and appointments for him, stared at Hinke and tugged at her left breast, which, although well covered by her bland dress, he could tell was ample. He wondered if her brassiere strap needed rearranging and tried to look away. But he couldn't stare when she did it again. A subtle tug to her left bosom. His eyes showed confusion.

"Special Agent Hinke, you might want to adjust your handkerchief."

Hinke looked down at his own chest. His white hanky was stuffed in his lapel pocket like a grade-schooler.

Mortified, he managed to say, "Ah, thank you, Miss Gandy."

He pulled out the square of white cloth, put it in his lap, and refolded it as quickly and neatly as possible. When he looked up, she gave him a wink. That's when he noticed her office was bigger than it first looked. A lot bigger. It was lined with four-drawer file cabinets stacked in two layers on two of the walls. He'd never seen that many file cabinets in one office. There was a rolling ladder for reaching the top drawers.

Nervously, Hinke combed his fingers through his short, sandy hair—trying but failing to look calm.

With a kindly tone, Helen said, "It'll be okay. He won't bite. And if he tries, there will be hell to pay from me." She winked again and then smiled, showing her beautiful white teeth. He acknowledged her with his bright blue eyes. When her phone rang, she gracefully picked it up and said, "Yes, Boss."

As Helen got up from her modest L-shaped desk, Hinke admired her profile from the side. It was fetching, especially for a woman of her age. He wondered what might be under the schoolmarmish dress she was wearing. The more he looked, her face, while not classically beautiful, was attractive. Maybe if her brown hair wasn't severely glued to her head? He noticed no wedding ring and thought, *Yes, I believe I'd like to explore that.*

Chapter 4 – J Edgar Hoover

When she turned to face him, her face lit up, and again, she playfully winked at him. He took a deep breath like he was going to swim an entire length of the pool underwater, then silently blew it out and followed Miss Gandy into J. Edgar Hoover's inner sanctum, which was through another anteroom. A lean, long-faced man, good-looking enough to remind him of Gary Cooper—yet there was a delicateness about him versus the macho movie star—was at the door and shook his hand with an overly firm handshake.

"Clyde Tolson, Associate Director. Thank you, Miss Gandy."

When Helen exited, Hinke followed Tolson into the next office. J. Edgar Hoover was sitting behind a large, dark wood desk adorned only with a blotter, a gold pen set, a phone, and a short stack of file folders.

Tolson's introduction was, "And you certainly know the Director."

Anyone on the planet who read a newspaper or magazine or went to the movies knew who Hoover was, but Hinke had neither met him in person nor seen him at FBI headquarters. His thin lips pressed together, Hoover extended a fleshy yet small, almost dainty hand across the desk but said nothing when he shook Hinke's. His big, blocky head was out of proportion to his body—buggy yet deep-set dark eyes, squashed nose, and chin like a worn-out boxer's. Hoover looked more like a well-heeled gangster or mafioso than the country's top cop. The two debonair dandies were both dressed in identical cream-colored, custom-tailored, double-breasted suits, the only difference being the hue of their silk neckties and perfectly starched handkerchiefs. Hoover's a dusty blue and Tolson's navy.

Hinke scanned the office. As neat as his desk was, Hoover's walls were jam-packed, helter-skelter, with photographs, magazine covers, award plaques, and honorariums. Hoover with presidents, Hoover with Hollywood celebrities, and Hoover with dozens of other famous faces. And many of only the Director's ugly mug, plus other memorabilia with "J. Edgar Hoover" in large, fanciful scripts.

Hoover picked up the top file, a personnel jacket. Hinke thought to himself, *Oh shit, this is it. I'm going to get canned.*

Tolson broke the silence. "Gentlemen, let's sit at the conference table."

Hoover opened Hinke's personnel file and started speaking a mile a minute (hence his nickname, "Speed"). Hinke strained to understand.

"Derbert Hinke. Interesting name. Fourth-generation American. Solid German stock like me. Lots of Krauts continue to be helpful to us, making rockets and bombs and the like—and helping us catch commies. At least the Nazis had discipline. The pinko Russkies sure don't."

Hoover stopped for a minute and read more of Hinke's file silently. Then his rata-tat-tat started up again as he picked out bits and pieces from his file:

"You redeemed yourself after Georgetown going to George Washington Law. My alma mater, too. District prosecutor, but then you enlisted. U.S. Army. Silver Star and Purple Heart. Wised up and joined the Bureau after the War. Good work in California with Ron Reagan, who's been terrific in helping us nab commies. That boy Reagan is going far. Hinke, we're going to hunt 'em down and put all the subversive red devils away until they rot or get the chair. You hear me? Forty and not married, but you're obviously no homo. Quite the lady's man. Marjorie Gale's a nice-looking tootsie. You should marry her."

Hinke felt dizzy trying to keep up with Hoover's high-speed snapshot of his life. He thought to himself, *How the hell does he know about Marjorie?* Then answered his own question. *Duh, he's the Director of the FBI.*

Hinke and Tolson sat opposite the Director. The conference table was shiny enough that Hinke could see his reflection and theirs. In the glassy wood, Hoover looked darker complexioned. It was widely known that Hoover was a closet homo, and there was also the rumor that he had mulatto Blood a couple of generations back. Hinke thought that wasn't too far-fetched. He figured neither of those things were ever mentioned in Hoover's presence.

In front of Hoover now was a plain manila file with a blue marking in the top right-hand corner. Hinke read it upside down: an art he'd mastered a few years back in the courtroom. It read "P."

Hoover opened the file and took his time flipping through what looked to be several eight-by-ten glossy photos. He studied each one thoroughly, his intense eyes lingering on each photo as if having second thoughts about sharing them with a stranger, as if they were his own secrets.

Tolson said, "Special Agent Hinke, you heard about the murders in New Canaan two weeks ago?"

"Yes, sir, the twin girls—and their teacher who committed suicide after killing them. Sad. Haven't heard much since."

Hoover and Tolson shared a quick, knowing glance. Hoover said condescendingly, "That's for a reason, Hinke. We took it over from the locals the next day, and the big papers agreed to downplay the coverage. When asked, the *Times* and any others do what I tell them."

Hinke didn't doubt that, but he held his tongue and wondered, *Why is the Bureau interested in a homicide case that's already moot?*

Hoover smiled faintly; his minuscule lips glued together. After selecting a few from the file, he put the photos face down on the table in front of him. Hoover and Tolson locked eyes, and then the Director flipped the first one face up and slid it in front of Hinke like he was playing poker in a Hot Springs casino.

Tolson said, "Identical twins Natalie and Nellie Haverford, age fourteen. This photo is one their family gave us, and there are lots more of these. Lovely lasses, don't you agree, Hinke?"

Hinke nodded affirmatively. Indeed, the two slender brunette teens, both in sky blue short-sleeved dresses a bit past their knees, trimmed in white, white socks, and black patent leather shoes, stood smiling in front of a colorful English-styled garden. They were dazzling.

With his perfectly manicured, stubby, uncalloused fingers, Hoover flipped over the next photo and slid it in front of Hinke and Tolson. Tolson said, "This and the rest are black-and-whites blown up from small Land photos. Maybe you've seen a Land? They're brand new. Cameras that automatically develop photos on the spot without the usual film processing. Not great quality, but it's good enough. Speed…I mean, Director. Why don't we show the first and last black-and-white for now?"

Hoover snarled but flipped it over.

Tolson said, "This photo was taken in the gaming room of the Haverford guesthouse, the Big Cottage."

Chapter 5 – The Pool Table

Easter Night, Two Weeks Earlier

New Canaan, Connecticut

It was a cool, cloudy, and breezy spring night with rain expected. She wore a light black leather jacket to match her black slacks and boots. She walked up the main driveway, then took a right to the Big Cottage. The Haverford Big House mansion was more than a hundred yards away. The two men followed several paces behind her. The gate lock, which they'd learned how to pick last week, was no problem.

Her husband cut the telephone line around the side of the Big Cottage, the only link to the mansion and the outside world, just in case. The front door to the spiffy forest-green guesthouse with white trim, made entirely of durable cypress imported from Louisiana, faced away from the main house, providing guests with privacy.

Perfect.

She could see lights inside the Big Cottage and pressed the doorbell. She waited, then rang it again. One of the twins—she could never tell one from the other after knowing them for years—looked through the peephole and opened the door.

With gigantic, stunned eyes, Natalie Haverford exclaimed, "Miss Priscilla, what a surprise! What are you doing here?"

She smiled. "I'm sorry about not telling you on Thursday, but your mother asked me to pop in on you two a couple evenings while they were on vacation. She gave me a gate key. This is the first chance I've had to make it over. I hope you don't mind. I'll only be a short while."

Priscilla stepped into the guesthouse hallway. Besides her purse, she carried two fancy Macy's shopping bags. "Oh, and I brought you both surprises that I'll give you in a bit."

Nellie and Natalie looked at each other, neither thrilled that Mom had pulled a fast one on them to have them spied on when she and Dad were vacationing in Cuba. But after all, their parents had acquiesced and let them stay in the Big Cottage by themselves. It was only Miss Priscilla.

"Miss Priscilla, who's taking care of your little twins?" Nellie inquired of the headmistress as they sat down in the luxurious living room decorated with fine antiques, original Impressionist French art, including a Van Gogh and a Renoir, and Oriental rugs. Both girls were dressed in identical silky, navy blue PJs and white robes. They were exquisite young ladies, and she always knew they'd turn out to be spectacular.

She answered, "Oh, my second cousin, Patricia, is staying with us." She pulled a photo out of her small purse for the Haverford twins to see.

"They are too cute!" Natalie squealed.

Priscilla said, "Maybe one day you girls can take care of them for us."

"Okay, if you promise they won't pee on us," Nellie laughed.

Priscilla chuckled. "No guarantees, but I think boys are more dangerous when it comes to pee."

They all giggled. Natalie told her headmistress, "We've made hot chocolate and popcorn. Would you like to stay for a bit? Mom said we could stay up till eleven."

"I'd love a cup of hot chocolate, and buttered popcorn is my weakness." Each took her by the hand into the kitchen, where they chatted, sipped elegant Swiss hot chocolate, and munched on popcorn that Nellie made in a big skillet.

"Girls, I've heard through the grapevine that you like to play pool and are pretty good. Let's play a couple of games, and then I'll be off."

"Miss Priscilla, how could you know that?" asked Nellie.

"Ah, a little birdie told me, but I'll let you in on a secret. I used to be a decent player a long time ago. I warn you; I take no prisoners." The girls laughed.

They led her into the large, dark, paneled game room that had a pool table in the center—a room large enough to also fit a ping-pong table, dartboard, and two smaller tables for chess and checkers.

Priscilla said, "Okay, how about eight-ball? I'll play you two, and you rotate."

Natalie racked the balls, and each of the three comely females held a stick.

Priscilla pocketed the nine and two balls on the break, then smiled at each. "Pure luck."

Natalie told her sister, "Nellie, we're going to have to play our asses off to win. Oh, sorry, Miss Priscilla."

"Everything between us tonight, girls, is secret."

Back and forth, the Haverford girls played well against their headmistress in a competitive game. Smartly smacking the balls with their custom cue sticks and leaving only the eight-ball and the two-ball.

Priscilla said, "These pool balls are beautiful and so unusual. Do you know where they're from?"

Nellie told her, "Papa said they are one-of-a-kind custom balls made of ivory by a man in the City."

Priscilla pocketed the two-ball, then made a tough carom and sank the eight-ball last. "Rack 'em up again, girls, but the rumors are true.

You are accomplished billiards players. I'm going to use the ladies' room. No peeking in the bags," she grinned.

They pointed her down the hallway and said in unison, "Yes, Miss Priscilla."

Priscilla went to the front door and flicked the outdoor light twice. The door was unlocked, and the two men entered without a sound. The three walked into the gaming room together. The twins' eyes widened. Like Priscilla, the tall men were dressed in black from head to toe.

Natalie asked, "Miss Priscilla, what are they doing here?"

"Girls, I think you've met my husband, Reginald. You can call him Reggie. This is his second cousin, Nicholas—or we call him Nick." In turn, each man took a proper bow.

Priscilla said, "They're pool players too – but mainly here to help you both indulge in your fantasies—the ones I know you discuss with each other and Tommy."

"Miss Priscilla, what are you saying? What fantasies? You're talking crazy!" Nellie exclaimed with more than a bit of fright. I'm going to call the main house, and you need to leave right now."

"Oh, my dears, don't bother. The phone no longer works. We've gathered here to make all you want—and more—come true. Then we'll be gone."

"What the hell are you talking about?" Natalie shrieked.

Priscilla ignored her question. "For starters, we'll need you to remove your robes and PJs and then put these on. She pulled a sheer black gown, sheer panties, and fancy high heels out of each bag. "I told you I had surprises. Then these two amazing men will teach you extraordinary games, a lot more fun than pool. They'll make you forget about Tommy; I promise."

Both twins tried to bolt down the hallway but were caught by the two men and dragged back to the gaming room where they were placed on the pool table. The twins' eyes locked in mutual terror. They screamed.

Chapter 6 - The Polaroids

Two weeks after the murders

Washington, DC

In the first black-and-white photo, the naked girls lay parallel to each other on top of a pool table—gagged, with their hands over their heads and feet tied and legs hanging off the edge. Their eyes open; they were alive in this photo. Hoover's tight-lipped smile cracked open a fraction. Hinke could tell he was enjoying his morbid porn show. Hoover ignored a few photos and then turned over the last one in the stack and slid it across the table.

Hinke glanced at the photo and momentarily shut his eyes. But sitting in front of J. Edgar Hoover, he made himself stare at it. The heinous finale was shockingly gruesome. His eyes lost focus, and he fought his gut reaction to put his hands over his face or mouth or both—and to look away. He could taste the bile rising.

The dead twins were laid out on their backs on the pool table. Blood splattered over their naked bodies and the felt of the table. Positioned parallel to each other. Gags off. Arms now perpendicular to their bodies. A hand of each touching the other. Throats slashed. Long cuts carved the length of their bodies and under their breasts. Legs now open with black crosses impaled inside each. Bloodied banners now at the side of each body. Hinke peered into Hoover's steely slits. It was clear the Director was relishing his show-and-tell.

After a pregnant pause, Tolson observed, "See the banners at the outside of each girl in the last photo? With all the dark blood and quality of the black-and-white photos, they're hard to see. Unfortunately, the New Canaan coppers disturbed the crime scene. The idiots tromped through the blood on the floor. They removed the black crosses from the bodies. They took the banners off the table. Then, they covered the bodies before additional photographs were taken. There are dozens more crime scene and autopsy photos in the file, but the Land photos tell the story. Here are photos of the black crosses and the banners themselves."

The grotesque, black wooden crosses had sharp points at each of their four tips. They were hideous, foot-long weapons. He held up color close-ups of the red banners; the familiar Communist logos, bright yellow with hammer and sickle, were spotted with the Haverford girls' blood.

With conviction, Hoover said, "Now maybe you see why the FBI got involved? Sheriff Yates in New Canaan, an old friend, gave me a call when he saw the Bolshevik banners. It's the commies on a murder rampage!" he yelled and pounded the table.

Tolson put the small black and white photos next to their corresponding enlargements. "They were cleverly taped in an envelope underneath the top drawer of the nightstand in their bedroom. The killer or killers used one of the new Land cameras while in the guesthouse."

Hinke nodded once more because that's what he thought he should do as he tried to process all the stuff they'd thrown his way. He decided to join the conversation for the first time. "The murderer or murderers left the Land photos at the scene? The teacher who killed himself—why in the world would he leave pictures of the murders anywhere, much less the guesthouse?"

Tolson ignored Hinke's question for now.

"The teacher was shot once in his right temple at point blank range—in his apartment a couple miles outside New Canaan. Found the afternoon after the murders by a friend. Muldoon taught at Greenwich Academy and was the Haverford twins' math teacher and academic advisor. Apparently, they met with him at least once a week after school. A note from the twins was found in his apartment inviting him over Easter night—and to be there at midnight. Their parents were on holiday in Cuba."

In disgusting bad taste, Hoover added, "He didn't go to the Haverford estate to play Monopoly."

Tolson said, "The note wasn't signed; it was typewritten. Two days later, we found Nellie's diary in her mansion bedroom, and it confirmed that Muldoon had been doing more than tutoring the girls in advanced algebra; things seemed unconsummated.

Hoover cackled, "Teaching them anatomy instead of math, no doubt."

Hinke thought to himself, *Jeez, how can they be this cavalier about the slaughter of two beautiful girls?*

Tolson continued, "They were murdered in the guesthouse. A couple hundred yards from the mansion."

"Who found the girls?"

Tolson said, "The girls didn't arrive for breakfast at the mansion by 9:30 a.m., and the guesthouse phone wasn't working. The line was cut, no doubt, by the killers. The housekeeper walked down to the Big Cottage. She saw the dead girls in the pool room. Ran out and back up the hill. A maid called the police. They'd been dead for approximately twelve hours. Muldoon's death had all indications of a suicide. A 22LR revolver was on the bed beside him, and powder burns on his face and hand. No apartment neighbors heard anything. By the looks of the Dewar's bottle, he was sloshed, and our boys confirmed that. Oh, you may want to know, Muldoon was a decorated soldier like you and a lacrosse jock in college."

Hinke saw the two most powerful law enforcement officials in the U.S. look at each other as if they were communicating telepathically.

Tolson told him, "Please excuse us for a few minutes."

He and the Director exited through another anteroom at the back of Hoover's office. The deviant photographs on the table beckoned Hinke to look again. He wondered, *"How could God let this happen to these beautiful girls? But heck, He let millions of Jews be massacred in Nazi death camps. The Auschwitz carnage I saw with my own eyes. What were two girls in His grand scheme?"*

When Hoover and Tolson came back in, Hinke took the initiative—having no idea what impression he was making on them other than he hadn't been ushered out yet. "Was there physical evidence that Muldoon was in the Big Cottage?"

Tolson answered, "The short answer is no."

Hinke went out on a limb. "Okay, based on the little I know, it sure looks like more than one perpetrator was involved."

The Director and Tolson stared at him like they were waiting for more.

Hinke told them without seeing the photos from the Muldoon crime scene, "It doesn't sound like a suicide to me. First, an ex-military guy like that would've eaten his 22LR or put it under his chin, not blasted through his temple—and probably not in bed."

Hoover clapped once. His thin lips almost formed a smile. Tolson combed his fingers through his perfectly slicked-back hair, then said, "Yes, over a couple weeks, we've done a lot of investigating already. We're not convinced Muldoon killed the girls." Grinning like the cat that ate the canary, Tolson continued, "We concur that his death wasn't a suicide."

Hinke couldn't resist: "From what you've both told me, it looks like we're being taunted by a group that is audacious enough to leave murder photos at the scene and kill with impunity. Maybe commies or maybe another group?"

Then he knew he'd made a mistake. Hoover interrupted; his tinny voice spit-fired faster than ever—

"Hinke, nobody fucks with the goddamn Director of the Federal Bureau of Investigation, ever, and gets away with it. I don't know what role Muldoon played in all this, but I'm certain this is part of a new, dastardly Kremlin plot, one we've not encountered before. We must be diligent. We must get after them today!"

Hoover held up the color photos of the banners in both hands.

"My God, Hinke, they're rubbing shit in our faces. These monsters mean to strike fear into the hearts and minds of all white Christian Americans. Their end game is to destroy our God-fearing democracy and control all continents. I cannot let that happen. I will not let that happen. And fuck the CIA. I've decided to keep all specifics confidential at the Bureau and out of the news until we find out exactly who is responsible for these atrocities. Muldoon, dead, doesn't give me what I need. Whoever *they* are, they'll be dealt with harshly. Do you understand, Hinke?"

Hoover glanced at Tolson, the two again seeming to communicate with each other without speaking. The Director had worked himself up into a lather—his words galloping faster as his nearly unintelligible voice railed against a yet-to-be-determined group of bad guys. With Hoover's uptick into near hysteria, Hinke barely nodded but got the gist.

He responded by rote as he did to his old drill sergeant, "Yes, sir!"

The Director plopped back into his big leather desk chair. Tolson inserted himself once more. He put two gold cross necklaces in front of Hinke and said, "Curiously, these two identical necklaces were found on the pool table in an area not covered by blood. We don't know a lot more about them other than they didn't belong to the Haverford girls. Both have the letters "KAA" engraved on the back.

After a few moments of silence, Tolson told him, "Hinke, we're putting you in charge of a new operation to make sense of all this and find the Communist infidels who murdered the Haverford girls; discover what their plans are; and put a stop to them. You'll report directly to Director Hoover and me, but Miss Gandy will be your daily liaison. I believe you'll find her helpful."

Tolson stood. Hinke did the same and extended his hand to the Director.

Hoover chirped again, "Find the commie bastards, Hinke. Get the sons-of-bitches!"

Again, Hinke blurted almost involuntarily, "Yes, sir!"

Tolson added, "Lou Nichols, who I'm sure you know heads PR, has complete control over the public story. For now, it remains a double murder and suicide. Is that clear?"

"I understand. Yes, sir. Thank you, sir."

Chapter 7 – Marilyn Monroe

He opened the door into Miss Gandy's adjoining office and closed it behind him. Sitting in the seat he occupied sixty minutes earlier was an exquisite platinum blonde, dressed to the nines, who looked familiar. Before he could say anything, she gave him a gigantic smile, showing her perfect, pearly white teeth—her lips glistening with ruby-red lipstick.

She said, "Mr. Hinke, it's nice to see you again." She remained sitting and extended her lovely hand. Every pore of her skin gushed sensuality. He shook it. "Marilyn Monroe?"

"I'm impressed that you remember me. We met at the Tam O'Shanter in the City of Angels last year. You were with Ronnie. All the girls fawn over Ronnie. Frankly, I think you're better looking— and probably a nicer guy, too."

After giggling, she added, "And he's kinda small if you get my drift."

At age twenty-four, her smile was breathtaking and persona otherworldly. Hinke's face flushed with heat.

"Miss Monroe, it's good to see you again as well. I certainly do remember. Small world."

"Sure is, especially out in LA, but I guess in DC, too. It's Derbert, right?"

"Yes, ma'am, that's me, but please call me DH."

With a huge smile, she replied, "Well, okay, DH, call me Marilyn." It was hard not to stare at her sumptuous cleavage.

Miss Gandy's phone rang. She got it on the first ring.

"I'll tell Miss Monroe you're ready for her, Boss."

Hinke's eyes were transfixed, consuming Marilyn's curves. Touching the brass doorknob, the blonde bombshell started to turn it, then stopped. Her face lit up again. She took three steps straight toward him and planted her moist red lips on his cheek.

"I do hope we meet again one day soon, DH."

Hinke was too overcome to say anything. His eyes focused on her ass as it swiveled gracefully into the anteroom connecting to Hoover's office. When he finally looked around, there was Helen Gandy. "Nice-looking woman, don't you think, Special Agent Hinke?"

"Hard to argue with that."

"Miss Monroe and I had a wonderful time before your meeting concluded. She's as smart and funny as she is gorgeous. How did it go with the Boss?"

"I got the job. Now I gotta figure out exactly what that is."

"Congratulations, Agent. Don't worry, I'll help you. You know Marilyn Monroe through Ronald Reagan?"

"A little. He introduced us one evening in LA. Predicted she was going to be a big star."

"Of that, I have no doubt." With her index finger, Helen indicated, "Come here a minute."

Hinke walked around her desk. She took a hanky out of her purse and stood up, her breasts almost touching his chest. She gently held his chin and daintily dabbed off the red lipstick imprint on his face. Her perfume was heavenly. Standing by Helen's desk, Hinke realized he was lingering and returned to his seat. He thought to himself, *Wow, I'm guessing Marilyn and Helen both have great boobs.*

With a playful smirk on her face, Miss Gandy looked at him—more seductively than any woman had ever done, and said, "Girls shouldn't tell all their secrets, Special Agent Hinke, but Miss Monroe and I share the same measurements up top."

Hinke's face burned crimson.

"Marilyn is a striking 36-24-34. She's less than half my age. I can't compete with her waist or hips anymore, though mine aren't too bad. But boobs, yes."

Hinke did a half-double-take. Flabbergasted how she could know what he was thinking. Was he being that obvious, ogling her tits?

Helen winked at him, then reached into her top drawer. She held out a key. "The key to your new office. If you ever lose it, a replacement will cost you five dollars."

Before he could say "thank you," she handed him a scrap of paper with a four-digit number on it.

"The Director's extension. Memorize it and give it back to me. *All* his calls come through me first."

He looked at the number and memorized it. Her fingers lightly touched his when she put it in his hand. Her touch electric. Instead of staring at her breasts, his blue eyes locked onto her liquid brown ones.

"Besides the new office, you'll get a salary bump of two pay grades, though your title remains the same."

"Thank you, Miss Gandy. This is all a bit overwhelming but pleasantly surprising."

"I had no doubt you'd be the perfect candidate. You were a skilled prosecutor and have done well at the Bureau. And there's..." She stopped for a moment and didn't continue her thought out loud, which was, *It was I who chose you, Derbert Hinke.* She pointed to the door at the other end of her office. "Tomorrow, I'll show you the files and evidence for the Haverford case."

"Miss Gandy, I'm sure my new office will be splendid, but could I ask a favor: a large freestanding chalkboard? It's how I work."

"I'll have one brought to your office today."

Helen got up from her desk and shook Hinke's hand. The handshake lingered.

With a smile and twinkle in her eye, she said, "But of course, you'll owe me..."

Hinke again felt his face flush.

With another sultry smile, she said, "I look forward to working closely with you, Agent Hinke. One more thing before you leave."

She put another small piece of paper in his hand.

"Memorize this too, then dispose of it. Never call that number from an FBI phone."

"You have my word."

After shutting her door, Hinke stopped and read the short note. He was flummoxed.

He took the elevator down to the third floor and located #336. He slotted the new key into the lock and opened the door. The first thing he did was walk to one of three large windows and pull up the blinds. A room with a view out onto the traffic of Pennsylvania Avenue. A glorious sight despite the dreary weather. *Hot damn, DH, you've finally made the big time!.*

Wandering around, going from window to window, Hinke finally noticed what was on his big walnut desk: a bottle of his favorite bourbon, Very Old Fitzgerald, a heavy glass tumbler, a bottle of sparkling water, and a plate with a napkin over it. He removed the napkin and breathed in the aroma of pastrami and cheese with onions on rye and crispy potatoes. Plus, a slice of cheesecake, all from Sal's Deli, a couple blocks down. His favorite lunch place.

He grabbed the bottle, cracked the seal of the Old Fitz, and poured three fingers. The first sip glowed all the way down and made him grin. Eating his delicious meal, he pulled out the note from Helen. There was a DC phone book in the drawer of his new desk.

"I'd like to order a dozen roses and have them delivered today around 6:00 p.m. to an address not far from you. I have an account, Derbert Hinke. Add a five-dollar tip."

"Deliver them to the usual address, Mr. Hinke?"

Already feeling guilty as hell, he said, "No. The address is 1025 Dupont Circle #4. Put: 'Thanks, DH.'"

"Consider it done, Mr. Hinke."

Holding his Old Fitz in one hand and a piece of chalk in the other, Hinke began to jot down a few early observations:

- Twins' bodies mutilated and positioned the same way

- 2 black wooden crosses used as sacrilegious weapons

- 2 commie banners

- Several Land photos of the murders—taken by the killers

- 2 gold cross necklaces with "KAA"—not owned by the twins

He walked back to the windows and enjoyed the rainstorm outside.

After Marilyn Monroe left, J. Edgar Hoover walked into Helen's office and sat in the chair opposite her. It had taken her years to convince the Boss that when no one else was around it was okay for him to be in her office. Before he could speak, she said, "Boss, Marilyn is not new meat for you to keep under surveillance and serve up to McCarthy if she doesn't play ball and get you enough juicy dirt on the rich and famous. She can be a Hollywood star but needs a big role. She told me she thinks Darryl Zanuck is considering her for his upcoming production. Why not keep the FBI out of her life, at least for now? There may come a time when she'll be invaluable."

Hoover said, "That Marilyn Monroe, she's one good-looking tootsie, but sure has a mouth on her for a youngster."

Helen chuckled. "If you only had more agents who were half as smart as her."

Hoover ignored her comment, but as he walked back to his office, Helen said, "I'm going to get Zanuck on the phone. I'll buzz him in. Tell Darryl you need a favor. In return, you could have McCarthy lay off going after his troop of supposed commie actors and writers. Marilyn Monroe gets the starring role, and he pays her at the rate of his best actresses."

Hoover said nothing more and returned to his inner sanctum. Darryl Zanuck was the most powerful of the Hollywood moguls. His star-power influence, though, was notches down from J. Edgar Hoover's. She called and got Zanuck's secretary. "Director Hoover for Mr. Zanuck."

Helen didn't remember the voice. Darryl went through bimbo secretaries like Hemingway went through booze. The new version made a mistake and said, "He's in a meeting right now and can't be bothered. Can I get a number? I'll tell Mr. Zanuck you called."

Helen had trained dozens of secretaries of the rich and powerful to get their bosses to jump like trained circus animals when she called them in the name of her boss—and was able to get along famously with most. She didn't like to strong-arm newcomers, but this was a priority, and she was in no mood.

"I didn't catch your name."

"Melody. Melody Sneed."

"Melody, I'm going to give you exactly two minutes to get Mr. Zanuck on the phone, or I promise you'll be fired by the end of the day."

The shocked girl started to mumble, but Helen cut her off.

"Two minutes, Melody, for Mr. Zanuck to get on the phone with FBI Director Hoover."

Her voice trembled. "Yes, ma'am."

Helen hung up. Almost two minutes later, Darryl Zanuck called. "Helen, you nearly scared the shit out of my new secretary."

Not wanting to chitchat with the head of 20th Century Fox, she said, "Mr. Zanuck, I'll connect you to the Director now."

"Edgar, it's a treat to hear from you. How are things in the Capitol?" In his ultra-posh, top-story Hollywood office off Sunset Boulevard, feet up on his mammoth desk, Zanuck rolled his eyes and doubted this would be good.

Hoover said evenly, "Darryl, I need a favor."

"How can I help?"

"I hear you're considering casting Marilyn Monroe for the lead role in your next picture."

"Edgar, she's a possibility. I've got a couple of other starlets who'd be perfect. I haven't decided yet."

Hoover said flatly, "Now you have."

Zanuck hesitated, "Edgar, I don't know. She's awfully green."

"Darryl, just get it done. In return, you have my word that neither the House Committee on Un-American Activities nor McCarthy will go after any of your people. Call Helen with your list."

He wasn't sure Hoover would make good on that but said, "Fine, Edgar."

"She's going to be a big star for you," Hoover said and hung up.

He called Helen, "Miss Gandy, it's done. She got the part."

Helen was aware the Boss fancied himself as a movie mogul, albeit a non-Jewish one. If he weren't

Director of the FBI, Hoover would have given his right nut or maybe both nuts to be a Hollywood bigwig more than anything. He'd have Marilyn Monroe play the lead in all his movies. He loved all things beautiful. He'd be free to do anything sexual or otherwise.

"Thank you, Boss. One more thing…well, a couple of things. I'm putting both Special Agent Hinke and Marilyn Monroe on the NS (No Surveillance) list."

"Okay, Miss Gandy. Oh, and about Hinke, I think I made a good choice—if he finds the commie murderers."

You certainly did, Boss."

Solicitously, she cooed, "Boss, Special Agent Derbert Hinke can do that and much more you if you let him."

Chapter 8 – Miss Gandy

The next morning Helen Gandy beamed when Hinke walked into her office.

He bid her a "good morning" but tried to hide his disappointment that she was wearing another frumpy dress, and her hair looked more severely pinned to her skull. Hinke thought, *What got into me yesterday? She must be at least ten years older—maybe more.*

She saw his face, listened in on his disappointment, and said, "Miss Monroe mentioned to me yesterday what a shame it is that women here have such a strict dress code. Don't you agree?"

"I sure do."

"Tell you what. I'll get you a cup of coffee and then show you the files in the conference room."

With a cup of coffee in hand, Hinke followed her back through her file cabinet-lined office to a modest conference room. *Did she get the flowers? Maybe I shouldn't have sent them?*

Not missing a beat, Helen told him, "The roses are beautiful. Thank you, Agent Hinke. Let me show you what we've got here. I'll be busy most of the day and will check in on you later. For now, please keep these files in the conference room. But feel free to come and go."

She was gone, but Hinke daydreamed about her in naughty ways.

He looked over the conference table: a short stack of FBI investigators' files, the Land photographs, enlargements and other crime scene photos, and clear bags containing the hideous black crosses, the blood-spattered commie banners, and the necklaces. He drank a lot of coffee, wrote a lot of notes, and did a lot of pacing.

Late that afternoon Helen opened the door and asked, "Was the information helpful?"

"Yes, the FBI investigators seem to have done a good job in a short amount of time. But I have questions."

She replied, "I would hope so since the perpetrators haven't been caught yet."

This time Hinke winked at her, then pulled out a chair, and they both sat, not three feet apart, at the conference room table.

He asked, "Have you read these files?"

"Yes, but not every word. I know the gist of what's in them."

"And?"

"And what?"

"Who do you think the bad guys are in this case?"

She gave him a kindly smirk. Special Agent Hinke, I'm a secretary, not an FBI special agent." "Besides, you wouldn't want me to put you out of your new job."

"Touché." Hinke smiled. "But I know you're much more than a typical secretary, and I'm guessing you're smarter than at least ninety-five percent of the agents in this building."

Hinke picked up the clear plastic bag with the identical gold cross necklaces and said, "These are puzzling. Found on the pool table in 1950, in a spot not soaked with blood but confirmed as not the Haverford twins' necklaces. Both have the letters 'KAA' on the back."

"Let me look." She let the necklaces fall out of the clear bag into her hand—and considered them closely, flipping them front to back. Her brown eyes widened, and she put them on the table.

"My, this is strange." She couldn't take her eyes off the necklaces.

"Why do you say that?"

She took a deep breath and said, "Could be a huge coincidence, but I may know whose necklaces these were."

Hinke was all ears.

"I believe it was 1911. Katherine Ann Abercrombie and Kaitlyn Anne Abercrombie, beautiful twin sisters, disappeared from Port Norris, New Jersey—where I grew up. Simply vanished. Assumed kidnapped, then probably worse. No bodies, no clues, no motive, nothing. They were a couple years older, but I remember they loved to spend time at the wharf. A local legend is that pirates spirited them away, and they became *The Mermaids of Port Norris*."

"Fascinating story. You say they were twins?"

"Yes. Can you excuse me? I've got to go check on the Boss before he leaves."

Before she left, she handed him another small note. He waited until she left to open it. With trepidation and anticipation, he unfolded it. It said: "7:00 PM this evening."

Immediately, Derbert Hinke got the jitters like a teenager going out on a first date.

Before Hinke left, he knew he'd first have to make the call. "Hey, babe, how was your day?"

Unenthusiastically, Marjorie said, "It was okay. How about you?"

He hesitated, not sure what excuse he'd use but went with the old standby. "Marjorie, I gotta stay late and work tonight.

"Derbert, how late? I'm already making your favorite dinner. Meatloaf, escalloped potatoes, and apple pie."

"I don't know, babe. I'm on a new thing that Hoover himself wants done. I was in his office for an hour. And I have other news."

"Wow. I'm impressed. What news?"

"A secret for now. Listen, I promise to come over tomorrow evening. Leftovers sound good—or I'll take you out to eat if you want. You name the place."

She moped. "I understand. Call me tomorrow?"

"I will."

"Okay, I love you."

"You're the best. Good night."

Home after taking a cab instead of the bus, he ripped off his suit, jumped into the shower, and scrubbed as quickly as he could. Once out of the shower, he shook his head at himself in the bathroom mirror. *Jeez, DH, this woman could have her grandkids, for God's sake!*

He shaved for the second time that day and then wondered what the heck to wear. He decided on a crisp white shirt and dark slacks. He checked himself out in the mirror and nodded approval. Almost out the door, he ran back and grabbed a couple of rubbers, then told himself, *I'm not thinking that's an issue.*

His five-year-old Buick was parked a half block down. With most of the traffic thinning out, it took him less than ten minutes to turn onto Q Street off Dupont Circle and park near the Cairo Apartments. He gave himself a little leeway to find her place and not hurry. He rode the elevator up to the Cairo's sixth floor. He took one deep breath, exhaled, then rang the bell at 606. He was nervous as hell.

Helen Gandy opened her door with a radiant smile as he stood at the threshold of her flat. Helen, the frumpy, middle-aged secretary of J. Edgar Hoover, had transformed into Cinderella.

She looked ten years younger, maybe more. Her sleeveless black dress cut tight, its hem reaching a bit below her knees. Her black heels, high. Her black stockings, nylon. Her cleavage rivaling any female valley he'd ever peeked into. On the top of her ample bosom, he could set teacups. Her lipstick, ruby red. Her eyelashes long. her hair, dark brown, straight, shoulder length, and flowing. Her perfume not from the 5 and 10 or Kresge.

He stared, speechless. Her warm smile grew. He finally stammered, "Miss Gandy, you look..." He tried to search for the right word and came up with "Splendid."

He then told himself, *Way to go, asshole. What was that? I should have said gorgeous or beautiful or incredible or anything else.*

Helen said, "Thank you for coming over, Derby. May I call you that?"

"That's swell, ma'am. I haven't been called Derby in a long time."

"I'm Helen in here."

Hinke thought, *God, I must get this woman to bed.*

Helen gave him a knowing wink. She took his hand and led him into her flat. Roomy, neat, unusual, pricey furnishings. Not exactly what he expected.

Her smile was radiant yet sultry, and she said, "Relax, Derby. We've got all evening. Have a seat on the sofa. I'll be back with drinks. Vodka martini with an olive?"

"Perfect."

Walking away, the backside view in that tight black dress was as good as it got. She brought a batch of martinis in a shiny chrome-finished pitcher and handed him a matching martini glass. On the tray were two cocktail picks with two plump olives skewered on each. Instead of inserting one pick into his martini glass, she slowly sucked the olives off, rolled them around with her tongue, and then plopped them one at a time into his drink and handed it to him. He'd never seen that in his life. He decided to play. He speared one and pointed it into her mouth. She sucked the olive off the spear and swallowed it.

They sipped their martinis. She sat close enough on the sofa to touch her crossed leg with his. He felt his cock lurch at the mere touch.

"Helen, may I ask you a question?"

She grinned, "Shoot. What would you like to know?"

"I hear you're an FBI legend like your boss. The word in the hallowed halls is to never fuck with you. I don't know much about you other than you are a highly respected secretary with a lot of influence. They say you're a spinster, never married, devoted exclusively to Hoover. Is any of that true?"

Helen couldn't help herself and giggled. "That's a lot of questions, Derby. I've worked for the Boss since 1918—before the Bureau was the Bureau. I handle many things that few, including the Boss, know of. I'm devoted to my work. I'm not married and never have been. When I first started working for the Boss, he told me he didn't want a married secretary. I promised him I wouldn't, and I've kept that promise."

Gracefully, she picked up her martini glass and took a big sip.

"Yes, Derby, it's best to never fuck with me, but you, sir, I do expect you to fuck me."

Hinke could take a hint. Sitting on the couch, he kissed her deeply while moving her skirt up her leg. She stood and turned around.

"Will you please unzip me?"

Hinke stood and followed her directions. Her black dress fell to the floor. She turned toward him. A see-through black brassiere barely covered her impressive breasts. While her body wasn't Marilyn Monroe's—in a black corset, garter belt, black stockings, and no panties hiding her luxurious brown triangle—it was maybe better.

In silence, she unzipped his fly and undid his belt. He was plenty ready.

Hinke asked himself, *What in the world have I gotten myself into?*

Chapter 9 – The Chalkboard

The following day when Hinke entered her office, Cinderella Helen was no longer. Now middle-aged Helen, she wore her uniform of a loose, lifeless dress and her hair pinned up, smashed against her head.

Helen immediately saw his disappointment, but it mattered not.

Awkwardly, after last night's incredible sex, Hinke said, "Good morning, Hel...then caught himself and started again.

"Good morning, Miss Gandy."

"Good morning to you, Special Agent Hinke. I hope you slept well last night?"

"Like a baby."

"Good to hear. What can I do for you?"

He wanted to say, *Give me another blowjob like last night*, but said, "Coming by to see if I could take the files and evidence to my office?"

She chirped, "Already there."

"Thank you, Miss Gandy."

He didn't know what else to say. He exited to the third floor. When he unlocked his office and turned on the light, he saw the files he'd started to examine the previous day were perfectly laid out on his conference table. On top of the stack of files was a note that said, "P files. Keep locked in your office." The flip side of the note said, "Next Tues. Same time." Hinke grinned and felt a twinge in his nether region. Then he grabbed his legal pad and reread his notes from the day before. He dove into the files again and wrote more.

By late afternoon, the files, photographs, and pieces of evidence were scattered over his conference table and desk. Hinke paced, then stopped to look out over Pennsylvania Avenue. In his mad scientist-investigator mode, it was time for the chalkboard, which he'd flipped around. He grabbed a piece of chalk and wrote in giant letters, "WHY?"

He paced.

Underneath, he wrote in a column

"Not about $."

Next, "Not about jealousy?"

He picked up one of the Communist banners and wrote:

"Commie political statement—doubtful."

"Revenge? For what?"

He picked up one of the black-and-white enlargements and wrote, "Sicko sacrifice? But why?"

He looked at the mess on his desk and conference table, smiled, and added: "To piss off Hoover?"

Then, more darkly he wrote, "Murder for fun and games?"

He picked up the photo of the Haverford girls in front of their garden, then the two gold cross necklaces.

He put them down and wrote under the board header:

"GAME?"

"TWINS?"

He stopped by Helen's office the following day to ask a favor. Again, she was Helen, Hoover's secretary, but he immediately fantasized Cinderella Helen. Before he could say anything, she said, "It's good to believe in Cinderella, don't you think, Agent Hinke?"

Hinke was nearly floored, but recovered and said, "Miss Gandy, I need to go to New Canaan. Can you make the arrangements for me?"

"Certainly. When would you like to leave?"

"If possible, this afternoon."

"Fine. I'll book you a flight to LaGuardia and have a rental car for you at the airport. It's a nice drive up into Connecticut. I'll book you a hotel room."

"Perfect."

"Returning?"

"Let's leave that open. It's a short trip, but I'll be back by Tuesday afternoon. I have a date that evening."

Helen winked at him. "What a coincidence. I, too, have plans. Your itinerary in Connecticut?"

"Let's see. Friday morning I'd like to meet the sheriff, who the Director knows. Then I'd like to see the Haverford Estate Big Cottage where the girls were murdered. In the afternoon maybe you can get me an appointment with Priscilla Loncart, headmistress of the Greenwich Academy. The agents' notes say she was out of town when they were interviewing. I'm assuming she knew the girls and the teacher."

He hesitated, then told her of another person. "That one might be difficult; and perhaps I could be a journalist instead—to get me in the door. And I'm going to play by ear talking to the Haverfords and their housekeeper.

Helen smiled and told him, "Give me an hour and a half. Pop in before you leave the office, and I'll have your arrangements made."

He winked. "Thank you, Miss Gandy."

Chapter 10 – The Sheriff of New Canaan

The same day

New Canaan

His short flight from National to LaGuardia was uneventful. He used it to start formulating questions for his visit. From LaGuardia, Hinke drove northeast to New Canaan. Nice country he'd never seen. After getting out of New York, it was skinny two-lane roads all the way. Spring greenery and flowers in bloom. A pleasant day in the low seventies.

New Canaan was a crisp, clean New England town—its downtown streets, business establishments, restaurants, public buildings, and landscaping all prim and proper. All a cut above. Most striking, he noticed that the cars, driving and parked, were late-model automobiles: Chryslers like the rental he was driving, Studebakers, Chevrolets, Buicks, Mercurys, and Fords. His quick assessment was that he couldn't afford to live there, even with his recent raise.

Traveling and jumping into a new case, Hinke liked to arrive at his destination the day before and do a little exploring to get the lay of the land. He checked into the Taft Hotel, took an hour's nap, and ate a fabulous meal at a small Italian restaurant, Alito's, a block away. He'd explore the town the next few days—and maybe he'd find a small gym where he could work out. He'd copied his chalkboard thoughts onto his legal pad and spent an hour jotting down additional notes in preparation for tomorrow. The main question was, "Why?"

The following day, after breakfast at the hotel, Hinke walked the couple blocks to the New Canaan Police Headquarters, which was housed in an impressive three-story brick building. There, he met Sheriff Eli Yates, his navy-blue uniform was perfectly pressed and his shoes spit-shined. His matching hat on his desk. Yates was a tall, slender, white-haired man with crystal blue eyes. Hinke figured sixty-ish. He accepted the sheriff's offer of a cup of coffee, which was promptly brought by a secretary into his corner office that looked out onto Main Street.

They both sat at a small, round conference table. In his clipped New England accent, Yates said, "The Director's secretary, Miss Gandy, didn't tell me much about why you're here other than to see the crime scene and take a fresh look. And that the Director would appreciate any assistance I could provide you. Which I will certainly do."

But Hinke immediately sensed he preferred not to do so.

The coffee arrived. Hinke said, "Thank you, Sheriff. As of a few days ago, these murders are now my sole charge and responsibility."

Yates nodded, wondering what that meant.

Hinke said, "I've reviewed all the crime scene information and the notes of the agents who were here after the murders. But you were first on the scene. What was your initial impression?"

Yates didn't hesitate. "Barbaric. Unimaginable. I was the one who pulled the hideous black crosses from the girls. Though, in hindsight, I know I shouldn't have. Such desecrations. But it was like God told me to do it."

Hinke thought, *"Jeez, a holy-roller type."*

"Water under the bridge. After seeing the Communist banners, you thought it would be wise to call the Director?"

"Yes, and I figured the Bureau had a lot more experience with this kind of thing."

"Like what, Sheriff?"

"Like...it seemed, I'm not sure this is the right word…. staged?" The girls were in precisely the same positions, with the same wounds, their hands touching each other. The black crosses. It was eerie and ghastly."

"Sheriff, do you think one person could have pulled off what you saw?"

"Highly unlikely."

"On that point, we agree with you. Only you and your two deputies saw the complete scene before the crosses were removed from the girls? Is that right?"

"And Mrs. Crumbie."

"Yes, of course, the housekeeper, whom the previous agents interviewed.

"Then that afternoon, you got a call about Tommy Muldoon, found dead in his apartment several miles away by a friend. What was your impression of that scene?"

"Looked like a suicide. Assumed the note next to him would be a suicide note. I didn't touch it, but I could read enough to realize it was an invitation from the Haverford twins for Muldoon to visit Easter night. FBI agents had arrived from New York to work the twins' murder scene. I figured they'd want to process the suicide scene, too. We stayed an arm's length away."

"Sheriff, you've been doing great work under tough conditions, and I mean that. But Tommy Muldoon didn't commit suicide. He was murdered. Multiple clues add up to that conclusion. The main one being how the bullet entered his head. An ex-Army guy would never shoot himself in the side of the head, or for that matter, in bed. He'd be sitting or standing with the gun in his mouth or under his chin."

"Okay," Yates said warily.

Hinke said, "I'm going to be straight with you: Hoover wants it to be commies. It would be high-profile PR for the Bureau if and when they're caught. Lou Nichols thinks this could be bigger and better for the FBI than the Lindbergh case."

Yates had not fallen off the turnip truck recently. He said, "But you're not buying that, are you?"

When necessary, Hinke fibbed and said, "I'm keeping an open mind."

Hinke had thought about his situation, and the obvious became clearer. Hoover could care less about finding the twins' and Tommy Muldoon's murderers—unless they were commies. Hoover would love to get headlines producing jaw-dropping Red Scare PR—with the FBI making dramatic arrests and saving the country from commie infiltration. The Director was willing to put a small bet down to catch the Communist perpetrators. Muldoon was dead and didn't count, regardless of how he was involved (and Hinke felt sure he wasn't). Hinke was that small bet.

If Hinke got the commies, Hoover would take the credit. Hoover would be on every newspaper and magazine once again, which was fine. If Hinke failed, it wasn't a big deal for Hoover or the Bureau. Little was public about the murders, and no more would ever be public if commie murderers weren't found. The double murder/suicide would become cold cases. And the victims would likely never get justice. And who knew what would happen to him?

The sheriff had seen the banners and was predisposed to the bad guys being commies. He now knew, though, that Tommy Muldoon likely did not die by his own hand. Hinke was ninety-five percent sure the commie flags were red herrings (no pun intended) and that Hoover was wrong. He could try and do a good job convincing him of that—the problem being he'd need to find the perpetrators sooner rather than later. He hoped his strategy of doling out bits of information via questions to a few New Canaan townspeople might point him in a direction; he would tell his interviewees their conversations needed to be confidential—knowing full well they wouldn't be. It was a gamble. He didn't want to completely piss off Hoover, Tolson, Nichols, or Yates.

The good news: The sheriff was clearly engaged and told Hinke, "Maybe Muldoon was part of a commie ring. His buddies could have killed him as a loose end after he did his deed. I didn't know Muldoon, and I don't know any commie types around here. But I'm sure there's plenty in Hartford or New Haven or the City or Philly or lots of other places on the East Coast.

Hinke replied, "Yes, all good thoughts. But, we haven't found any political bent to Mr. Muldoon. Nor do we have any physical evidence putting him at the murder scene." But he thought, *"There was a good chance he was there after the twins were murdered; he came home and got murdered by the same perpetrators."*

Hinke started to mention the Land photos that he was sure the FBI agents hadn't told Yates about. Also, he might have seen the necklaces on the pool table but would know nothing about them. He decided to hold back – not offering the sheriff any more details, at least yet.

"Maybe a cell of commies set him up, and he became an unwitting pawn," Hinke said. "The thing is, commies I've run into skulk in the shadows using their lies and persuasion and propaganda to win hearts and minds. If you're a commie subversive, why do you commit three complex murders and likely invite the wrath of J. Edgar Hoover and disgust the public more? To what end? What could you gain?"

Yates said, "I don't know."

"Me neither. Or maybe a nastier group set up Muldoon. But why kill the twins? Nothing is adding up in any of the three murders. Though, I'm betting the banners were a ruse."

Yates nodded and said, "I understand why you're here."

Hinke thought, *"That's a positive sign of cooperation, and he doesn't know the half of it."*

Then he told Yates the cold, hard truth. "For now, the story remains a double-murder and suicide."

Yates gave him a sardonic smile. "Though it isn't, is it? Though that's the way I hope it stays."

Hinke replied, "Right, even though it isn't—at least until I find the sons-a-bitches who killed both the twins and Muldoon. If I don't figure it out, it will stay that way."

The sheriff leaned back in his chair and said, "Hinke, I'm not going to blow smoke up your ass on this. I was hoping you were sent here to put a bow on this thing, wrap it up for the parents and townspeople; and put it behind us. The murders have been tough on everyone but particularly the Haverfords and Mrs. Crumbie. Could I ask that you not interview them again?"

Hinke thought for a minute, " I have the notes of other agents who talked with them. That's fine for this visit. And Sheriff, I'd appreciate it if this conversation remains between us."

Yates replied, "And I'd appreciate it if you keep me informed of your progress."

"Absolutely."

The sheriff stood and picked up two keys on his desk. "The large one is for the gate, and the other for the side door of the Big Cottage guesthouse. Here's a simple map to get you to the Haverford Estate. A tall, black wrought iron fence surrounds the property; you can't miss it. The guesthouse is on the right; the mansion, also called the Big House, is straight ahead up the hill."

"Thanks, Sheriff. After I visit the crime scene, I have an appointment with Priscilla Loncart at the Greenwich Academy. Any background you could provide?"

He grinned like a Cheshire cat. "You'll see for yourself, but she may be the most beautiful woman I've ever laid eyes on. Her family is said to be one of the wealthiest in New Canaan and maybe the state. She hardly needs the money, but I know she was a teacher for a few years at the Academy, then became headmistress. Maybe close to forty. She gave birth to her first children a couple months ago.

"Children?"

"Twin girls."

"Okay, thanks again."

As Hinke turned to leave, the sheriff asked, "How long do you plan on being in New Canaan, Hinke?"

"This visit, probably no more than a few days. I'll be gone by next Tuesday at the latest."

Hinke exited feeling that the sheriff wanted to add, *"Don't let the fucking door hit your ass on the way out."*

Chapter 11 – The Guesthouse

With gray clouds now replacing the early morning sunshine, Hinke followed the map. The homes got more majestic by the minute. He arrived at the Haverford Estate, which had to be behind the tall, black iron fence and wooded fence line. He slotted the big key into the gate and pushed it open. Drove through and came back to see if the key worked on both sides. It did.

A couple hundred yards in the distance he could see part of the palatial Big House, the Haverfords' white brick mansion. He drove up the paved driveway until he came to the guesthouse to the right. A sprawling, one-story ranch. He used the other key to get in. The interior was in perfect order but smelled of potent cleaners.

He walked up the hallway until he got to the gaming room, where the girls were murdered. The wood floor had been scrubbed of blood. Few others would notice, but he could see faint outlines of the stains. He flipped on the light as he entered. The stains were more prominent as he approached the pool table with a cloth cover over it. He pulled it off. The green felt was blanched and ruined; no doubt when trying to wipe off the twins' blood, it would need replacing. No clues on the pool table. He wouldn't be surprised if the table was gone by his next visit. Hinke stepped back from the table, looking for what; he wasn't sure. Here at the scene, he could conjure up the Land photographs, but this time in color: the ornate pool table, its leather pockets, the Tiffany light. Then, the pool table was sprayed with blood. The twins' bloody bodies were laid out on the table.

Though it felt a bit sacrilegious, he thought, *"What the fuck?"* He grabbed a ball rack and a cue. He circled pocket to pocket and gathered up the balls. They were unusual—made of ivory with the ball number inside a star. Three were missing: the eight-ball, the two-ball, and the cue ball. He rechecked each leather pocket. No balls. He wandered about the gaming room and opened a few cabinet drawers. No balls.

Using the one-ball as the cue ball, he quickly ran the table. It reminded him of playing pool at Sonny's Bar in Georgetown, which he used to frequent before the War. He re-racked the balls, put the cover back on, and walked back into the hallway. A strange rattling noise was coming toward him from his right. What in the world? He looked down. Instinctively, he reached and grabbed it before it passed him—the missing two-ball.

"Who's there?" he shouted.

He peered down the hallway in the direction from which the ball had come. Out of the darkness walked two girls. They stopped several yards in front of him. The beautiful, liquid-like apparitions smiled. Nellie and Natalie Haverford. He tried to walk closer, but his feet didn't respond.

"He shouted, "Who did this? Please tell me who killed you."

Holding the two-ball, he could only watch as the apparitions walked back in the direction they came from—and were gone. Only then would his feet move again. He ran down the hallway after them. Nothing. There was nothing in the other rooms off the hallway. Nothing unusual anywhere.

He had to ask himself, *What the hell just happened?*

Hinke strode back to the entrance of the gaming room. The cover of the pool table was off. Thirteen balls were positioned dead center in the shape of a cross. This felt creepy. He ran into the living room and kitchen, where he checked the pantry. He ran down the opposite hallway and poked his head into three other rooms and a bathroom. He re-examined the gaming room, the two rooms off the hallway, and another bathroom. There was no one else in the house. He needed to get out of there.

Sitting on a stone bench in front of the cottage, the stark reality hit him: no one would believe what he saw. If he fessed up to what he'd seen, he'd be sent to St. Elizabeth's looney bin and probably fired, regardless of what Helen Gandy had promised about protecting him, and no, the last few minutes had to remain his secret.

He rolled the two-ball in his hand and claimed it as his. He'd pooh-poohed the supernatural his whole life. He was surer that there'd been no commies involved in the murders. No, he was up against something much eviler than any minions directed by the Kremlin.

Hinke got up and walked along the imposing ten-foot black iron fence in both directions. In spots, the stately maples, oaks, and other vegetation blocked any visibility to the fence from the road. Maybe the killers had a gate key, but if not, he figured they could have easily picked the lock.

Back in town, Hinke grabbed lunch at a little restaurant near the hotel. As he ate a BLT with fries and drank iced tea, he reviewed what he'd seen. *"No, I wasn't hallucinating. It happened."*

Chapter 12 – Tommy Muldoon

Two weeks prior—Holy Thursday

Greenwich, Connecticut

Headmistress Priscilla Loncart made a point of bumping into the Haverford girls when they emerged from class before lunch.

"Ah, how are my favorite twins?"

"We can't wait for vacation!"

Priscilla put an arm around each and asked, "What are your Easter plans, girls?"

Nellie and Natalie were so excited that they kept interrupting each other. "Miss Priscilla, our parents left Monday for Cuba and agreed that we could stay in our Big Cottage, by ourselves, until they get back next Friday. It's been fun, but it'll be better when we're out of school."

That news excited Priscilla more than she could say—finally, an opportunity. "My, that does sound like fun! Who looks out for you?"

Natalie told her, "Mrs. Crumbie has meals for us up at the Big House. She comes down with cookies at 9:00. Of course, we never go to bed then." The twins both giggled.

Priscilla smiled. "Of course not."

"We had to promise not to let anyone in the gate—and not to go out unless we told her where we were going. And not after dark. We've been good about that. They looked at each other, and both grinned.

"Happy Easter, girls. I'll see you in a week."

Priscilla walked quickly to her office, shut the door, and stared down at the school grounds through her large picture window. She knew about the twins and their minor hanky-panky with Tommy Muldoon in the tutoring room after school. They were both teases who were driving him nuts. A hidden bug and transmitter had confirmed this, and she'd intercepted a couple of salacious notes that they'd written and put in interoffice envelopes, which ended up in his mail cubby—after Priscilla read them. She'd been trying to figure out an angle. The note was typed using one of the typewriters in the typing classroom. Excellent!

Tommy—

We want you to visit us Sunday night at midnight. We're staying alone in the Big Cottage, which is the first building you'll get to, way before the Big House. We'll leave the gate unlocked. Drive in, then close it again. On the right, park in the back. We'll leave a light on.

We promise lots of fun!

Natalie & Nellie

Then, she typed a duplicate in case it was needed.

Sex with two beautiful teenage twins had to be the ultimate dream for Tommy (and a zillion other guys). She bet that he'd show at the Big Cottage. Tommy wasn't critical, but it would make it a lot more fun. She'd been racking her brain about how and when to get the twins in a solitary place. Then it fell in her lap. No doubt, a gift from her Dark Lord. Her family would be happy, but maybe not about including Tommy Muldoon. Too bad.

She folded the note once, as the girls had done in previous notes, and put it in a beat-up interoffice envelope with a fastener tie. On one of the black lines, she mimicked as closely as she could how the girls wrote, "MR. MULDOON." She kept "From" and "Date" blank. On the way, she said hi to a couple of her teachers, stopped at the bank of teachers' mail slots, and fetched the other mail in Tommy's slot.

A few minutes later, she walked down to his math homeroom and poked her head in. "Tommy, your mail. Thought I'd drop it by." She'd been careful to stick her envelope in the middle of the others.

He probably didn't have to but stood when he said, "Thank you, Mrs. Loncart. You didn't have to do that."

"Do you have plans over Easter, Mr. Muldoon?"

"Going to a friend's parents in Greenwich for Easter dinner. I may visit an old army buddy of mine in the City for a couple days next week. Not sure what else."

"Excellent—have a Happy Easter. See you the week after next."

"Happy Easter to you too, Mrs. Loncart."

She turned and was gone.

Tommy thumbed through the mail he'd not picked up for a couple days. A few one-page school announcements and three interoffice envelopes.

One, he immediately knew who it was from. His heart pounded. A note from the Haverford twins.

He tried not to jump up and down after reading it twice. *"They wouldn't tease me, would they?"* He discarded the thought as he sat back down in his desk chair. *"No guy on the planet wouldn't be jealous"*.

Priscilla had the place and time—figuring they needed to be there ready to pick the gate lock around 9:30. In case Mrs. Crumbie was late with cookies that night, one of them would watch until the coast was clear. They'd be in and out and gone in an hour. If Tommy showed up at midnight or a bit earlier, that would be great. Whatever she could do to muck up the works of anyone trying to figure out who killed the twins and why—she would do. Tommy was a monkey wrench, and She wanted to throw it at law enforcement and see what happened. It wasn't about the perfect crime; it was about a fun, challenging crime consistent with the Teachings and her mother's rules.

Chapter 13 - Greenwich

Greenwich, CT

It was a pleasant drive down to Greenwich on a beautiful spring day. There are two lanes all the way, not a lot of traffic, and lush rolling hills, fields, and forests. The main building at the Greenwich Academy, deemed the most elite girls' school in Connecticut, was three stories and brick with a large semicircle of white columns. It trumpeted tradition and old money.

Priscilla Loncart's was a generous third-floor corner office. No frou-frou; rather, dark wood with colonial art and furniture. Hinke felt like he was on a hot streak with women. There was his lovely, young girlfriend Marjorie, the surprisingly sexual Helen Gandy, and bombshell Marilyn Monroe. But none could hold a candle to auburn-haired Priscilla Loncart with her gorgeous face and comely figure. She extended her perfectly manicured hand.

"What can I do for you, Special Agent Hinke, on this beautiful afternoon?" Her perfume was intoxicating; her eyes were dark but sparkling. She sat down on her leather sofa. Hinke couldn't avoid watching her cross her legs as he sat down in the adjacent leather chair.

"Mrs. Loncart, FBI Director Hoover asked me to take a fresh look at the Haverford twins' murders and the death of Tommy Muldoon. Not closed cases yet."

"Please, call me Priscilla."

"Okay, I'm DH. A hike from New Canaan to Greenwich. I didn't realize…"

"Only a half-hour drive. I do it each school day. Not too bad unless it snows."

"You live in New Canaan, too?"

"My family has lived in Connecticut since the 1600s. The Haverfords have been here for the better part of the last couple centuries. They made their fortune in sugarcane, now mostly from Cuba. My family made it in shoes, lumber, and other businesses."

"Priscilla, can you tell me a bit about Tommy Muldoon?"

She feigned distress. "I can't believe he's dead. Tommy was one of my first hires three years ago when I became headmistress after teaching history here for several years. A wonderful teacher."

"Any troubles with Mr. Muldoon?"

Wistfully, she said, "No, he was one of my best. Tommy was well-liked by students and fellow teachers. It's a terrible loss."

"Did he have a temper?"

"Not that I ever saw. But they are saying it might have been bad memories of the War that triggered him to murder Nellie and Natalie?"

He ignored the begging question and asked, "He was the twins' math teacher, and he tutored them?"

"Yes, but not because they had a difficult time in his subject. On the contrary, they wanted to jump ahead a couple of grades into Advanced Calculus. They were not only beautiful and vibrant girls; they also had amazing minds for mathematics."

"That's unusual for girls. When and where did he tutor them?"

"Typically, after school, a couple times a week in the small tutoring room, only three offices down from here."

"Priscilla, I will try to put this delicately. But have you ever had any inappropriate teacher-student issues at the Academy?"

"DH, we pride ourselves in making sure our students are always safe." She hesitated. "A couple years ago, there was an incident."

"Tommy Muldoon?"

"No, not Tommy. Another teacher who I immediately fired. We only have five male teachers, and female math teachers are hard to come by."

"I'll bet. Never my best subject. You have a lot of adolescent girls and had a good-looking, young teacher with them five days a week. You never heard about any crushes girls might have had on Muldoon? Like the Haverford twins? Maybe he came to you asking counsel about a girl or two who was, how should I say, getting a bit too flirty?"

She smiled. "Yes, that did happen a couple of times but not with the Haverford twins. And yes, he was an attractive man. Such a waste."

"I'm assuming Tommy didn't have his own office. Correct?"

"Only a few teachers with the most seniority do, but no, he didn't have his own."

"Where would Tommy get his interoffice mail?"

"Here, I'll show you." She got up, and he followed. The view from behind was world-class spectacular.

They walked a short distance down the hall. Several dozen wooden slots along the wall, most with brown, reusable envelopes with tie fasteners and other mail pieces—and a bin and table for sorting.

"Our not-too-fancy mailroom." She smiled, then explained the process of collecting outgoing envelopes from the wood pockets on the outside of classroom doors. "Or a teacher could drop it in the bin herself or himself. The envelopes are sorted by one of the secretaries."

She pointed out the slot that said "Muldoon." "Haven't had a chance to remove that."

Back in her office, he asked, "Was Tommy political in any way—like belonging to a fascist, or Communist, or another group?"

"Not that I know of. I've read that Hoover and the senator are going after commies."

"McCarthy. He and Hoover share a hatred of commies." He did not add that they were both equal opportunity haters of any non-white, non-Christian.

"What if I were to tell you that Tommy Muldoon got a note from the Haverford twins inviting him over late on Easter night to rendezvous at their Big Cottage? Maybe you knew their parents were out of town?"

He wasn't sure if she looked stunned or not. "No, I didn't know."

"Yes, a note inviting him to Haverford's Big Cottage was found at his place. And one of the girls' diaries indicated they'd done more than math problems in their afterschool tutoring sessions."

She stammered, "Oh my goodness, gracious. That's horrible. My school would be disgraced if that got out."

Hinke noted she sounded a lot more concerned about her school than the twins and Tommy Muldoon dying.

"Relax, Priscilla. It's possible Tommy Muldoon didn't murder the twins."

He let that sink in, then said, "Could be that a commie group set Tommy up to take the fall, then killed him."

"What? Tommy didn't commit suicide?"

"Not likely."

"How could that be?"

"Sorry, that's FBI business. Here's the thing, Priscilla: It might not have been a band of commies either."

"Then who?"

"That's why I'm here for a few days to start figuring out."

"But why kill those beautiful girls?"

"Good question, and I'm telling you, their murders were heinous. If all of this is true, the killers—and it had to be multiple—had to know things that only Tommy and the twins knew."

She said, "The note was intercepted?"

"That would be my guess."

"Or he got the note in his home mail?"

"I don't think so. It was on a full-page, half-folded piece of paper. I think it was in one of your brown reusable interoffice envelopes."

He gave her a minute—then went out on a limb. "Priscilla, the murderers left photographs of their grisly work at the scene."

She gave him her most horrified look. What?"

"You've heard of the new Land cameras that let you take a picture, and it develops automatically?"

"I have, though I've not seen one. Why would any murderer leave such evidence at a crime scene?"

"Why indeed? The killers went to a lot of trouble to make these murders happen and left photos."

She shook her head, feigning disbelief.

"Thank you for your time, Priscilla. I know you have a school to tend to. It's been a pleasure. I'll be in town for a few days; I'm staying at the Taft Hotel. Please let me know if you have any other thoughts about the murders. And if you could keep all this under your hat for now, I'd appreciate it."

"Certainly, DH. But do the Haverfords need to learn about the note and the rest? They will be more devastated."

"No, at least not now."

"Thank you again."

Upon Hinke's departure, Headmistress Priscilla Loncart grabbed the bottle of Macallan Scotch and a tumbler from her desk drawer. She took a sip and felt her gut glow. She'd never felt this satisfied in her life. Not even after giving birth to her twins. She was playing on the bleeding edge, and she knew it—and that it might never get any better than this. Indeed, FBI agent Hinke was a perfect player. He was intelligent and charming and easy on the eyes. She knew that her physical assets got his attention. Indeed, they'd meet again before he left New Canaan.

Chapter 14 – The Gossip

The same day

New Canaan

Hinke walked up the steps to the impressive veranda of a two-story house. She sat in a white wicker chair and extended her hand. Stella Vickers was in her mid-sixties with a short, stocky body—and an unforgettable face (not in a good way) with a Pinocchio nose, wrinkles crowding her overly sharp features. Hinke thought she'd make a great Halloween witch—with little makeup. "Mr. English, so nice to meet you."

"Mrs. Vickers, I must admit before we start that my name is not Paul English, and I'm not a writer." Immediately, he pulled out his gold shield and said, "My real name is Derbert Hinke. I'm an FBI special agent. You're not being investigated, but I'm looking at the three murders three weeks ago from a couple different perspectives."

"Oh, my lands," the city's gossip queen exclaimed. "You mean two murders and a suicide, though. Their teacher killed those beautiful girls. The coward, I hope he burns in hell. Horrible, all horrible. We haven't had a murder ever in New Canaan in my time, and I only recall a couple of suicides."

Hinke ignored her comment and said, "Director Hoover has decided to keep the cases open for now. I'm here to take another look for him."

He handed her one of his cards with Hoover's name and watched her eyes light up. "If you have any issues or further observations, call that number to reach his secretary, Helen Gandy."

Positively starry-eyed, she asked, "You know Mr. Hoover?"

"Yes, I report to him directly."

"Oh, my lands. Is he not the best copper ever!"

Hinke made himself fib, "He sure is. Mrs. Vickers, they say you know more people and what's happening in New Canaan than anyone. We need your help. Call me DH, by the way."

Mrs. Vickers answered, "That's true enough, though I can't possibly know all people and places. But I know most within about twenty miles."

Sitting in the adjacent wicker chair, Hinke deflected and smiled. "You have a beautiful home, Mrs. Vickers."

"Why, thank you, DH. Needs a bit of paint here and there. Harder to keep up the house and gardens and whatnot at my age. My husband, Alvin, died five years ago; God rest his soul."

He told her, "Director Hoover thinks that the murderers might be Communists."

She was dumbfounded. "Sakes alive, however could he think that?"

"Well, let's say that there were commie symbols found at the murder scene."

Her eyes got wide. "You don't say.? What kind of symbols?"

"Mrs. Vickers, I can't say more right now."

Her wheels were spinning. "Oh, my goodness, you mean Mr. Muldoon was a Communist?"

"Not as far as we know. But maybe you've heard rumors about his political views?"

"I knew he was an Academy teacher, a good-looking young man—a decorated war veteran. Wait, you're saying that Mr. Muldoon was or wasn't the twins' murderer? I thought that was all decided."

He ignored the question for now. "Mrs. Vickers, do you know any people in the area with Communist leanings?"

"Umm. We have our share of liberals who voted for Roosevelt and Truman, but I haven't heard of any commies. There are a handful of free-thinker architects who've decided to make New Canaan their playground and have built a handful of the strangest houses you could ever imagine. They're called the Harvard Five. They could be commies, I guess. I've heard they throw wild parties poolside."

She took a sip of her iced tea. "Oh my, DH, I haven't gotten you a tea. My maid Elsa will get you one." She wobbled to the door and yelled for her, then went inside. She disappeared for a couple minutes and then returned with her black maid holding a tray. She put the tea on the table. "Now, where were we?"

He looked her straight in the eyes. "Mrs. Vickers, it could be that Mr. Muldoon didn't kill his two students."

Eyes wide, she asked, "What? Oh my, you are going after Communist killers elsewhere?"

"Maybe...or other killers."

Her eyes bugged out. "But you said Mr. Hoover thinks it's commies."

"Well, the case is fluid."

"Not commies, not Mr. Muldoon. Oh, my gracious."

"Mrs. Vickers, here's my theory right now. The same person, or likely people, murdered the girls and Tommy Muldoon. His suicide was a set-up."

Her hazel eyes lit up. "Oh my, this is like an Agatha Christie murder mystery."

"I'm afraid it is," he smiled. "But real life. That's why I'm here. Thought maybe you might have an idea or two. But, of course, you must tell no one about our conversation."

"Of course not. I will try to think like Hercules Poirot. First, what could be the possible motive?"

"An excellent question, but I'm ninety-nine percent sure it wasn't about money."

She barely nodded her head. Hinke poured himself a bit more tea, debating if he should open the next can of worms or not—then told himself, what the heck.

"Mrs. Vickers, are you aware of any witchcraft practiced in New Canaan or in the area?"

She looked at him quizzically. "Why in the world would you ask, DH?"

He purposely hemmed and hawed until she couldn't stand it. "I know you'll keep this in strict confidence."

She nodded and crossed her heart. She sat on pins and needles for Hinke to give her a juicier scoop.

"There were two identical pieces at the murder scene that might have an occult meaning."

He had clearly thrown her for a loop.

"Lordy, please tell me what they were. Please," she begged.

"I'm sorry, Mrs. Vickers. I'm sure you understand. I can't at this point. I've probably said too much already."

Disappointment written all over her face, Mrs. Vickers told him, "DH, I don't believe in witches or witchcraft and the like, but I know the fear of them was rife among early colonists. More witches were put to death in Connecticut than in Salem, Massachusetts."

"Is that so?"

"DH, I've not heard of or met any witches in New Canaan. That would be barking up the wrong tree. And I think Mr. Poirot would advise that as well."

"Oh, I didn't mean to give the wrong impression, Mrs. Vickers. Witches aren't on my radar."

She asked, "DH, do you believe in witches?"

"Never met one," he smiled, wondering if she included any supernatural. In that case, he fibbed.

"If you're interested in more witchcraft poppycock, I've heard there's an excellent collection of books about that subject in our New Canaan Public Library."

He stood. "Thanks, Mrs. Vickers, for your time and hospitality. Remember, mum's the word on our discussion. I'll be at the Taft Hotel if any more ideas pop into your head."

Slowly, she stood and told him, "This is exciting, DH, and I heard your admonitions." She then moved a thumb and finger across her lips to indicate her mouth was zipped.

As Derbert Hinke walked to his car, he smiled and thought, *"I doubt any of them will be able to keep their mouths shut about our discussions. Mission accomplished."* He would let his interviews marinate over the weekend while he did some sightseeing and research – and see what else he could learn by Monday. In the Big Cottage, he'd seen the twins' ghosts; of that, he had no doubt. But he'd also sensed an Evil that wasn't playing tiddlywinks.

Chapter 15 – Dinner with Priscilla

Hinke took Saturday off; he needed to clear his head about the twins' murders. He got up late, ate a decadent brunch, found a small gym to work out at, took a nap, had couple cocktails, ate a wonderful dinner and was asleep by 9:00.

Sunday morning, after breakfast, he got a few tips from the hotelier about sightseeing around New Canaan. He was fascinated by the modern look of several houses designed by the Harvard Five, the group of avant-garde Harvard architects who were using New Canaan as their laboratory. The houses were unusual but, he thought, spectacular. They all used a lot of glass on their exteriors. The Philip Johnson Glass House—its exterior walls totally glass—was his favorite.

He drove by the Haverford Estate again. He felt another pang of guilt that he'd not introduced himself to the Haverfords when he visited the Big Cottage. But he hadn't wanted to intrude since the other agents had talked to them and found the diaries. That said, any melancholy the Haverfords harbored would likely be exacerbated if new rumors of the murders started swirling around town. He was sorry about that.

Back at his hotel, he felt better after a change of clothes and sipping a martini at the hotel bar. With some rest, he was getting a better picture of New Canaan and the murders. He asked to see a menu. The bartender placed a phone on the bar. He stretched the cord and told him he had a call.

"DH, it's Priscilla. I know it's short notice, but how about dinner on me at your hotel in about an hour?"

His recent luck with females continued. He replied, "I'd love to."

The New Canaan rumor mill was on fire: Muldoon killed the girls; he didn't kill the girls. Muldoon committed suicide; he didn't commit suicide. He was found with a ton of money; he was found with valuable pieces of art. It was part of a secret cell of commies who killed the girls; the girls had a secret lover who became jealous of Muldoon and decided to kill them all; it was all the doings of an evil coven of witches who used the twins in a ceremony with Muldoon's help, then killed him. And on and on…

Priscilla Loncart knew she must get close to Hinke to better hear his thoughts and throw more into the bubbling cauldron of New Canaan blather. Before leaving, she kissed her baby twins—and then her husband Reginald, who was in his office. "Esmerelda is watching the twins. I may not be back until tomorrow morning."

With no surprise or anger, he said, "Don't play this too cute and screw it up."

She kissed him again on the cheek. "Reggie, darling, You know I love living on the edge."

Priscilla drove her black Rolls-Royce Phantom to the hotel, which was only five minutes away, and told the maître d' to park it for her. She handed him a twenty—in case he wasn't on duty later. Hinke was at the bar drinking his second vodka martini. She winked at the bartender and said, "I'll have the same."

It was a long mahogany wood bar with a bronze-framed mirror that ran forty feet. Nice leather barstools. From his stool, he stood and was instantly mesmerized.

"Mrs. Loncart…I mean, Priscilla, you look fantastic."

What she heard him think was, *"She'd be very fuckable."*

Now that her baby fat was one hundred percent gone, she wore her tightest red skirt, silk blouse with the hint of a black brassiere, red blazer, and red high heels. She was sumptuous, her perfume exotic.

She offered him her hand and then put both around his right hand. She sat on the stool next to him. "DH, have you been enjoying our fine town?"

He gushed about the Harvard Five's modern home architecture and about New Canaan and what an intriguing place it was. She listened and suggested, "Why don't we go to our table?"

It was a cozy, dimly lit, two-person table near the window. With no prompting, the waiter brought fresh drinks. Hinke couldn't help but think, *"Yeah, I know, Marilyn Monroe's lips were on my cheek not long ago, but Priscilla Loncart may be more magnificent."*

As his eyes devoured her, she said to herself, *Ah, now a much better view directly into his mind.*

"DH, have you made progress on your FBI investigations? Do you think…"

He interrupted. "I'm sure Tommy Muldoon was set up and didn't kill the twins."

With as much sincerity as she could muster, she told him, "I'm relieved to know he won't be blamed for the murders. This hasn't been great PR for my school, but it could be a lot worse."

"I understand. But his name has already been dragged through the mud. Unless I find the murderers, his name will never be cleared."

Priscilla had known there was a less risky scenario in which she hadn't made Tommy Muldoon a player. That changed when her bugging of the tutoring office indicated fun and games with the Haverford twins. The opportunity became too delectable to pass up after she found out about their Easter vacation alone in the Big Cottage—an almost perfect setup. And if Tommy didn't take the bait, the plan would work. She prayed to her Dark Lord, thanking him for his largesse. So far, so good.

She looked him dead in the eyes and said, "You'll find the murderers. I know you will."

With her confidence and kindly, classy manner, he felt revitalized in his quest. Priscilla ordered for both. Quail in plum sauce, crispy new potatoes, and Caesar salad. They discussed a wide variety of topics, from politics to sports. She admitted that three months earlier, she'd had her first children, twin girls, and that they had changed her outlook on life. Hinke admitted he was trying to get up the courage to marry his girlfriend but hadn't been able to pull the trigger after three years. She smiled and said, "Well, maybe that should tell you something, DH. I'm guessing there's another woman?"

Hinke thought, *"No, I'm not going to mention Helen to her."*

"Perhaps."

Priscilla smiled but let it go.

Time flew as they talked—but no more about the murders. They'd drunk a bottle of Bordeaux and were on to after-dinner drinks and dessert. Those eyes of hers were remarkable; they shimmered as if they were a myriad of black diamonds. He'd never seen anything like them. After her last bite, matter-of-factly, Priscilla leaned forward across the table, displaying her cleavage, and said, "DH, let me see your room key."

"What the heck," Hinke thought. He dug into his pocket and put it in her hand. Regally, she stood, straightened her tight skirt, and said, "Give me ten minutes to freshen up before you knock." He watched her swivel as she pranced to the elevator. She looked better than a million dollars.

Hinke could hold his liquor okay but realized he was decently drunk. This wasn't what he was expecting. He waited eleven minutes and took the elevator up three floors to the top floor. But he couldn't remember his room number. After frustrated pacing, he realized that 316 was the one. He knocked twice before the door opened. There stood Priscilla Loncart, like Aphrodite, totally naked but for her high heels and her shiny black necklace. An auburn goddess from head to toe. She took his hand and led him to the bed.

He knew it was a bad idea, but hers was an amazing pull unlike he'd ever felt before. There was no way to resist her.

The next morning, Priscilla awoke in her own bed to the sunlight, which danced across her body. Her dutiful husband, Reggie, entered with a cup of coffee. He didn't have a classically handsome face, but he was tall and dark. She figured two out of three ain't bad.

"Thank you, my dear."

"How did it go with the special agent?" her husband asked

"He's making our *Game* more fun than I could imagine, but it's more dangerous sooner than expected. I read his notes while he was passed out last night."

"After you fucked him…"

She ignored the comment. "He knows the commie thing was pure crap—and that Muldoon was a pawn, at best. Worst case, he thinks the murderers live nearby and that they knew Muldoon and the twins. We both may be suspects."

He briefly closed his eyes.

"But…" She smiled broadly. "…it's clear he has no idea of any motive; it's already driving him crazy. And he doesn't have any proof. In bed, his thoughts were garbled, but I heard, "I'm a horn dog; what would Helen say?"

"Maybe you should nip this in the bud?"

"No, we'll let him play—at least for now. Come on, think of the *Game*, Reggie! It will be fun to play it out as far as we can. We'll go down in the annals for the sheer audacity of what we're doing. Mother would have been thrilled that I've taken her Teachings to heart."

"Can't get out over our skis on this, Priscilla," he said seriously.

"You worry too much," she smirked and beckoned him to bed. But not before telling him she was in the mood for cocaine, too.

Reggie knew that was always a good sign.

When Hinke woke up the next morning, she was gone. Gently, he sat up. Thank God his hangover wasn't too awful. He remembered pieces of last night. She was riding on top of him, bucking up and down, looking him dead in the eyes. Her almost pitch-black, sparkling eyes were otherworldly. While his hands groped her generous breasts, he couldn't help but notice her bouncing necklace; an unusual pendant made of sparkling black stones with small red accents.

Mostly recovered after a long, hot shower and hearty breakfast, including three cups of coffee, he went out to the veranda and sat in a rocking chair—and let his thoughts flow without writing notes. He decided to spend a couple hours in the town library but needed his notes and briefcase. When he got back to his room, it had already been cleaned: new bed sheets, linens, fluffed pillows—plus chocolates and mints on the bed. More of the festivities from last night were coming back to him—but in bizarre fits and starts. No question, Priscilla was great in bed. That much he remembered. He smiled. *"Oh, how I do love the ladies."*

His well-worn, leather, stand-up briefcase was on the only table in his room. But the snap was undone, and it was unlocked. He never left his briefcase like that. Ever. He reached to the back folder compartment where he always kept his legal pad. It wasn't there. Panicked, he turned the briefcase upside down and let it all fall out onto the table. Pens, pencils, paperclips, and a rubber (which he didn't use last night), plus several other files and thankfully, the legal pad.

He was relieved but puzzled about the lock clasp and the location of the legal pad.

Chapter 16 – Witches?

At the New Canaan Library, he walked up to the front desk, not exactly sure what he was going to say. A bespectacled, trim, middle-aged lady smiled politely and asked, "May I help you?"

He made it up on the fly with a slight Southern accent and extended his hand. "I'm Duncan Osburn, from Savannah, a salesman passing through your lovely town. I've always been fascinated by witchery and the occult. My town is full of it. I've heard that there were more witches executed in Connecticut than in Salem."

She interrupted. "Monnie Maples, head librarian. And you are correct. New Haven and central Connecticut have a much darker history than Salem."

"I wondered if you could point me to a few of your books. I'm not a scholar, only a hobbyist. I'm looking for books that I could perhaps thumb through to get a flavor of the history of witches and the occult in this area."

Her eyes brightened. "While Yale has the most amazing collection, we've been building our own and have excellent references. I'd be glad to show them to you."

"Splendid, Miss Maples. I'll be in your debt."

She led him through a row of stacks, then pointed him toward four shelves packed with books about the occult, including two shelves devoted strictly to witches in New England. Others were more generally about the occult and witchery in the US and abroad.

He thanked her and picked out a handful at random. Expecting to be bored, he thumbed through the books and became immersed, reading bits and pieces and perusing the black-and-white illustrations. A wild goose chase—for what, he didn't know.

Most illustrations were crude, but one caught his eye: a female lying on a stone slab, three devils surrounding her. One, looking more female than the others, held a black cross above her head. The sketch was entitled *"The Devil's Sacrifice."*

Hinke stared at it for several minutes, then did a no-no he'd have been whipped for and maybe kicked out of school back in the day. He ripped the page out, folded it once, and slid it into his coat pocket. He could have looked at this collection a lot longer, but feeling guilty as hell, he put the books back on the shelf and strode back to the main desk. There, he thanked Miss Maples. "A fascinating collection. Wish I had more time."

He turned back as he walked out. "A question, Miss Maples. I'm curious: do you think there are witches around the area today?"

He was shocked when she said, "I do." She then turned her head and disappeared into the stacks.

Back in his car, he looked at the black and white sketch again and thought, yes. Indeed, the Brevard murders had been sacrifices. While the commie banners were red herrings to get Hoover's attention—the black crosses, the Land photos, the necklaces, the phantom pool ball—those were real clues. He said out loud, "The assholes are leaving breadcrumbs for me to chase after." Then wished he were as wise as Hercules Poirot.

Chapter 17 – Get Out of My Town

After confirming his travel reservations, eating a late lunch, and taking a nap, Hinke was awakened by a phone call. Sheriff Yates wondered if he could drop by the station. Hinke told him he'd be glad to in a half hour. He walked over to the New Canaan Police Headquarters—trying to anticipate what was on the sheriff's mind. Guessing it might not be pleasant.

In the sheriff's office, Yates didn't ask if he'd like coffee. Instead, he opened a cabinet and brought out a bottle of bourbon and Scotch with two glasses. "Pick your poison, Hinke."

Hinke pointed at the bourbon. Yates poured, then sat down behind his desk. Hinke took a seat in the nearest chair. After a big pull on his Scotch, Yates asked, "You've been enjoying our town, Hinke?"

"A fine place, the type I could live in one day after big city life— if I could afford it." They both laughed.

"Hinke, I'm going to cut to the chase. You've instigated wild rumors about the Haverford twins' and Tommy Muldoon's murders. As the defender of public safety, I don't need that."

"Sheriff, I asked questions of a few people to see what I might learn. I spread no rumors."

Yates popped the bottom of his Scotch hard enough on his desk to jettison some of it. "The hell you didn't. Did you find the commie or whoever did the murders?"

"Not yet, but…" Yates cut him off.

"I want you to promise that you'll return to DC and recommend that, in light of Muldoon's suicide and murders of the twins, the investigation will end."

Hinke wasn't expecting this level of pushback and tried to dial back his anger. "Sheriff, I promised that I'd keep you in the loop, but there's been nothing to report yet. I don't have one suspect. If I did, you'd be the first to know."

The sheriff punched back, "I want you gone tomorrow, and I don't want to see you again in my town. Ever."

Hinke had to bite his tongue to avoid flinging a diatribe of expletives at the sheriff. But he knew he'd struck a nerve somewhere in New Canaan—and it wasn't Yates.

"Hinke, this is a small town. We need to let sleeping dogs lie. Muldoon killed the girls and then committed suicide like your FBI boys originally said. I'm sure that Director Hoover has plenty of commies for you to chase down elsewhere."

As he drank the rest of his bourbon, it was evident to Hinke that Yates had already called Hoover or would shortly. He knew he couldn't burn this bridge but was thinking, *"Sheriff, are you remotely interested in who killed these girls and what happened in the Big Cottage that night? What if these killers do it again?"*

Hinke stood tall and left Yates' office. He walked back to his hotel and into the bar. Then decided on room service instead. He needed to write down as many ideas and thoughts as possible before any faded away. He went to bed early and had pleasant dreams of Helen, not Priscilla.

Chapter 18 – Helen and Derby

The following day

Washington, DC

The second time he visited Helen in her flat, he brought a bouquet of yellow roses. Nervous as a cat on a hot tin roof from a week of anticipation, he exclaimed, "It's good to see you again, Miss…Helen." She was eye-popping again, this time with a martini already in hand.

"Come in, Derby." She handed him the martini. "Do you like this little outfit I got by special delivery yesterday from Marilyn Monroe? Wasn't that nice of her?"

"No question Marilyn had good taste—with a lot of naughty baked in." He followed Helen inside. She wore a flattering, gauzy pink gown over a white half-brassiere, little panties, and matching pink heels. Her lips again glistened like a shiny apple; her big brown eyes were accentuated with carefully applied liner and mascara, and her dark hair was combed out, spilling to her shoulders.

Helen looked good enough to eat—and that he would do. He stepped closer, pressing his body against hers, grabbed her ass with both hands and kissed her. Helen broke off the long embrace and giggled, "Derby, I've got cooking to do."

"Okay, but please tell Marilyn to send more…or I will," he chuckled.

Unable to take his eyes off her as she sashayed into the kitchen, he asked if he could wander around. "Explore to your heart's content. You might want to visit my guestroom office."

She retreated to the kitchen. He considered the spacious living and dining rooms more closely on this visit. Hinke was no interior decorator. He guessed you'd call her taste in décor eclectic. Furniture, rugs, paintings, and pottery were unlike anything he'd ever seen. Fascinating pieces from, it seemed, all over the world, including a beautiful set of long warrior swords maybe from the Orient? Lots of shades of reds, maroons, whites, blacks, and grays. Not anything he'd seen in any DC home he'd been in. Lots of pieces, yet the room didn't seem jam-packed, and it all meshed. An extension of the private Helen.

He peeked around the corner where she stood in front of her stove in her sheer lingerie. "Helen, where did you get all the beautiful things in your apartment?"

She smiled. "I receive gifts off and on from many people who—should I say—need access to the Director."

"Helen, you can't be influenced, can you?" he kidded.

She laughed but then said, "Maybe off and on…"

The first time he'd been there he hadn't visited her office, which doubled as a guestroom. Photographs of famous people were neatly arranged on all four walls. Holding his vodka martini, he circled the room and looked more closely. Most were signed photos not to Hoover but to "Helen," or "Helen Gandy" or "Miss Gandy." Every president since Coolidge and several first ladies, Ginger Rogers, Dorothy Lamour, Shirley Temple, Greer Garson, Cary Grant, General George Patton, Gary Cooper, Grace Kelly, Hedy Lamar, Henry Fonda, Judy Garland, W. C. Fields, Ethel Merman, Joseph Kennedy, Bobby Jones, Babe Ruth, Ted Williams, Milton Berle, Jimmy Stewart, Walter Winchell, Marlene Dietrich, Lucille Ball, Desi Arnez, and, of course, Marilyn Monroe…plus many more.

"Ah, I see you found my gallery." Helen brought the silver pitcher of cold vodka. She looked more desirable than last week if that were possible. He had to have her before dinner. She poured him another martini.

"You must get a kick dealing with all these luminaires," he commented as she sipped her martini in her eye-popping lingerie.

Her phonograph in the living room was playing Sarah Vaughan's melodic jazz. He was in heaven.

She laughed and said, "While I finish in the kitchen, take a peek at the file, too." She pointed to an FBI file on her desk.

He noticed a "P" designation on the cover. It was chock full of eight-by-ten photographs. He flipped through several and looked around the room again. Many of the icons who were hanging on the walls appeared in the photographs he thumbed through. A Who's Who of famous people: wives having sex in a variety of places, positions, and outfits. Men and women, not with their spouses. Not with members of their own sex. One famous wife with several large Negro men. A well-known politician with a sheep. Doing things he'd never seen. And much more…

She came back and grinned, "Only a small sample from the boss's P for Personal and O/C for Official/Confidential files, that are fruits of thousands of hours of Bureau surveillance. She winked. "He likes to keep his minions of gumshoes, like you, busy. I'm kidding. The Boss is a pervert. More than you could imagine. But a little kinky might be fun? Don't you think, Derby?"

He smiled and said, "I'm game."

She took his hand and led him back into the living room. "Sit down, Derby. It'll be another fifteen minutes. If you'll oblige, I could use an appetizer first." Within a minute, her head bobbed up and down in his lap like a buoy in a wavy sea, and her red lipstick wallpapered his erection—until the appetizer was served, thick and warm onto her lips and face.

"You taste good," she said, curiously rubbing most of his essence into her skin as she'd done last week and then licking her fingers. She knew what he was thinking and said mysteriously, "Trust me, it's the closest thing to the Fountain of Youth there is on earth."

Antipasto, lasagna, spinach salad, and rolls with a tasty Classico hit the spot. Helen regaled him with stories about the people in the photos on her wall and in the file—while Hinke asked several questions, which she always had an interesting answer to. The subject of Marilyn Monroe came up.

"I worry about that young lady," she told him. "Heavenly looks, sexier than all get-out, plenty of smarts, nice gal, but she has a blind spot when it comes to dating the right men. The Boss wants to turn her into one of his stool pigeons. But I've taken her under my wing."

She led him to her bedroom. After two hours of sex better than any he'd had in his life, perhaps partly inspired in part by the "perverted" photographs (Hinke could not get enough of Hedy Lamar and her dark proclivities), he turned his head on the pillow and asked, "Helen, I've heard that a few special agents are called 'Gandy dancers.' I'm not another one of those, am I?"

She could not help playfully smirking. "Why, Derby, I do believe you're jealous."

His face went crimson. Heat steamed from each pore.

"I've helped many special agents over the years. Purely professional. Favors can come in handy. You're the only one on my dance card, Derby, and nobody dances like you."

He believed her but was troubled. Before he could ask the question, she answered it. "Derby, don't worry about surveillance. The only two people in the world who the Boss truly trusts are Junior, his nickname for Tolson, and me. That's it. We're the only two – other than the Boss – who can put anyone on the exclusive NS, No Surveillance, list. You're already on the list. Marilyn is, too, but that's harder for me to monitor since she's usually in California."

She changed the subject. "Derby, how about we go over a few ground rules in the event you decide to continue as we've done this week and last week?"

He wondered what she'd say next as she sat naked, Indian style on her bed. "Derby, you weren't picked out of a hat. I put together the shortlist, and it was obvious you were the best man for the job. I'd already put you at the top of the list. Your interview with the Boss was your first meeting about the Haverford murders. When you walked into my office, I knew you were the only one. You'll do a fine job."

She touched his hand and continued, "I need a man like you. If you want to continue, here are the two rules: first, this relationship will need to be a solemn secret between you and me. We both want to keep our jobs."

She continued, "Derby, I'm not a young woman, but I promise to fulfill your desires the best I can for as long as I can. You can see other women, but the second rule is you can't get married. It would be too complicated."

His head propped on the bed pillows. He considered Helen's brown eyes, and a part of him shouted, *"This is nuts. Okay, the sex is off the charts, and she's maybe the nicest, smartest woman I've ever met. But for God's sake, she's a lot older. And she's Hoover's secretary to boot."* But he stayed silent.

Helen continued, "I suggest we get together one designated evening of the week, but only at my place. I understand this means giving up things you may have wanted. Derby, I know you have concerns. Think it over if you'd like. One more thing, though. The Boss will never harm you or get rid of you while he and I are at the

Bureau. And you will remain on the No Surveillance list. Those things I promise regardless of your decision."

It wasn't a complete no-brainer, but after another round of extraordinary sex with her that night, he readily agreed to her terms.

Lounging naked next to him, she said, "Derby, I know you wanted to talk with me about your trip to New Canaan tonight. Tomorrow at 10 a.m., you'll get an audience with the Boss, Junior, and Lou Nichols. And I'll be in the room."

"Helen, I can do that, but the murders weren't done by commies. No way."

"Of course, they weren't. But you know that's what the Boss wants. We'll see what happens in the a.m."

Out of the blue, he asked, "Helen, do you believe in the supernatural? The world beyond what we can usually see or hear or sense?"

"But of course."

"And in the supernatural, there is Good and Evil? God and Devil continuously battling for the hearts, minds, and souls of humans?"

"Definitely."

"Angels and devils that can revisit their territory here?"

"No doubt."

"Helen, I'll give my pitch to Hoover that the killers aren't the commies he hoped for. I think he won't like it. This case is about Good and Evil. I saw the twins, or rather their supernatural beings, or apparitions, or ghosts. I spoke to them, but they didn't answer who killed them. They rolled a missing pool ball down the hallway at me. They formed a cross using the pool balls in the middle of the table. Helen, this whole thing is about twins and crosses and Good and Evil.

Commies aren't part of it. But if I ever admit all that, they'll cart me off to St. Elizabeth's nuthouse."

Chapter 19 – Hoover, Hinke & Helen

The next morning, Hoover sat implacably behind his desk. Tolson and Nichols sat opposite Hinke at the conference table. Assistant Director Lou Nichols, he'd not met in person but recognized him from pictures in the press. He'd read in a few magazines and papers that Nichols was the best and most feared PR guy on the planet and next in prominence in the FBI after Tolson and Helen. Hinke reached his hand across the table to the bespectacled, slightly paunchy guy, who looked about Hoover's age. "Special Agent Hinke, it's a pleasure."

Helen stood against the far wall, which already felt like an inquisition. Hoover started, "I hear you had an eventful visit to New Canaan, Hinke. Did you find my Communist killers?"

Hinke only got to "Sir…" before he was interrupted.

"Hinke, Yates called and told me you indicated to him you didn't think commies did the murders. And that people in New Canaan are running around in a panic saying it might be commies, or witches, or a whacky unknown group; that Tommy Muldoon wasn't the killer and didn't commit suicide—and all sorts of other nonsense."

"Sir, I told the sheriff that Muldoon's death wasn't a suicide, which you and I and Mr. Tolson already discussed. Yates called you originally because of the banners. I told him it was *possible* it wasn't commies. I talked to a few others in New Canaan but only asked questions."

"Hinke, I'm going to ask you again: Did you find my commie killers?"

"Sir, can I have a few minutes to tell you why it's not commies who killed the twins or Muldoon?"

Hoover jutted out his chin out and looked over to Tolson, who nodded.

Grudgingly, he said, "Get on with it then."

"Sir, your other agents checked out Tommy Muldoon, and I asked around, too. It wasn't impossible he had commie contacts, but locals said he had no political leanings as far as they knew. Sheriff Yates said there aren't any commies around New Canaan that he knew of. No doubt there are commies in the big East Coast cities. No one had anything bad to say about Muldoon; he was a popular teacher and a handsome guy. Yes, it looks like he had an inappropriate triste with the twins at school, but that goes more to prove he'd never harm the girls if, indeed, they did invite them."

"What are you saying?" Hoover barked.

"I spent time at Greenwich Academy, where the girls were students, and Muldoon was their math teacher, trying to figure out how Muldoon got the note that was found in his apartment—the note inviting him to the Big Cottage."

Then, a curveball. "I'm not convinced the note was from the twins."

Hoover's face was reddening by the second. "Hinke, you're batshit crazy. I read the note. It was from the Haverford sluts, for God's sake."

"Sir, I don't necessarily think that. It was typed with no signature. Anyone could have typed it. This anyone, though, apparently needed access to the internal mail delivery at Greenwich Academy Muldoon got a note that told him to show up that Easter night at the Big Cottage where the twins were. I think they were already dead when he got there. Then he knew he was in deep shit unless he covered his tracks the best he could. The problem was that the twins' killers were at his place when he got home. I don't think Muldoon played a big role in this carefully plotted scheme, other than he had a connection with the girls—which, at first blush, made it all seem reasonable. I think Muldoon himself was a red herring—which became evident during my trip."

Hoover bellowed, "For Christ's sake, Hinke, you're babbling in riddles."

Hinke kept plowing ahead. "Miss Gandy recognized the necklaces found on the Haverfords' pool table as possibly belonging to twin girls she grew up with in Port Norris, New Jersey."

Hoover turned his head and shot a glance at Helen. "That true?"

She nodded affirmatively.

Hoover refocused on Hinke, who added, "The two gold cross necklaces, both with KAA initials for twins, Kaitlyn Ann and Katherine Ann Abercrombie. Two beautiful teen girls kidnapped in 1911 and never found."

"Goddammit, Hinke, now you're saying those are connected to the murders in New Canaan?"

"I'd like to investigate more. Don't you think it's highly coincidental the necklaces were found at a murder scene thirty-nine years later? Like commies or Muldoon would have ever done that?"

Hoover was about to pop a blood vessel in his forehead, but Hinke continued, "Sir, the point is: If commies were going to make a violent political statement, which frankly is not their modus operandi, they could, I guess, leave the all-too-obvious commie banners. But the rest of it: the black crosses used as mutilation weapons, the Land photos, the necklaces, the intrigue—none of it makes sense for commies. All that and the complexity of these murders became more evident when I was in New Canaan. Those are real clues that can help us find the killers. Sir, I think this a sick game a group of killers is playing. It's about twins. Muldoon himself got conned, but not by the girls, who likely knew nothing about his invitation. And why would they? The killers constructed a phony conspiracy and made his murder look like a suicide. I admit it's convoluted but also darkly ingenious."

With his usual arrogance, Hoover shouted, "Hinke, if not commies, who, goddammit?"

I think the killers are in New Canaan or the area. I think they—or at least one of them—knew the twins and Muldoon. And they could get access to Greenwich Academy's internal mail system. What I don't know is why they killed the girls in such a bizarre, ritualistic way. I want to dig in more—in New Canaan—since I now have the lay of the land. I want to visit Port Norris to see if I can find out more about the Abercrombie twins. I want to investigate the occult and witchery angle to see what role the black crosses might have played."

Then he realized he should have left out the last sentence.

"Goddammit, Hinke, stop! Witchery? Have you lost your marbles!" He got up and motioned the others to follow him to the far anteroom. The last time he sat in Hoover's office, he wondered if he was history when Hoover brought out his personnel file. This time, he felt sure the outcome wouldn't be good.

Ten minutes later, the four single-filed back in, Hoover leading the pack, Helen last. He sat behind his imperial desk; Tolson and Nichols again took their seats at the conference table from Hinke. Helen stood in a far corner.

Lou Nichols hadn't said a word so far, but it was immediately evident that this was now his show.

He was smooth. "Agent Hinke, may I call you Derbert?"

Hinke said, "How about DH?"

"DH, it is."

"Let me be brief. We're cutting our losses at this point and sticking with the original story—the one I gave to the *New York Times* and other big papers: Tommy Muldoon, the twins' teacher, was a deranged former soldier who, in a fit of jealousy or rage, raped and killed the Haverford twins, then committed suicide. On the surface, it is a perfectly reasonable story that is already widely accepted."

Nichols paused and then said, "When the Director first told me about the commie banners, I visited the murder scene and also saw it as an excellent opportunity to paint another picture of the FBI as the heroes vanquishing the latest Red Devil threat: the FBI finding, maybe killing or jailing the commies who did the dastardly murders—their kind dedicated to destroying our democracy." He stopped for a moment.

"But that meant we needed to catch real commies and ideally be able to link them to Muldoon. As you know, we did initial investigating and found nothing in Muldoon's background and didn't hear anything about commie activity in the area. But the Director was adamant, so Miss Gandy suggested another look at the whole kit and caboodle. Your work was excellent, and your arguments that the murderers weren't commies are compelling."

Hoover yelled, "Goddammit, Lou. It could have been a crazy outside commie group."

Tolson interjected, "Possibly, but regardless, we've decided to let sleeping dogs lie and stick with the original story."

Hinke tried to remain calm but said, maybe too loudly, "Though that's not what the fuck happened?"

Tolson took over. "Hinke, there will be no more investigations by you of these murders. We're shutting the book on any future investigations."

He begged them, "All I ask is a couple more weeks in New Canaan. Please, I can find the murderers."

Slowly, Hinke scanned each of them eye to eye, including Helen. "You're telling me these murder cases are over because it wasn't commies? You cannot be serious." The sound of silence was deafening.

Hinke closed his eyes and started shaking his head, then exploded, "Where is the justice for these girls, for God's sake? And for Tommy Muldoon.? This case is all about the games these murderers play— and twins are at the heart of it."

He stormed out through Hoover's office, the anteroom, and Helen's office and headed to his office two floors below.

In his three decades at the Bureau, J. Edgar Hoover had never been talked to like that by a subordinate. "I'm firing his ass. I will accept no insubordination. Hell, I may get his butt put in a grungy DC jail."

The only person on the planet who could reel Hoover in from where he was at that moment was his longtime paramour, Junior. Tolson told him, "Speed, easy. He's a good agent. Just upset, and frankly, he has a right to be. He was doing a job and got caught in a vise. Our vise."

Tolson looked at Helen. "I want you to talk to him and tell him he can work whatever interesting cases come to light out of the main office or others. You'll feed him a steady stream. He can pick and choose what he wants. He'll get a next-grade salary bump. Can you get him under control and get him to let this go?"

Helen told the three, "I'll do the best I can. But I'm weighing in here that this is fucked up."

None of the three had heard Helen utter a curse word in her life and were stunned. Helen turned and left.

Stoically, smiling, Hoover said to Tolson and Nichols, "She'll handle it; she always does."

Pissed off, Hinke stomped to his office and poured a big bourbon. He thought about those who wanted it to be a double murder and suicide – a closed case. Sheriff Yates wanted to restore the peace and tranquility of his little rich town. The townspeople had already read the story in the *New York Times*—and would soon forget other gossipy rumblings about the deaths. The Haverford parents didn't want to be put through any more grief. Despite Hoover's visceral hatred of anything commie, Tolson and Nichols realized the smart thing was to kill the truth—instead of going with Hoover's gut, him shouting "commies" from the rafters and then not finding any. A cold case was OK with them, and if they got lucky down the line, that would be peachy. For Helen, Hinke wasn't sure? Regardless, he knew it was all happy horseshit. The killers were out there. Likely no one was going to be happier than them.

Helen knew she must keep Derby busy to have any chance of him staying at the Bureau. He wasn't going to like being removed from his murder cases after only two weeks—through no fault of his own. To rid him of the temptation, she had his Haverford murder files and evidence moved back to her office. Best case, she knew it would take Hinke some time.

On Saturday, Helen decided to get radical. She went on a voracious shopping spree in Georgetown—unlike any she'd done in her lifetime. Money was no object. She had her hair styled like younger women were wearing theirs. She got her fingernails and toenails manicured. She bought a whole new chic wardrobe. If she was going to challenge the female dress code for the FBI, she was going to go full out. She was inspired by her friend Marilyn Monroe, who was aghast after finding out about the FBI female dress code.

She'd told Marilyn, "The Bureau doesn't hire women as special agents. The Boss doesn't think they belong. There was one female agent when he became director in 1924. Alaska Davidson was her name. The first day on the job, he fired her and told me, "There won't be another cunt special agent while I'm Director. Females don't have the right stuff. They're here for typing, filing, answering phones, cleaning, cooking, and other such menial work."

"Such an enlightened man," Marilyn had editorialized sarcastically.

The current twenty-page dress code policy manual edicts on professional and conservative apparel for female secretaries and administrative staff. Dresses or skirts below the knees with blouses and a jacket, all the way to the neck—in muted dark or light, but not bright colors. No flashy jewelry. Sensible shoes, never high heels. Nothing that accentuates one's figure, making all dress dull and devoid of femininity.

The same weekend

New Canaan

Sitting on the second-floor veranda with their silver cups of mint juleps, Priscilla told Reggie, "The special agent has been neutralized. You were right that he was becoming a nuisance and too dangerous. Such a pity."

"Is he dead?"

"Reggie, you worry too much. No, he's not dead. It will work out better this way, trust me. He'll be kept under control. Soon, he'll forget all about it. Besides, he could play in the future."

She held up her cup, which Reggie bumped with hers.

It was a beautiful spring day as they sipped the potent drinks through straws. She asked, "Reggie, darling, don't you think it's time all of us got a permanent change of venue? Away from New Canaan. I'm tired of the snow and cold weather. And this place is so boring. We need a new place for our girls to grow up—maybe as southern belles," she chuckled.

He sucked on his mint julep and listened.

"Come on, Reggie, let's put some geographic distance between New England and a new destination. A place where we can more readily expand our business interests. I admit it was exhilarating— getting revenge for our Dark Lord and eliminating three persons-of- light. It has revitalized me—and I think you as well. Perhaps a clarion call to get on with the *Game*, the whole *Game*?"

Reggie took a Cuban cigar from his nearby humidor, trimmed it with his cigar cutter, and lit it. "Did you have a place in mind, my dear?"

She told him her suggestion.

He nodded. "This would be a big deal, but I'll check with the others."

They again clinked cups.

Monday

Washington, DC

When Hinke didn't show up to work at 8:00 a.m. sharp, Helen worried. She'd waited a few minutes in his office before going back to hers. On Friday he'd walked out of the meeting mad as hell, and she couldn't blame him. She hoped he hadn't eaten his gun or ended up drunk in a DC gutter. Or worse, maybe he eloped with his girlfriend, Marjorie. She came within a whisker of having him surveilled over the weekend but had promised that would never happen.

Helen got to her office a few minutes later than usual but earlier than most. A handful of early birds in the hallway did double-takes as she strode regally to her office on the fifth floor. Helen had a mountain of political capital with the Boss but had never used any of it. That Monday morning, she decided to spend a bit.

Contrary to popular belief, Hoover was not an early bird. Others could do the workaholic hours. He typically entered her office around 8:30 a.m., barely acknowledged her, then walked through the anterooms to his office. She made a point of standing on the file side of her office versus sitting behind her desk when he entered. Though Hoover was a flaming homosexual, he delighted in the beauty of the feminine form, clothed or unclothed. Hoover's stash of female porn, much that was in her P files, was world-class. When Hoover opened the door, she turned toward him.

His look was priceless. Absolute incredulity.

Helen smiled at him and said brightly, "Good morning, Boss."

The Director looked at her up and down. She'd broken too many FBI dress code violations at one time for him to count. He was speechless.

She wore a teal pencil dress that looked like it had been painted on, black silk stockings, teal high heels, and a diaphanous white blouse with a wisp of a bra underneath.

A long time ago, she'd worked months with Hoover to help his stuttering, which she'd help erase ninety-five percent of the time. But not now. He could only stutter, "Umm, Miss…Ga…Ga…Gandy. Wha, wha, is ga…going on?"

She did a slow twirl for him. "Do you like?"

His eyes were confused. He found his tongue. "Miss Gandy, this is not some sleazy downtown joint…"

"Boss, you're right, but it's also nothing like your private collection of porn in my office."

She handed him a short one-page document.

He went back to stammering, "Wa…wa…what is this…?"

"It's the FBI's new Female Dress Code Policy for professional and administrative females, which supersedes the policy dated January 31, 1925. It's a start."

Hoover read the short document with disbelief. Basically, it said that FBI females could wear any professional, attractive attire—skirt or dress and any style top, blouse, or coat—without limitation on colors, shoes of any height of heels, and any stockings. Hair could be worn in any style.

The last sentence above the signature line read, "Any issues with regard to this policy will be arbitrated solely by Helen Gandy, Executive Assistant to the Director."

Before Hoover could say anything, Helen added, "Boss, think what it will do for female as well as male morale."

He steadied himself. "Helen, you cannot be serious!"

She interrupted him, took the document from his hands, put it on her desk, handed him a pen, and looked him in the eyes. "Let's get this done."

Hoover knew she'd won. He leaned down and signed the document and said without his stutter, "Helen, I don't like this one bit."

She told him, "Boss, trust me, you'll get used to it, and it will brighten your days and the days of your FBI employees. I'll get it posted throughout the building this morning. Oh, and Boss, I'll be back at my desk in an hour. Laura will take calls in my absence."

Looking nothing like the arrogant prick he typically was, Hoover slunk through the anteroom into his office. Helen smiled and wondered what he'd say about the next quantum leap: hiring women as special agents. Perhaps it was a bridge too far right now, but she knew it would happen.

Helen strode down the third-floor hallway from the elevator like she was a model on a runway. She drew more than a few stares. She loved it.

Hinke's door on the third floor was locked. She opened it with her master.

After waiting fifteen minutes, Helen was pacing in her new high heels. She wondered, *"What if he's gone entirely AWOL?"*

Ten minutes later, though, Hinke turned the handle and entered his office.

She stood in front of his desk and did a twirl. "What do you think of the new FBI dress code?"

Hinke could only smile.

She told him, "Lock the door."

He was more than happy to comply. When he turned around, she was unzipping and slipping off her skirt. She sat on the top of his desk, her legs spread.

He approached her and stood between her legs.

She unzipped his suit pants.

Tongue in cheek, he said, "Helen, you know this is highly illegal."

Her reply: "I don't care. Just fuck me."

He wanted Helen more than he'd wanted any woman in his life. She slid him inside her and moaned. Hands gripping her legs, he moved in and out slowly, teasing, then upped the pace. She told him, "Fuck me harder."

That morning, when Hinke had hopped on the bus from Georgetown, he had no idea what to expect. For all he knew, he was already fired, but the lobby guard waved him in. In his office, he'd gotten the surprise of his life.

Post-coital, with her sitting on his desk, he asked, "You really got the female dress code changed?"

"That I did."

"And Hoover?"

"Derby, I can be persuasive, especially with the Boss."

He joked, "And you didn't need to fuck him."

She laughed and knew that things with Hinke would be under control—and fun for a long time.

When Hinke arrived in his office the following morning, he needed to look at the crime photos from the Haverford murders. He knew he was off the case, but he was compelled. Photos, evidence, murder files, and notes about the murders were in the bottom two drawers of a locked four-drawer file cabinet.

The drawers were empty.

To his credit, he didn't get pissed off. He slumped in his desk chair and thought: "Probably for the best. I need to make a clean break from the case."

On his desk was a typed list of various ongoing FBI investigations: a few in the DC-Baltimore area and others in New York, Miami, Chicago, and San Francisco. None looked like what agents called "Fuck You" cases whose only objective was to dig up dirt on the rich and powerful to provide leverage whenever Hoover needed it.

"No doubt Helen had provided the list. No doubt she had his Haverford files moved as well. Were they now back in Helen's office where they initially came from? He wished that he at least had his notes. Ask her? Maybe, but not on their weekly night of fun and games."

Chapter 20 – Card Tricks

The following Tuesday night

Washington, DC

Walking into Helen's flat, the anxiety he'd experienced his previous two visits was gone. The anticipation was more intense. Helen oozed sensuality in a red and black teddy, garter belt, stockings, and heels. After they sipped martinis, Helen knelt between his knees and gave him the blowjob of his life. Again, instead of swallowing, she swilled and let the cum leak from her mouth into her hands. She slathered it on her face and neck. "Trust me, it will help keep my skin young for a while longer."

He was baffled that cum could be a skin cream, but he was all in.

She kissed him and went back to the kitchen to tend to dinner. He'd already been fascinated by her "celebrity" guest room, a photo museum of the rich and famous. He read more of the cordial notes to Helen. Incredible. On the nightstand next to the guestroom bed, he spied a couple of decks of unopened Bicycle playing cards. He walked back out and asked, "Helen, okay if I open a deck of cards I found?"

"Of course. Let's play a game after dinner."

The lamb chops, homemade rolls, and Caesar salad with generous anchovies were delicious. She promised ice cream and Kahlua later. They sat on the living room sofa, and Hinke had a hard time not putting his hands on her again but announced, "It's been a while, but I used to be pretty good at card tricks."

Helen said, "I love card tricks! You go first."

Hinke removed the jokers and shuffled several times, then fanned the cards face down on the table. "Okay, pick a card. Don't show me."

Hinke unfanned the cards while Helen looked at her card, cut the deck, and told her to slide her card in. Then he told her to cut the cards as many times as she wanted. She did several times. Then he flipped and fanned the cards face up. He slid out the Six of Hearts. "Is that your card?"

She clapped. "It certainly is. Amazing!"

Helen couldn't resist a chance to show off. "Okay, let me try."

She shuffled with the acumen of a dealer in Hot Springs. She fanned the cards face down as he'd done.

"Derby, think of a card."

"You don't want me to pick one?"

"Nope. Don't touch the cards. "Just think of one."

She unfanned the cards and shuffled them several times. Then she put the deck on the table and fanned the cards face up.

"Helen, you aren't doing it right," Hinke insisted.

"Humor me," she grinned. "You're thinking of one card, right?"

"Yes, okay."

She fingered through the open deck and pulled out the Queen of Diamonds. "Is that the card you were thinking about, Derby? Be honest now."

"Yes, but that's impossible. Neither of us touched that card until you pulled it out."

Helen smiled. "Okay, let's try again."

"This time, I want you to think of two cards and only those cards. Let me know when you've got them in your brain."

"Okay, but this is crazy."

She went through the same procedure. Hinke never touched the cards he chose to think about. Again, she shuffled several times.

She asked, "You're thinking about only those two cards?"

"Yes. I promise."

Helen fanned the full deck face up and picked out the Five of Hearts and Eight of Clubs.

"Those are your cards?"

"Unbelievable! Can you teach me that?"

She poured him a Kahlua.

"Derby, let me tell you a story about a girl from years ago. She was five years old when she realized she could read the thoughts of others. In their small backyard, she and her friends would sit in a circle on the grass and play a game. She told them to think of a number or a letter, or think of a color, or think of almost anything and then whisper it to one girl without letting the others hear. She was never wrong when they told her to guess.

"Word got out about the young girl, and she got offers from strange people, including a few carnivals, to do strange things. Her mother was embarrassed; she told her daughter to stop her wickedness. When she was seven, her father whipped her with his belt when she told him that he shouldn't lie to Mother about Julie, a cute girl in his office; she knew what he did with her. He threatened to do the same thing with her if she didn't stop listening to the Devil. But she had a hard time controlling those thoughts back then. When her father's naughty desires drifted to her -- as they sometimes did – she would flee to the water—glad that she always had a safe refuge. But then, one night, when she was twelve, her mother was out playing bingo. Her father was drunk, as he usually was in the evening. He barged into her bedroom.

"He outweighed her by more than a hundred pounds and was much stronger. He ripped off her pajamas, pushed her down on her bed, and thrust himself inside her. It was painful, but that's when she realized she had another power, and she used it. His evil eyes staring down at her went blank. She rolled out from under him, put on a robe, and went to sit in the living room until her mother arrived home. She told her mother to go to her bedroom. There she found her husband with his pants off, lying dead as a doornail on her daughter's bed."

Her mother ran back to the living room and screamed at her. "What have you done? What have you done, you little slut!"

Her mother refused ever to see her again.

"This power the girl had, what was it?" asked Hinke.

"It was not until a couple years later that she discovered what she had done. It was an occult power called Black Widow. If any male entered her without consent, she could invoke it. Immediate death. Faster than golden frog poison, the deadliest on earth."

"And what became of the brave girl?"

She smiled. "She became a mighty woman. But she had to wait many years until one night, she became Cinderella and was whisked away by the handsome prince. She hoped the story would have a happy ending."

"I hope that, too." And then she kissed him.

Part 2

Chapter 21 - Post Hoover

22 years later, May 2, 1972

Washington, DC

*I*n the words of Bob Haldeman, who personally delivered the news to his boss, "J. Edgar Hoover is dead,"

Richard Nixon exclaimed, "Jesus Christ! That old cocksucker."

...In the words of Special Agent Derbert Hinke, when he heard the news, "For twenty-two years, we fooled the old cocksucker. Our affair right under his nose."

...In the words of Helen Gandy, when she heard the news, "Now I've got a ton of the old cocksucker's files to cull, collate, hide or destroy."

To the chagrin of few and the joy of many, John Edgar Hoover, Director of the Federal Bureau of Investigation, died in his own bed early morning on May 2, 1972. He was seventy-seven years old. Hoover had joined the Bureau in 1918 and in 1924 became interim Director and ruled the roost as Director for forty-eight years. Unquestionably, the most powerful bureaucrat in the history of the United States. And arguably, in the history of Western civilization.

Six days after the old cocksucker's death, President Richard Nixon officially named the monstrosity Hoover had obsessed about for years the "J. Edgar Hoover Building." After endless changes and millions of dollars of budget overruns—most dictated by the Director—his "baby" across Pennsylvania Avenue from the Department of Justice would not be one hundred percent completed for three more years. Hoover never got to enjoy his own baby.

Nixon was ecstatic that the Director was stone-cold dead, as were the seven presidents who preceded him—all of whom Hoover had terrorized at one point or another. Cheering from Heaven or Hell. Like

Joe McCarthy and other politicos of the day, Nixon was a creation of Hoover (and not the other way around), though the two had been estranged the last two years. Nixon pondered firing the Director a year before his death but gagged at the possibility that Hoover could destroy him with God-knows-what dirt his FBI gumshoes had dug up or fabricated. Reluctantly, he put that thought out of his mind. At last, Hoover was dead and buried. Hoover was no longer a thorn in Nixon's side. Hallelujah.

But not so fast. Hoover had woven himself deep into the Bureau's DNA: some good, a lot more, bad. Very bad. Dead, but he wouldn't be finished for many years. As first evidenced by the Watergate fiasco that started within a month of his demise. Watergate was a seminal event in American history Hoover's Bureau had its illegal fingerprints all over and helped destroy Nixon's presidency. Nixon was only one of the many to feel Hoover's ungodly wrath after the Boss's corpse lay rotting in the Capitol Hill cemetery. Richard M. Nixon resigned as president of the United States on August 9, 1974. Nobody fucked with the Director, dead or alive, and got away with it.

All those stories about a woman standing by or behind her man (and providing him a real backbone): that was Helen Gandy for Hoover. Young Helen had been an unknown quantity but ended up being a superstar. Her employment was arranged in the strangest of ways. Hoover's first interview question to the comely twenty-one-year-old in 1918 was a statement. "You can't be married while you're working for me. Understand?"

"Yes, sir."

She'd stood by her man for forty-eight years, but it wasn't love; it was the dead opposite of Tammy Wynette's song "Stand by Your Man."

"Sometimes it's hard to be a woman
Giving all your love to just one man
You'll have bad times
And he'll have good times
Doin' things that you don't understand."
Thanks to Helen, Hoover did things he'd never understand.

Inexorably, through the years, Helen made herself indispensable to Hoover and, thus, the FBI. Hoover was the FBI.

She controlled Hoover's calendar and screened every phone call. After reading them, she kept Hoover's most private Personal (P) and Official Confidential (O/C) files in dozens of file cabinets in her office, but any individual file was virtually unfindable without her homemade, handwritten cipher. She did much more with her special talents. In his presence, Helen read his thoughts and was always able to calm him or plant an option, a suggestion, an alternative, a new idea…especially when Hoover was wavering. Some Hoover acted on. Others not, but there was no question, she'd arguably had become the most influential **female in the United States in 1972.**

That year, Helen was seventy-five years old but looked sixty and was as sharp as a tack. In the two weeks after Hoover's death and state funeral on May 4, the day Hoover's lead-lined casket toppled and nearly killed two of the pallbearers, Helen had never been that busy. She had her marching orders from the dead. Some she would carry out. Others, she would not.

For decades, J. Edgar Hoover wielded his power with dirt or what he called "the goods," and he collected mountains of it over five decades. With dirt came leverage and raw, hardball power—and a comfortable, though not flashy lifestyle; he lacked for nothing. With Helen's help, he discovered dirt was the most treasured of any currency, especially in DC. She encouraged him to weaponize it. And you could never tell when a friend could become a foe and vice versa. She was the weaponizer.

The volume of letters, top-level correspondence, dossiers, documents, audiotapes, videotapes, and photos exploded in the '60s and until his death. Much of it illegally obtained—and much of it sexually explicit. Stuff that could make or break careers, imprison or allow freedom, create wealth, or take it all away, or kill, or grant life. Whatever it took to coerce, threaten, bully, and strike fear into people at the highest levels of government, business, or any organization. Helen continuously triaged hundreds of P and O/C files to multiple locations; her office was reserved for the crème de la crème of Hoover's "goods." None of these files made it into the Bureau's new, impressive NCIC database. Hoover, the egomaniac that he was, was sensitive to the fact that a lot of his personal and confidential files might tarnish his legacy forever. Yet he stubbornly held on to them to the bitter end. He left it to others to destroy or hide the most incriminating (to him) once he was dead. It was a monumental task.

On the day of Hoover's death, Helen went into high gear. She was chauffeured to 4936 30th Place in Northwest DC. Hoover's spacious, two-story, red-brick residence had been bequeathed to his colleague, confidante, and homosexual partner, Clyde Tolson, who had been in poor health for some time. That day, Helen split time between the office and his home. In her FBI office, she triaged the P and O/C files, plus others warehoused by top FBI loyalists. Thousands of the less confidential but damning files got marked D for Destruct.

All in all, it was a collection of "information" more incendiary—to more people—than one of Truman's nuclear bombs.

Helen had already extracted the information she wanted for her own purposes. Those included "the goods" on a handful of old Bureau friends/loyalists and enemies in case they might come in handy down the road for Derby. Then there was the robust set of explicit photographs and videos of the Boss and Tolson, unlike anyone had ever seen them together. Years ago, the Boss had returned to her a confidential file on Errol Flynn and mistakenly stuffed a few of his Director-Eyes-Only photos of himself and Junior in Errol's thick file before he could get them home. The photos dispelled any doubts about Hoover's sexual proclivities. Truman Capote and many others knew the obvious. Capote nicknamed the two top boys at the FBI "Johnny and Clyde." The Boss had been too embarrassed to ask Helen what had happened to the photographs and assumed she'd put them in a safe place.

There were tons more juicy files. Over the past year, Helen had begun culling these crown jewels from P and O/C files on a few dozen of the most famous and infamous people, living and deceased, who, for better or for worse, had crossed Hoover or his path while he was alive. No doubt some of that information would shock the masses and debunk assumptions long held by the US public based on stories fed by Lou Nichols to heavy hitters at newspapers, magazines, radio stations, and new television broadcasters, who in turn spun them to the gullible American public. Big lies, courtesy of the FBI and John Edgar Hoover, that had never seen the light of day.

May 16, 1972, was a windy, rainy day in the nation's Capital as it had been twenty-two years earlier. On that day, he was reassigned from his first crummy office in the Department of Justice basement to a decent office after Hoover promoted him to solve the Haverford murders. The day he'd met Marilyn Monroe again—the day when Helen had entered his life and never left.

After Hoover croaked, technically, Derbert Hinke remained the head of a Special Operations Unit that the Director had established. After his death, it seemed strange he'd only spoken to the Director a handful of times over the past twenty-two years; Helen ran interference when Hoover asked about the murders in 1950—but that only lasted a year. She got Hinke assigned to cases, some in the DC or Baltimore field offices and others across the country, to provide him a change of pace. She was his savior on all things Hoover, and he never worried about being sent to Anchorage, or a clerk job, or worse, getting thrown out on the street. Helen had it covered.

With a half tumbler of Old Fitz in front of him, Hinke sat in his comfy office chair, now perfectly molded to his backside, which through regular exercise didn't look half bad compared to the scrawny butts and big guts of other elderly politicos that he'd seen in the sauna at his gym. Proof that he was aging gracefully. Better proof was his effortless ability to get into the panties of women two or three decades his junior. After many travels to California, he fell in love with it and hoped in his next life he'd get to attend college at Berkeley or Pepperdine or UC Santa Barbara. Go figure Ronnie Reagan, known back in the day as the informant "Ronnie the Rat," was at the political pinnacle in California. Would Ronnie remember him after all these years? Probably, the consummate politician he'd always been. He wondered how many people knew – or cared – he'd been an important, backstabbing snitch for Hoover's FBI.

Hinke enjoyed the Old Fitz but wished he had a baggy of good pot. Better yet, a few Thai sticks. His adventures over the last two decades had broadened his horizons and opened his eyes to new pleasures. Hinke became an FBI go-to guy on home-grown terrorists, several of whom he'd helped put in prison—while bumping into the most radical side of the hippie generation.

One night the previous year, he'd gotten an anonymous tip on the location of Bill Ayers, co-founder of the Weather Underground, who were mostly white college-age, early-twenties kids who liked to blow up stuff to make a political point but not kill anyone. Misguided anarchists but hardly instruments of the Kremlin. He got intel that Ayers was supposed to show up at a Baltimore dive called Benny's Bar to raise cash for his cause. Probably a longshot, but Hinke decided what the heck. He'd do it alone. A no-no, he was aware. He dressed down and wore an Orioles cap. He spied Ayers inside and then guessed where Ayers would egress. For two hours, he waited in a putrid, dark alley near the back door of the bar. Bingo. When Ayers appeared, Hinke drew his Smith & Wesson .357 Magnum and cocked the trigger after Ayers was fifteen feet ahead.

"Bill Ayers?" Hinke had startled him. "Federal Bureau of Investigation. You are under arrest for destruction of US property including buildings at the New York Police Department, the United States Capitol, the Pentagon -- and assorted other crimes."

The lean, long-haired, mustachioed Ayers calmly turned and said, "Fuck you, pig."

Hinke was familiar with the phrase.

"Mr. Ayers, you're under arrest. Last time I'm going to say it." His gun pointed at Ayers' heart. "I want you to kneel and put your hands behind your head."

Ayers faced Hinke and smiled. "Good luck with that." He turned his back and started walking down the alley. With his back turned, he stuck the middle finger of his right hand in the air and shouted, "Peace, man."

Hinke didn't particularly want to shoot a young guy in the back or give chase. But it was his job. Hesitating, though, he made a rookie mistake, distracted by Ayers calling his bluff. The next thing he knew, he was lying in the wet grime of the old brick alley behind the bar. His head was pounding after being hit in the back of the head by a lug wrench. He presumed by a member of the Weathermen or a sympathizer.

Picking himself off the soiled bricks, Hinke told himself, *"I'm getting way too old for this shit. This never happened."* He never told anyone other than Helen about it.

Hinke was never sure why he'd given Ayers a pass that night. He'd have gotten a commendation even if he'd shot the prominent Weatherman in the back. But he didn't want to. He'd met enough of these supposedly dangerous criminals, proliferating across college campuses and elsewhere as the war in Vietnam disintegrated in front of the millions of Americans tuned into Walter Cronkite each weekday night. How many times had he heard Robert McNamara's latest body count of gooks killed? But then there were the staggering, ongoing body counts of American kids. Despite all the American propaganda, he, too, wondered why the hell his country was in Vietnam. The worldwide commie conspiracy argument had worn thin with this WWII vet.

Chapter 22 – Twins Murders Redux

October 1973

Washington, DC

Hinke sat down at his desk with a cup of coffee in hand. There was a wide, green-lined computer printout of recent major crimes with a section circled in blue pen:

Not that all crimes nationwide were reported—nor typically reported expeditiously, if at all, since reporting was voluntary. But the Bureau's new NCIC Data Processing was as good as it got in 1973. Public news sources were attached when available.

The top page read:

Crime Report—Friday, October 10, 1973

Two females reported missing in Anniston, Alabama by the Anniston Police Department

Identical twin sisters, Cherry and Merry Blount, age 13, 5'4", 105 pounds

Last seen about 19:30 EA Wednesday, October 8, after leaving local football game wearing red and white cheerleader uniforms and red cheerleader jackets

No contact to date

Possible kidnapping

No suspects to date

Contact Sheriff Frank Filmore at 256-APOLICE if you have any information about these girls or their disappearances.

Clipped to the printout was a single black and white photograph transmitted from the *Anniston Star*, showing the Blount girls standing side-by-side, looking like mirror images. Smiling, holding their pompoms. Cute girls by any standard.

He had no idea why, but he walked over to his file cabinets and unlocked the bottom drawer on one. He was taken aback; the Haverford files and evidence that he hadn't seen since 1950 were back. Had to be Helen's doing. And the printout. He never ceased to be amazed about what Helen knew— after Hoover was six feet under.

He stood with his coffee and walked to the window. Usually, a dark, dreary day was relaxing for Hinke, but not now. His mind raced. *Teenage twins kidnapped. Could it be possible? Kidnappings related to his twins' murder case years ago? These kidnappings were in Alabama—a long way from New England. Come on, DH.*

But what if...?

After the Haverford twins were murdered, Hoover had been certain the commies would kill again. Hinke agreed but knew it wasn't commies. Hoover was gone. All bets were off. Hinke was getting involved again in the murders, past and maybe present.

He called both the Atlanta and Birmingham Bureau offices to see if the Blount kidnappings were on their radar. Both FBI offices knew about the case. But being thirteen-year-olds, the twins were on the cusp of requiring automatic action, per the Bureau's definition of "tender years" (twelve or under). It was apparent both offices were slammed and could provide only minimal backup. Hinke, himself, had been swamped for the past year with domestic terrorist cases, but he'd trained another agent to take over his heavy travel workload. He needed a breather at home. That was out of the question now.

He pondered how to best become part of the mix, sooner than later, without being heavy-handed. Off and on, while the Director was around, he pulled the "Hoover card," indicating he worked directly for him. Which immediately cut through any bullshit and red tape. After the Boss kicked off, Hinke retained his special operations status—thanks to Helen. He knew that a lot of local cops were none too keen about the Bureau or other Feds barging into their jurisdiction. Others were thankful for any help they could get. He wondered which group Frank Filmore fell into, but regardless, he would tread lightly.

Not knowing anyone in Anniston or Birmingham, he pocketed his Hoover card and instead called an old acquaintance in the Atlanta Police Department, Jerry Clarkson, who'd helped him investigate a couple of professors at Georgia Tech. In turn, Hinke checked the P and O/C files for interesting goop on Atlanta big-timers who'd run afoul of the law. Information that helped APD get a crooked real estate developer with a major drug problem and multiple mistresses to roll over on a bigger fish.

"Jerry, how the hell are you? What's it been, a couple years? Deputy Chief now? Congratulations!"

In his smooth southern drawl, Jerry said, "DH, thought you'd be fishing in the Keys or having fun by now. Atlanta's booming; crime's booming more; cops' pay never booms. A few of us have nicer offices and, if lucky, have a decent-looking secretary who gives blowjobs. Kidding, yeah, in my next lifetime. I gotta deal with more and more shit on my desk. Many days, I wish I were out there chasing down bad guys."

"Jerry, I can tell you the chasing is overrated. Getting nastier everywhere. I may hang it up in a couple more years if I haven't kicked off before then."

They made more small talk until Hinke asked, "You heard about the girls who disappeared in Anniston, Alabama?"

"Yeah, the twins. Don't sound too good since nobody's heard squat. Probably a niggra or niggras did it. If they catch 'em, them Alabama boys ain't going to bother with no trial."

Hinke thought about commenting but bit his tongue. "Anniston's not far from Atlanta, is it?

"'Bout an hour and a half drive, give or take, depending on traffic."

"You know Chief Frank Filmore?"

"Umm, I met him at a police conference a couple years back, but I don't know him all that well. Why?"

Hinke tried to say the least he possibly could. "Filmore is the case contact on the Bureau's Major Crimes report I got about the kidnappings. Jerry, I'm reaching here, but when I saw it, I had déjà vu on a case I worked in New England a lot of years back. Maybe nothing, but I wondered if you could get me an introduction to grease the skids? I don't want to show up and piss off him or the Alabama SBI boys."

"Sure, I'll put in a call and tell him you're not a typical dickhead Fed."

Hinke laughed. "Gee, Jerry, thanks. Lemme know if you ever need a dickhead Fed to get your ass out of the frying pan. "

The Atlanta deputy chief chuckled. "This likely kidnapping I'm guessing is a big shit deal in Anniston, but it's Friday in the South. Who knows what the cops will be doing on the weekend"

"Yeah, if I don't hear from him by the end of today, I'll call him Monday. Thanks again."

He needed to re-review the Haverford files and evidence to see what he might glean. He found it puzzling that he hadn't tried to dabble again in the murders in over two decades, but Helen had made it clear not to. His desire to finish what he had started had wilted on the vine. Maybe this was the spark he needed. He placed the files and black crosses, the gold necklaces, and the two-ball on his conference table. As he circled the table, he felt that old desire to march forward and catch these killers.

A couple months earlier he'd attended a lecture given by Howard Teten who would go down in the annals of FBI lore as one of the first special agents to espouse a "criminal profile" and almost singlehandedly established the FBI Behavioral Sciences Unit at Quantico. Hinke was intrigued and mentioned Teten's new approach to a few colleagues, who howled with laughter at the idea of finding completely unknown criminals by using half-baked, warm-and-fuzzy psychological crap. That was for pussies who were afraid of working hard and getting their hands dirty.

Hinke saw no contradiction in tried-and-true investigative procedures and profiling. It didn't displace figuring out the perpetrator's MO but instead piggybacked on top of it to provide a better insight into who the perpetrators were. Through additional deductive reasoning, profiling could help investigators understand the behavioral and personality manifestations of a killer – starting at the crime scene.

His thoughts drifted back: What *type* of person (or, he believed, persons) could/would want to murder female twins in that horrific, ritualistic way? Physically and psychologically, who were these people? Why torture the girls, then kill them, and pose the bodies? And leave the bodies and evidence at the crime scene? And take pictures of them alive and dead? What was it about these teenage girls that attracted the killers? Where would the killers likely have been living at the time of the crime and where now? Not much was known about what made these killers tick, and that's what Teten and his colleagues were studying.

Hinke considered talking to Teten but decided for now the Haverford case was his and only his—since the alternative was turning over all the files, notes, and evidence he had. Those belonged only to him while he was investigating the case.

After twenty-three years, he was re-engaged. He must get to Anniston.

Chapter 23 – Anniston, Alabama

Three days prior: Wednesday, October 8, 1973

Anniston, Alabama

At least one of the three had been in Anniston off and on for eight weeks. The bug they'd put in the girls' bedroom had been most helpful in eliminating times when they'd have no chance. It became a game of waiting and watching. Watching and waiting. Necessary drudgery. Hopefully, when the girls were attending school it would provide more opportunities, but none thus far. Then earlier that day, they'd heard the girls' plans for the evening. All hands on deck. The woman smiled. Their van was no longer Zimmerman's Carpet Cleaners, which had given Mrs. Blount a free cleaning of all rooms in her house two months earlier. It was transformed into a midnight-green van with bogus Georgia plates and no other markings. They'd been taught patience, but it was wearing thin, especially with the two men. Maybe tonight after the football game if they were lucky. Then there was Matty Elder.

In the passenger seat, the man flipped through a half dozen color photographs of the twins, photos he'd selectively lifted from their bedroom. Not too many to be noticed missing; better quality than the black and white photos where they'd discovered the Blount twins in their middle school yearbook. Only one of the many yearbooks they'd collected for a hundred-mile radius around Atlanta. A fruitful source of information now put to use. As he looked at the photos again, he felt himself stiffen.

Two months prior—August 1973

Atlanta, Georgia

In the subterranean room, she spoke to the three. "Few ever get this chance. You three are prepared to play *Game of Twins*. Revenge is yours; revenge is ours. Revenge is the Dark Lord's. Play fiercely but never in haste. Never forget the *Game* behind the *Game*. Now go." They nodded while the two infants slumbered in the corner.

Three days after the Blount twins disappeared—Midnight, Saturday, October 11, 1973

Atlanta

After following him from his Buckhead condo to downtown, they parked on the other end of the same level in the dingy garage off Peachtree. It was a three-hour wait in their Mercedes until he got off the elevator shortly after midnight. Thankfully, there was no one else they could see as they drove toward Elder. They parked in the adjacent spot to his fire engine red Chevelle Malibu. Matty Elder never had a chance. As he pulled the car keys out of his jeans pocket, one grabbed him from the front and the other punched him hard in the kidney—knocking the wind out of him. As he buckled, one wrapped silver duct tape around his head, covered his mouth, and pushed a syringe into his neck. The other popped the trunk and chuckled, "Looks like Matty was thinking about getting out of Dodge." He moved the two pieces of luggage to the back seat. Quietly and efficiently, they dumped him into the Chevelle's trunk. The man with the scar on his forehead drove Matty's car. The Mercedes led—both headed in the same destination, due west.

Sunday, October 12, 1973

Anniston

When he woke up, Matty was handcuffed on the floor of a large room with no windows. No furniture except for one chair. Footsteps on the stairs got louder. He knew he'd seen the two men somewhere.

They sat him up in the chair and didn't bother to blindfold him. Both assured him he'd be okay; they only wanted to ask a few questions. Then they'd get him back to Atlanta. He responded, "Yeah, that's great. It's a big misunderstanding, I'm sure." Neither responded.

A week prior

Atlanta, Georgia

Matty Elder hadn't met with her in person for nearly three years. Only phone calls from payphones, and those, infrequently. When he was sixteen, she was the older college girl, and he'd fallen head-over-heels. But part of the deal had been no one-on-one contacts unless she requested. Then a week ago, at the big cocktail party at the DeVries' mansion, they stood eye-to-eye. It had been inevitable they'd meet eventually since their families ran in the same social circles. He was surprised it hadn't happened sooner.

He saw her minutes after arriving. She was with her uncle, Raymond, the best-looking guy there, even among the bevy of handsome homosexuals. She was more gorgeous than he could have imagined. Stunning in a backless, short black dress with tantalizing cleavage, her rich brunette hair worn up and perfectly coiffed. Striking, black jewelry. She was perfectly balanced on ebony high heels, no stockings necessary. He made eye contact, and she nodded toward the large outdoor porch. It had always amused him: him a Matty and her a Maddie—he'd always thought they would be always linked.

It was there that he knew for sure.

He'd watched them interact at the party. He could tell she worshipped him, her uncle who was one of the top financiers in Atlanta with an impeccable reputation. When Raymond winked at her it was much more than any uncle-niece thing. He'd be shocked if uncle dearest weren't doing her. He was jealous. She was the most exquisite woman he'd ever slept with. It broke his heart. She'd helped make him a bundle of money on his own. But seeing them both like that, he knew what he'd suspected: Raymond was the Ghost.

On the big brick terrace that overlooked an arboretum of a backyard, she kissed him lightly on the lips, her beautiful face lighting up. "Matty Elder, you've grown into a hunk of a man. Turn around. Lemme see all of you. A young, blue-eyed Paul Newman!"

He managed to get out, "I don't know about that, but you look amazing." He blushed.

She did a twirl. "Not bad for a gal who already has two kids, right?"

"What?"

"Yep. Twin boys! Thad and Jeremy.

"Well, congratulations."

They made small talk, but his thoughts were scattered as he sipped his champagne.

"Matty, what's bothering you?" she asked, gently touching his forearm with two hands.

If he told her, now, he had no idea what would happen to him. He was in too deep. He should have gone to her first, but they'd promised a lot of money. His employers-to-be wanted him to pave their way in Atlanta and run it, but first they wanted the identity of the Ghost. Matty's signing bonus: $1,000,000 in cash. No doubt, they would then kill the Ghost.

She said she needed to get back to the party and told him to call her for lunch soon. They'd catch up. She kissed him again on the cheek and walked back inside, wondering, *What the hell is he keeping from me"* An accomplished mind-reader, she'd only heard static, nothing to clearly divine. Other than his fear was deafening. She heard only, "The Ghost, I hate him. And "a million dollars." Maybe Matty had deduced who he was? Then she got the idea of three instead of only two.

Two hours later, Matty made the call to Chicago. He was in—but needed another couple days to be sure of the Ghost's identity. They weren't thrilled but agreed. He was stalling. None of his options were great: fall on his sword with Maddie and beg for mercy; get the info ASAP to his new partner; or fly as far away as he could, preferably to another planet. Yet he could only think about her and the Ghost.

In the basement of the rental home outside Anniston, two men stood before him. One tall and chiseled, with jet black hair, maybe later twenties. The other was also about the same age, dark-haired, a bit shorter and stockier and had a prominent scar above his left eyebrow.

The tall one said, "What didn't you want her to find out, Matty?"

"Pardon? No idea what you're talking about."

"Sure you do, Matty," he smiled. "We'll give you exactly one minute to reconsider."

Why didn't he go to her instead of being seduced by out-of-towners promising more power and big bucks? What the hell was he thinking? He was making more money than he could ever spend. How do these guys know he's keeping a secret? On the edge of hyperventilating, beads of sweat popped out and dripped down his forehead.

If only he hadn't gone to the party!

Hearing nothing, Scarface backhanded Matty across the face with brass knuckles, whiplashing his neck to the side and jarring loose two teeth that Matty spit out. Blood drooled from his mouth. Next, he grabbed Matty's cuffed hands and bent the left middle finger back, little by little, then more, until it snapped.

"What the fuck!" Matty screamed, staring at his wobbly, left middle finger. "Fuck!" he yelled again louder, but there was no other audience in the basement of the upscale rental home.

"Hey, just a little dislocation—easy, buddy. It'll be fine in a few weeks. You should probably see a doc and a dentist, though," said the tall man.

In a calm voice the tall guy said, "Matty, let's get back to it. I'm going to ask you again. What were you keeping from her? Next is the middle finger on your right hand."

His left hand on fire, his face throbbing, Matty tried to catch his breath and babbled that he'd been contacted by the Carmillo brothers out of Chicago. They planned to set up shop in Atlanta and wanted him to help. Promised him a lot of money if he could tell them who the Ghost was. They said they were going to take out the Ghost, then take over the whole operation."

The tall one stood up and spoke louder. "Matty, your finger is barely hanging on. Your face looks like hell. How do you know the Ghost?"

Matty blurted out, "I didn't until the party, but he was there." His two captors looked at one another.

"Please, I've told them nothing about the Ghost. No harm no foul. I'll call the deal off. Please," he begged.

"Matty, the Ghost, what's his name?"

Matty gave them a name, then equivocated a little: "But I'm not entirely sure."

Neither reacted. The two looked at one another and stepped away from Matty's moaning. The tall guy said, "Back in a few minutes."

Matty's hand hurt like it never had—more than his face. He whined to the tall one, "I need something for the pain. Come on, man!" No response, and after a minute, he too walked upstairs, leaving Matty, his hand and face throbbing, alone in the basement.

Ten minutes later they both walked back downstairs and told Matty that if he played ball, they'd have him back in Atlanta tonight. Scarface handed him two Percocets and a Budweiser. A Bud had never tasted that good. He hoped the Percocets would kick in fast. The tall one said: "Matty, the rules are simple: You do double what you did last year. You never contact the Carmillos again. We'll take care of them. You never mention the Ghost again—or who you think he is. If you ever have an issue again about anything, you talk to her first. Got it?"

"Got it," said a relieved Matty Elder. Scarface took off the handcuffs and the three walked upstairs. In the kitchen, he handed him a big baggy of ice.

Scarface added, "Oh, Matty, one more thing. We need to know where your list is. It's yours. We just want to look it over."

His customer list was his lifeblood, but he knew they'd find it sooner or later. He told them.

"Perfect," said the tall guy. "Let's get back home to Atlanta. We'll pick up the list, then get you some medical care, too."

In the gravel driveway, the tall man smiled and put his hand on Matty's shoulder. He handed him the keys to the Chevelle. "Matty, go pop the trunk."

The Percocets were kicking in. He thought, *Holy shit, I talked my way out of a tough spot again.* He sometimes amazed himself. It was going to be okay. But then it hit Matty Elder. The tall guy looked amazingly like Raymond. Not exact, but a younger version.

As the three stood behind the trunk of the Chevelle, Scarface said, "There's another thing you need to do."

Matty said, "Absolutely. What?"

"You seeing and being here with us. It didn't happen."

"Already forgotten," he told the two, now remembering their names, Franklin, and Nigel.

Franklin said, "Might be hard to forget things like that—the Ghost and us and her. You know she's my wife, don't you, Matty?"

Matty was puzzled but not for long. Franklin pinned his arms from behind. Nigel pulled a Gerber Mark II knife from the sheath on his belt and in an instant sliced Matty's neck from ear to ear. The shock on his face, the two men thought, was priceless. He fell and flailed like a hooked fish out of water for maybe twenty seconds. Then stopped. Lots of blood, but not enough that it couldn't be covered up with a bag of fresh gravel they'd found in the white building. They tossed his body into the trunk and spread the gravel.

They'd picked out a couple spots to dump the car with Matty's body but decided to add their own wrinkle to the Game. In no hurry, they went back inside and shared a good Bordeaux with Russian caviar and crackers while playing a game of eight-ball. How apropos given the history they'd been taught to honor their Dark Lord. Her idea of taking the two old pool balls and then one from the set in the Victorian, they had to admit, was a nice touch. Neither was sure that it had been worth the risk—mixing their drug business with the other family business and the Game – but shrugged it off; they were worrying too much.

They bid adios to the pretty house they'd stayed in, off and on, for three months. One drove the Mercedes, where they stowed his luggage; the other drove the Malibu—to a natural boat launch site on the Choccolocco Creek, which looked more like a small river than a creek. Excellent place to launch a small fishing boat or canoe into the water. It was below road level enough so as not to be obvious, and no cars passed at this hour. It was easier than they'd thought. Only two minutes to get the Chevelle into a position. Scarface turned on the ignition and put it in drive, hopped out, and shut the door as the other pushed the car down the slight incline. The back end flopped up and then the car headlights dove headfirst and disappeared into the gurgling, inky water. Piece of cake. They noted the mile marker again and headed toward town to use a payphone. Then jumped on I-20 East toward home, where they knew the Blount twins were waiting for them.

Chapter 24 – The Pool Ball

Monday, October 13, 1973

Washington, DC

On Monday morning, Derbert Hinke got a heads-up call from his cop buddy in Atlanta, who told him that Frank Filmore would be calling. Knowing how things often happened on southern time, though, Hinke wasn't holding his breath. Surprisingly, a few minutes after he hung up, the sheriff called. "Agent Hinke, Jerry Clarkson over in 'Lanta give me yer name. I thank we might need hep down here. SBI boys 'greed."

"What's up, Sheriff?" He tried to remain calm. It had been more than two decades without so much as nibble, much less a solid lead.

Filmore told him, "Earlier, we fished a car outta the Choccolocco Crik southeast of the city. If yer not familya with Anniston, the crik's more like a small riva in places. Good white watta too. Bran new Chevy Chevelle Malibu, red with them black rac'n stripes, ya know, all souped up. Plates were 'Bama but showed as stol'n. Runn'n the VIN by DMV but nutt'n yet. Hail, now that it's drip-dried, it looks like a brand spank'n virgin. Nice wheels."

Hinke waited while the sheriff harangued a cop on his end.

"Sheriff, you didn't call me about the Blount disappearances?"

"Sorry, Hinke. Gitt'n to that. I'm trying to git my depady's fat ass mov'n to stay with the SBI sons-a bitches before this becomes a fuck'n circus. They patched me through to you—I'm out at the crik. Calling about gett'n fingerprint hep. I heared it's possible when a car's been in the watta. Oh, yeah, there's a dead body in the trunk."

Hinke nearly gasped. "One of the twins?"

"No, sir, that's what we was first thank'n when we pult up the car. Mebbe they'd both be thar. Nope. Body of a male in the trunk. 'LLooks like from ID in his wallet, name's Matthew Elder of 'Lanta, Georgia. I already contacted the 'Lanta Police Department. Said they'll gt an investigator here by tomorrow morn'n if not earlier."

Hinke tried to figure out where to go with the conversation. "Sheriff, I'm not going to BS you; it's possible, but it's a stretch to get decent prints from a vehicle that's been submerged. That said, watch what you touch inside. Anything inside that might indicate the girls were in there?"

"Nope, no sign of the girls from what we seen. SBI's got a few divers check'n out the crik to see if there's any more bodies or anything else. Thar' sump'n in the glove box, kinda strange."

Hinke waited.

"An eight-ball."

Hinke's eyes and mouth opened in surprise. "Pardon me? You mean like a billiards eight-ball?"

"Yep, a pool ball in the glove box roll'n round all by its lonesome. No car papers or nutt'n. Just the ball."

His heart raced, and he unglued the phone from his ear to take a moment. With one hand over the speaker, he blew out a long breath to get his bearings as he heard the sheriff ask, "You thar?"

He put the phone back to his mouth and ear. "Apologies, Sheriff, secretary walked in with a message. Can you describe it?"

"It's a goddamn pool ball. Ya know, round, smooth, black, and white with an eight on it. About the size of one of my nuts. Kidd'n. You played eight-ball, ain't ya? Gotta get the eight-ball in last, or you lose the game."

Hinke fought to remain calm. As politely as possible he asked, "I mean, Sheriff, is the ball solid black with a white circle and eight in it?"

The sheriff cleared his throat and spit out a hawker of Red Man. "Sorry, didn't mean to be a horse's ass, Hinke. Here, lemme git a closer look for the F...B...of...I. And yeah, it's bagged. This one here's black with a white star and black eight inside it. Looks sorta old, too. Yellowish. What the hell difference does it make what the pool ball looks like?"

Hinke was certain it was one of the missing Brevard pool balls but realized he was making too big of a deal about the ball. "Curious, Sheriff. I collect old billiards stuff. Sounds like an interesting one."

He switched subjects. "The guy in the trunk died by drowning?"

"Don't look that way to me. Looks like he got knifed in the neck. Think'n he don't gotta a lotta blood in him anymore. Gotta wait and see what the ME says. Hail, don't know what state he got kilt in."

Again, Hinke was surprised.

"Listen, Hinke, I got two girls done dispeer'd and now a guy from 'Lanta kilt. That's more goin' on here in a few days than a month a Sundays. I'll take whatever hep I kin git."

Hinke told him, "I'll get you a couple of our best fingerprint guys there tomorrow. Oh, and I'll get in touch with the Birmingham and Atlanta Bureau offices. You mind if I make a trip down there with our crime scene boys tomorrow?"

"More the merrier. Do all that and the fine city of Anniston, we'll treat you like a king."

"Great. Were you able to find the VIN on the vehicle?"

"One of my deputies found it looking through the inside dashboard."

"Good. Can you get me that and the driver's license info? Also, could you transmit photos of the car, the dead body, and the eight-ball to me as soon as you can? I'll get you a number to send them."

"Anythang else, pardna? You definitely gotta weird thing for pool balls."

Hinke ignored his comment. He figured if he could help on the murdered guy, supposedly from Atlanta, he'd have a better shot investigating the twins' kidnappings.

"Sheriff, what's the latest on the twins?"

Over the next several minutes Filmore filled him in. No headway yet. No doubt the girls had been abducted. Not the runaway types. No contact and no ransom demand. Both knew that wasn't good. The twins were popular thirteen-year-old beauties. Cheerleaders. Auburn-haired, freckled, green-eyed, five-foot-four, and 105 pounds. Identical twins. The girls usually walked back home from school through a hilly, wooded city park wedged between the football stadium and their neighborhood. Only a ten minute walk. Probably where they got grabbed. They left right after the game and didn't wait for their boyfriends, both on the Bulldogs team, or anyone else. Both boyfriends had airtight alibis. No stalker types anybody knew or an abduction in years around Anniston. It was around dusk, maybe seven. Been running down possible leads, but nothing. SBI divers hadn't found any other bodies yet.

Hinke knew the girls wouldn't be in the creek.

Filmore asked, "Hinke, Clarkson told me you had a case like this one?"

"Teenage twins murdered a long time ago, but not in your neck of the woods, Sheriff. Up in Connecticut outside New York City. Cold case. Any tie to your kidnapping would be a longshot. I know you've got to get back to work."

"Here, I'll put you on the line with one of my deputies to get you the VIN and driver's license info."

"Thanks, Sheriff."

Hinke had the Haverfords' two-ball. He hadn't yet seen the eight-ball that Filmore described, but he knew it was part of the Haverfords' set. Leaving one more missing ball. Standing in his office, he rolled the old ivory two-ball in his hand and smiled. *Okay, motherfuckers, you want to play, I'm all in.*

After talking to the deputy, Hinke put a director-level stat request into FBI Intelligence and Data Processing. He was, in turn, transferred to a special agent named Caroline Knopfler.

After introductions, Hinke said, "I need help, ASAP."

Her pleasant voice was calm and professional. "What can I do for you, Agent Hinke?"

"I've got the VIN of a late model Chevelle Malibu that's part of a murder investigation. Car found in a river outside Anniston, Alabama. Plates are stolen, but I have a Georgia driver's license number that was on the body of the guy murdered. I need you to check out any relationship between the victim and the vehicle—and anything else you can find out in the next couple hours. Priority."

"You got it, sir."

"Wait, I also need you to call Sheriff Filmore in Anniston and give him instructions for sending facsimiles of the car, the VIN, and the pool ball."

"The what?"

"The pool ball, Knopfler. Trust me, he'll know. Here's the number…"

"Yes, sir."

Within an hour, Knopfler called Hinke back. "I'll run a report up to your office with the facsimiles when I get those. The car belongs to a Matthew Elder, age twenty-one, who lives on Delmont in the Buckhead area of Atlanta. The 1974 model Chevelle Malibu was purchased six weeks ago with cash for $3,300 at Jim Ellis Chevrolet in Atlanta. The car hadn't been reported as missing yet. Elder hadn't been reported as missing either until this morning when Anniston Police called Atlanta Police."

Before he could get out his next question, she told him, "Matthew, AKA Matty Elder didn't have a police record, but I dug a little more. His name popped up in a few Atlanta drug cases. No arrests, but he could be a player."

Hinke was impressed. "Thanks. I gotta call the Crime Lab to see who we can get to Anniston tomorrow to check out any fingerprints."

"You're welcome. Let me know if I can do anything else."

An hour later, Special Agent Caroline Knopfler knocked on his door holding a folder of facsimiles. *Oh my, she was stunning.* A conservative dark dress suit, but he could tell in an instant it was heaven under all that. Tall, blonde, blue eyes, stacked—a more classic face than Marilyn Monroe. *Jeez,* Hinke told himself, *down boy. She's thirty-ish, give or take.* He'd never been able to help himself when it came to beautiful women. Helen had always accepted that—with the caveat that he wouldn't marry. A different relationship to say the least, but it had worked for them for twenty-three years.

Knopfler handed him the folder, and he leafed through, but he was only interested in one page. It was at the bottom. A grainy photo of the unusual eight-ball found in the glove compartment. "Bingo," he said involuntarily.

"That's what you were looking for?"

He nodded. "For a long time."

"Will that be all?"

"Yes, thanks, Agent Knopfler."

Leaving Hinke's office, she had two thoughts: *1) What in the world was going on with the pool ball? And 2) He's an awfully attractive older guy without a wedding ring.*

Under normal circumstances, Hinke might have asked the attractive blonde to join him for a drink. Perhaps another time. His brain whirred. *They're fucking with us*, he said to himself. But then realized it was worse than that: *They're fucking with me.* No one else who was investigating Elder's murder or the Blount twins kidnappings would have any idea what the eight-ball meant. No one else could connect any dots from the Haverford murders to the Blount disappearances—and then back to the Abercrombies. For now he intended to keep it that way.

Chapter 25 – APD Detective Hollis Delacroix

Tuesday, October 14

Anniston

Hinke had enough juice to finagle an FBI jet to fly him and the fingerprint guys to Anniston. On the way, he jotted down several profile thoughts in his worn, little notebook. They flew into Anniston Regional, a nice small airport, and rented two cars, one for him and one for the fingerprint boys, and headed into town.

Detective Hollis Delacroix of Atlanta PD was a striking Negro, maybe late twenties? Or was it "black" now? Hinke wasn't sure but knew that in the South there were names much worse. Delacroix was taller than Hinke, and at six-four looked like he could play Othello on Broadway or a rangy defensive end for the Redskins. He was the one black guy among a dozen white guys in the little Anniston PD office. He was hard to miss.

Coming around the corner from the little break room, Hinke overheard one of Filmore's deputies say to another cop, "Hell, I know Bear has a few darkies play'n for him down in Tuscaloosa. But I cain't believe 'Lanta sent us a nigger cop." Hinke wanted to punch the cracker but instead gave him a scowl that could kill. The cop was a coward and got his drift, turned, and walked away without saying another word. Hinke walked up to Delacroix and introduced himself, and the detective did likewise.

"Call me DH, by the way. I brought the Bureau's top fingerprint guys to see what they can find on the car."

"That's great. Underwater prints?"

Hinke nodded. "Sometimes retrievable. This Matty Elder guy from Atlanta it was his car. Photo on his license looks like the dead guy. He doesn't have an arrest record, but his name came up in a few drug cases."

"You already know more about Elder than I do," Hollis admitted.

"Yeah, but I got a head start and a lot more resources. I'll get you the photos and reports that Anniston PD has—if they don't give them to you. In a nutshell, Elder was in the trunk of his own car with his throat cut and bled out in the trunk. My two cents: whoever killed him wanted him to be found. The water was only six or seven feet deep."

"DH, before you arrived, I saw a pool ball I heard was found in the car; the only thing found in the car. Weird."

Hinke wanted to avoid discussion of the pool ball. "Yeah, I'm going to check with the sheriff and take it back to DC. See if it can tell us anything, but I doubt it." The ball had already told Hinke that he was back hot on the trail of the killers.

He told Hollis, "Not a lot for us to do here. The FBI crime scene guys are going over the car in a nearby garage. Body is at the morgue. Listen, why don't you let the Bureau find any next of kin and get you that. Then a family member can ID the body."

"That would be great."

"Let's go visit Matthew Elder."

The morgue was only a couple blocks away in the local hospital. Hinke had asked the sheriff to call ahead. Seeing dead people never bothered Hinke, but he didn't know about Hollis. A small room with the typical tile floor, the morgue was as cold as death and reeked of it. They were met by the county coroner, the white-haired Dr. Julius Bloom.

After introductions, Bloom wasted no time telling them that he wished a family member would get Elder's body out of his morgue and into the ground. He slid the body out of its steel container and flipped the sheet to expose Elder's face.

Elder's body was nearly the same color as the sheet. The two law enforcement professionals stood on either side. Without prompting, Bloom gave the short version of his findings.

"Haven't done an official autopsy yet, but I'm ninety-nine percent sure he died quickly from the single incision across both carotid arteries. As you can see, one slash from one side of the neck to the other. Likely bled out before he was found in the trunk, where the water washed away any remaining blood."

Hollis asked the ME, "The cut looks perfect. Who could do that?"

Bloom said matter-of-factly, "A killer who knows what he's doing and has a sharp knife."

Hinke said, "Got it. Thanks, Dr. Bloom."

That night in Anniston, Hinke guessed that Hollis would dine alone at a dive or not eat dinner at all unless he offered an alternative. When they walked into Al's Steaks, the cute hostess looked Delacroix up and down and said she'd be right back. A couple minutes later she arrived with a heavyset middle-aged man in an ill-fitting powder blue sport coat and a paisley tie that hung halfway down his sagging gut. The manager sized up the two big men, one older and white and the other younger and black, in their dark suits. Hatred oozed from the fat man's bulging eyes. Per Helen, not dissimilar to when Hoover used to talk about Martin Luther King—or any blacks. Hinke guessed Delacroix had seen that look many times before. A look that he admitted he'd never had to deal with. Hinke figured he wouldn't have lasted long as a black man and wondered how they did it. Survive, much less thrive. A few black men like APD Detective Hollis

Delacroix were ostensibly thriving, but he guessed that his life with a badge was no picnic.

Hinke fibbed to the fat man, "Sheriff Filmore recommended your place as having the best steaks in town."

The manager gave a reluctant nod and left without saying another word. The petite blonde gave a fake smile and directed them to a table in the far back of the dimly lit restaurant, where it would be a miracle if any waiter could find them.

But the steaks and baked potatoes were excellent. Hollis' career came up, and Hinke remembered he was a stellar defensive lineman at Rutgers and wondered why he didn't go pro.

"I played plenty of football over the years; I needed to make a difference. I took a couple criminal justice courses in college, and my professor, who was white, told me that I'd do well in law enforcement. So here I am on my first murder case in Alabama. With no leads."

"Hell, you're just starting. The leads will come. Back in Atlanta, you focus on Elder. Filmore and the Alabama SBI can focus on, well, investigating what they see fit in Anniston. But he's mainly worried about the kidnappings."

"And what about you, DH?"

He told the bare minimum. "Had a murder case of teenage twins in New Canaan, Connecticut, a long time ago – hell, maybe not long after you were born. They weren't kidnapped like the Blounts; they were killed at home. But I'm going to look at the Blount kidnappings. I hope the girls aren't dead, but I'd guess they are or will be shortly. A stretch to link the twins cases or link your murder to the Blount's kidnappings," Hinke lied. "But keep me posted on your investigation, and I'll do likewise. Never know."

Hollis talked about his family and his new baby girl, Suzanne, who was born two months ago. Hollis showed the agent wallet photographs of a remarkably beautiful baby and his Chinese wife, Mei. Bedazzling to say the least. Photos like these made him think about Marjorie and the kids they could've had. He knew she had three grown sons now. Hinke had no family stories but told a few colorful ones about his former boss that he'd heard from Helen.

Hinke picked up the check. "Hollis, you got a decent place to stay?"

Hollis winked at him. "Dewdrop Inn has been a Green Book place for a lotta years. I had an old copy; figured it would make things easier here in Alabama."

"Green Book? What the hell is that?"

"It's sorta the bible about where black folks can safely stay and eat meals, mostly in the South."

"No shit?"

"No shit."

"Doesn't all that stuff piss you off?"

"Absolutely, but I gotta pick my battles carefully. It's a long-term game…"

Hollis asked, "Will I see you again tomorrow?"

Hinke said, "I'll be around in the morning."

Hollis said, "Good night, DH, and thanks again for the help."

Right off the bat, Hinke knew Detective Hollis Delacroix would go far. He had a powerful, yet calm, gentle giant way about him. And a deep voice with no accent. Sharp as a whip. Hinke had a warm feeling that he'd maybe made a new friend—who would be his first-ever black friend. Hinke hadn't ever seriously asked himself the question whether he was prejudiced. He didn't think so, unlike most agents who believed lock, stock, and barrel Hoover's perverse reading of the Constitution that granted Anglo-Saxon, Christian men status above all others. He was thankful that Helen had steered him away from the most egregious Gestapo-like investigations. But to be honest, he'd done nothing to further better race relations. Maybe he could atone. Or not. How good a friend could he ever be? He'd already told a big lie to Detective Delacroix.

Two weeks later there was no word on the Blount girls. No ransom demand, no suspects, no one saw them after they left the game. No leads. Nada. Hope dimming that the girls would ever be found alive. Hinke read the daily Alabama SBI reports but had no new wisdom. According to Sheriff Filmore, it was like the Blount girls had simply vanished. For now, Hinke would keep the eight-ball under his hat. He'd told Filmore that he'd take it back to DC and see if FBI experts could find anything worthwhile. He was sure they wouldn't; he didn't bother to have it analyzed. The eight-ball, like the two-ball, was off the books and now tucked away in Hinke's locked file cabinet drawer. That left one more missing ball.

Saying nothing about the eight-ball connection, though, he knew he was passing a point of no return. If that ever became known, he'd be run out of the Bureau on a rail or put in jail.

He smiled. He didn't give a rat's ass.

Chapter 26 – Dinner in Atlanta

Two weeks later

Atlanta

Hinke wanted to know if there was anything else to be gleaned from Matty Elder's murder. Thus far, he'd heard zip on his murder from Hollis. But then, Hollis had heard dick from him. All the pieces of these multiple crimes were as clear as mud. Like trying to read an eye chart with the wrong lenses. He'd talked with Hollis Delacroix once by phone but decided to fly Delta down to Atlanta, take him to dinner, and see if he knew anything that might help the twins' cases. Hollis's case was secondary, but Hinke was still betting that the kidnappings and the murder -- happening within a few days of each other – was no coincidence.

They ate at the Colonnade in Buckhead, not far from where Hollis lived. Hinke felt bad about not inviting Hollis' gorgeous wife, but the detective had taken the hint that they needed to meet alone After a tasty, medium-rare chateaubriand and all the trimmings, the veteran FBI agent and the young Atlanta detective sat sipping Black Jack. Like two longtime buddies, they chatted about this and that before getting to the murder of Matthew Elder. Hollis told him about the young, never-arrested cocaine entrepreneur last seen at Pittypats Porch in downtown Atlanta that Friday night before his body was found in Anniston on Monday. Hinke was all ears.

"Bartender said he was alone but was chatting up the babes. Bought a lot of drinks for others; paid a couple hundred in cash and exited about midnight. Didn't look like he left with anyone that he could recall. He grew up in the West Paces area and attended the Westminster School, the bluest-of-blood private, pre-collegiate institution in Atlanta. Personable and preppy good-looking, always in a Polo, khakis, and Italian loafers, Matty became a stud dealer while still in high school. Supposedly he got the exclusive franchise—in the

Northwest Corridor, one of the wealthiest areas of Atlanta. A gold mine for any drug dealer."

"Who'd he work for?"

"Not even the narcs know for sure, but they hooked me up with a low-level drug snitch. Sleazy white guy had no doubt Elder was part of the Ghost's organization. The Ghost is the invisible big hitter in town, hence his name. If I am to believe Narcotics, they don't know who he is. But there was an unsubstantiated rumor that Matty got approached by a big Chicago narcotics player who wants him to jump ship and facilitate their entry into the wild west Atlanta drug market. All hearsay."

"Maybe this Ghost got pissed off and had him whacked?"

Hollis took a sip of his bourbon and replied, "Definite possibility."

Hollis wondered about Matty Elder. He'd been a popular, successful, apparently nonviolent drug dealer for a big chunk of Atlanta's young and rich; no doubt thought he was bulletproof. The killer, or he bet killers, went to a lot of extra trouble to murder him. Matty didn't drive to Anniston, Alabama, himself and then end up in his own trunk.

It was like Hollis was reading his thoughts when he said, "DH, why Anniston, Alabama? There'd be a hundred better places than a shallow river in east Alabama to dump Matty Elder's body and keep folks wondering. If it was a drug whack thing, why not make an example and put a pool ball or worse in his mouth or up his ass—and leave him in a downtown Atlanta alley?"

Hinke lied once more. "I don't know, but he was meant to be found."

Of course, Hinke knew why Elder had ended up in Anniston. The killers were comingling their crimes, making their game more challenging—not unlike what they'd done with Tommy Muldoon in

New Canaan. Hinke didn't know why the Blounts were snatched from Anniston. Other than they fit the beautiful teenage twins victim profile. They weren't too far from Atlanta if that's where these assholes lived.

Then he came back to his question: *Why murder the twins?*

Hinke guessed that this Ghost who ran a big drug business was mixed up with the group who was fucking with him. But for now, Hinke would let Hollis chase the Ghost.

Sipping his Jack, deep in thought, Hollis said, "I've been wondering about the eight-ball, DH."

He got Hinke's attention.

"You agree whoever murdered Elder left the eight-ball to be found?"

Hinke needed to tread carefully but answered, "No doubt."

"I know you said your lab didn't find anything useful, but I was curious."

After lying again about the lab, Hinke listened. Hollis told him, "Found the phone number for Max Billiards in Elder's address book. I visited the pool hall up Peachtree near the new Perimeter. An old Jewish guy, Max Heimer, owns it and doesn't see too well. I had a couple photos of the eight-ball. He said Matty Elder came in once a week. Good player, but he didn't play high stakes. Max said it looked like an old ivory ball, a design he'd seen in the '20s in New York City. Collector's item now. But Max told me Matty wasn't a collector as far as he knew."

Hollis said to himself, what the heck, and told Max, "That eight-ball was found in Matty Elder's glove box. His Chevelle was found in a river in Alabama. Matty was in the trunk with his throat cut." Max looked dumbfounded. "I left him my card in case he had any thoughts on who might have done that. I asked around the department if anybody's heard about a pool ball as part of murder. Got nothing. I thought about going to the press, but my boss said it would just attract lots of loonies. Probably true."

The killers who left the eight-ball were sending a message, but to whom?"

Hinke had to shut this down quickly. "I don't know, Hollis; I suppose law enforcement. Maybe some new type of bad guy's' calling card? I just don't know. Tell you what, I'll get a search done of our NCIC database for 'pool balls' or 'pool' and see if anything falls out."

"Yeah, okay, that would be great."

Holding his Jack, Hinke felt shittier. Hollis had done good detective work and was busting his ass trying to find Matty's killers – also the Blounts killers. All Hinke had done was tell more lies.

Hollis wasn't going to let this go. "DH, you told me a little about your case years ago. New Canaan is a rich New York City bedroom community, right?

"Yes, high class."

"Did pool play any part in those murders?"

"Nope." He maybe lied too quickly.

The lies kept slithering out of the exemplar FBI agent's mouth like a snake's tongue—and more smoothly under the cover of booze.

"Hollis, I don't have a single suspect or motive for the twins' crimes. Keep at it." That was the truth, but Hinke felt he was getting closer. Sipping Jack, the two men went silent. Hollis was lit. The detective slurred out, "Feds got this tab." The two were the last to leave the Colonnade. Hinke could already tell he was the more seasoned drunk and offered to drive Hollis home. Hollis quickly agreed.

A couple minutes later Hinke let him off in front of a well-kept one-story brick home on Delmont in the heart of Buckhead.

The big cop said, "I'd invite you in, but I'm sure my wife and baby are asleep."

"Another time, Hollis. Let's keep in touch."

Hollis Delacroix was drunk as a skunk. He fumbled with his key but managed to unlock his front door, then immediately slipped off his shoes. Bracing himself on the hallway wall, he tried not to stumble while tiptoeing to the nursery. Anyone who'd ever seen her always did a double-take. He'd never laid eyes on such a beautiful baby but tried not to brag. Her straight black hair and light caramel skin were much closer to her mom's black hair and porcelain skin than his curly hair and coal-black complexion. Leaning down over the bed rail, he kissed her on the forehead. She wriggled but didn't wake up. He wondered what Suzanne Delacroix would become one day. Hopefully, she would make a living far away from the world where he'd cast his lot.

After taking off his clothes and brushing his teeth, he climbed carefully into bed; his precious wife didn't stir. Drunk but wide awake he stared up at the ceiling and closed his eyes. He wondered why Matty Elder's face had looked familiar when he'd first seen his photo. Then realized he'd seen him a few times as he walked through his Buckhead neighborhood. He remembered Matty playing frisbee with a hot babe in a bikini in a courtyard on Delmont. A white boy neighbor down the street was a big-time dealer and now dead. Why should he be surprised?

He thought about the veteran FBI agent and their conversations. He liked Hinke but knew in his gut he was holding back. He wished he'd gotten home earlier and melded his body to hers. Instead, he fell into an alcohol-induced sleep. With startling dreams of water and drowning.

Chapter 27 - The Rules

Sunday, October 31, 1973

Atlanta

As she waited, the young woman examined the Haverford Shrine, which she'd viewed many times since she'd been a child. At first, it bothered her, but as she learned more, she gained appreciation. The hexagonal glass display case contained a few dozen photographs of Nellie and Natalie alive and dead, their nightclothes, other underwear, their jewelry, and one of the pool cues.

The Abercrombies case had a few clothing items, but most striking were the photographs; the clearest were black-and-whites, long before Land/Polaroid cameras.

In the Blounts display case was a pile of clothes and several photos, not yet organized. After two weeks, the twins were again secured on the stone sacrifice table. She'd watched while the two men took turns with each of the Blount girls for several days. The twins were drugged but only enough not to be a problem. The sacrifices were special: the first in twenty-three years and the first ever here.

She walked across the huge room. On the wall hung a large plaque. She knew them by heart but reread the Rules. The words were burned into a simple square of lacquered pine wood, accented with overlapping silhouettes of two identical girls.

Game of Twins—The Rules
April 30, 1912
Find and sacrifice the next twins:
Draw the enemy close
Wreak havoc, have fun
Escape to live another day
Rest and wait
'Til the next two

Always fight & destroy the light
And always encourage Our Evil

She and the two men heard their leader walking down the marble steps into the cavernous subterranean room. She kissed each of them on the lips and told the three, "You played with aplomb! Your names will be remembered for all time. Your rewards will be great." She faced the young woman and told her, "You will take my place one day." The young woman's eyes showed surprise, then pride. To the two men, she said, "Make your requests for whatever you want." Both men beamed.

The older woman continued, "But then rest. The wait will not be long. It seems that you will be the first to play twice. An honor never bestowed before—and may never again. Realize, though, we have poked a sleeping bear. He will be a formidable foe who will test you. He is approaching and could be our ruin—if you are not diligent. If you are, you will have great fun." The three shook their heads in acknowledgment.

She rang upstairs and within one minute, the tall Negro appeared with a silver chalice and silver goblets for each. After filling the goblets with dark red wine, she offered a toast: *"Game of Twins."*

"Game of Twins," they chanted in unison.

Chapter 28 – More Breadcrumbs

November 12, 1973

Washington, DC

He was being led. That much was obvious. But why and why him?

At age sixty-four Hinke figured he'd be long gone in another few years—or hell, he had a heart condition – he could drop dead any day. No time like the present to get on the stick after finally getting a lead. Hollis was working the Elder murder case out of APD. The Alabama SBI was working it across the state line. SBI was working the Blount abductions with Anniston PD. Independently, they had little. Hinke was the only one who could see the big picture, the only one viewing the crime spree in Anniston as the handiwork of the same criminals.

By 8:30 a.m., he'd already downed three cups of the Bureau's delicious coffee. One more than his morning quota. He had a hard time sitting still. He'd checked in Friday by phone with Detective Hollis Delacroix in Atlanta and Sheriff Frank Filmore in Anniston to see if there was anything new in either set of investigations. There wasn't. He couldn't concentrate. He read the Post and memorized the latest Redskins statistics. The mail arrived at 9:30 a.m. A few unimportant interoffice blurbs, an invitation to an Investigative Techniques conference in Williamsburg, and a six-by-eight-inch brown envelope, hand-addressed, with no return address. The postmark was Birmingham, Alabama. Inside was a thin color brochure from Crimson Realty Company in Anniston, Alabama. "Anniston's #1 Realty Company 12 years in a row." Professional but not glossy.

In the small brochure were an array of properties for sale and rent. He was surprised that several looked attractive. As he flipped through, one was circled in black pen. It was a white, picturesque Victorian home, seemingly alone on in a beautiful hilly, wooded setting. No others were circled.

His chin braced on his hands. He pondered and smiled.

Another breadcrumb.

He was compelled to play. He made a call to Crimson Realty and asked to make an appointment to see one of their advertised properties, tomorrow, if possible.

Hinke always had a bag of essentials and set of extra clothes in his office. He asked Fay, one of Helen's former assistants, to get him a ticket to Atlanta and have a car take him to National. No flights until 2:00 p.m. to Atlanta. Uneventful flight, but it all swirled in his brain. He picked up his Cadillac rental, checked into the Omni, got a nap, and dined at the Prime Meridian. He'd like to see Hollis but didn't want to discuss his visit to Anniston. Not yet anyway.

The next morning Hinke drove to the office of Crimson Realty on the outskirts of Anniston. He kept on the lookout for Filmore who he didn't want to see. The less time in public places the better. He wasn't Derbert Hinke this visit. He was Robert McGuire, a New York writer looking for privacy and a change of venue. He'd used several aliases over the years; it was no stretch to become Bob McGuire, author of historical fiction novels.

His 10:00 a.m. appointment was with Joan Richter, whom he told yesterday he didn't have a price range in mind. The kind of prospect Joan loved to show around. She said that she handled the best upscale rentals in the area. Based on his criteria, she knew three good rental properties that might fit the bill he'd described. But really there was only one.

Joan was a medium-height, forty-ish bleached blonde with a tad too much eye shadow and mascara. But a friendly, oval face and not a bad figure. On second look, not bad at all and no ring on her finger. Her genuine southern drawl was to die for. Along with her killer smile. He already had no doubt she was a successful real estate agent.

Driving to the first property, she filled him in on a little history of Anniston and the area being a cultural center for several decades. People were proud that Anniston hosted the Alabama Shakespeare Festival. She told him about the Anniston Army Depot and Fort McClellan, supposed to be secret, but well-known locations where the Army housed a vast amount of the country's chemical weapons. She did not mention the horrific attack on Freedom Riders in Anniston only a dozen years ago. Hinke heard what she was saying but was already falling in love with her soft, melodic accent, honey to his ears. Her perfume, enchanting.

The first properties were northwest of the city up off 431—about twenty minutes from Anniston's quaint downtown. Both were decent, sparsely furnished, single-story houses off the beaten path on skinny, pot-holed secondary roads but visible from the road. One had a barn that could maybe fit one vehicle. The other had a two-car open garage. Both were being renovated but should be available soon. Joan wanted to give him a couple of comparison points. Hinke played along.

They ate a late lunch at a mom-and-pop burger joint outside of town. Joan told him more about Anniston, which she called "the hidden jewel in Alabama." She asked him about his family, and he told her he had a son who was twenty-five. He got divorced years ago. Never remarried. This provided a lead-in for her to give him the short story of her volatile marriage to a local banker. No kids. Now divorced herself. Money not a huge problem, she implied, but she liked working and had to support her lifestyle. He told her to call him Bob and not

Mr. McGuire. She heard that but called him "darl'n," and he thought this lady was more than average attractive; her soft, syrupy drawl was driving him nuts.

After their leisurely, late lunch, Joan looked at her watch and said in her heavenly accent, "Darl'n, we better get going. I've been saving the best for last." She winked at him and headed back east across 21 north of Fort McClellan. The day had been a classic of autumn, but it was already late afternoon with the sun and temperature dropping.

The countryside of east Alabama, he didn't realize, was on the edge of the Blue Ridge Mountains. Even with the hardwoods having lost their leaves, the terrain was beautiful, and it was a spectacular day. Pines towered over the rolling landscape. He hadn't seen any houses for fifteen minutes when Joan pulled into a gravel driveway, then used a remote opener to swing the iron gate open. "Nice, huh?" she smiled. "Not too many places I know have a gate like this, and I know you want your privacy. If anyone is visiting the house, they must call ahead to get in. Property backs up to the Mountain Longleaf National Wildlife Refuge. Not that far from the city, but it don't get more private."

The tires on her BMW crunched the gravel, kicking up a smokescreen of dust behind them, but Hinke saw no house. She turned and smiled. "Don't worry, darl'n, we're gett'n there." It was another couple minutes of a winding, hilly road until Hinke spied the white Victorian with sky-blue trim, looking better than the brochure. The house was set on the top of a hill, framed by taller hills—or, he supposed, small mountains painted with majestic pines. It was breathtaking.

"Nice, huh?" said the southern blonde, looking better by the minute, while he listened to her gentle lyrical rhythms. "Lemme show you around back. You mentioned it might be nice to have a garage or barn to keep your car. This baby has both."

Without going in yet, he knew this was where they had staged it all, the kidnappings and Matty's murder. High-end, off-the-beaten path with lots of privacy from any road or property.

Hinke was glad he'd brought a jacket, and she put on her sweater. The sunset glowed pink and purple in the west. He had no idea how she could walk in the gravel with high heels but guessed with years of practice it was easy peasy for her. In addition to the Victorian, there was a bright red barn with white trim and no signs of wear. Next to it, a freestanding white building.

"Hell, you could have a party with a hundred or more people in here," she said, swinging the barn doors open. There were a few stalls on each side and a tack area, but not a speck of dirt or hay on the cement floor. He followed her to the plain white building. Pristine and plenty of room for a small fleet of cars. He nodded his head in approval. *It's perfect*, he thought to himself. She told him, "It was going to be an office and guesthouse, but they changed their minds."

As they walked to the main house he asked, "Joan, who's 'they'?"

"The owner, Alfred Brantley. He and his wife only lived here one year before she got real sick. Went to a big hospital in Atlanta, but they couldn't save her. Pancreatic cancer, bless her heart. Alfred decided he couldn't live way out here by himself, and he moved to their place in Naples. An older guy who made a bundle off his radio and TV franchises."

"He rents this out?"

"For now. Not exactly sure why since he doesn't need the money. He told me one time, 'Joan, no one ever owns anything. We're all only renting while we're here.' The price keeps the riffraff out, and I make sure of that," she giggled. "Don't worry, darl'n, I know you're not riffraff," and she winked at him again like Helen used to all those years inside J. Edgar Hoover's domain.

"You think he might sell it?"

"Maybe, if the price was right and if Alfred liked the buyer. I know he'd like you. But that's a whole 'nother conversation. How 'bout we take a spin around the house?"

Inside it was traditional but with great taste. Rich colors, dark wood trim, ornate crown molding, antique furniture, and Persian rugs. Gently, she took his hand and led him across the foyer from the formal dining room. "Check this out." Dark walnut walls and a gorgeous billiards table, several cue sticks lined up in their stand with blue chalk. He stood with a wry smile, staring at the table.

"What's the matter, darl'n?"

"Oh, sorry, the room reminded me of…" His voice trailed off.

The downstairs master bedroom had one of the most enormous bathrooms he'd ever seen and looked like it was all marble—or granite? The kitchen glittered with copper pots and pans hanging from a square chandelier above the oven in the middle of the room. They walked upstairs, where it appeared that another decorator had taken over. The three bedrooms were country rustic light pine, colorful quilts, warm woven rugs, and pictures of outdoor scenes and animals. They were done with impeccable taste. They walked down the stairs to the basement, and he toured the perimeter. Not much except a wall of empty wooden wine racks, a water heater, and a laundry area with a sink, washer, and dryer. The dull gray walls were blank, and the cement floor immaculate, like the barn. Nothing stood out. Back on the ground floor, she asked, "So whadya think?"

"It's magnificent" and thought, *Entirely possible Matty Elder and the Blount twins could have been here not long ago.*

She had her sweater on, and Hinke saw she'd undone two buttons of her blouse. It got his attention. "Knew you'd like it. Ready to get back?" She hadn't put on the hard sell, at least, not yet.

Walking out of the house, Hinke thought, *Hell, I could retire here easy, maybe with a lady like Joan Richter. If only I had the bucks of Robert McGuire.*

The grapefruit-colored sun was diving fast when she started down the long driveway back to the gate.

Preemptively, Hinke said, "Joan, I like it a lot. Tell you what, I'd like to spend a few hours tomorrow on the property by myself, look around and maybe sit down and relax, and try to write. Sorta kick the tires by my lonesome. I'll pay you a month's rent in advance, which is yours even if I don't take the place. Will that work?"

Driving, she glanced over a little warily.

He pulled out his billfold and told her, " In cash. If this doesn't cover it, you let me know." He counted out twenty Franklins that he'd taken from FBI petty cash.

Her eyes lit up when she glanced over again. He handed her the money. With one hand on the wheel, she nonchalantly folded the bills over once and squeezed the wad between her breasts. Glancing over, she noticed his eyebrows rise. In her sultry southern voice, she said, "What? Where else do I put it while I'm driving?"

Hinke grinned and said nothing but wished he'd been the one to slot the bills between her boobs. He'd be glad to retrieve the money for her when they stopped. She broke the silence. "I'm on a roll with that place. Wish I had more listings like it."

"How's that?"

"My last client paid me in cash, too, for three months and a deposit. A couple weeks ago, told me to keep the deposit. Vacating early. Three months was up at the end of October. You're in luck if you want to move in. Whenever you want it."

"A high-roller guy?"

"No, a gorgeous young woman. Blonde with more curves than Sharon Tate. Maybe mid-twenties at most. Kinda gal any guy would drool over. But I only met her twice in person. She wore sunglasses both times. Elegant and sorta mysterious. Like you. She said her privacy was important. I never ran into her around town."

Deflated, he asked himself, *A woman? That didn't make any sense, but he decided to give it a shot anyway.*

"You remember her name?"

"Why do you ask? You aren't drooling, are you?" she kidded.

"Nah, like to hear what she thought of her stay."

"Penny Ardmore from Birmingham Alabama, but she sure didn't have a southern accent."

"You got a phone number?"

"Nope. Said she was moving after her stay in Anniston and didn't have one. She only had a P.O. box."

"Maybe you got her driver's license or plate?"

"Nope. Usually, I do on lesser properties, but it was a lot of cash up front: $5,000."

"Wow. Can you get me her P.O.?"

"Sure, darl'n."

Hinke hesitated for a minute, wondering how far he could take this line of questioning. "Nice Beamer, Joan. Curious what kind of wheels did the rich girl ride?"

"Dark green van, not sure the make. Plates were orangey. Maybe Georgia? Said she was an artist and needed to bring all her stuff. She was going to get a couple relatives to help her move it into the barn. I told her I'd get a couple guys here and not charge her, but she insisted she had it handled. Left the place spic and span. Didn't need a cleaning service, and nothing was missing. If only all my clients were like her."

He wanted to probe a bit more. "Joan, that reminds me, is there a phone in the house?"

"Sure, phone service is included. Long-distance calls are extra."

"You remember if you charged her extra?"

Driving as daylight disappeared, she said, "Jeez, darl'n, if I didn't know better, I'd think you were a cop with all the questions you're ask'n."

He chuckled and gave her a sheepish smile. "As an author, I can get a one-track mind. Wanted to talk with her if possible before I make any big commitment."

She looked over at him again, and he had a hard time not sneaking a peek down her world-class cleavage. She knew he was looking and smiled. "Okay. I was giving you shit. No, as a matter of fact I thought it was strange she didn't make any long-distance calls."

They drove a couple more miles through the unlit darkness. She switched gears. "Bob, I'd sure like to take you out to a nice dinner tonight, maybe to Al's. Great steakhouse." And with her liquid blue eyes staring into his, she said, "If you need a place to stay, I've got plenty of room."

A vision of him with Joan flashed into his brain. Not unpleasant. But he needed a good night's sleep and not get ensconced in anything around Anniston right now.

"Thanks, Joan, but can I take a rain check? I need to get back to Atlanta this evening. I'll be back here about nine tomorrow morning. If I can borrow the gate opener and key, I'll get them back to you tomorrow afternoon. And we'll take it from there. Okay?"

With more than a little disappointment in her lovely voice, she told him, "Sure, darl'n, and I'll get you the address."

Silence for the next few miles until they reached Crimson Realty. It was torture watching her, from behind, move in her tight skirt as she walked up to the door and unlocked it. "You com'n in, darl'n?"

What could he do but follow? Inside, she removed her sweater, her curves looking curvier after she flicked on a light. His eyes were glued on her ass as she slowly walked in front of him and then over to a set of file cabinets. She paraded back and handed him the house key and gate opener and a piece of paper with a Birmingham P.O. address. Instead of shaking hands with her, he bent down and gave her a consolation kiss on the cheek, knowing he could have had much more that evening. But she did one better, grabbing the back of his head with both hands and planting a big wet one on his lips. He had a hard time not reciprocating.

"Sure I can't change your mind, darl'n? I love the quiet, tall, good-looking types." She lifted his right hand and placed it on one boob, then the other. "I'm not asking to get married." She looked up into his eyes. "Just tonight?"

Hinke was horny and torn and would have loved to spend the night with Joan. On the edge of temptation, he bit his lip, smiled at her, and let himself out.

When the door shut, Joan Richter counted to ten then said out loud, sarcastically, "Sure, darl'n, another time."

She regretted she wasn't getting laid tonight but smiled, regardless. She'd done her part and would get a $5,000 cash bonus, which the woman known as Penny Ardmore told her she'd have by tomorrow. Plus the two grand from Bob. That would pay for her next couple luxury cruises and who knew? Maybe she'd meet a rich guy like Maguire or whatever his name was.

Three months ago, Penny Ardmore gave Joan Richter similar rental criteria as Robert McGuire—adding she'd wanted a pool table in her rental. The real estate agent found one that she rented and had carted in for two hundred bucks. The cost was a rounding error.

Chapter 29 – The Victorian

Tomorrow came too quickly with his wake-up call at six. Hinke got a good night's sleep but felt groggy. It was against his religion, but he brewed an in-room cup of coffee to hold him over. Driving his rental Caddy, he eased into the Atlanta traffic, which was already at a standstill at 7:00 a.m. He stopped outside town at a little diner and bought a big cup of real coffee and a pastry. He didn't feel patient enough to sit down and order breakfast. His anxiety increased as he drove I-20 West. He passed a bunch of gas stations with dozens of cars waiting to fill up. Damn gas shortage. OPEC was a pain in the ass for anybody who drove. He was grateful he had three-quarters of a tank.

Unlike yesterday, the sky was slate gray. It was windy and downright inhospitable when he opened the gate and wound his way up the long, gravel road to the stately Victorian, now starker against the unfriendly sky and tall, almost black pines. Inside, though, it was warmer. Joan must have turned on the heat yesterday. He removed his coat, realizing he had no plan for what to do. The property, she said, was thirty acres with the house, barn, white garage, lots of forest, and grassland. Way too much territory to cover in the morning hours—or ever.

He decided to start in the basement. Much cooler than the main floor. He turned on the lights. Deadly silent with the dank, familiar smell of being underground. He walked the perimeter again, but this time got an eerie feeling that made the hair on the back of his head stand up. Nothing ever spooked him, but the tough special agent was uneasy. He trotted back upstairs. The door to the top of the basement was shut. He was positive he hadn't closed it. He checked to see if it swung by itself but didn't. With his memory faculties not what they used to be, he decided he must have shut it.

He walked into the billiards room. A Tiffany-type lamp hung over the ornate table. A lamp not unlike the one in the Haverfords' Big Cottage. He'd always loved the sound of billiards: the pop of the cue tip hitting the ball, the soft thud of the balls against the sidewalls, the clack-clack-clack of the balls ricocheting off each other, then plopping into a pocket. Playing pool, with its strict confines, always took him to another world where he could forget everything else.

He grabbed the rack and placed it on the table. He went pocket to pocket fetching the balls and placing them in the rack, always with the one-ball at the top of the triangle. But he was missing the cue ball. He walked around the table stuffing his hand down into the leather pockets and finding nothing. He used the one-ball to break and played for a few minutes.

Then it hit him. He could almost hear them laughing "Gotcha," but thought, *Could it be possible?* He walked down the hall to the oversized master bedroom on the main floor. It was traditional with a mammoth dark-wood four-corner king bed and a comforter that matched the royal blue room trimmed with white and green; two sitting chairs with a matching table; and bookend nightstands on each side of the bed.

Hinke opened the top drawer of the nearby nightstand. Empty. He pulled out the drawer. Nothing inside or on the bottom or outside. Nothing on the interior or back exterior of the nightstand itself. He shook his head, castigating himself, wondering what the hell he was thinking.

Prepared to be disappointed, he walked around the big bed to the nightstand on the far side. Inside was a black bible but nothing else visible. He pulled out the whole drawer and almost dropped it. There, taped inside against the back of the drawer, was a pool ball.

Not the missing ball from the set in the house. A yellowed ivory cue ball. He should've had gloves on but ripped it out and pulled off the tape.

The last missing pool ball from the Haverfords' pool table years ago.

Only he would know the significance of it—yet it proved nothing. No one else would believe it anyway; no reason to tell anyone. Another breadcrumb from the scum who had kidnapped Cherry and Mary Blount, killed Matty Elder, killed the Haverfords, and likely the Abercrombie twins, too.

He sat down on the massive bed holding the old cue ball, rolling it around in his palm.

His next thought: "They" includes a woman. Interesting. Joan had mentioned "relatives" were going to help Penny Ardmore. He'd never find a Penny Ardmore in Birmingham, Alabama. But maybe "relatives" are real? Would that explain the sixty-two years of these strange kidnappings and murders? He'd brought a basic kit for fingerprinting and could spend the rest of the day going room to room in three buildings and scouring the property for a grave or graves. But he wasn't going to find anything. The killers-kidnappers were too good for that.

On his way out he couldn't help checking out the basement again. The door was open. He knew he'd closed it. Before he went down, he debated fetching his Smith & Wesson .44 locked in the trunk of his rental but decided to leave it.

"Okay, who the hell's down there? Federal Bureau of Investigation. Coming down," he yelled. Before hitting the light switch he looked down the basement stairs. At the bottom, he saw the floating luminescent outlines of two girls beckoning him. As if in a trance, he walked down slowly, unarmed. This time he smelled chemicals. Chloroform? By the time he got to the basement floor the two apparitions were in the middle of the big room, facing him, smiling.

He'd seen a few more photos of them after he'd arrived in Anniston. Unquestionably, the Blount twins.

As he started to say, "Please tell me…," they turned and walked away from him until they disappeared into the far wall, leaving him in the dark.

Hinke climbed the stairs, shut the door, and sat in the small living room of the white Victorian. He didn't think he was going nuts. His world of it's-only-real-if-you-can-rationally-explain-it, which he hadn't revisited since seeing the Haverford twins' ghosts twenty-three years prior, was now completely shattered. He was dealing with the world of the unexplainable, a world he'd always had trouble accepting. It scared the crap out of him. When he finally stood again, an hour had gone by. It was clear that the Blount twins were dead, whether they died in that basement or elsewhere. He wished he could at least tell their mom. Maybe one day he would.

He had to take another look at the billiards room. He should have been shocked but wasn't. The balls he'd left scattered on the table were now in the shape of a perfect cross. All balls from that set, including the cue ball that had been missing.

He shook his head.

Then, walking back down the hallway to the front door, he heard a rumbling.

It was coming at him. The two-ball. It had been on the pool table with the others only seconds ago.

Twice he'd had two-balls rolled at him. *Two for twins? Why not?* He was a believer.

Hinke had a decision to make. Maybe Joan remembered more about the woman or the van? Perhaps he could get a sketch artist? Maybe, but she said the woman wore sunglasses, no doubt, to hide her face. Was she a blonde or a brunette or a redhead today? Had she made herself look younger or older? Maybe the phone records from the line in the rental? That, he could get checked out but was likely a waste of time, as would sending in an army of FBI crime scene investigators to cover the entire Victorian, its ancillary buildings, and the thirty-acre property.

Besides, trying to marshal any significant Bureau resources, he knew would mean a clusterfuck of FBI and other law enforcement boys tripping over each other's dicks while the bad girl and guys vanished. That being moot, though, unless anyone would take him seriously, which he doubted. Another unpleasant possibility. He'd been withholding evidence from the original Haverford case, the Blount abductions, and the Elder murder. He wasn't going to end up in the slammer. He'd eat his piece first. He was all in. This was his baby. It wasn't a hard call.

Hinke drove back to town to drop off the gate opener and key. He was relieved Joan was out showing a property and left her a short note. "Joan, Thanks again for yesterday. I'll be in touch. Bob McGuire."

But Robert McGuire would be gone. As Joan Richter knew last night, long gone.

Earlier that day while Hinke was in the Victorian, on the small mountain inside the wildlife refuge that overlooked the beautiful, solitary home, a man in camouflage with high-powered binoculars watched. He saw Hinke enter and stay in the house for two hours. In his right hand, Hinke gripped what he was sure was the old cue ball. He smiled. He was positive Hinke had found the other breadcrumb. Later, he'd go back and make sure. Now, the game should get a lot more interesting. She would be thrilled.

Part 3

Chapter 30 – The Invitation

Six months later, April 15, 1974

Washington, DC

On Easter Sunday, Hinke got up late. He'd had a few too many cocktails the previous evening. When he separated his head from the pillow, he knew he was going to pay the price. Living alone, and last evening, unfortunately, sleeping alone because his girlfriend was out of town at a wedding, he couldn't conjure up a beautiful woman to fetch him aspirin and coffee in bed. Not bothering to put on a robe, he ambled his 215 pounds as daintily as possible, first to the bathroom, then to the kitchen, where he started a pot of coffee. With his pounding headache easing a bit, he walked to his front door to get the *Post* in the hallway. Pushed under the door was a small envelope addressed to Special Agent Derbert Hinke. No return address or name. He plopped down at his dining room table and opened it; inside was a notecard with fancy black calligraphy. It simply read:

Thank you for playing

Game of Twins

He got up to get a cup of coffee and sat back down at his kitchen table with the note in front of him. Yep, it was abundantly evident that since 1950, he'd been part of a sick, murderous game whose objective was to sacrifice female teenage twins. "*Game of Twins*"—catchy and dead on.

But what did those words mean, and why now?

Egging him on to keep playing?

Warning him; a harbinger of a darkness to come? More twins murders? His own murder?

Making light of his futile attempts to find them?

Telling him this game was about to be over—or that it was starting again in earnest?

Maybe all the above?

He posted the note on his refrigerator. He would ponder more when he was not hungover. He was starving. After frying sausage links and a couple of eggs, he devoured that with two slices of honey toast and orange juice. Once upon a time, he attended Mass on Easter Sunday, but that stopped years ago. He wasn't sure why and wasn't interested in analyzing his behavior right now.

With food and more coffee in his belly, he felt much better and stepped into the shower. Usually, he felt any tension or anxiety dissolve away after standing a few minutes under the hot spray. Not this time. He dried off, walked into the kitchen, and poured a few fingers of whiskey into his empty coffee mug. He'd known for a long time, but now the killers had made it official: all of it was linked to the Haverford murders in 1950, then to the Blount disappearances last year—and back to the Abercrombie kidnappings in 1911.

Chapter 31 – Twins Murders in Georgia

A day later (the day after Easter Sunday), April 16, 1974

Woodstock, Georgia

Sitting on the edge of his bed, Barron Brevard felt disoriented and unsteady after only a couple hours of sleep. It couldn't be true. Wearing his rumpled clothes from last night, he walked into the living room and stood in front of the recently painted, full-length portraits of his beautiful twin daughters. The tall, rough-hewed but distinguished businessman, who'd been told more than once looked like a well-aged version of the Marlboro Man, looked like shit in the adjacent mirror. He wanted to cry but couldn't. Not yet, anyway. He stared at himself in the mirror and asked, *What the hell did I do to deserve this?*

After brewing a pot of coffee, he called the offices of Stuyvesant, Knight, Fitzpatrick & Burns and asked for Ted Davies. He'd never needed Ted for criminal law, but the two had met at several Atlanta functions and gone skeet shooting together a couple of times. He'd heard Ted was *the* guy when it came to criminal law. His secretary, Valerie, said, "Oh, Mr. Brevard, I can't tell you how sorry I am for your losses." The news of his twins' murders was too late to make the *Atlanta Journal and Constitution*'s morning edition, but there had been a short piece on TV that morning. It would be the ubiquitous lead story news tomorrow. She explained that Ted was in Charleston working on a case and wasn't expected to be back until early evening. Barron asked if he'd call him when he could. Later was okay since he'd be out most of the day. He intended to search for Thor for as long as it took.

"Yes, sir. Again, my condolences."

At noon in Charleston, Ted broke away for a few minutes to call his office.

Valerie told him, "Mr. Davies, Barron Brevard called. You may not have heard yet, but his twin daughters were found murdered last night."

"What?" Ted was startled. How could that be possible? But the top criminal attorney in Atlanta knew when it came to murder, anything was possible. "What happened, Val?"

"Not much news yet. They were found on a farm in Woodstock near Mr. Brevard's. Cops think they have the murderer in custody. Anyway, Mr. Brevard would like you to call him. "Later is fine," he said. "He'll be out most of the day."

Valerie gave him Barron's home number. He thanked her and hung up.

Holy shit, Ted Davies said to himself, not being able to imagine how he'd feel if something terrible happened to his son Kip, who was a teenager about their same age. Kip had met the beautiful twins, and Ted knew his son had been smitten.

He re-entered the conference room to continue depositions in the murder of a wealthy Charleston physician. He had trouble focusing on his case. He wanted to hear more about the murders but then wondered: *Why would Barron want to talk with me? Could he have done it?* That thought crossed his mind, but he dismissed it. *Maybe he was under suspicion simply because he was a family member?*

Ted tried to reach Barron when he got to the Charleston Airport about 5:00 p.m., but there was no answer. He asked the only stewardess on the thirty-seater prop plane for a couple mini-bottles of Makers before they took off. After downing the liquor, cut with a little Coke, he tried to doze, but the bumpy ride and his remembrances of the Brevard twins interfered with any sleep. "*Jeez,*" he thought, "*the guy's had two wives die on him, and now he's lost his only two kids. What were the chances?"*

After landing in Atlanta at 6:30 p.m., he went to the Delta Crown Room and found a quiet space with a phone. But not before ordering a double Makers on the rocks. This time, Brevard picked up.

"Barron, it's Ted. Val told me the bad news. Please accept my condolences and those of everyone in the firm." Barron's bank was one of Stuyvesant-Knight's most significant clients and had been for two decades.

"Ted, I've been out all day looking for our dog, who disappeared with the twins yesterday. Haven't found him yet. At least it's keeping me busy."

"Barron, tell me what you know about the murders and how I can be of assistance."

Brevard spent the next ten minutes telling him what he knew (ninety-five percent not given to the press at this point), with Ted politely asking a few questions. God, he was relieved Barron had an alibi and wasn't involved.

Ted asked, "This Orville Johnston, you knew him? Your daughters knew him? Tell me more." Barron filled him in and said, "I was going to have Orville over for dinner next weekend with the girls. Hell, they thought it was terrible he'd never been invited for a meal. Maybe if I'd invited him for Easter...," he said, his voice trailing off.

Did Johnston have an alibi? Had he been charged yet? Davies wanted to ask—and a bunch more questions—but decided to lay off for now.

"Ted, I want you to defend Johnston. I'm ninety-nine percent sure he's innocent."

"Why do you think he's innocent?"

"No doubt in your line of work, you read people well, and I think I do, too. I know him well enough. I talked to him last night in his jail cell. He was devastated and could barely speak. He told me point blank that he didn't do it. With a look in his eyes that said, 'I'd never do that in a million years."

Ted Davies wanted to interject that he saw it all too often. People who had murdered in rage or other mental state and honestly believed they didn't do it. Others could fool the best—even with a lie detector test. Then there were a few he knew who weren't criminals—for whom Ted enjoyed getting real justice.

He told Barron, "I'll drive up to Canton first thing. Lemme talk to him a bit, and I'll give you my take. We can take it from there. I'm sure it's been a long day for you."

"Thanks, Ted."

Barron hung up, poured himself a big Scotch, and collapsed onto his buffalo skin couch. I can't believe they're gone, he told himself for the hundredth time. "My babies," he moaned and then sobbed, uncontrollably.

Ted Davies left a message with Valerie telling her to reschedule his Tuesday morning. He'd drive straight up to Canton and not be in the office until maybe noon. He hoped that Barron was right. If not, and he helped get Johnston off, Ted wasn't sure he could live with that.

Chapter 32 – Mareissa & Matilde

Earlier that same day

Atlanta

The Monday morning after Easter, Detective Hollis Delacroix heard a couple homicide cops yakking in their cramped, grungy break room in downtown Atlanta PD headquarters. Between their coffee slurps and stuffing Krispy Kreme donuts into their yaps, he caught a few comments about twins murdered in Cherokee County last night. Detective Virgil Stockman held a transmission copy that included a photograph of the girls all dressed up like they were in a beauty contest. "Looks like two tasty young pussies bit the dust. Damn waste. Hey, you ever done twins, cock breath?" Stockman asked his partner. Jimmy Gilligan chimed in, cupping both of his hands and jerking them up and down. "Not me, asshole, but I'd guess your two palms could count as twins."

"Blow me," Stockman told him.

"Yeah, maybe later in the squad car if you've got better porn than last time."

Hollis looked at the transmission they'd left on the counter. Photographs of striking, blonde teens but only sketchy information that the bodies were found on the land of Orville Johnston, a Negro who lived outside Woodstock, who'd been arrested. He grabbed a cup of coffee and walked back to his desk. Last year he helped a Woodstock cop out of a serious jam he got into downtown. He'd heard the cop left the Woodstock force, so he called his ex-partner to see what else he could find out.

Hollis got a female dispatcher and waited a couple minutes for her to locate Woodstock Deputy Sheriff Louis Giles.

"Hey, we're a little busy up here today."

"I heard. The murders last night."

"Bad news travels fast."

"Saw a short blurb this morning on the wire. Wonder if you could tell me a little more. Longshot but there might be a tie-in to another case I know of."

He knew Sheriff Sumner wanted to keep the details quiet, but Hollis seemed like a trustworthy guy. Hell, maybe Johnston was involved in other crimes, too.

"Mareissa and Matilde Brevard, who lived on a big ranch outside Woodstock, were out hiking with their dog after Easter lunch yesterday. Fourteen-year-old twins of an Atlanta heavy hitter who owns a big spread on the edge of Woodstock. No contact for several hours, and we had a lot of areas to search: rolling farmland, but also lots of water, woods, old mines, and grist mills. Found 'em dead, sliced up, on the land of an old farmer, Orville Johnston, who was drunk and passed out at the scene. I was the first one there. Nigger's going to get fried," he said, forgetting whom he was talking to and already feeling like shit.

Giles tried to bite his tongue. "Holy shit, pardon my French, Hollis. My apologies."

Delacroix had heard countless racial slurs—before and after he'd become a cop. He hated it. Most times, he knew he had to ignore it but not with Giles. "Louis, I wouldn't want to drive up to Woodstock and kick the living shit out of a short little white boy."

Giles hoped he was kidding. He prided himself on not being a stupid-ass, knee-jerk bigot, and he knew he fucked up. He apologized again.

After a minute, the Atlanta homicide cop let him off the hook," We're good,"

Giles breathed a sigh of relief.

Hollis said, "Okay, but I need to make a phone call to an FBI guy in DC. You remember that case in Anniston last year? Girl twins went missing in October. Never found, presumed kidnapped and murdered. About the same age as the Brevard girls. This FBI agent's been working the Anniston abductions case and will want to know about these murders. Maybe your guy kidnapped them, too."

Giles knew his boss wouldn't want the FBI involved but felt guilty about slandering Hollis.

"The girls' dad is hyper-sensitive about the press. We gotta keep it low-key."

"No problem at all. His name's Hinke. Special Agent Derbert Hinke. Goes by DH. Good guy up in DC. Old pro. I'm going to give him a call. Thanks, Louis. I'll let you get back to it. And if we need to talk with your boss, let me know."

Giles said goodbye and would cross his fingers that Sheriff Billy Rae Sumner wouldn't be too pissed about him inviting a Fed from Washington, DC. *Nice work, Louis. You'll be a two-bit cop in this hick town till you're fifty if you're lucky.*

Hollis Delacroix was already looking up Hinke's number in DC and was glad he was in. He got to the point. "DH, it's Hollis. Late last night twin teenage girls got murdered in Woodstock about thirty miles north of the city. Thought you might be interested."

Hinke jolted upright in his chair. *Holy shit, he'd been right in his premonition.* The thank you note he got yesterday was an announcement that they were going to murder again. And they were taunting him—daring him to play their *Game of Twins*. Unfortunately, he was already too late to stop them.

"Just got off the phone with Woodstock Deputy Louis Giles, pronounced Lou-ee. 1 let him know you're coming. Don't know him all that well, but he seems like a good guy. I'd drive up too, but I gotta be on a case today and probably in court all day tomorrow."

"Did he tell you anything else?" Hinke asked.

"Not a lot. Happened on the land of a black farmer who's in custody. He passed out at the scene, which apparently was grisly. The twins were mutilated by a knife or a sharp object. The farmer hasn't spoken -- other than to say he didn't do it."

Hinke's heart pounded like a bloodhound who'd caught the whiff of an unmistakable scent.

Hollis asked, "Maybe this is like the old double murder case you mentioned?"

Hinke ignored the question (adding it to his growing bucket of fibs and outright lies) and said, "Thanks, Hollis. Tell the deputy sheriff I should be there by mid-afternoon. I'll try to call you later."

Hinke contacted a friend of a friend of Helen's and reserved an FBI Gulfstream to fly him ASAP from National to Hartsfield. On the flight, he had profiling on the brain.

He'd read more of Teten's work and attended another lecture. He and Patrick Mullaney were charging ahead, challenging the FBI status quo with their brand-new Quantico Behavioral Sciences unit. They'd looked at several historical mass murders done by the likes of Jack the Ripper, H. H. Holmes, and others. They were applying their nascent profiling to several current cases. The lecture was where he first heard two terms: "unsub," who was an unknown perpetrator of a crime, and "serial killer," an unsub who murders premeditatively and exhibits patterns over time with their multiple murders. Often with no apparent motive.

The time between crimes—1911 to 1950 to 1973—he no idea how to explain, but the killers were telling him the three were related. Would these latest twins murders also fit the pattern? He again thought about going to Quantico and let them in on his cases—but held back. *If Teten or any of the others believed his story, they'd want everything he had. That wasn't going to happen. No one was going to fuck up his investigations.*

That was the day Derbert Hinke told himself, *"I'm dealing with serial killers. And this new methodology of profiling is going to help me catch them.* Daydreaming, he thought, *Maybe one day I can give a lecture at Quantico about these serial killers and how I profiled them."* Then thought, *"I better worry about catching them first"*.

Chapter 33 - The Granite Crime Scene

The same day

Woodstock, Georgia

By two-thirty, he was driving his Cadillac rental up 85 past the Perimeter and up 400 into the north Atlanta burbs. He was famished and stopped for a Coke and peanut butter cheese crackers at a truck stop after getting off 400. He needed to double-check the directions he'd tried to divine from a map of the metro Atlanta area. Back in the Caddy, he drove up Highway 92 into the dinky town of Woodstock, Georgia. Driving at a snail's pace he rolled down the car window and asked a wide-bodied woman in baggy overalls and a flannel shirt, "Ma'am, can you point me to the police station?"

"Block down. Cain't miss it."

"Much obliged."

Looking much like it had a half-century ago, Woodstock had its own train stop, and he could hear the distant rumbling and whistles. He parked across from the station, whose minuscule size matched the quaint town. Inside it, though, was a bustle of activity. He was more than a little out of place in his Brooks Brothers attire, which he hadn't bothered to change before leaving DC. A little woman, maybe about his age asked, "Hep you, mister? We're up to our asses in alligators after those horrible murders last night."

Hinke pulled the badge out of his lapel pocket. "Special Agent Derbert Hinke, FBI. Deputy Giles is expecting me." The tall, impeccably dressed FBI special agent wasn't hard to miss. The short, sturdy young cop, dressed in a butternut uniform and gear, cowboy boots, and Stetson, walked up, stuck out his hand, and introduced himself. "Deputy Sheriff Louis Giles. Hollis Delqua mentioned you'd be dropp'n by." Looking carefully at the big man's tanned face etched with wrinkles, Giles' first reaction was: *"This guy's been around the block and won't take any bullshit."*

Hinke shook hands and introduced himself. "Appreciate you taking the time." He didn't beat around the bush. "Mind if we see the crime scene, Deputy?"

"You got it. Call me Louis."

"I'm DH."

Walking out the door to his Dodge cruiser, Giles told the FBI agent, "Just got back after going through the Negro's house and barns; a couple county cops have been blocking the road leading up to the land near his house. Nobody's found anything new other than what we found last night. We got enough to fry him, but if we can find more evidence, that'd be nice. You think the murders might be related to them girls gone miss'n from Anniston a few months back? Hell, maybe he buried them all on his farm?"

Hinke managed to say, "You never know," but he'd already heard enough to think, *"In your fucking dreams you've got the right guy"*

Louis drove a Dukes of Hazzard-like white Monaco with a line of red, white, and blue lights crossing the middle of the hood. No flashers needed or wanted as he chauffeured Hinke to the crime scene on the north edge of Orville Johnston's land.

Hinke listened while Giles told him more about the Brevard girls and their prominent father. It was well known that whatever Barron Brevard wanted, he got. Big-time Atlanta banker but spent a lot of time on his Woodstock ranch with his girls. They all liked to ride horses. Heard the girls had modeled in Atlanta. They were that good-look'n. Seen 'em a few times. A shame..."

With no traffic on the narrow two-lane road, Giles stopped ahead where there was a white cop car with his rainbow row of lights turned on. "Mack's guarding the back way into the property nearest the murder scene."

Giles got out and asked, "What's the haps, Mack? This is Special Agent Hinke of the FBI. Come to visit the scene."

The rail-thin cop with gun-metal wire rims tipped his cop hat. "Sheriff told me to stay till dark to shoo off any TV or other types that don't belong, then I'll get relieved. I'm hungry as hell. Haven't seen nobody yet except you two all day."

Giles thanked him and said he'd make sure to get him food and a break. He turned left onto a one-lane gravel road that forked more times than Hinke could keep up with. No question they were in the boonies. But pleasant boonies. Hinke doubted he could ever live out here, but it was sure a lot more peaceful than Washington, DC, or Atlanta or any city he'd been in recently. Giles kept driving on the bumpy one-lane round. It was a rural terrain Hinke doubted he couldn't navigate his way back to civilization from—but could tell from the sunlight they were driving west.

"Where the heck are we?" Hinke asked.

"Only a couple miles northeast of Woodstock as the crow flies, in Cherokee County. This was the only good way to get out here. Not too many folks live out this way till you get closer to the lake."

Now on a hilly, bumpy path of packed red clay, Giles told him, "Almost there," as he turned the cruiser off the gravel onto a wild grassy field. "Need to hike a few minutes from here. Too many rocks that could fuck up my car—then I'd have to pay for the damages. Hope it don't ruin your city shoes."

Not sure what to expect, Hinke emerged from the car and took in the pastoral panorama: beautiful pristine country with rolling hills spotted with intermittent stands of pines and hardwoods, wild grasslands, long strands swishing gracefully in the light breeze. A rock bluff toward the north with dense forest below it. To the south it looked like endless pastureland. Like a lush English scene. He stared at the stone bluff on the other side of the forest. *Thinking, it would be a great view from up there.*

Giles pointed toward the dual rock formation with two giant Georgia pines straight ahead, swaying a bit in the breeze. The sky was crystal-blue; this place, though, reeked of death.

Hinke knew this was it.

There were two massive pieces of granite, like vertical arrowheads, black with white and red flecks. Between them: a low, flat natural table of the same colored granite at a slight slant. Stonehenge-like. Probably colonists and early Americans clashed with Cherokees and other tribes in the nearby fields. Maybe others died on this altar of black rock?

Hinke stepped under the crime scene tape to get a close-up view of the rectangular black slab. The blood from last night was barely perceptible, having soaked into the prehistoric bed of stone. He bent down and noticed bits of coagulated blood on the long grasses around the big rock. Mother Nature would cleanse the rest when She got around to it.

The idyllic countryside was a place of horror last evening.

"You were first on the scene. What did you see last night, Louis?"

"Hell, we had dozens search'n toward the old mica and gold mines and a few of the deserted mills. Too much lake for a couple hundred guys to cover much less a few dozen. Could've been look'n there till the cows came home. But we got lucky."

"Right around midnight I saw a bright flare in the far distance. I drove toward the light, but when it fizzled out, I saw another faint light up ahead. Not a flare. Got out my car, got my shotgun out of my trunk, and went on foot. The light got a little brighter. I had my flashlight on but was careful getting to where we are now. I saw Johnston on the ground. Unconscious. Liquor bottle not far from him. His jeans and fly were open with his black cock out. An old revolver and a ballcap near him, about right here." He pointed down to the grass a few feet from the huge, flat rock. "The light I saw was a flashlight turned on that was leaning against Johnston."

"Louis, can you tell me about the girls—how they were murdered?"

Giles gathered himself for several seconds and then said, "I had a hard time look'n. They were lying on the rock, arms out and feet taped. The worst was the black crosses, stuck into them between their legs. I sent up a couple of my own flares, then called it in on my walkie-talkie."

Giles started to break down. Hinke waited, his own skin crawling. The all-too-familiar photos of the Haverford twins were burned into his brain from decades ago.

"I wanted to pull those things out of 'em, but I got a blanket and a poncho from my trunk and covered the bodies."

"Louis, tell me more about the wounds you saw on the girls."

"They were sliced straight down the middle of their bodies, then across under their breasts. Not a stitch on. Then it looked like they had their throats slashed. Same wounds on both."

Hinke asked, " Exactly how were their bodies positioned?"

"It was spooky. They were laid out the same. On their backs, arms straight out to their sides, an arm's length. An arm of each touching together. Legs straight and feet duct-taped. Not sure but looked like they'd had tape on their mouths too; maybe ripped off."

Virtually identical to the Haverford murders in 1950, twenty-four years ago. Hinke looked away.

"DH? You okay?"

"Yeah. Wondering, you find the girls' clothes, shoes, jewelry?"

"Didn't find anything that belonged to them."

"Deputy, where do you think the twins' stuff went? Just disappeared?"

"I don't know."

"You find a murder weapon?"

"Nope. I found a couple big knives in Johnston's kitchen. Spic and span."

"Duct tape?"

"Didn't find any. Maybe Johnston buried it all on his farm."

Hinke could barely hide his disbelief. "Uh-huh. Anything else?"

Giles said, "I didn't find nothing unusual at his house and or barns. Still look'n for their dog."

"Their dog?"

"German shepherd, Thor. He went everywhere with 'em. No sign of the dog."

Hinke said, "Maybe shot the dog and buried it with the twins' stuff?"

He realized he needed to tone down his sarcasm. Giles said nothing. Hinke did a slow 360, perusing all directions. "Do you know when these murders happened?"

"Haven't heard. Between 2:00 p.m. when they left their house and when I found 'em close to midnight. I'm thinking late afternoon or early evening."

Hinke replied, "When it was light. These mother-fuckers have balls."

He tilted his head back to see the two immense pine trees only about ten paces from the rock deathbed. A couple feet at their base, their branches not starting until about fifty or more feet up, like they belonged in a thick pine forest instead of out here alone with the three big pieces of granite. The tops of the two tall, identical trees swayed gently in unison. Twin trees. But as he tilted his head farther back to see the tops, his off-and-on vertigo kicked in. He stumbled to one of the pines for support.

"DH, you okay?"

"Yeah, I'm fine."

Hinke steadied himself and scanned the bluff overlooking Johnston's property—and then back to the flat rock. A good line of sight. The bluff was at least 150 yards away. Maybe a hundred or so feet high, an almost ninety-degree wall dotted with shrubs and small trees.

"Louis, what's up on the bluff?"

"Not sure. No nearby roads. Probably city or county owns it."

"You got binoculars?"

"Yeah, but they're back in the car."

"No problem."

Hinke was now sure the twins had been assaulted and killed in broad daylight. A lot could have gone wrong with that plan but apparently didn't. The killers were upping their game from New Canaan and Anniston. A perfect, out-of-the-way venue for dramatic outdoor murders in Woodstock. Leaning against the pine, Hinke asked, "Louis, who has the crime scene photos?"

"I took a few with my camera, which weren't great. Gave them to the sheriff. No doubt there are others I ain't seen yet."

"Tell me more about Orville Johnston."

"I didn't know him but knew who he was. I heard more about him this morning. Owned this big piece of property, about four hundred acres, apparently given to him by one of the founders of Woodstock after the War Between the States. Name's Johnston, too. Guessing there's a mixed-blood story. They say Orville fought in WWII with a Negro regiment, was a decorated soldier, and had been a farmer ever since. Widower who used to have a couple young'uns but both died of a disease. Then his wife died a few years back. Used to run a big operation but now tends to the farm himself. I heard he was friendly with the Brevard twins.

"What do you mean, 'friendly'?"

"Heard they liked to hang out on his land and fish in his ponds. He knew 'em for years."

"Sure doesn't sound like the kinda guy who would just decide to butcher and kill two girls he knew."

"Unless he went sex-crazed."

Hinke covered his eyes with his right hand and shook his head. He thought, *No way. Not in a million years.* The murderers knew exactly where the girls were going to be and when. They had the audacity to kill before the sun went down. They lured the black man to this spot and set him up.

He wasn't surprised in the least. Same wounds, same body placements, same crosses, another set of beautiful twin teens. Had to be the same killers who had the same modus operandi that was never published in public accounts.

"Louis, how do you suppose Johnston got here from his house?"

"There was a horse standing by the trees when I got there; assume his."

"So one guy, one horse, two teenage girls, and a protective dog show up here in daylight, and the twins get murdered?"

"I guess."

"Did he confess?"

"Heard he told their dad he didn't do it. He ain't admitted jack."

The girls' father had already talked to Johnston. Interesting.

"Don't worry, DH, they'll get him to confess."

Then make it quick and lynch him the old-school way? Hinke thought.

Hinke's feelings were bittersweet like when a long-suffering loved one or friend moved on. Two more teens brutally murdered—but definitive evidence of a link to the past. His deceit must continue as surreptitiously as possible. His excitement escalated the closer he got to the killers.

Hinke knew the Georgia cops wouldn't bother with tox screens or rape kits, which were extremely rare anyway. Perhaps a doubt or two creeping into their brains that this thing could unravel? No, on second thought, these numbskulls had already made up their mind, but he had to ask.

"Did Mr. Johnston have an alibi?"

"Said he went fish'n by himself up at Lanier and got back about 7:00, fixed dinner, and was relax'n on his porch when a lady called him around 8:00 to help and join the search.

"Louis, I'm going to walk around a few minutes, then let's go visit his house. That okay?"

"Sure, DH, I'll go call in. Take your time. Meet me back at the squad car."

On top of the bluff, the gigantic orange sun was sinking into wavy layers of yellow, orange, and purple.

Standing ankle deep in the wafting wild grass on a delightful spring day in Woodstock, Georgia, in 1974, Hinke looked back at the mammoth slab of granite where the girls had been murdered the night before. Two angelic apparitions hovered directly above the stone where they were butchered. This time, the smiling translucent figures of the Brevard twins; he just knew. Both were pointing to the bluff to the west, the outline of the sun above the bluff almost gone.

He had a hard time taking his eyes off them. Entranced, he was slow to turn and look in the direction they were pointing. On the bluff stood three hooded figures. Three outlines stood out in stark relief against the gorgeous late afternoon sky.

Unfortunately, Hinke's long-distance sight had deteriorated (he was too proud to let on). When he squinted harder, they were gone. He glanced back to the granite slab, but the twins were also gone. No doubt, like the Haverfords, were sacrificed—and likely the Blounts, too. Twins sacrificed. Why?

They enjoyed watching their game evolve. Murder voyeurs. He knew they could kill him anytime they wanted. At his age, he didn't give a damn because come hell or high water he was going to find them and make them pay.

He was getting closer.

193

Chapter 34 - Orville Johnston

Back at the car, Giles said, "Orville's gonna pay for what he done." Hinke ignored his comment and suggested, "Let's go see his house."

They took another winding fork of gravel road that rambled south for about a few minutes until Giles' headlights hit the picturesque country house. No crime scene tape anywhere he could see.

"Sheriff, you got a flashlight?"

"Yep, on my belt."

Both heard a dog bark. The girls' dog?

It was laying down on the porch and not too concerned about the two strangers. Raised his head and half-heartedly barked when they approached the house. Derbert Hinke walked up the steps to pet the animal. A friendly old sheepdog whose collar read "Sarge" with a phone number, probably Johnston's. He patted the old dog on the head, and kneeling there, knew exactly what he was going to do.

"Louis, you included the house and barns as part of the crime scene?"

Giles told him, "Hinke, we only got two other deputies. Got a Canton cop keeping an eye down by the main road to keep the riffraff away. Not sure how long he'll be there, though. I took a quick spin through the house and barns earlier. Noth'n of interest I could find."

"I want to look around," Hinke told him.

The house was a modest one-story that looked well kept, the paint shiny like it was brand new. The window shutters were dark blue. A matching tin roof. A wrap-around porch with one rocking chair and Sarge. It was a picturesque country farmhouse like Norman Rockwell might have painted.

Hinke walked over to the nearest barn; there was another behind it. Giles followed, showing the way with his flashlight. The red barns were trimmed in white, similarly idyllic, with a few fenced fields. He could see three quarter horses in one field, a couple dozen cattle in another, and another with donkeys—or were they mules?—he could never remember the difference. He wondered who the hell was taking care of the animals.

What Derbert Hinke knew he needed to do, he needed to do it without Giles. "Is there a key?" asked Hinke.

"Yep, I put it back earlier under the cushion on the rocking chair. I'll fetch it for you."

"No, that's okay. I'll get it."

Seeing the pack of cigarettes in the deputy's uniform pocket, Hinke suggested to Giles that he grab a smoke and maybe check out the barns again. "Louis, I know you went through the house. Maybe another set of eyes. I'll look around."

Giles didn't need his arm twisted and walked out while tapping the bottom of his Winstons.

The key was there. Sarge looked up at him with curiosity. Nice dog; poor guard dog, though. Hinke entered and flipped on the hall light. Johnston's home smelled of pipe tobacco and Old Spice, comfortable, and lived in. The old pine floorboards creaked as he entered.

The inside was as tidy as the outside. Hinke couldn't resist going there first. He walked down the short front hall and found the small main bedroom. He stood in front of an old dresser and looked at the black and white photograph of Orville Johnston—he guessed, with his wife and two young daughters. A lovely family with only Orville left.

Hinke sat down on the double bed, which was covered with a thick, colorful patchwork comforter. He took a deep breath, then leaned over and pulled out the drawer of the old nightstand. Inside there was only an old leather-bound King James with gilded edges. He took the bible out, then pulled out the whole drawer and flipped it over. Nothing on the bottom or back. He knelt and looked at the inside back of the nightstand. Nothing. "Dammit!" he muttered out loud.

He put the black bible back in the drawer and put the drawer back into the nightstand slot. So much for that idea. He'd hoped to find a trove of photographs—like the killers had left in 1950 in the bedroom of the Big Cottage. And where'd they'd left the cue ball in the bedroom of the Victorian in Anniston.

He checked out the other little bedroom with bunk beds, the single bathroom, the living room, and kitchen—not expecting to find anything unusual. He stopped and was drawn back to Johnston's bedroom. He again pulled open the nightstand drawer and picked up the King James Bible. He fanned the pages. Inside the bible was a rectangular cut-out. A perfect rectangle that held several photographs.

Hinke's hands shook. To calm them, he clasped them together for a minute. It had been happening more in his sixties, especially when anxious. His heart was beating like a bass drum; he could barely catch a breath. He hoped his angina wouldn't kick in.

He removed the stack of photographs and slowly flipped through them, first a few four-by-six color prints; the rest, small color Polaroids probably done with the latest Polaroid SX. The first print was of Orville Johnston standing outdoors with Mareissa and Matilde Brevard dressed in cut-off jeans, white tops, and boots. All smiling. He wondered who took the photograph, or maybe it was a timer photo they'd set up. Then a couple more with the girls in green bikinis with a pond in the background, looking like they were maybe out on his property.

The color Polaroids told another story.

In broad daylight, the beautiful Brevard girls were laid out naked on the black granite rock; their long legs, wide apart, feet dangling over the edge. Their heads each tilted back like they were drugged but maybe alive? Duct tape covered their mouths. Their flat bellies shiny and slick. Another photo of each girl from a slightly different angle.

Then worse. Three more Polaroids that could have been taken by the Cherokee County crime scene photographer post-mortem. The girls positioned exactly how Giles had described – as if two crucifixes were joined together. And the black crosses.

Minus the flags; on a granite rock outdoors instead of a pool table; but otherwise exactly like the Haverford instant photos from twenty-four years ago.

But then more Polaroids.

Different twins standing for the cameraman. Wearing only the top of their Anniston High red and white cheerleader uniforms. In the next photo, the Blount twins lay naked, restrained on a smooth rock table; it looked like it was indoors. In the final photograph, they were dead, spotted with spray, perpendicular wounds, throats cut; in the exact positions as the Brevard girls. And a hideous black cross in each.

Hinke had to make a quick decision. He'd handled each photo by their edges only. He left four photographs on the bed; the rest he slid into his suitcoat pocket.

He couldn't take his eyes off the photo of the Blount girls on the stone slab. Indoors. The slab maybe three feet tall and longer than a pool table. The floor shiny with a black and red pattern. He was entranced and didn't hear Giles enter the bedroom.

"What did you find?"

"Found them in a cut-out in the middle of the bible—in the nightstand. Got lucky. Well, I mean *you* got lucky."

His smooth, round cheeks and small brown eyes scrunching up, the prematurely balding Giles broke his stare from the photos and looked quizzically at the older man. "Whaddya mean *I* got lucky?"

"In Orville Johnston's house, you found photographs that should put the final nail in his coffin. Guessing that won't hurt your career one bit. With the murder on Johnston's property; Johnston, knowing the girls; having their blood on him; being found at the scene—and now these pictures in his nightstand. Plenty to convict. No reason to get in the way of that train, right, Deputy?"

Warily, he said, "I suppose not."

An awkward silence.

"Who are the girls in the other photo, DH?" Then Giles answered his own question. "They're the twins from Anniston, aren't they?"

Hinke's expression told him he was right.

"Johnston didn't kill either set of twins, did he, DH?"

He'd clearly underestimated the deputy sheriff but made no acknowledgment.

"Louis, I want you to take the three Brevard photos. He carefully stacked the three, touching only the edges. *You* found these in Orville Johnston's bedroom in this bible. That's the truth, and you should get the credit." He slid the fourth color Polaroid in his suit coat pocket with the others he hadn't mentioned to Giles.

Hinke let that sink in a moment, then said, "Let's get a bite to eat. Nothing's going to change over the next hour. Then you can get the photos to your sheriff. I have a proposition for you."

"What kind of proposition?"

"We'll talk about it over dinner," Hinke told him, evasively.

On the way out of Johnston's home, he found a bag of dog food in the pantry and put a big bowl of food and water on the porch for Sarge—and hoped a kind soul would come to care for him.

Chapter 35 - Hinke & Giles Make a Deal

In the squad car, Hinke asked the deputy how he knew Hollis Delacroix. Giles told him the story about Marv Pfeugel, his not-too-bright, hard-drink'n ex-partner, who a couple years earlier got into a scuffle in a downtown Atlanta bar. Blew away a brother with his .357 Magnum. A couple boys had pulled knives on Marv, probably after he'd yelled a racial slur or two.

Marv said he'd pulled his piece and shot one dead in self-defense. He was being held in Fulton County Jail; the brand new black city prosecutor was loaded for bear to charge him on Murder Two—make an example of a white cop from the sticks. Hollis investigated and after talking to the bartender who snitched for him once before, thought it was bullshit. He convinced a witness to come clean in exchange for cutting slack for a cousin heading to Milledgeville. "More to it but, yeah, fortunate. A black cop saved my partner's sorry white ass. Marvin went back to farming, where he's better suited. Hollis is a good guy, and we've fished a couple times since then."

Giles chuckled. "Like most Negroes, Hollis can't swim a lick, which I give him shit about. Always wearing a big life preserver in a boat or when he's anywhere near water. But he's a helluva fun fish'n buddy. I'd help Hollis out anytime, but gotta admit chauffeuring a Fed around in the middle of a double murder case may be beyond the call of duty." Both laughed.

Louis took him to Della's; a hole-in-the-wall ribs joint off 92. "Best pork ribs you'll ever suck off the bone and all the trimmings," he told Hinke.

"Love ribs," Hinke said.

Inside, they sat on wooden benches at a beat-up, graffitied wooden picnic table. Louis ordered a sweet tea and Hinke a longneck Bud. Giles ordered a full slab, fries, slaw, and green beans for each.

Before the food arrived, Hinke told him, "Louis, I'm going to propose a win-win for the two of us. What we say is between me and you, off the record. Agreed?"

Intimidated by the FBI agent, with trepidation Giles said, "Yes, sir."

"Good."

"This is a long story, but I'm going to cut to the chase. I've been tracking these killers since 1950, and this whole thing, I think goes back to 1911."

"You're kidding, right?"

"Nope. Deadly serious."

"Twenty-four years ago, the Haverford twins, who lived in New Canaan, Connecticut, were murdered in almost the exact same way as the Blounts and now the Brevards; plus their murders have a connection to twins from New Jersey, kidnapped and never found. In 1950, Hoover, personally assigned me the Haverford case.

"J. Edgar Hoover?"

"The one and only."

"No shit?"

He held out his hand to show him the ring. "This baby was Hoover's. I've been good friends with his secretary for a long time. She was nice enough to make sure I got it. First ring I've ever worn. But not sure I like this big rock on my finger."

Giles had seen the ring earlier but not up close. "That is too cool!" said the young deputy. "Can't ever see me owning something like that."

"Here's the thing, Louis, there's nobody else on the planet who can make the connections among all these murders, including anyone else in the Bureau. My files aren't in the FBI crime database. After hearing what you know and visiting the crime scene, I'm not surprised what was found in Johnston's house. Louis, I'm the only one who can solve this. If it becomes a media shitstorm—and a bunch of law enforcement organizations including the Bureau, SBI from multiple states, and local cops from multiple jurisdictions join in—I'll never get a shot at the murderers. Nor will anyone else. And it may sound crazy to you, but I've got to keep playing their game to have any chance. They call it *Game of Twins*."

Louis Giles nodded his head, trying to understand what he'd heard, but not sure he was following all of it, especially the game shit. The huge rib slabs plus cornbread and bowls of the sides arrived. Hinke ordered another Bud while Louis tore off a slathered rib and started gnawing.

"Louis, my proposition is this: "You've got three photos of the Brevard girls found in Johnston's bible, which is icing on the cake for what your sheriff and the rest want."

"I don't know, DH. More I thought about it, it would be awful hard for one guy by himself to murder them and maybe their dog, too," said the deputy before attacking another deliciously messy rib.

Hinke smiled and nodded affirmatively. Indeed, Louis Giles had not fallen off the turnip truck yesterday.

Hinke continued, "But a lot of people are going to overlook that theory, don't you think? And let's say you don't turn in the Brevard photographs to your superiors, Johnston is in a bad spot anyway. In fact, the only way I can see an out for him right now is for me to figure this out ASAP before he gets the chair or whatever they do in Georgia to convicted murderers." Hinke knew he was reaching here; the odds of Orville Johnston getting executed quickly, if the powers-that-be wanted it so, were good.

"But I need the Blount photo to have any shot at doing that." At least for now, it does not need to see the light of day." Hinke didn't mention the other photos in his pocket.

"I'll pay you $3,000 in cash for the Blount photograph and your silence about it and any of our conversations. The Brevard pictures are yours to do as you like with them."

Louis Giles almost spit out a mouthful of coleslaw, and his eyes popped wide open. *Hell yeah, I could use three thousand bucks.* Then it hit him. An FBI agent offered him a bribe that could get tied to a host of illegal stuff like obstruction of justice, bribery, evidence tampering, theft of evidence, conspiracy, and possibly worse.

Hinke excused himself to take a piss and let Giles ponder his offer. Giles couldn't help fantasizing about the money. Three large could get him a house down payment or a helluva a nice car or boat. Maybe he could finally convince Cheryl he was the guy. And she'd be sucking on his bone for life.

Back from the head, Hinke sat and said solemnly, "Louis, part of this that may concern you is not telling the Blount family right now. But I promise you that will happen." He kept selling. "Look, I've been at this a long time. I think we can save other girls' lives. We can maybe save Orville Johnston's too. Regardless, you get a big pat on the back from your sheriff and who knows, maybe a promotion or a raise, and you benefit financially with no one the wiser. What do you say?"

Louis Giles sat silent for about a minute, gnawing on a rib, and let it all sink in. It wasn't all adding up for him. Unless Hinke could pull a quick Hail Mary out of his ass, he knew Johnston was dead meat, any way you cut it, with or without the photos. Desperately, Hinke wanted to win this so-called game he believed he was playing with the bad guys. And Orville Johnston wasn't a bad guy. Hinke was in his sixties, for Christ's sake; hell, he could be a little senile or delusional.

But it was a lot of money.

He extended his hand and said, "Deal."

"Great." Hinke took a last swig of beer and told the deputy, "My check tonight."

Outside the little clapboard restaurant, the temperature had dropped after the sun disappeared. Giles tapped out a cigarette and cracked a wry smile and said, "DH, how do you know these bad guys who have been leading you around won't punch your ticket for grins?"

"I don't. But I'm thinking they won't try until I have them dead in my sights. Which I don't yet. Then I become expendable. The game's definitely rigged in their favor, and I'm outnumbered."

Giles saw the old FBI agent smile. Hinke wouldn't have it any other way.

In the deserted dirt parking lot, Hinke popped the trunk of his Caddy rental, spun the combination on his metal briefcase, and extracted three rolls of bills. Hinke handed him the money and said, I need you to do another thing for me, Louis. Once this blows over, I want all the Brevard case files and evidence. For safekeeping. I don't trust anyone else to have them."

Giles considered the request and chose his words carefully. "Might not be that easy. They won't all be kept in Woodstock."

"I'll double the money once I get the files and evidence. Three grand more."

Giles tried to pretend he was playing poker with his Friday night buddies but wasn't sure he was pulling it off. "I don't know, DH."

Hinke bit his tongue but was in no mood to dick around. He twisted off the big, bejeweled ring that Hoover once wore. He knew it was valuable but didn't give a rat's ass if it helped get him closer to finding the murderers.

"Maybe this will help convince you? The Madagascar dark blue sapphire, alone, is worth more than the cash I gave you. Here, put it on."

"You're kidding, right?" The ring mesmerized the deputy as he worked it onto his right ring finger.

Louis Giles looked at it on his finger. He had a feeling this might be the biggest decision of his life when he said, "I'm in."

Stoically, Hinke told him. "Remember, Deputy, I know how to find you."

Giles drove Hinke back to Woodstock to get his rental car and told him he'd be calling the sheriff about what *he* had found. A wry smile. Hinke said, "Think I'll go back to my hotel and fly out in the morning. I'll probably be back in a few days but keep me posted."

"Yeah, I will, thanks."

It was a few minutes past 11:00 p.m. when he valeted and checked into the Omni. Too late to call Hollis Delacroix at home. Once he knew more, he'd give him a call; he was trying to figure out what to say—since he'd already told him a handful of lies. Unwinding them would be much harder than telling them.

It had been a long day. He was beat. Hinke took a hot shower and put on his long blue PJs. A habit for years, regardless of what bed he slept in. He used the key to open the well-stocked minibar and grabbed a couple airplane-sized bottles of Jack Daniel's, then propped himself up in bed. He cracked the labels and with one hand poured both into a short glass. The first swig he felt all the way down. A couple more and he finally felt relaxed. But when he closed his eyes, he saw exactly what happened on Orville Johnston's farm.

The movie in his head played in slow motion until the twins lay dead. The three figures on the bluff were laughing. He opened his eyes again and took another sip of Jack. Unconsciously, he walked to the closet and pulled the Polaroids from his suitcoat.

He slipped on his readers and sat up cross-legged on his bed with his whiskey. He flipped over a half-dozen pictures of the Brevard and Blount twins like they were playing cards. More than a little déjà vu from the first time he met the Director and saw the Haverford twins' pictures. Hoover would have loved these photos, too—sick bastard that he was.

After a couple minutes as he continued to examine the photos, two sets of the beautiful teen twins on the edge of death, his penis hardened involuntarily. He hopped out of the bed and thought, *My Lord, am I a pervert too? Like Hoover? Like the killers?"*

He turned off the lights and got under the covers. The Jack got him to sleep quickly, but a couple hours later he jerked upright and woke in a cold sweat; his brain on overdrive. Hinke knew the Game was escalating. No similar kidnappings or deaths for twenty-three years. Then two in less than a year? How could it be otherwise? He needed to find these killers ASAP.

What the heck happened today? He knew he was obsessed but couldn't help himself. The Game had him in its grips no different than if he were a drug addict or alcoholic. He kept telling himself, "I'm the only one who can connect the dots. I'm the only hope. If Johnston gets executed before I figure out the murders, that was a calculated risk. Johnston would be a sacrifice for the greater good: saving more girls in the future. Hinke had to capture as much of the Brevard and Blount evidence as he could before it fell into the dreaded black hole of law enforcement, where it could disappear forever.

He'd made a deal with a young cop he didn't know well. Since the eight-ball in Anniston, he'd broken too many laws and told too many lies…he'd lost track. He was taking risks he'd never have considered even a couple of years ago. He didn't know who these people were or why they were killing twins, but knew he was breathing down their necks—and it was going to get a lot more dangerous.

Chapter 36 – Barron Brevard's Edict

The same night (the day after Easter)

Woodstock

It was nearly ten o'clock Monday evening. Barron sat upright on his sofa, but like a man propped up in a coma. He heard the phone ring once, then two more times. Reluctantly, he walked to the twelve-foot-wide foyer to answer it. It was the sheriff saying that he'd like to come over. It was important. Brevard didn't want to see anyone but told him okay.

He hung up knowing only two things: the murderer must be caught and die; and Orville wasn't the murderer. Hoping the girls' German shepherd was alive, he yelled out his open front window, "Thor, where are you, big boy? You're all I've got left to remember them." His cries dying in the blackness.

Sumner came alone. He rang the doorbell and was greeted by Brevard's tired but steely blue-gray eyes. His face was unshaven and long silver hair tousled. "Come on in, Sheriff," he said. "Drink?"

"Sure, Barron, bourbon."

Sumner took off his cowboy hat and slipped the bible underneath it when he sat down. Brevard poured himself another Mortlach and a healthy Bulleits for Sumner. He asked, "Any sign of Thor?"

The hefty man with the bad black toupee said, "No, sir, not yet."

"Makes no sense," muttered Barron.

"Barron, you know the murder scene was on Johnston's property. We found blood on him that is no doubt your daughters'. He was drunk as a skunk and had his big black pecker hanging out of his pants."

"Goddammit, Sheriff, I know all that! Did he confess?"

"He ain't said nothing other than he didn't do it, but I kin assure you he did the murders."

"And you know that how?" Barron said with anger in his voice.

Sumner put the bible on the shiny wood coffee table. "Barron, Deputy Giles was doing more checking around Johnston's place a couple hours ago. This bible was in his nightstand. When Giles opened it, he found these."

Sumner extracted photos from the cutout in the bible. He handed them to Barron and said, "I'm sorry, Barron. Cain't tell you how much."

He looked at the top photo, his beautiful twins, dressed in shorts, sleeveless tops, and tennis shoes, flanking Orville Johnston, in his jean overalls and a white shirt and boots—their arms hugged around him. The three other photographs were color Polaroids. Brevard winced in horror.

"Barron, he took the pictures; he's the murderer. No doubt about it now. Don't need no more investigat'n. Fuck'n niggers can't keep their hands off our women. Cherokee County needs to the same thing Forsythe County did back in 1912 after them darkie boys killed and raped that little white girl. Ain't been one nigger living in that whole county since. They all got rounded up and booted out or lynched. They know how to treat damn niggers there."

Brevard wasn't listening; he stared at the photos before him. There had to be an explanation for the mutilation and deaths of his twins, but now he didn't care. His only thought was revenge.

The two men sat in complete silence except for the crackling fire that Barron had started—not for warmth but to keep him company.

Sumner had no clue what else to do or say. He sipped his bourbon and looked around the massive living room adorned with Southwest furniture, Indian pots and rugs, and a few old guns displayed on the rustic wood walls.

After a couple minutes, Brevard laid the bible on top of the burning logs in the middle of his twelve-foot-wide stone fireplace. Then he picked up the photographs and one by one tossed them into the inferno.

Sumner yelped, "Barron, Jesus, what are you doing? That's evidence!"

With somber calm, Brevard told him, "Don't worry. You won't need the evidence."

He stood up and walked to the wall across from the couch where Sumner sat. From its hook he lifted off a western painting of Indians hunting buffalo with bows and arrows on a golden prairie, ominous thunderclouds, and lightning flashes in the background. He spun the tumbler on the wall safe right, left, right. It opened, and he extracted four healthy stacks of bills and tossed them, one by one, to Sumner.

"My daughters' murders and legal proceedings would be a media circus for a long time, Sheriff. That's not going to happen. There will be no trial. Do you understand what I'm saying? Twenty grand. You divide up the money however you see fit but make sure you give five to Giles for finding the pictures. When it's done—and the sooner the better—I'll double it. Oh, and another twenty thousand if you find Thor alive. Do I make myself clear?"

Sumner said, "Yes, sir."

"Failure is unacceptable, Sheriff. This conversation never took place, and my name is never to be mentioned. Nor will yours. And no discussion of what you know or saw about the murders. I will be out a good part of tomorrow but will be awaiting your news." He wrote down his private business line phone number and another number where he could be reached in an emergency.

"Sure, okay, whatever you say, Barron. Whatever you say."

After shutting the ten-foot-tall seventeenth-century Mexican church door, Barron slumped into his favorite leather chair near the fireplace. The dying embers now seemed like the story of his life. He was too angry, too depressed, too sad, too exhausted to cry more right now. He knew his revenge wouldn't bring back his twins, but he didn't care. He only wanted it all over ASAP. But he had no idea how he'd carry on.

Unfortunately, he had another call to make. It was past eleven o'clock and he made the call.

In bed, Ted Davies answered on the fourth ring.

Chapter 37 – Ted Davies

"Ted, it's Barron. I know it's late. I was wrong about Orville Johnston."

"In what way?"

"He's their killer, Ted. No question."

Ted couldn't be more surprised and disappointed at the same time. "What's happened since we talked a few hours ago, Barron?"

Haltingly, Brevard managed to tell him about the photographs found inside a bible in the bedroom nightstand of Orville Johnston.

Silence on both ends.

"Barron, that does sound incriminating." Ted hesitated and sat up straighter in bed, his wife having already pulled the covers over her head. "But Barron, didn't you tell me that Johnston got set up?"

"I thought that was possible, but this new evidence changes everything. Hell, Ted, I saw the goddamn pictures he took with my own eyes. I was a fool to believe him."

Ted could rattle off a half-dozen rebuttals to that statement but didn't. Instead, he said, "Barron, he's going to need an attorney."

"That's not going to be you, Ted," Barron said authoritatively like he was running a boardroom meeting.

Ted Davies was utterly deflated. He'd already fantasized that this could be his *To Kill a Mockingbird* case. But the partner at Stuyvesant Knight could never take the case after one of his firm's most prominent clients had told him to stand down. And the PR if he were to defend an accused murderer of a big client's two kids? Bad publicity could indeed be bad publicity. He couldn't afford to let that happen. Yet Ted sensed something amiss.

He made another pitch to the grieving father. "Barron, how about I go up to Canton for an hour on my dime and then give you another read on Johnston?"

"Ted, this conversation is over," and Brevard hung up.

Ted was dog-tired after a long, long day. He sat up in bed racking his brain what he could do. He came up with zip. His wife eased the comforter off her head and stared at him. "What's wrong, hun?"

After a minute he finally answered, "I think I just agreed to send an innocent black man to his grave."

Barron thought, *It's all my fault. I should never have let the girls run around like wild Indians all over Cherokee County. I should've known Orville Johnston, the niggra he was, could do this.* He'd appointed himself judge, jury, and executioner. He believed in God but didn't trust Him to handle this the right way. He hoped he would not be judged too harshly. He felt bad about yanking Ted Davies' chain and vowed to make it right with him.

Brevard's head pounded with pain. He hadn't gotten his brain around the fact his beautiful twins were dead. Now, the aftermath was becoming a mess. Life was unfair; death was more so for his twins.

Chapter 38 – The Money

The same evening

Canton, Georgia

After showing himself out of Brevard's ranch house, Woodstock Sheriff Billy Ray Sumner climbed into his squad car and put the stacks of cash on the front seat. He smiled down at the windfall and lit up a Marlboro. He chuckled and did the math in his head: He'd give Giles $2,500, not $5,000, and he'd be happy with that. He'd offer Cherokee County Sheriff Joey Condurelis $5,000 to get the dirty work done—that could include the warden, guards, and prisoners. With $2,500 more after the deed was done—Condurelis could keep that for himself. Billy Ray would end up pocketing $10K—then another $20K bonus. Thirty thousand for himself. Sumner was drooling over what he'd do with the money. Hell, if he could find the dog, it would be another $20K. He was thinking a brand-new top-of-the-line fishing boat and gear, a couple rifles he'd had his eye on, and a first-class trip to Las Vegas—to start. And his involvement was already over. Man, he hated that those girls died, but today was like Christmas in spades.

It was nearly 11:30 p.m. when Sumner got up to Canton to talk to Joey, who wasn't too thrilled about getting out of bed. But after he heard Sumner's proposal and took the initial $5,000 in cash, he was happier than a pig in deep shit. Sumner knew that Joey and lots of his relatives were the backbone of the Klan in North Georgia. "Hell, Billy Ray, putting down an old nigger rapist-killer of white girls, I could probably get a hundred volunteers for free." But Joey understood that this needed to happen inside the prison and be well thought out and be traceable to neither. They shook on the deal.

Before Sumner zoomed up to Canton, he had Giles meet him at the Woodstock police station where he gave him $2,500 (not $5,000) as a "bonus" for finding the photos at Johnston's—with absolute instructions not to mention the money or the pictures (now non-existent).

Giles could hardly believe his largesse for the day: $5,500 in nontaxable cash, a promise of $3,000 more from Hinke after he got the murder files to him, and the spectacular ring that might be worth more than all the cash.

Louis called his girlfriend and told her he'd be home around midnight. She told him she was bushed and in bed. He needed a couple of beers to decompress. He didn't trust leaving the cash in his squad car. He wore a jacket with cash stuffed in two pockets.

He sat on a barstool in Joe's, the only bar open late in Woodstock, and sipped his Bud, pondering the day—and staring at the big, beautiful ring on his right hand. J. Edgar Hoover had worn it. *If that don't beat all*. He had a hot chick keeping his bed warm at home and enough money that he now felt good about finally popping the question. After his first beer, he felt a calm satisfaction like when he was in the dugout after homering off the kid from Marietta now pitching for the Dodgers. Better than an orgasm. Even one Cheryl made happen.

But halfway into his next Miller, Orville Johnston crept into Giles's thoughts. He wished he hated Negroes like most of his white friends—who truly did hate them for no good reason. He had learned to fake racism and use the "N" word to get along in the presence of other whites. But he had a few good Negro friends he'd met playing ball and liked them better than most of his white buddies. He'd never heard anything bad about Mr. Johnston in his life. It wasn't surprising to him that Hinke didn't think Orville did it.

The old black man was getting reamed, and he was helping. But, the power of rationalization was strong. Giles kept telling himself

Johnston was a dead man anyway. Plenty of evidence to convict without the photographs. Per Hinke, there was no way to exonerate him unless he could quickly find the murderers—but who knew how long that could take? Hinke had hunted them for twenty-four years, for God's sake. No, Louis Giles was no savior. He would not get in the way of the freight train of traditional racist southern justice barreling down the well-worn north Georgia tracks. No way. Too much at stake. He was no dummy, either; he had a feeling there was something else going on with this double murder—stuff that he didn't want to know about. None of his business.

But on his ride home he couldn't shake the thought he was helping sign the death warrant of an innocent man. After unlocking the front door, he said, "Babe, it's me."

He didn't hear anything and tiptoed through the kitchen/dining area to the tiny second bedroom, where he pried up a floorboard under a throw rug and deposited the money and the ring—at least until he could figure out the story he'd tell Cheryl and others.

He marveled at his good fortune meeting her at a Lake Lanier bait shop a year ago. She had a good job as a paralegal in Roswell. She was funny and for an unknown reason liked him. And she liked to fish and fuck! With or without clothes she made his dick hard, constantly. A hundred ten pounds of luscious curves, dark hair tumbling to her waist, and as beautiful a face as he'd ever seen in these parts. He knew exactly what other guys were thinking about when they saw her. Now, maybe he could close the deal and not wind up with a homely bitch who'd be a 250-pound blob in a couple years. Cheryl liked to keep trim and had been encouraging him. He'd lost fifteen pounds in the past couple months. He adored her.

He took off his uniform in the dark and climbed into bed. "Baby, where have you been?" she yawned as he touched her bodacious melons through her frilly gown, then dug a hand under her tight buns.

"Work'n on them murders. Think they got the right guy, a Negro farmer, doesn't live too far away. I'll tell you all about it tomorrow." Louis realized he'd said "they" and not "we." He wanted to tell her all about his day but needed to ponder what he'd tell her.

She reached back and found him already stiff. "Baby, I was touching myself earlier think'n about you. I've got a place for that," she told him and nuzzled her bare buns up to his crotch. That woke him up. As always, sex with Cheryl was world-rock'n. She begged for more, but he was out of gas and promised more in the morning any damn way she wanted it.

His dream was world-rock'n too—but not in a good way.

Louis always had lots of wild dreams and had bought a couple books to help him interpret them. He yearned for the rare wet ones, especially the one with Cheryl and her hot mom, but hadn't found any way to replicate that. Tonight his dread started out much like a dream he'd had off and on for years:

It's a lazy, sticky summer afternoon down by their favorite swimming spot on the Chattahoochee, the one with the best rope swing ever. A dream he'd had before. Darius Jeffries, a black boy they played football with, and the other guys tolerated okay because he could run like the wind and catch any pass thrown in his direction. They ride their bikes there. He knows Darius can't swim a lick. One of his asshole friends pushes Darius in. He flounders around till Louis gets to him. The others yuk it up drinking beers that Frankie stole from his pop. But this time Darius grabs him from behind. Screaming, "I'm drowning." Louis can't get out of the horse collar around his neck. They are both going down, deep down into the cold, dark water. He can't breathe. He's suffocating and knows he's going to die. He wakes up; his body jerks upward.

Cheryl said, "Baby, you had a bad nightmare," and snuggled against him again. When he knew Cheryl was asleep, he got up and went into the little bathroom between the two bedrooms. He flipped on the light switch and stared at himself in the mirror. He didn't like what he saw. The nasty dream no doubt germinated from the real-life fact that he saw his friend, Darius, hanging by his neck from a big oak tree a mile outside Canton. At school earlier that day, one of the real lookers, Jeanne Fulbright, had asked Darius, who was a math whiz and football star, to help tutor her after school. And that's all he did, but a few of boys saw them sitting alone in the classroom. Plenty enough to hand him a death sentence. The nausea built up until he puked in the toilet. He crawled back in bed, stared at the ceiling, and asked himself, *"What the fuck did I do today?"*

Chapter 39 - Orville, Matilde and Mareissa

The previous day, Easter Sunday, 1974

Woodstock

It had been a spectacular mid-April Georgia day. Powder-blue skies accented by wispy white clouds and a mild, warm breeze. A day only God could craft. He believed in God and Jesus, but Orville hadn't gone to church since his Lizzie passed five years ago. Figured he'd been to enough church services in his life. Instead, every Sunday he sort of obeyed the Sabbath by taking at least half the day off. After reading Easter scripture from his bible, he headed out to Lake Lanier for a day of fishing. The peace and tranquility of being on the water, only gifts God could give. And he caught four stripers.

He got home late afternoon, cleaned the fish, fried one up, and made biscuits and coffee. He ate and retired to his front porch, where he let God's Peace sink in more, especially this wonderful Easter Sunday. It was starting to cool off; he brought out the shawl Lizzie had made him years ago. He started reading *Black Boy*—for maybe the tenth time—but dozed off with his dog Sarge at his feet.

The phone ringing in the kitchen woke him. He was disoriented and tried to shake out the cobwebs. Unusual for him to get any phone calls, but especially after 9:00 p.m. The phone rang several times before he got to the kitchen and picked up.

A female asked, breathlessly, "Is this Orville Johnston?"

"Yes, ma'am, it is."

She started in at a rapid clip. "Mr. Johnston, sorry to call this late. My name is Sally Black—you may not know me, but I live a couple miles from you. We live over on the other side of the Brevards. You know them?"

"Yes ma'am," he told the woman. He didn't remember hearing the name or the voice but more and more well-to-do white folks had begun migrating to the Woodstock area from the city and elsewhere. He knew few of them. Several times he'd been offered decent money for his land but if he sold it, he had no idea where he'd go. He loved his farm and hoped to die there. But never say never. There might be a price he couldn't turn down.

He said, "I do a little business with Mr. Barron from time to time, and I know his two daughters cuz they hike and fish on my land with their dog."

"They do?" she asked, again sounding agitated. "We could use your help. The twins went missing a few hours ago after their midafternoon Easter meal. We're getting as many people out looking for them as we can."

"Matilde and Mareissa are missing?"

"They haven't been seen in over six hours."

Orville Johnston thought about the delightful, lovely young ladies he'd known since they were skinny little tikes. Now blossomed into true beauties. But he hadn't seen them since the freaky late snow in early March. "I'll do whatever you want me to do, Miss Black. Were they walk'n or rid'n? I suppose Thor was with them?"

She sounded more anxious and hurried. "Hiking with their dog is what I was told. We're not too organized, Mr. Johnston. We're trying to get as many people out looking tonight as we can. Can you please search your own farm first?" she pleaded. "I was told you have a big place. We'll send others to help you if we can, but we're sending most to search near the lake and where the old mills and mines are. Mr. Johnston, do you have a CB radio?"

"No, ma'am, I don't." It seemed lots of folks who had trucks or drove a lot—or had nothing better to do—were getting them, but he never saw a good enough reason to have one.

"If you have any news, can you call the main Woodstock police number?"

"Yes, ma'am, please tell Mr. Barron I'll be out look'n, and we'll find 'em."

"Thank you, Mr. Johnston."

Orville considered the best way to cover his four hundred acres. A farmer his whole life, he'd been planting less and less the last few years, now primarily raising a few dozen cattle and a handful of goats. His land was an eclectic mix of relatively flat land once packed with soybeans, oats, hay, and wheat (cotton in days gone by) and grazing fields for his cows, a few sturdy stands of pecans, and untouched rolling hills with wild grasses, flowers, and a few acres of pine forests that he only used for his own wood. And a couple decent-sized ponds he let the Brevard girls and other kids swim and fish in.

On the prettiest part of his land were the granite boulders and two majestic pines that he hoped would be there forever. But there was too much geography on the north end of his farm to bounce around in his old truck. He could drive down to the highway and then up and around east, but that would be a lot of walking for him with his right hip aching worse than normal today. He decided to ride his buckskin, Lulu, and navigate by the moon and stars and his big flashlight.

He wanted to get going fast but knew it could be a long night. He brewed a pot of coffee while he put on his boots, his favorite leather jacket, and his Braves ball cap that an old friend got signed by Henry Aaron himself. He grabbed a box of Animal Crackers, beef jerky, the thermos of hot coffee, and a long, galvanized flashlight, then saddled up his fifteen-year-old quarter horse. Inside his saddlebag, he put his old army revolver, a WWI Colt 1911. Standard issue to colored troops in the Second World War, where it had served him well. He stuck a couple flares into the saddlebag in case he needed them.

Other than in the War, there was only one time in nearly three decades Orville used a gun against another man. It was the year before he went to Basic Training. He was at the house one evening, his family visiting friends in Alabama when he heard vehicles rumble up their gravel driveway. Immediately, he fetched his Colt M 1900, an early semi-automatic he'd won in a poker game down in the city. When he walked out onto his porch, he was faced by two dozen good ole boys dressed in white robes with hoods, the robes bordered with crimson crosses on their chests. One stepped forward and said, "We've decided it's time to clear all niggers out of our county like Forsyth did a long time ago. You can leave now, or we'll kill you as sure as were stand'n. Drop the gun, nigger."

What happened next became part of Cherokee County lore.

He could see these white boys weren't well armed. Their mistake. Must have figured their numbers would be plenty enough to overtake and maybe hang him. They'd lit their torches, and he saw only two with rifles, not yet aimed at him.

With his handgun lowered, Orville Johnston told the Klan boys, "Look, you all are tresspass'n. I'm going to give you exactly ten seconds to turn around and get back in your cars and git off my land. We'll forget this ever happened."

The Klan leader laughed, and Orville waited. Under their cowardly hoods, he knew they'd be knocked off their game.

Suddenly, two shots rang out. Orville Johnston, who could down a racing squirrel from twenty paces with most any handgun, shattered the action of both rifles, splitting each in half, rendering them useless, only doing some damage to the fingers of the boys that had gripped them. The pieces fell on the gravel. It took all of one and a half seconds. The two boys with the guns screeched. They all froze. Normally a mild-mannered man, Orville yelled, "If you or your kind ever come onto my property again, those bullets will go through the eye slits in your sorry costumes. Now git."

The Klansmen scrambled for their vehicles and were gone. The Klan gave friends of his trouble from time to time, but never him.

Gingerly, Orville Johnston hoisted himself up on Lulu and headed northwest. The fact that Thor accompanied his owners was a good thing. He'd never seen the girls without their trusted German shepherd. But maybe not so good if Thor hadn't made it home yet. Orville felt a queasiness in the pit of his stomach. He said the Lord's Prayer and prayed for God's Peace and Presence and Protection for Mareissa and Matilde Brevard, truly God's gifts who, off and on, filled a bit of the dreadful loneliness he'd gotten far too accustomed to without his wife and daughters.

After speaking to Johnston, the woman on the phone, whose real name was not Sally Black, smiled and hung up. All on script. She was confident it would play out with the right ending but not sure how they'd get there. Ah, but otherwise the *Game* would be no fun. Now, as the old man rode his horse out onto his farm, she needed to hustle to his home and get a few things done.

Five minutes later she was at the house but knew there was the matter of his old beast. Why canines often bothered females of her bent, and rarely males, she'd always thought unfair. But knew it was written into their story since the Beginning. She smiled, aware that as a female of her Tribe (she loved the Indian reference), her advantages were more significant. If the dog were a problem, she'd take care of it.

The bugs they'd put in his house near the kitchen phone and in his bedroom along with her periodic surveillance had provided plenty of information about Johnston and what he did and when. The four bugs in the Brevard residence gave them more invaluable information. None of the three, though, were naive enough to believe that people's daily patterns were always the same.

She walked from the nearby woods, past the barns, and up to his front door. The old dog must be too feeble to offer resistance—even to her type. He was snoring and didn't acknowledge her presence as she approached, as quietly as she could.

She entered the house and quickly checked the small rooms. There was a thick photo album on the coffee table in the little living room. Wearing medical gloves, she picked it up and flipped through it. It was chronological from when Johnston was a Negro boy to more recent. The last pages were an unexpected bonanza. Johnston in his farm clothes, his wiry, muscled arms around the giggling Brevard girls dressed in white T-shirts, and short blue jeans and boots. Then more photos with the bald, old black man with twins in their lime green bikinis. She grinned and thought to herself, Maybe the old man had fun thinking about them. Black men she'd always found so attractive. One day she'd have one of her very own. She bet Orville Johnston had been a catch in his day—with his glistening smooth, strong, pulsating blackness, now weathered with age. A stark contrast to the long-legged, virginal blonde teens, their long locks lifted by the wind as the photos were taken.

She found the bedroom and opened his nightstand drawer. No bible, which was fine. She had an old worn one with the middle pages carefully cut out where she could insert a few of the farmer's album photos with her fresh Polaroids and a couple others that should get Hinke's attention.

It took her only five minutes. Opening the door, she faced the grizzled cur, now with teeth bared, eyes blazing with menace. "Get away from me," she shouted. Terrified, she was able to ease the tranquilizer gun out of her coat pocket. Sensing an enemy, the dog lunged at her. She pulled the trigger, aiming at the meat of his body. The dog yelped and retreated. Within a half-minute it was a lump of fur on the porch floor.

Before leaving, she knelt and gave thanks. The excitement and anticipation was making her wet. This Game was more fun than the Blounts! But there was so much to do. She replaced the old key under the rocker cushion and walked to the backyard, where they could see her better with their binoculars. She used the walkie-talkie, then jogged back to her pickup truck hidden a football field past the three barns on his property. Thus far, on this Easter night, things couldn't be going more swimmingly.

Not fifteen minutes after the woman left his farmhouse, Orville Johnston's phone rang again. The man at the other end let it ring at least ten times but there was no answer or machine to leave a message. Maybe Orville was already out looking? He hoped. He wasn't sure why he hadn't called him until now, but knew he wasn't thinking clearly and needed to get a grip on himself if they were to have any chance of finding the twins. Barron Brevard hung up to rejoin the search party and would tell the police to contact Orville.

He was an acquaintance, not a friend, but Barron Brevard thought a lot of Orville Johnston and had bought cattle from him in years past. Orville bargained thoughtfully and fairly. His kind of man. A no-

nonsense man. A nice man. Always a pleasant smile on his weathered face. A quiet man who favored listening over talking. A man, though, who struck him as one tough hombre in the white man's world of rural Georgia. One of the most notorious places in the country for its horrific treatment of African Americans. And he'd heard the epic story about Orville singlehandedly facing down a troop of Klansmen.

Barron knew the old man had been nothing but kind to Matilde and Mareissa.

Only with the exuberance of youth, Matilde and Mareissa Brevard had told Orville about their explorations usually within three miles or so of their ranch. Their favorite area being the old mines and mills that he'd searched as a kid but hadn't seen in decades. Those two twins were the most tomboyish girls he'd ever met. They loved to hike, run, hide, explore, collect stuff, and take pictures with their fancy camera, and have fun. They delighted in showing him the treasures they'd found old bullets, belt buckles, pieces of guns, and all sorts of Civil War relics; Cherokee arrowheads, tomahawk heads, pieces of pipes and pottery; small lumps of mica and gold flecks, and a few small nuggets; dozens of butterflies and rattlesnake rattles.

Never had he seen two girls with that much curiosity for God's green earth and how it all worked.

One afternoon while he served them lemonade, they told him they were going to be archaeologists. He didn't doubt it one bit and reminded them there were plenty of historical things to find in America without visiting all the continents. But he could tell they wanted to go everywhere in the world they possibly could go. They were adventurers. He liked to tell them the local history, especially a few of his mama's stories going back to the Civil War. They listened like he was the only person in the universe. But mainly, he left the twins to themselves to explore because that's how he'd always loved it as a kid.

Their favorite place to sit and talk on his property was on the northwestern edge where a huge piece of rectangular black granite, about three feet tall and fifteen feet long, was shielded by two massive boulders and two towering pines, by far the tallest on his property. The majestic trees were over a hundred feet tall and only ten feet apart. It was the Brevard girls' private place where they liked to be alone. A place he called "The Table."

Orville Johnston headed toward there.

Six months earlier

Cherokee County, Georgia

One of the two men discovered them and told his cousin. Neither could believe their good fortune. They were hiking and looking down from a bluff a mile or from their recently purchased property. It seemed too good to be true, but neither believed in coincidence. Leggy beauties with long, wavy, blonde hair to mid-back, T-shirts, no bras, short shorts, and boots. He was ninety-five percent sure they were twins. Their binoculars were trained on Matilde and Mareissa Brevard. Names they learned after following them back to their grand ranch home a couple miles away and checking them out in their own library of school yearbooks. One was a veteran of multiple tours in Vietnam with MACV-SOG recon, Command, and Control North. His cousin had been sent abroad to train with Mossad, heads above any special operation military in the world. Plus, the finer points had already been drilled into them by their fathers. They surveilled the twins off and on for nearly four months. They took turns and mapped out a strategy. One thing they'd learned since Anniston was that three people were best.

Outdoors in the broad daylight would be doubly dangerous compared to what they'd pulled off in Anniston. They would be breaking new ground and taking the *Game* up another notch. The old farmer's property was perfect. The girls' favorite place more perfect. That's where it would happen. Not far, but far enough off the gravel road that bordered the northwest section of the farmer's land and no other close access. It was like their Dark Lord had put the sparkling black altar there specifically for them. One day it too would be theirs. They could grab them at any one of several spots depending on where the girls hiked. That Barron Brevard was a well-known businessperson, not only in Cherokee County but the city of Atlanta, amped up the difficulty more. They sought the toughest challenge. Their deeds would be legend and their rewards beyond comprehension.

Easter Sunday, April 14, 1974

Woodstock

Riding on Lulu, Orville called for them, "Matilde, Mareissa, it's Mr. Orville!" But his calls seemed swallowed by the darkness. Off and on a coyote howled, but that's all he heard. He was having a hard time imagining the two resourceful young ladies getting lost or hurt on his property. He hoped they'd already been found elsewhere but hadn't seen any flares or heard sirens or anything else. He didn't want to think about the possibility that one of the old mines had collapsed on them—or that any harm had come to the girls. He eased Lulu to stop, stuck a finger up, and yelled to the Lord, "If anything happens to these girls, I promise there will be Hell to pay!"

He rode north and then west on the flattest land. Then he saw them. The loblolly pines that had survived winds and rains and droughts—and men's saws—since the Civil War. Their branches didn't start until high up their trunks. A surveyor he knew said they were 115 feet tall; unusually tall, majestic, and beautiful—and identical—like the Brevard girls. Mother Nature at her finest. He hopped off, tied Lula to one of the gigantic trees, and walked around the nearest, massive triangular granite boulder.

He wasn't prepared for what he saw next.

A dull, dark tarp covered the table of granite between two huge boulders. The tarp was staked down at each corner, each tethered to the ground. "Lord Jesus, please no, please no! No!" he shouted out loud. He didn't want to look underneath but yanked up two of the stakes and pulled back the tarp.

Then, he caught a whiff from his past; a nasty odor he'd too often smelled as a soldier. He turned away in horror and disgust as he pulled off the whole tarp, exposing what was underneath. It wasn't the smell of mere death, but the stench of violent death. Years ago he'd seen humans killed and their bodies left in the worst ways imaginable: babies, children, women, men, enemy Japs, and lots of his own buddies. Images and sounds and smells burned into his brain, too terrible to speak to Lizzie of them. The uneven line of shrapnel embedded in the right side of his body, like a dozen hot pokers melting his skin. He remembered that too.

"Lord Jesus, why not take me instead?" Orville looked straight up into the heavens and moaned, "Why not me, Lord!"

He stood holding the flashlight looking down at the bodies of his beloved friends, Matilde and Mareissa Brevard. Obviously gone. Dead eyes, throats cut, bodies drained of blood, perpendicular slices across their naked bodies, impaled with black crosses. Bodies laid out in the shape of crucifixes.

Orville stood looking at the bodies he didn't know how long; maybe he was in shock. Then he re-covered them with the tarp. He walked over to Lulu to get the emergency flares from his saddlebag. But as he pulled out the flares, a man behind him hissed, "What did you do to the girls, nigger!" He heard the click of a gun pressed to the back of his head. Then the world went black when he felt a powerful hand press into the side of his neck.

Chapter 40 – The Killers

"Nice the old man played along," said his companion. And that no one's found them yet, but we're way out on the bleeding edge tonight. We got to get hustling."

"Yeah, I know. Let's do this and get out of here."

They dragged him to the rock beneath the girls' feet. One took a fifth of Jim Beam and poured it out on the grass. He opened the black man's mouth and poured some liquor in, knowing it wouldn't be digested but it would certainly smell and look like Johnston was shit-faced drunk. For added effect, they unzipped his fly and left his dick hanging out. Then popped him with a dose of Rohypnol in the groin. They folded up the tarp and put the tent stakes inside it—leaving the bodies alone in the cold night air and leaving Johnston's flashlight leaning against him. It could be minutes or an hour until the light was seen, but hopefully before coyotes or other creatures ravaged their bodies—their handiwork. Then one said, "Let's make sure they find the girls sooner than later." He picked up one of Johnston's emergency flares. His partner said, "Oh hell, why not," and laughed.

They set off one flare, then made a quick call using the walkie-talkie. And heard, "Roger that." They picked up their gear and the folded tarp and moved on foot, jogging back south to get to the pickup place. Within ten minutes they'd rendezvoused and were driving on Highway 92. The three of them wondered how this would play out for the old man, the FBI agent whom they hoped would get to Atlanta soon, as well as the cops and the rest of them. Regardless, their job was done for tonight. They weren't sure what was going to happen next, but the game was going to be fun!

Below the twin pines, by the granite boulders, Orville Johnston lay unconscious. His autographed Hank Aaron Braves cap on the ground next to him with the empty bottle of bourbon and flashlight and his revolver.

The Brevard twins were elsewhere for eternity.

It was almost midnight when Barron got the news they'd been found. He'd been out since 7:00 p.m.

Searching with dozens of others near the old mines and lake when Sheriff Sumner located him and they talked over the police cruiser intercom.

"You know Orville Johnston's place about a mile southeast of yours?"

"Yeah, sure, I know Orville. Girls know him, too. I called him before I left to have him check his own farm, but he wasn't in."

"We're out on Johnston's property by a couple big rocks and pines on the northwest end. Where the bluff overlooks the top edge of his land. Barron, your girls, I'm sorry, they're dead."

"No, that can't be." His voice trembled like every ounce of energy had been sucked out of him. He felt unsteady. He lost his breath and leaned against the car with its lights flashing. "That can't be," he wailed, then hung onto the police intercom but could say no more.

Finally, he pushed the button and asked, "What happened, Sheriff? Tell me."

"They were murdered, Barron. It was bad—real bad. No matter what you say, I'm not going to let you come near here. I want you to go home with the deputy, sit down and have a drink, and he'll drive you up to Canton in an hour."

"Goddammit, Sheriff, how were they murdered!"

Sumner wasn't going to tell Barron Brevard much but offered, "They were both stabbed to death. Johnston did it. He was near the scene passed out drunk with blood on him. His dick was hanging out of his pants."

"Orville Johnston? No way!"

More silent static on the radio. "What'd he say?" Barron asked.

"Nothing yet. He's woozy right now. Got him in custody. I'm going to take him up to the county jail in Canton instead of Woodstock. They can handle this better than us."

Brevard asked, "What about their German shepherd, Thor?"

"We ain't found him yet. Barron, go back to your house with Deputy Giles. In an hour or so, he'll bring you up to Canton and get it over with. And we'll figure all this out, I promise."

He mumbled, "Right, Sheriff," and handed the police radio to the deputy, who talked with Sumner for a minute and then drove to Brevard's place only a few minutes away. Barron rarely took advice but decided he didn't want to see the crime scene.

At home Brevard invited the deputy in, but Giles said he needed to stay in the car to monitor the police intercom. "Sir, I'll let you know if there's anything new about your dog."

Inside, Brevard poured a couple bourbons. He hadn't asked the deputy because he knew he'd say no but walked back out and handed him the drink. "It's okay, deputy, we all need one...or maybe a full bottle, tonight."

Giles thanked him and took the glass, but only to be polite.

Barron Brevard collapsed on his sofa. He'd always thought he was good at reading people. He couldn't fathom Orville Johnston murdering his daughters in cold blood. Especially a man they often spoke about, a man who'd told them he loved them like his own daughters, who'd died many years ago. He had a hard time catching his breath again; anxiety drowning him. He gulped down his bourbon.

He needed to get a grip. He called his lady friend, Judy Dean, principal at Dean & Smith Public Relations, who'd been out to the ranch earlier for Easter dinner. He needed to make sure this didn't become a circus.

"Judy, sorry to wake you so late," he said, his voice cracking.

"Barron, you sound terrible. What's the matter?"

"They're gone."

"Who's gone, Barron?"

"The girls were murdered," he sobbed.

"Oh my God, Barron. No. Oh my God. What happened?"

He managed to get out what he knew. "But I don't think the Negro farmer did it."

"Barron, I'll drive right up, baby. You need company." She knew this story could get racially toxic in a hurry.

"Judy, I'm going up to Canton in a bit to identify the bodies. Come up in the morning; I'll need you to handle the press. The less said the better."

"Okay, I can help," the PR pro told her boyfriend. Any way you cut it, this was going to be huge news for TV, radio, and print in Atlanta and beyond.

"I'll tell the Woodstock and county cops. They don't speak to the press; only you."

"I'll be up to Woodstock early tomorrow."

"Thanks, Judy."

He'd barely remembered the ride up to Canton. He was numb and unable to speak with the young deputy. The morgue was conveniently located in the prison building. It was a room that only fit two exam tables and six cold chambers. He smelled the mixture of chemicals and death. Judiciously, the medical examiner pulled out two chambers, then only exposed their faces. Pale white but at least not damaged like the rest of their bodies. Barron bent down and kissed each of his twins on the forehead, then left without saying a word.

In the hallway, Barron told Sumner, "I want to see him."

"Barron, I think that's not such a good idea right now."

"I don't give a shit."

Sumner led him down two hallways at the Canton County Prison to the guard's desk. "He needs to see the old niggra."

The fat man with the pumpkin face and round spectacles half grinned. "Okay, but don't be kill'n my prisoner tonight. His time's a com'n soon. He's gonna git fried. Last cell."

Brevard told Sumner, "This is between me and Orville Johnston." The sheriff turned and exited.

The old man was laying on a thin cot. He sensed Brevard's presence in front of his cell. Orville stood and looked him straight in the eyes. "Barron, I'm sorry about Mareissa and Matilde. I feel bad. Can't imagine how you feel."

"What happened, Orville?"

"I went out to search for 'em a little after nine. A lady, said her name was Sally Black, called me and asked if I'd search my property. I don't know her, but she said she lived by you. I rode around and went up to the twin pines up north on my farm where they liked to spend time. I found 'em dead on the big rock. Worst thing I'd ever seen. Especially the black crosses. I was getting a flare from my saddlebag when a guy grabbed my neck from behind. Next thing I remember, I'm on the ground stinking of bourbon. I haven't had a drink in thirty years. I didn't know what was happening. A few minutes later a couple deputies came runn'n and put me in cuffs. You gotta believe me, Barron. I loved those girls like they were my own daughters. I wouldn't hurt them in a million years."

Barron Brevard detected no duplicity in the old man's face; only sadness.

"Got any idea who killed them?"

Orville Johnston had never mentioned to anyone what he'd seen up on the bluff overlooking the northwest piece of his land. He figured no one would believe him. Maybe Barron would.

"Barron, I don't know, but I'm think'n it's the bunch that I've seen a few times the past couple years. Dressed in outfits like the Klan, except black. Black robes with hoods. That ridge looks right down on the big granite rocks and tall trees. I couldn't tell what they were doing from where I was. I could only see them against the moonlight. I'm sorry, Barron," the black man sobbed.

"Where's Thor, Orville?"

"Never saw him, and I never saw the girls without their dog close by."

"Where were you earlier today?"

"Went up to Lanier to fish early and got back late afternoon. Then I had a relax'n evening; fried up the fish and had early dinner, got comfortable reading on my porch, and nodded off till I got the call."

Brevard told him, "Never heard of Sally Black."

Barron Brevard was having a hard time thinking straight but told Orville, "Listen, I'm going to call the best criminal lawyer in Atlanta. Not sure how long it'll take to get him up here. It's late. Tomorrow or Tuesday latest, but don't repeat any of that to the sheriff or anyone else. You got that, Orville?"

Orville nodded, his arms hanging on the cell bars.

Outside the prison, Sumner started to ask him, "Barron…," but got cut off.

"Tell me about the black crosses, Sheriff."

Sumner hesitated. "Barron, I don't think you wanna know."

"Goddammit, Sheriff, tell me."

The sheriff described the crosses and how Deputy Giles had found them.

Barron cringed.

He asked, "Do you know a Sally Black who lives around here?"

"No, sir, sure don't."

"You ever heard of the Klan or a Klan-type group with black robes meeting on the bluff that overlooks Orville Johnston's farm?"

"No, sir," he told Barron. He didn't add he was a card-carrying member of the local Klan himself, and they only wore white.

Would Orville make up a story like that on the fly? Barron doubted that. His tears had been real when he looked him straight in the eyes. He was sure Orville Johnston was telling the truth.

"Sheriff, I don't think he killed my girls."

"Say what?"

"You heard me."

"Barron, that's crazy."

"You need to get your boys finding more evidence, Sheriff. You got the wrong man."

238

Chapter 41 - Prison

The same night

Canton

Orville Johnston lay on his back on a smelly, grimy hard bunk in the Cherokee County Prison in Canton, praying because he didn't know what else to do. Before he'd arrived in his cell in the wee hours of the morning, he'd been kicked, hit, spit at, and berated by cops, prison guards, and prisoners. They gave him water but no food. He was starving, but he'd get by. The word had spread quickly. Prisoners bellowed, "Lynch the nigger—after we cut his dick off" and untold other epithets. At least tonight they'd put him in a cell by himself at the end of the row.

After fighting the Japanese in New Guinea, the North Solomons, and Bismarck Archipelago in World War II, not much fazed Orville Johnston. Years ago, though, he'd seen a boy he'd walked to school with; his hands and feet nailed to a big live oak, his face bloody and battered. Only a few miles from where he was laying right now. He didn't want to die that way. A blast of voltage didn't sound good either; he prayed, "Dear God, please not like this."

Despite the abuse and hateful words in the jail, Orville figured he was a lot safer on his side of the bars. He conjured up a little hope. Barron Brevard was a good man. He had promised the best attorney in Atlanta would represent him. Orville cogitated. He'd been set up for the murders of Mareissa and Matilde. But who and why? He was a God-fear'n Christian man but given the chance he'd take the murderers apart slowly, limb by limb, if he could.

First time he saw them it was sundown about a year ago, when he was riding Lulu: about a dozen dark-hooded figures standing against the slate blue/gray sky on county land, the bluff overlooking the place where he'd found the twins' bodies. Each was holding a black cross high in the air. The breeze kicked up and there were rumblings of thunder, then the sky lit up. They were gone. Whoever they were, he knew they were up to no good. These killers he guessed made the Klan look like choirboys.

He managed to fall back asleep but not before he heard from a few cells down, "Old man. You gonna be dead, niggra." Then a loud cackling: "Only a matta of time, boy. Only a matta of time."

Chapter 42 – Asheville

Tuesday, April 16—6:15 a.m.

Atlanta

Ted Davies lay in bed waiting for the inevitable 5:45 a.m. alarm. Usually, he'd lollygag for a few luxurious minutes before getting up, but not today. He shot out of bed. He'd changed his mind. His morning appointments were canceled anyway. Maybe he'd explain it away as a hunch—looking out for his client's best interests. But if Barron Brevard found out, he knew that even being a partner, he could get tossed from his firm. Hell, worst case, he could retire early and live on the pecan farm he'd bought years ago. Before his wife got up, he made a pot of coffee, showered, put on his lawyer attire, ate a banana, and was off at 6:15 a.m. But instead of going to the office, he headed up Peachtree, much less of a bitch going north than south in the morning. Then veered off 400 to Woodstock.

The same day—6:30 a.m.

Woodstock

Barron Brevard got up early Tuesday morning and decided to escape the horror at least for the day. Yesterday he'd called Judy and told her he couldn't handle company yet. This morning he called and told her he'd be out of town but would be back later. She asked, "Barron, where are you going? When will I see you?" But the line was already dead.

Barron had no idea where he was going—other than away from Woodstock and Atlanta. He cooked himself eggs over easy, sausage, and grits; then got dressed and headed out to the big barn that housed a few of his hobby vehicles: an MG convertible, a Jag, and a Ferrari that he hadn't driven for ages. And a couple classic bikes. He took the cover off his black 1953 Harley-Davidson Panhead Chopper Bobber. Good day for a bike ride. He grabbed a wad of cash and a well-worn black leather jacket and his best shades. Fuck the helmet.

He headed north. From his ranch in Woodstock, he cut over toward Roswell and rode up west of Lake Lanier on Highway 19. Perfect day to be on his favorite bike. Not too hot, not too cold. A little overcast and not too bright on his aging eyes. He'd heard about new advances in cataract surgery but kept procrastinating. Along with many other things. Traffic wasn't too bad as he biked into the Smoky Mountains of North Georgia. He wasn't going the fastest way to his destination, but he was in no hurry. He felt at peace for the first time since Sunday night.

He headed toward Asheville, a place he and his second wife, Rachel, the twins' mom, went to get away from it all for a couple nights. Horseback riding on the ranch, she'd died seven years ago from an allergic reaction when the inhaler she needed was depleted. He didn't think he could ever feel that bad again—until his daughters were murdered.

Behind his back, he'd heard that many hoity-toity Atlantans scoffed at Rachel as his trophy wife. She was statuesque, blonde, and beautiful—and sixteen years his junior. She also had a Doctor of Philosophy in Archaeology from Cambridge—and was a part-time lecturer at the University of North Carolina, specializing in pre-Revolutionary American Indian culture. And he couldn't have imagined a better mom. So fuck'em all.

At the Grove Park Inn in Ashville, they loved to ride horses, play tennis and golf, and hang out at the pool. But best of all, they loved sitting close together sipping martinis, in front of one of the inn's two mammoth stone hearths. Rachel always insisted they stay in room 545, the room where the Pink Lady stayed before diving to her death decades ago—and supposedly haunted the room and floor. Despite being a person of science, she believed in spirits and twice told him she'd seen her waft by. Barron wasn't buying it. But he wasn't complaining. The legend of the Pink Lady seemed to bring out the wildest versions of his Rachel in bed.

The same day—6:45 a.m.

Canton

When Ted arrived at Cherokee County Prison, the parking lot had only a sprinkling of cars. Ted had been there a few times, but it had been a while. Despite being a criminal attorney, he hated prisons, all prisons. Only society's worst criminals should be in them, but that's not how the system works.

He would have to lie to get inside. Surprisingly, the entrance door was unlocked, and there was no one at the front desk that early. He mashed the button to announce he was there. Nothing. The two sets of double metal doors bordering the front desk were obviously locked. After another minute, he tried again. The double doors to the right burst open, and a hulking man dressed in a poorly kempt brown uniform, with a baton on his hip and a bad attitude on his ugly mug, emerged.

Ted extended his hand. "Ted Davies, Orville Johnston's attorney. I'm here to see him." The guard didn't reciprocate. Instead, he looked at Ted like he'd love to kick his ass back through the front door and into the parking lot.

"Don't think so, mista."

The guard had to be at least six-two and three hundred pounds. From ten feet away, his body odor was like a family of dead possums.

Ted Davies, Esquire, had hit a big-fat-southern-white-boy brick wall. Plan B: He took out his wallet and extracted two fifty-dollar bills. He slid them onto the counter in front of the hulk, who picked up the bills. But he wasn't impressed. "Let's see the rest of your cash, counselor," he demanded.

Ted had another couple hundred in various denominations.

"Gimme the rest of it."

Ted didn't care about the cash but shot back, "I'll give you the rest payable when I leave."

"No, counselor. Give it to me now. Then you can see your nigger."

The hulk had called his bluff.

He opened his wallet and let the hulk see him pull out the rest of his money and put the bills on the counter. He grinned, snatched up the money, and looked at his watch. "Thirty minutes with the old nigger. Then you gone. But you gotta promise you won't kill him—because for that, you'd have to stand in line." The hulk guffawed.

Ted could only nod after the hulk's declaration.

"Follow me."

The gigantic man pressed a wall button that opened the door into the main prison. Ted followed him down the hallway; the big boy made two turns and unlocked a door with a thick glass window. "Stand and spread 'em." The hulk's meat claws pawed up and down Ted's thousand-dollar suit, lingering at his crotch. "Stay here."

A couple minutes later the door to the sparse interview room opened. Orville Johnston had his hands handcuffed in front of him. "You now got twenty-five minutes," said the hulk. He didn't take the cuffs off. Davies started to protest but held his tongue. Thank God, the bozo left.

"Sit down, Mr. Johnston. Sorry about the cuffs. Barron Brevard sent me," he fibbed. "I'm a criminal attorney with Stuyvesant, Knight, Fitzpatrick & Burns in Atlanta. We don't have a lot of time."

The man in front of him held his head high. His big brown eyes were clear and intelligent. Orville said, "Thank you, Mister Davies. I appreciate it. I knew Mr. Brevard would send a lawyer like you."

As with all people he defended, Ted Davies was initially less interested in what Orville had to say—and more in how he said it – and his body language. He looked Orville in the eyes and asked, "You're being treated okay, in prison here?"

Orville didn't answer right away, his shoulders straight, his hands steady, his eyes blinking as they should—but there was a faint tic at the edge of his mouth. He responded, "Yes, sir, they're treating me fine."

"Bullshit, Orville, I don't believe that."

Orville gave him a wan smile. "Okay, Mr. Davies, fair enough. I've been cursed at, beaten with a baton, not fed. No big deal. What else would you like to know?"

"Did you kill Mareissa and Matilde Brevard?"

"No, sir, I did not. Mr. Davies, my little girls both died of chickenpox a long time ago. Then I lost my wife. I loved the Brevard twins like they were my own. I'd never harm them, ever, but I would harm whoever killed them."

Davies knew that question had been asked thousands of times to men accused of murder. But unlike the huge majority, Davies knew Orville was telling the truth. "I believe you. Tell me about Sunday night."

"I was out fishing at Lanier most of the day. Got home around 7:00 p.m. Ate dinner, then dozed off in my rocker outdoors. Phone rang. A lady, who said she was Sally Black, told me the Brevard girls were missing and asked if I would help search my property. I kept calling their names and rode my horse Lulu up to the northern edge of my farm. To a spot they liked. Not sure what made me go there first. It was bad, Mr. Davies. Real bad."

Trying not to break down, he described how he'd found them. Ted Davies himself was shocked at the sheer evil of the scene he described. The minutes ticking by, Ted glanced at his watch a couple times. "Orville, do you have any idea who murdered the twins?"

"Maybe," the black man answered. He told Ted about the black-hooded men on the bluff that overlooked that part of his property. "I didn't have a good feeling about them the couple times I saw 'em. Like they were the Devil's helpers—worse than the Klan."

Ted Davies felt a cold shiver down his neck.

Both men heard the rattle of keys and the door unlock. "Orville, don't talk to anyone about your case. Nothing, until we talk again. You may get charged today or tomorrow. I'll try to figure out bail."

"Thank you, Mr. Davies. I already feel a lot better."

But Ted was sure if Orville had heard his late night conversation with Barron, his feeling wouldn't be the same.

The hulk entered the interview room. "Time's up, counselor." Then looked at Orville. "I'll be back for you, nigger."

Ted and the hulk walked back out to the drab, institutional lobby. Ted thanked him, but then as he reached the front door, he heard the hulk mutter," "Fuck'n nigger lover. Waste a time. He's already dead."

Standing in the little parking lot outside the prison, Ted Davies felt nothing but shame. Purposely, he'd not told Johnston he was his attorney, at least yet; he'd have to finesse that. He knew much better than Barron when a client facing life and death legal consequences was telling the truth or not. Barron's first instinct had been right. But he'd changed his mind. Now it was up to Ted to change it back again. He knew that wouldn't be easy.

The same day—8:30 a.m.

Atlanta

In his Corvette, Ted drove faster than usual against the traffic to the City Club instead of his office. In the lush men's lounge, he called the three numbers he had for Barron. First, he left a message at his home in Woodstock. Next, his secretary at his Atlanta office said that she had no idea but gave him his girlfriend's number. A woman answered, "Judy Dean speaking." He didn't know her other than she was Barron's girlfriend and was considered a high-powered PR type. He asked if she knew where he was. He needed to talk with him as soon as possible.

"Ted, honestly, I have no idea. He said he was going to get out of town, but I don't know where he went. He said he'd be back later—whatever that meant. I'm worried about him."

Ted caught himself before getting into a lengthy conversation.

"Have him call me, please." He left two numbers. "Thanks, Judy."

What do they say…? "Sometimes you get what you ask for—then wish you hadn't asked." Like a criminal attorney presented with an obviously innocent man, but one who had all cards stacked against him.

Ted started to leave the club but instead walked into the main dining room and sat down at his usual table by the window. Not a soul in the huge room; only dozens of tables perfectly set with white linen and silver. He gazed out onto the Peachtree traffic below.

Then heard, "Mista Davies, how long you been sitt'n, sir? Sorry, didn't know you was here. What kin I gitcha?"

He smiled at the elderly black waiter whom he'd known for thirty years. What he wanted to say was that he needed advice and counsel. Instead he said, "Chucky, I need breakfast: maybe Eggs Benedict, with the trimmings. No hurry on that, though; first bring me a short Bloody Mary—a lot of clear, not a lot of mix, and two limes."

"Yes, sah." Charles Lincoln Justice walked to the bar thinking, *Mighty early for Mr. Ted to be cocktailing. Wonder what's the matta?*

Theodore Davies knew he'd put himself in a pickle. A skilled chess player, that was not typical for him. Maybe the booze would provide insight. It never had, but, hell, there was always a first time. Breakfast was good; the second Bloody was doing its thing. As Chucky picked up the dishes, Ted got up the courage to ask, "Chucky, I need your advice. Put the dishes down for a minute. Have a seat."

They were the only two in the dining room. The old waiter looked puzzled but then grinned. "What is it that I could help you with, sah?"

"You heard about the girls that got murdered up in Woodstock?"

"Yes, sah, terrible thing."

"They're saying a black man, Orville Johnston, a reputable farmer, killed them. I know he didn't do it."

Chucky's eyes twinkled, and he waited for Davies to say more.

"The girls' father, Barron Brevard, who is a big client of my firm, told me to represent Mr. Johnston."

Chucky lit up. "That's good; you'll get him off. I know Mr. Barron, but he's not here real often. Met his pretty daughters once."

Davies nodded. The black man saw the pain in his face. "What is it, sah?"

"Then, he told me not to be his lawyer."

"Not sure I'm following, Mr. Ted."

"Yeah, not sure I am, either."

Ted Davies took a few deep breaths and asked with all sincerity, "Chucky, what should I do?"

The old black man who'd served him hundreds of meals and drinks didn't hesitate. "You'll do the right thing, sah. I know you will. You're a good man. You'll do the right thing."

Ted was going to ask what the right thing was, but he already knew. Why Chucky thought he was a good man, though, now that was a mystery.

Ted nodded. "Thank you, Chucky. I'll do what I can."

The same day—11:30 a.m.

Asheville, North Carolina

When Ted Davies left his messages, Barron Brevard was already a hundred miles outside of Atlanta, riding north into the Great Smokies. He took the longer scenic route. The hardwoods were starting to bud, and flowers were beginning to bloom. The air was fresh and, he hoped, soothing for his troubled mind. It felt good zooming down the highway alone.

Barron arrived at the majestic, stone hotel—not sure that many guests arrived at the Grove Park Inn on a bike. For now, he parked across from the main entrance. One of the older black valets remembered him. "Mista Barron, good to see you. How you doin'?"

"Hey, James." He hugged him instead of shaking hands.

"James, where can I leave my bike? Only stay'n for the day."

"Right where you are is fine. Hey, Mr. Barron, how are those beautiful twins of yours?"

James meant no harm; he obviously didn't know. But Barron could feel his face darkening and said nothing. He handed the elderly black man a twenty, patted him on the shoulder, and walked into the Inn. There was no escaping his grief. But he loved this hotel and always had. He decided to take a leisurely walk on the beautiful grounds and then relax on the Sunset Terrace and have a couple drinks.

The same day—11:00 a.m.

Washington, DC

After arriving at Washington National, Derbert Hinke cabbed directly to the DOJ building where he was housed, but probably not much longer. A couple years after his death, Hoover's new, butt-ugly building was almost ready to accept the first couple thousand FBI agents. Oh boy.

On the flight back, he'd been running through the events of the past twenty-four hours and making notes. He locked his office door, cleared his desk, and brought out the key photos and evidence from 1950. Plus, the Polaroids he found in Orville Johnston's house yesterday. He took his time sizing up each photograph and each piece of evidence.

Hinke had never felt more resolute about catching these sons-of-bitches. But he wondered what would happen to Orville Johnston unless he pulled a miracle out of his hat and found the real killers. He felt sorry for the old guy, but the horses were already out of the barn on that.

What Hinke didn't know was how fast the horses were.

Chapter 43 – The Conspiracy

The same day—3:00 p.m.

Canton

By noon, the plan was hatched. Earlier, Cherokee County Sheriff Joey Condurelis had met with Warden Carl Falcone and paid him two grand—with another two grand on completion. Carl loved running his little prison as the ultimate dictator, and he particularly loved meting out punishment to black prisoners. The idea of making good money taking out the nigger-rapist-murderer made him gleeful.

Carl's right-hand man was Dwight Greene, who at six-foot-five and 270 pounds, was a guard no prisoners (or other guards) would ever fool with. In turn, Greene, who always knew what was happening in the prison, picked inmate Arnie Yellman, who'd stacked time off and on for twenty years—most recently possessing a shoebox full of weed when a patrolman stopped him doing 110 on 92. The pitch to Yellman was a bunch of smokes, liquor, jerky, coke, and porn. Plus, the warden would go to bat for him at his upcoming parole hearing. But if he screwed up or anyone heard him blabbing would go to the top of the warden's "list" and maybe never see the light of day again. Yellman was on record as hating blacks more than anything else on the planet. Two years ago, he'd been beaten senseless by a couple black guys in Macon who demanded that Arnie pay his gambling bets. In Yellman's mind, there was no way the whole nigger race could ever make up for what happened to him that night in Macon.

Greene couldn't wear a gun inside the prison, but over the years, he'd become a connoisseur of shivs that he'd found and improved. He always had a couple on him. It was well known among the inmates that Greene could slice you with a shiv faster than a bullet. He'd slip one of his primo hand-crafted weapons to Yellman this afternoon.

He got none yesterday, but Orville was hoping for fresh air this afternoon. He never made it to the exercise yard. Dwight Greene stopped him and said, "Look, nigger, you're not too popular in here. No outside play with the boys. Go take a shower, then I'll get you back to your cell. Warden don't want you hung on his watch."

Greene smiled and opened the door to the communal shower. Greene told him, "I'll be back in ten minutes. Be clean and dressed." He slammed the door and locked it. Orville sat down on the metal bench built into the wall. Washing off a layer of stench from this place sounded good to him. He took off his institutional gray and white striped shirt and trousers and underwear. He hung it all up on a wall hook and turned on a shower faucet. Hot. His face and torso stung from the sheriff's beating yesterday when he wouldn't confess. Then two other Klan types, he was sure, broke a couple ribs. The water felt great as he closed his eyes and let it cascade over his bald scalp.

Three hours earlier, after lunch, Greene had passed Yellman a shiv and told him he better not lose it. It was classic crafted from a toothbrush, chicken wire, and sharp piece of glass; the handle well-wrapped rawhide and duct tape to hold it all together. One of the best he'd ever confiscated, the edge as sharp as any razor.

As the inmates got marched to the exercise yard, Yellman started pushing a black prisoner, who tried to retaliate, but he was a foot shorter and a hundred pounds lighter.

"Yellman, goddammit," Greene shouted. "No more playtime for you. Get back inside." But Yellman wasn't marched to his cell. Greene winked at him and opened the door to the shower room.

Orville heard the clank of the door opening, then the bang of it shutting. Naked in the shower, he turned around. The massive inmate gave him a toothy grin. "Mind if I join you, niggra? I know you're want'n a big white cock up your black ass."

As he stood in the shower on the old tile floor, Orville's back ached like hell, but the immediate rush of adrenalin nixed the pain. Brandishing the shiv, Yellman lunged at him. Orville dodged. On the way past, Orville pounded him in the back using a Japanese martial arts kick he'd learned years ago in the Army. Yellman was now a raging bull. "You're a dead niggra—you know that don't you? Before you croak, I'm going to cut your balls off and stuff 'em in your mouth."

Yellman charged him again. This time, Orville sidestepped and smashed his forearm into Yellman's wrist, knocking the improvised knife to the wet shower floor. Orville lunged for the shiv and got there before Yellman. He was up quickly and said, "Look, let's stop this now before anyone gets hurt."

"Like you're going to hurt me, niggra? More enraged, he yelled, "I'm going to finish it."

Orville was holding the shiv, but when Yellen came at him again, Orville slipped on the wet tile. Next thing he knew Yellman was straddling him, his meaty hands around his throat. He banged the back of Orville's head into the wet floor, but Yellman wasn't paying attention. With as much might as Orville could muster, he buried the shiv into Yellen's right side.

Greene and Falcone wondered why the hell Yellman hadn't emerged from the shower yet. They walked from the warden's office to check it out and unlocked the door. Orville Johnston stood naked before them while Yellman was on the tile, hollering at a hundred decibels.

Warden Falcone pulled his own untraceable handgun and pointed it at Orville. He was the little guy in the room, bespectacled and short and with a bad toupee, but he had the firepower. Orville backed up several steps.

Yellman wailed, "Goddam nigger cut me, I think bad."

"Shut up!" the warden yelled back. "Get the shiv out of him." Greene walked over and yanked the sharpened toothbrush from the prisoner's side. He screamed louder.

Falcone barked at Orville, "Get your clothes on and we'll sort this out." Then nodded, almost imperceptibly, to his head guard. As Orville put on clean striped pants, Dwight moved behind him and shoved the shiv deep into his kidney. Orville crumbled to the wet floor. The next stab went directly into his neck. Blood exploded in all directions and then slowly swirled over the tile floor, the life draining from Orville Johnston.

The warden nodded his head again to Greene. Yellman rolled on the floor, moaning, "Goddammit. I need a doctor. Get me out of here."

The guard smiled. "Sure, Arnie. Lemme look at your wound." He bent down and with both hands drove the shiv into Arnie's chest. The prisoner's eyes showed surprise and horror. He could only gurgle, then went silent on the shower floor.

Warden Falcone grinned. "Didn't go exactly like it was drawn up, but in a way better—the old nigger and his murderer-to-be, both dead. Two loose ends are gone. He told Greene, "Move the bodies closer and put another shiv in the nigger's hand and stab Yellman's body again. Make it look more real.

"Here's the story, Dwight: two inmates got into it. Likely a racial thing in response to the girls' murders. They managed to kill each other before we got there. You found them dead on the floor. Go get cleaned up ASAP, then come back to the shower. That's where you found 'em dead on the floor." The husky guard nodded and left.

The shower was running. Orville Johnston and his assailant, but not his murderer, Arnie Yellman, lay next to him on the cracked tile floor, soaked with water and blood. Their souls having departed in opposite directions.

The same day—3:30 p.m.

Asheville to Atlanta

The ride to the Grove Park Inn was pleasant. Not the ride back. Barron's dread increased with each mile. There was the memorial service on Thursday, and there was the empty house. And he wondered if Sumner had done his job. The ride made worse because, as the daylight faded, his cataract-diminished sight was fading as well. He slowed his speed to less than 15 mph compared to the ride up and took Highway 23 versus the scenic route. While he'd had only pleasant experiences at the Grove Park Inn, he knew of F. Scott Fitzgerald's sad story there in the 1930s. Trying to revive his career with chump-change writing assignments, trying to stop drinking, trying to get wacky Zelda cared for; trying to pay the bills, and failing at everything. The darkness of that story further clouded his return trip.

Barron was cruising along south of the North Carolina-Georgia border at a reasonable clip. Three deer bolted in front of him. By instinct and experience, he spun, balanced his bike, and managed not to fall. He wanted to get back and get the rest over with.

The same day—6:00 p.m.

Woodstock

Sumner called his deputy and told him he'd probably see it on the news. Orville Johnston had been shivved and killed in jail that afternoon. "Saved us taxpayers' money."

Deputy Sheriff Louis Giles was speechless; he hung up. It wasn't like he should be surprised, but until that moment, he felt like he was on the periphery of a conspiracy. Not in the middle of it. Technically, he hadn't found the photos that were given to Barron Brevard. And he hadn't been at the jail knifing Johnston. But only he and Hinke knew for sure it wasn't Johnston who had killed the twins. If he'd been inclined to save him, it would have been too late for Orville Johnston. He rushed to his bathroom and heaved his guts.

Then he had a call to make.

"DH, it's Louis. I know you wanted me to keep you posted."

"Hey, Louis, what's up?"

"Orville Johnston is dead. Got shivved in the jail shower by another inmate who died too."

Hinke had known it was possible—maybe likely—but the speed of the retribution was astounding. He'd underestimated the raw hatred southern white men had when it came to the smallest true or false innuendo or injury involving their women.

"Louis, thanks for the call. Remember what was asked of you."

"Yes, sir."

Hinke hung up. He couldn't have drawn it up this well; it was perfect. The Brevard investigations would be over and quickly forgotten by the public and law enforcement. They'd pinned it on the wrong guy, who was now dead. An unfortunate sacrifice. Now, he could hunt the real killers with total carte blanche. And he finally had avenues to investigate.

The word "sacrifice" stuck in his brain. After seeing the photos of the Brevard and Blount twins, he had no doubt that's what they were. He sat sipping his bourbon and then wondered if he still had it. The page he'd ripped out of the book in New Canaan years ago. He pawed around the file compartments in his briefcase. Folded up, it was there in the bottom of one. The girl on the stone slab. The two male devils. The female witch was holding a black cross. He put it next to the photos. Yes, his murders were versions of "Devil's Sacrifices."

It was time for Hinke to rock and roll according to his own drummer and fuck any consequences.

The same day—8:30 p.m.

Woodstock

Barron Brevard was bushed when he got back to his ranch. He hadn't spent that much time on a bike in one day for years. Getting off his bike, his back seemed frozen. His legs and butt throbbed. After checking on his animals, he went directly to the shower, then to his bar, where he took two Advil and downed them with a big Scotch. He had no doubt there would be phone messages.

The first, sent early that morning, was from Ted Davies. He was in no mood and skipped to the next.

He downed the rest of the tumbler and went to refill it.

The second was from Judy Dean. "Barron, call me when you're back. I want to come over tonight and be with you."

Judy was a smart, beautiful, sexy gal, but he had no desire to spend the night with anyone.

The third was from Sheriff Billy Ray Sumner. It was brief. "It's done."

That was the message he'd been waiting for. He walked around his huge living room sipping his Scotch—the gravity of what he'd perpetrated only now sinking in.

There were more messages, but he put the phone down and sat numb.

The phone rang, and he didn't want to answer but did. It was Judy.

"Barron, are you okay? I was so worried."

"Fine. I took a little bike trip to North Carolina and just got back."

"You probably haven't heard the news, then. Evening news had a short blurb, not many details. The black man who they think killed your daughters was found dead today at the Cherokee County Prison."

He tried to act surprised and hesitated. "Judy, that's not the way it should've happened," he lied.

"Well maybe it's for the best," she said. "You won't have to go through a big trial and all the other press hoopla. Barron, you're going to get asked about his death."

He knew that was true. "What should I say?"

She told him she'd handle it: basically he had no comment on Orville Johnston. He was too distraught grieving his twins. He'd appreciate it if people respected his privacy.

Of course, she was right. He wanted to say, *Tell them justice got done.* But he didn't.

"Barron, I can be up there in forty minutes, okay? You need company."

He'd never felt so lonely but said, "Thanks. Judy, handle the press inquiries, and I agree, ignore what happened to Orville Johnston.

Come up tomorrow anytime. Tonight, I need to be by myself and go to sleep."

"Okay, baby. Don't worry, I'll try to keep this down to a dull roar, but it will take a few days for it to settle down."

"I understand."

Barron hung up and realized then that even with Orville Johnston's death, it was going to take time for all of this to go away. Maybe it never would.

He poured more Scotch and sat in his shower—for how long he wasn't sure. When he got out, the phone rang again.

I shouldn't answer that, he told himself but picked up the phone in his bedroom.

With a tinge of sarcasm Ted said, "Barron, thanks for calling back."

"Goddammit, Ted, tell me what you wanted to tell me this morning. I drove my bike up to North Carolina. Got back a little while ago."

It had been short, but it was the lead story on Channel 2 News at 10:00 p.m. That's when Ted Davies first found out that Orville Johnston was dead.

"Did you know that Orville Johnston got killed in jail today?"

He didn't let Barron respond. "I went up to Cherokee County Prison early this morning and talked with him."

"God damn you, Ted. God damn you. I told you that you didn't represent him."

"I went up on my own dime to talk to him. And do you know what, Barron?"

"What?"

"You were right about Orville Johnston. What you told me the first time when you asked me to represent him. Orville Johnston did not kill your twins, Barron. I'm sure of it."

The anger, the grief, the disappointment, the confusion that Barron Brevard could not verbalize boiled up and overflowed. "Fuck you, Ted," and he slammed the phone down.

Ted Davies was not surprised by Barron's reaction. But what was he missing?

Shouldn't he feel relief, satisfaction, closure, peace? Whatever, for God's sake? But the fruit of Barron Brevard's revenge gave him none of those things.

Barron needed something other than booze to stifle his grief. He walked over to the stereo system and turned on his favorite FM station. Then, what were the chances? That catchy little tune Vicky Lawrence sang came on, "The Night the Lights Went Out in Georgia..." He couldn't help from singing it:

That's the night that the lights went out in Georgia

That's the night that they hung an innocent man

Well, don't trust your soul to no backwoods southern lawyer

'Cause the judge in the town's got bloodstains on his hands

Barron was the judge, and he had bloodstains on his hands, but at least this part of his nightmare was over. He prayed Ted Davies wasn't right. He didn't want an innocent man's death on his conscience.

It was almost midnight when Sheriff Sumner got a call from Lancy Adams, assistant pastor at the Church of Redemption and, in his spare time, head of the Ku Klux Klan in Cherokee County.

Sumner thought, *Lancy is such an asshole,* but he listened.

"Sheriff, Hallelujah that the nigger sinner was killed this afternoon. We have a good and righteous God."

"Hallelujah and amen, Pastor Adams," he said grudgingly.

"I thought it appropriate for our brothers to mete out more justice tonight, Sheriff."

Cringing, he asked, "Pastor, what the hell did you all do?"

"We torched the nigger's house and barns and animals. That land is now cleansed forever from sin. Free for white Americans to take back what is rightfully theirs."

Sumner thought about telling him what an idiot he was but the words stuck in his craw. After all, he'd perpetrated a much worse sin today, and he'd known deep down that Orville Johnston had been framed.

But hell, he'd get over it; he'd made a lot of coin today.

Chapter 44 – The Godfather

A week later—Wednesday, April 24

Woodstock

Barron Brevard decided this would be the day.

Off and on he was shell-shocked, morose, depressed, and so angry he could spit nails, but he'd stumbled through the initial trauma of his twins' deaths and the private service last week, the reception, the cards and flowers, the condolences, and the press that Judy had done a masterful job of handling, besides keeping him company the past week. But that day he told her he needed time alone.

He'd never tell Judy or anyone, but he had lost hope that he'd ever be okay again. Yesterday he'd given his ranch hands and his part-time housekeeper and cook, Margarita, two weeks off with pay. He figured it would be good for him to stay busy cooking and doing his own chores. Mostly, he wanted to grieve by himself. But by noon he wasn't sure of that.

There were two identical, stone urns on his eight-foot-high, rough-hewn cedar mantel. He poured the contents of both into a large black plastic bag, then put two handfuls back in the urns. He'd save those for the columbarium that he'd have built into the side of his stone home.

He headed out on his quarter horse, Jeremiah. It was cooler than usual with a healthy breeze from the northwest and fast-moving clouds. The fresh air was exhilarating. He was in no hurry as he periodically cast handfuls of his daughters' ashes onto the ground of his eight-hundred-acre ranch. Ground they'd both loved for their short fourteen years of life. Off and on, he could conjure up images of them riding alongside him. But he couldn't see Thor, their beloved dog. Each time he stopped his horse, he yelled at the top of his lungs. "Thor, please come back home, boy. Please, Thor, come back home." He rode to the far edge of his big ranch where he could barely see the tips of the tall pines on Orville Johnston's property. Where his daughters were murdered. The revenge bubbled up in his gut, but they were dead and gone – and so was Johnston.

Early afternoon, Barron returned with an empty bag. He put up his tack and grabbed a full bottle of Mortlach and a glass from his barn bar. He walked up to the house and sat on the big wooden swing on the porch. One of his favorite places where he'd always enjoyed sitting between Mareissa and Matilde, Thor at their feet. He drank and swung.

His head jerked up after nodding off for more than an hour. He needed more Scotch, then a hot shower, and maybe an early dinner. After pouring a half-tumbler and downing most of it, he walked through the anteroom straight into his huge bathroom, dropped his clothes on the floor, and turned on the hot spray. His rugged, rangy body clean, he craved a change of pace: a glass of Heitz cabernet from his stone-lined cellar.

Toweling off, he walked into his bedroom and froze.

It was wedged between the two pillows.

What was off? He ripped back the covers. The dog's head was severed, and fresh blood stained the sheets. He sat down and pet him between the eyes and down his snout as he'd done every day the last six years. He gathered himself and started to reach for the portable phone to call Sumner or Giles. But he stopped and put it back down. His daughters' beloved dog, was decapitated. Eerily like Francis Ford Coppola's *The Godfather*; a dog's head instead of a horse's head. A sadistic sense of cruelty beyond belief. Sitting on the bed, he sobbed.

After his cry, Barron had to face the cold, hard truth. Orville Johnston hadn't killed his daughters. The murderers were mocking him with the dog's head, freshly severed from his body. He had the wrong man killed. Realizing he'd been played, he could only shake his head in disgust at himself. He stood and looked in the mirror and didn't see the confident cowboy-banker-businessman who'd once taken Atlanta by storm. He saw an old man whose gray, grizzled face was permanently etched with sorrow, hatred, grief, and sin.

All that he loved in this world was gone.

A strange calm came over him. Methodically, he shaved and then picked out his favorite duds: broken-in Levi's, a crisp white shirt, a belt with a big silver and turquoise buckle, and Tony Lamas; he didn't bother with a Stetson.

He got a big black garbage bag from the kitchen and put his dog's head in it along with the sheets and bedspread. Behind his small horse barn was an old, unused well. He dropped the bag into it. Then he walked back to his barn and fed and watered his horses.

He walked back inside and poured a full tumbler of Mortlach. He got a piece of stationery and a pen.

Barron Brevard knew he had fucked up beyond belief, and he'd put himself in a box with no way out. If he told the truth, he'd spend the rest of his days in prison. Ted Davies couldn't prevent that. That wasn't going to happen. But if he didn't, he wouldn't be able to look himself in the mirror again. He chuckled at the irony of his success. "Wow, what a moron you've been, Barron."

Sitting on his wraparound porch, sipping his Scotch, he finished his short letter. Then went back inside for an envelope and stamp and walked the letter down to his mailbox, depositing it before the typical late afternoon delivery.

Back inside, he took his beautiful AH Fox double-barrel from the wall and grabbed two cartridges from a nearby drawer. He stood ramrod tall, all six-foot-four of him, in front of the foyer mirror, flanked by the recent portraits of Matilde and Mareissa. He said out loud, "Lord Jesus, I can't do this anymore and ask your forgiveness. Please let me join my girls and wife. I beg of you." Barron Brevard jammed the shotgun under his chin. Then he cocked and pulled the trigger.

The cowboy-banker, yet another victim of a game in which he had no idea he'd been playing a bit part.

Thursday, April 25

Woodstock

Brevard's body wasn't found until the next morning by Judy Dean. She hadn't heard from him and had left several messages. She decided to drive from the city to Woodstock; she had her own key. He lay sprawled on the wood floor in front of the foyer mirror. The shotgun by his side. Dark blood staining the wood, his white shirt splattered, his head mostly dark mush.

She screamed, "No, Barron, no!"

It was a media feast—the lead story on each of the Atlanta six o'clock news stations – and made the national news. Judy couldn't have stopped it.

Chapter 45 – The Apology

The same day

Atlanta

Ted Davies was playing in a scramble golf tournament at Calloway Gardens. He told Valerie that he wasn't available. Period. He'd be back in the office Friday morning. His team finished at 17-under and won in a scorecard playoff for first place. The golf tournament was great fun, but he'd stayed too long celebrating and was dead tired as he drove into the city at 9:30 p.m. He wanted to go in and relax in peace, which was possible since his wife was skiing with a few girlfriends in Vail, which was inundated with a big snowfall in late April. He wondered if she and her good-looking friends had recruited a few young studs to service them on their expensive getaway. He didn't give a rip. His son Kip was staying at friends through the weekend. He was alone.

Ted stopped at the end of his fifty-yard driveway, on Nancy Creek Road in the toney West Paces area of Atlanta, got out, grabbed the mail, and parked his brand-new black Beamer in the four-car garage. From there he entered their huge kitchen and turned on a couple overhead lights. He flipped through the mail. Only a couple bills and a magazine. And a letter hand-addressed to him.

He didn't recognize the handwriting, and there was no return address, but he noticed the postal mark. He opened it.

April 24, 1974

Dear Ted,

You were right. I was wrong. I'm sorry and owe you an apology. It wasn't Orville Johnston who killed my daughters. I fucked up worse than any human could possibly fuck up. Maybe someone will figure out who murdered my girls. I sure hope that they'll get what's coming to them in spades. The sons-of-bitches killed them and played us all like fools.

Ted, they had our dog killed. They left his head in my bed like the horse's head in The Godfather. I can't live with my horrible mistakes—and without my girls. Maybe see you again one day down the road. I hope with my twins, too, if I'm lucky enough to land on the right side.

Please forgive me,

Barron

Holding the short, handwritten letter, Ted Davies walked into the kitchen and grabbed a half gallon of cold Stoli from the freezer. He poured himself a full tumbler and rubbed a whole lemon around the edge.

Sounded like a suicide note. He paced the first floor of his 6,500-square-foot home sipping his Stoli. Walking past the TV in the living room, he turned it on. Pacing faster and guzzling the potent vodka, he heard Barron Brevard's name. He wheeled and spilled his Stoli. On the TV screen, he saw a photograph of super-suave Barron in a dark suit and another in his Marlboro man get-up. Then heard, "Barron Brevard, Atlanta financier and philanthropist, whose twin girls were murdered last week, was found dead in his ranch home in Woodstock this morning. His death an apparent suicide."

Ted downed the rest of his vodka and went to get another. He reread it a couple of times. Because of the dog's head, it couldn't have been Johnston who killed the twins. That made sense. But he realized it was more about what Barron did *not* say. *"Holy shit, Barron paid to get Johnston murdered. That's what pushed him over the edge. No wonder he blew his brains out."*

It only made Ted feel worse. Maybe he could've tried harder to convince Barron that Orville was innocent—before all of it spun out of control. Maybe he could've saved two lives. Maybe he should have demanded that Orville be better isolated and guarded. A black man—accused of murdering two white girls—in a white-racist-run prison in one of the most racist counties in the U.S. What was he thinking? Hell, he could've put a call into the Georgia attorney general, whom he knew well. But he didn't.

Barron Brevard's suicide note that drunken evening was a revelation to Ted Davies—attorney-at-law, the biggest swinging dick criminal lawyer in Atlanta—about who he really was. Since making Law Review at Duke, he'd always known he was going to be a star. He'd thought he was a decent guy, too, at least compared to most of the asshole attorneys he knew in Atlanta and beyond. Looking back, though, he couldn't help but chuckle. Who was he kidding? He'd always been phony as shit. Phonier than a lot of shyster lawyers who were at least upfront about their sleaze. How many scumbags had he successfully defended and facilitated their ongoing mayhem? After taking exorbitant amounts of their blood money. Too many to count.

After Barron was gone, Ted's wife left not soon after and hooked up with a ski instructor out west. Then it was a venture capital guy in a place south of San Francisco called San Leandro. She'd taken their young son Kip out west, too. Ted Davies loved his son and could've fought the custody battle and torn her a new asshole—but decided it wasn't worth the pain, especially to his young son. But more honestly, he didn't have the energy to be a part-time dad. His work was too important now. He had to atone for his monumental mistakes.

It took a while, but it was a steady downhill march from the top for Ted Davies. Orville Johnston often haunted his dreams. Barron Brevard would appear, but never with his twins, which he thought odd. His son Kip appeared sometimes, but he could never reach him.

Between his alcohol binges, Ted tried his best but couldn't find many "good" clients. That is, clients he knew were innocent and could pay. Eventually, he stopped defending any asshole he was positive deserved only the harshest of punishments. He believed he was fully capable of judging. He became the pro bono go-to guy in his firm across all types of law, not only criminal. A not insignificant asset to the firm since no one else wanted the cases. Most colleagues came to see him as a tragic figure to be pitied. Many laughed at him behind his back. His work was manic, often eighty or more hours one week, then he would go AWOL for days. His only short-term reward at the end of those days was as much cold Stoli he could drink and still be able to get out of bed or off the couch or the floor. He bought half gallons by the case, and a case didn't last long.

The partners put up with him for six more years, but, to a person, were relieved when Ted Davies took his own life in his study, alone at home. Though his gun was much more pedestrian, he opted for Barron's way out. And like Barron, Ted Davies left this world hoping for the best, but having no idea which side he'd end up on.

Chapter 46 – Delacroix, Giles, and Hinke

Like Ted Davies, APD Detective Hollis Delacroix found out about Barron Brevard's death on the tube. He'd never met the father of the two murdered twins and doubted Hinke had either.

Delacroix called Hinke at home in Washington, DC. "DH, what's going on?"

"Same old same old. You know us FBI goons. Trying to catch more rabble-rousers and left-wing bombers. Hoover lives on despite being dead." He chuckled.

"Thought you might be interested in this. Barron Brevard, the twins' dad, apparently committed suicide yesterday at his ranch. It's all over the Atlanta news this evening."

Hinke tried to digest. The dad lost it because of what happened to his daughters. Understandable. That could drive anyone over the edge. Then his mind whirred, *"Did he commit suicide? What else was going on here?"* He added up the deaths and disappearances beginning in Anniston last year. The body count continued to climb. He knew they were all linked.

"Thanks, Hollis. I appreciate the call. On my way out right now. I might be down to Atlanta next week. Can I take you and your lovely wife out to dinner? On me—you pick the place."

Hollis told him, "Yeah, would love that. If you can give us a day's heads-up, we'll get a sitter."

"Definitely. Thanks, Hollis."

Within ten minutes, the phone rang again. It was Louis Giles giving him the same news.

"Yeah, heard from Hollis Delacroix. Louis, tell me straight up. Was it suicide?"

"One hundred percent sure, DH."

Hinke asked, "Ever find their dog?"

"Nope, nothing. Big reward still but not sure how that'd get paid with Mr. Brevard dead now."

"Listen, Louis, I'm going to be in town next week. I'd like to pick up those files we talked about. That's not going to be a problem, is it." Not a question.

"Lemme know the day, and we'll figure out a time and place."

"Good. Thanks, Louis."

He was on the hook to get DH what he wanted. The Woodstock Police Department files would be a piece of cake. The ones up in Canton, he'd have to figure out. There was no reason to disappoint Special Agent Derbert Hinke.

Wednesday, May 1

Washington, DC

Hinke's mail was delivered mid-morning. One thick brown envelope. No return address. The postmark from Atlanta. He tore the top off and extracted the contents. It was a black dog collar. He didn't have to read the fancy engraved tag to know who it belonged to:

THOR

If found, please call Matilde or Mariessa Brevard

753-8966

24 Bells Ferry, Woodstock, GA

It was only 10:30 a.m. but Derbert Hinke pulled out a bottle of Jack and a glass out of his bottom drawer. He took a healthy gulp, then held the black collar and stared at the silver tag. They'd killed the girls' dog, too. Taunting him. They made the rules and held all the cards. He knew they were following him, but they didn't know what he'd do next.

Thursday, May 2

Atlanta

Deputy Sheriff Louis Giles kept rolling sevens. His latest good fortune: his boss asked him to get rid of all the Woodstock & Canton files about the murders. Giles figured it would take cash to make that happen, but he didn't pay a dime; hell, the powers-to-be wanted the twins' murders and Johnston's murder erased forever.

Hinke would add to Giles' cash windfall when he got the files. And he'd gotten an appraisal of J. Edgar Hoover's ring at a big Atlanta jewelry store. The estimate was jaw-dropping. He couldn't be in a better mood. On Saturday he was going to pop the question to Cheryl and let her go pick out the diamond ring of her dreams at Perimeter Mall. He fantasized about getting a blowjob in broad daylight driving his cruiser on the way back from buying it for her.

Hinke flew Delta to Atlanta and got into Hartsfield at 10:30 a.m. Deputy Sheriff Louis Giles met him at Minelli's, a little Italian joint a mile north of the Perimeter at noon. Hinke liked Giles and felt he could be trusted. But he decided that Louis knew way too much already, and he wasn't about to say more. They both ordered the lasagna lunch special and spent the time chitchatting about a lot other than the happenings of the last three weeks. Giles told him he was playing hooky for the day and going up to Lanier for a few hours.

"You fish, DH?"

"Not since I was a kid, but I liked it. A few guys I work with go to streams and lakes in Virginia and beyond. The rich boys keep their boats at Annapolis and fish in the bay and out in the Atlantic."

"Maybe next time, you can carve out a day and we'll go up to Lanier and catch us some striped bass or catfish. Whaddya say?"

"Sounds good."

They skipped dessert. "Let's get you fish'n after we finish our business."

From his cruiser's trunk, Giles took out a sealed banker's box and handed it to Hinke. "It's all I could find at our station and up in Canton, including the crime scene evidence."

"The crosses too?"

"Yep."

Hinke didn't bother to open the box. He transferred it to his trunk and pulled out an envelope of cash, which he handed to Giles. "Thanks, Louis. We're square now, right." he said more as a statement. "This stays between you and me." A firmer statement.

"You have my word."

Hollis chose a restaurant in Underground Atlanta where Hinke had never been. He thought DH would enjoy the sights. The last time he'd been there he walked right past Greg Allman and Cher. Another time, he did a double-take as Mick Jagger and Keith Richards traversed the merry crowd.

"Our reservation is at 7:30 at the Blackstone Inn. Not far for you but best to cab it, and it's coat and tie for guys."

Hinke decided to arrive a little early and explore one of Atlanta's most popular places, in south downtown. It was like he'd been transported to the French Quarter of New Orleans, minus the smells and grime and sleazy strip bars. Flickering gas lights, dozens of fine shops and restaurants done in traditional styles, and people enjoying themselves. Most adults dressed to the nines. Younger folks, though, in a wide variety of casual clothes. It was completely under street level; built on old railway tracks, he'd read, and earlier in the century covered over by the streets and buildings above.

For grins, he stopped at Lester Maddox's Gifts & Souvenirs shop. He didn't know a lot about Maddox other than he had been governor of Georgia in the '60s and now served as lieutenant governor under Governor Jimmy Carter. Strange southern politics. It was a cornucopia of souvenirs: red, white, and blue political buttons, flags, bumper stickers, southern candies, autographed photos of Maddox and other white guys he didn't know, and a host of other touristy trinkets. Near the cashier was an old barrel of what appeared to be long wood axe handles, and he took one out.

He asked the cashier, "What's up with these?"

"Governor Maddox used to have a temper if certain folks he didn't want entered his restaurant."

Hinke got it; he was in the South.

At the Blackstone, he asked for the Delacroix table. The maître d' told him the other two in his party hadn't arrived yet, but he was welcome to be seated. At the table, he checked the wine list. The past few years he'd started drinking more red wines from the United States. He'd been introduced to Stag's Leap cabernet, and there was a 1972 bottle on the list. Pricey, but who cared? Uncle Sam would get the bill.

The wine was decanting as the Delacroix's arrived at 7:40 p.m. Hinke stood, and Hollis stuck out his hand and apologized profusely that they'd gotten hung up, but Hinke only heard, "…and this is my wife, Mei."

Hinke was tongue-tied but managed to get out, "The pleasure is mine, Mrs. Delacroix. Call me DH."

Together, the Delacroix's were the most handsome couple he'd ever laid eyes on.

Hinke was mesmerized by Mei Delacroix. He'd seen her picture, but it didn't come close to doing her justice. The Chinese woman was tall, regal, and gorgeous – the shape of an amazing feminine hourglass in her tight-fitting black dress. Porcelain skin, ruby-red nails and lipstick, and pitch-black hair to her shoulders. Her intelligent, gigantic eyes at a slight tilt, and a color he'd never seen, like natural honey. He had a hard time not staring. She was as captivating as Marilyn Monroe, maybe more, in a far more exotic way. His first reaction was: that she should be in the movies. The second: Hollis Delacroix was one lucky guy.

Their waiter poured the Stags Leap as they chatted. Hinke mentioned he had stopped by Lester Maddox's Souvenir Shop on the way. They both grinned. Mei asked, "Did you buy me a cute trinket there, DH?" The lady had a sense of humor, too.

"No, ma'am, but I almost bought Hollis an axe handle. Thought he could add it to his other police weaponry." They all laughed. He toasted, "Hollis, you clean up good, but you obviously married way above your pay grade." Hollis grinned, knowingly, and they clinked glasses.

She playfully winked at her husband.

Mei asked Hinke, "Hollis didn't tell me exactly what brings you to Atlanta, DH?"

"Hadn't gotten a chance to meet his better half yet," he said truthfully. But then added, "There's a new case I'm consulting on with the Atlanta Field Office, but it's a quick trip. *A total lie.* Going back to DC tomorrow."

Hollis interrupted and chuckled, "Top secret FBI stuff, no doubt."

Mei asked, "Hollis tells me you're not married?"

"Never have been and not likely at my advanced age. Years ago, I was on the verge." His voice trailed off. "Guess I've always been married to my job…" Mentioning Helen – no reason to go there. But he felt a pang of remorse that he didn't have a wife and children.

Diplomatically, Mei dropped the subject.

Hinke recovered quickly and ordered another bottle of cabernet. They dined on prime rib and lobster, fried okra, rice pudding, and Caesar salad. Mei Delacroix had no problem keeping up with the two big guys, eating-wise. He wondered where in the world she put it. Hollis bragged on her, and he couldn't blame him. DH was all ears. After graduating from Georgia Tech at the age of twenty, by twenty-four she was already an associate professor in the Department of Physics, and her brilliant treatise on Chaos Theory, Hollis told him proudly, was second to none. Then about a year after being married she walked away from the scientific fast track at Tech. They both wanted children, and she had another calling. To her family and Christ and the work she could do for the least fortunate in Atlanta. With her luminous smile and perfect white teeth, she added, "And of course, now we have Suzanne."

Hollis recommended the key lime pie. Mei told her husband, "I'll take a bite of yours."

He told her, "No way. Order your own piece. I know you." She laughed and they smiled at each other like newlyweds. Hinke was jealous.

Hinke asked permission of Mei if he could talk a little shop with Hollis. She replied, "Please do. I like to hear about Hollis' work. He's so damn secretive."

Hollis raised his eyebrows. Hinke wanted to know if there was anything new on the Elder case. Hollis told him that he was on to other things and had helped solve the last two homicides he was assigned to. Hinke congratulated him. Hollis told him that the Elder case was now officially categorized as cold.

"You think it was a drug hit?" Hinke asked.

"I talked more to several narcs who know the drug scene in town better than anyone. After Elder's murder, more low and mid-level dealers were found dead, executed with a bullet to the head—maybe like the chaff was being separated from the wheat by the Ghost. They still have no idea who runs the Ghost Cartel."

Mei asked Hinke, "You think there's a connection to the Elder murder and the Anniston girls' disappearances? Nothing new on the kidnappings?"

"Unfortunately, no."

She followed up like she was a skilled interrogator. "Hollis tells me you had an old FBI case that might be related to what happened in Anniston?"

"A case in 1950 involving the murders of teenage twins up in Connecticut." *True.*

She lasered in and Hollis let her run with it. "You mean like the recent murders in Woodstock?"

"Teenage girls like the Brevards, but I've been unable to make a connection." *"A true pile of horseshit."*

Mei Delacroix wasn't done. "Do you still work on that old case, DH?"

"Not for a long time." *"Another pile of crap. God, how many lies am I going to have to tell?"*

Mei was no shrinking violet. She added softly but insightfully, "All these crimes could be related?"

Hinke deflected and grinned. "Hollis, maybe she needs to join you at APD?" They all laughed.

Hollis told Mei and Hinke, "Time to get home. Gotta be in court in the morning." Hinke paid the check, and they walked into the sounds of the Atlanta night. Hollis hailed two cabs. Before getting in their cab, the young detective stopped his older FBI friend and put his massive hand on his shoulder. "Hey, DH, you stay in touch. If you ever want to talk about anything, lemme know and visit anytime." Words Hinke realized would more typically have come from an experienced pro like himself to a younger man. Not the other way around.

He gave Hollis a wink and a hug. Mei Delacroix said, "Okay, my turn." Her hug he'd always remember.

In bed, Mei told her husband, "I like DH, but he told us a few fibs, and you know it."

"I know. I've got a couple ideas why he didn't give us the straight scoop. He's a good guy. He'll tell me in his own time."

"Hollis, all these murders and disappearances, they're related, aren't they, back to 1950?"

"Perhaps, and if that's true, that's a big burden DH is carrying by himself."

"Why by himself?"

"Umm, it just something he has to do alone."

He watched her beautiful breasts rise and fall as she sighed. "I'll pray for him."

"I will too, Mei. He's going to need a lot of them."

In his room in the Omni, Hinke walked to the mini-bar but hesitated and looked at the cardboard box. Then told himself, "If you're going to do this, DH, you've got to have your wits about you at all times." He shut the little refrigerator. He'd carried the box up to his room and was tempted to open it. Instead, he looked at himself in the full-length mirror on the wall. In his boxers, he stared at the now officially senior FBI agent who'd always done everything by the book—until he started playing the Game again. He wasn't proud of much he'd done recently but rationalized it was the only way he'd have a chance. He stared at the box but decided he was too tired to tackle it. He'd go at it full bore in the office tomorrow.

He was asleep in minutes but woke up in a panic. It was a nightmare he couldn't recall. He sat up, his chest hurting. He swallowed two nitroglycerin tablets. Finally, the sweat stopped, and the panic subsided. His heart slowed. His chest pain had eased. He got up and looked out the window of his thirtieth-floor room. It was nighttime but already early the next day. The big, bustling awakening city of Atlanta was their hiding place; he was sure of it.

Part 4

282

Chapter 47 – The Game is On Again

Four weeks later

Washington, DC

Derbert Hinke's office in the new FBI headquarters looked out onto E Street, the opposite side of the building from Pennsylvania Avenue. He missed gazing out on the grand street, though it was around the corner. Thanks to Helen, his new fourth-floor office was bigger than his old one at DOJ. It had that antiseptic, new smell—the paint, the leather on the chairs and couch, the lemony wood polish, and nary a hint of smoking. There was also a small conference table and chairs, a bank of empty bookshelves, a few potted plants (though he had no idea who would water them), and a tasteful cabinet where he stored a few bottles of his favorite booze. The only things truly important, though, were already elsewhere: in a file cabinet with its own combination lock.

Two weeks ago, he'd decided to set up shop in a more private location in the basement of the new FBI building. His current office became his break room where he could drink and pace while looking out on the city. As he sipped his Old Crow while staring out on the late afternoon traffic, he had decisions to make.

At least the storage room had an extra high ceiling that didn't set off his claustrophobia. And, without a phone, it was quiet. The john and the coffee were inconvenient, but it was good exercise walking back and forth down the hall and up a floor to both. He wanted and needed a spartan existence; his "war room" was the only place in the building where he took off his coat and tie. He couldn't leave the crème de la crème information—photographs, documents, notes, and evidence—out in broad daylight upstairs even if he had a locked office. He wanted to always be able to see any piece of key case stuff in front of him. Along with four long folding tables, he had one folding chair and two grease boards. Right now, his war room was a disaster with Styrofoam cups, soda cans, lunch wrappers, boxes, and paper napkins on the floor. One day, he'd have to break down and do a little cleaning—at least before the stuff got ankle-deep. Why Hinke was neat at home but elsewhere was a slob he attributed solely to him wanting to make a good impression on the babes he entertained in his Georgetown flat. He knew if his place was neat, if he cooked up a little dinner, if he had a good bottle of wine, he always got laid—even at his age.

Retired for nearly two years, it had taken Helen only one call to get him keys to the unmarked sub-basement storage room. A room completely off-the-grid, with no windows and no room number. Plus, she arranged a cushy teaching job at Georgetown Law funded by the FBI at full-time pay: "The First Amendment and Political Protest in the United States." Hinke hoped the heckling wouldn't be too brutal but was looking forward to his first class in a few weeks.

What would he have done without Helen in his life?

Helen had made it clear that no favor was ever too big—but also that she was otherwise in retirement. For the past few years, she'd made no sexual demands of him, and their once white-hot sex had fizzled to ashes. She knew that Hinke needed to be with women younger than her. He always had.

Helen spent a lot of time at her condo on the beach in Jacksonville, where she loved to fish, walk the beach, hunt shark teeth, and enjoy the sunny outdoors. She would pop back to DC from time to time, and the two longtime friends and lovers would eat dinner at Helen's and enjoy each other's company, but Helen liked her new freedom without the burden of J. Edgar Hoover, who never had a clue how influential she'd truly been.

It took two weeks of reviewing, organizing, and distilling key information. If viewed by an outsider, he probably look like a mad scientist in his laboratory.

He organized the photo table chronologically: several dozen photos from 1911 to the present day made his cut, with a nametag, location, and date of death for all deceased, showing the critical photos from each date. He'd never tallied the total but was struck that at least thirteen people (that he knew of) had either been murdered or committed suicide—or were tied to the kidnappings or deaths of the Abercrombie, Haverford, Blount, and Brevard twins. The Brevards' German shepherd was another casualty. The small Polaroids and photos had been blown up into eight-by-tens, but he'd not taken the risk of ordering enlarged copies for the most recent acquisitions from Cherokee County. He further divided the photographs into those left behind at the murder scenes—and others from law enforcement and other sources.

The idyllic beauty of the four sets of twins was remarkable. Heartbreaking that they were gone and never got a shot at living past their teen years. The post-mortem body positions of the Haverfords, Blounts, and Brevard twins were remarkably similar, as were the crucifix wounds cut into their bodies. To his best knowledge, none of the murder details ever became public— so there was no way they were done by a copycat.

On the evidence table, he laid out: the gold necklaces, which he was sure had belonged to the Abercrombies sixty years ago; the three pool balls (all from the Haverford Big Cottage but each found in a different location); the dog collar and most strikingly, the two sets of all black crosses. He wondered what had happened to their jewelry and clothes and other belongings. He'd bet a lot of money they became valued souvenirs. Now the killers' keepsakes.

The third table had his notes, case documents, FBI records, and police records from New Canaan, Woodstock, and Cherokee, as well as his records from 1911 in New Jersey and from Anniston. The fourth was his workspace, where he could examine and re-collate any of the information other than chronologically.

Hinke was on information overload. He had to bite the bullet and write a profile of these murderers, whom he was convinced were all linked for at least sixty-three years – and probably more than a century. He had a lot of disparate notes in his small notebook. It was time to boil it down and see what he had.

He needed to find actual evidence he could use.

With a damp rag, he wiped clean two of his whiteboards: one for his "profile" of the murderers and the other for what the hell he was going to do to find these murderers. At the top, he taped the "*Game of Twins* announcement" the killers had sent him. Even with the high ceiling, he started to get that yucky, semi-nauseous feeling he got in his old DOJ basement office. He needed a drink to relax. He headed toward the door, but in passing the black wooden crosses, two pairs each in clear plastic bags, he stopped.

Fascinating, horrible, evil things that frankly gave him the willies; he didn't like to handle them. In fact, he couldn't remember the last time he'd touched their wood surfaces. He forced himself to take the Haverford crosses out of their bags.

They were sixteen inches long and eight inches wide, each being about a half-inch thick. Both sets made of carved hardwood and painted with a black lacquer. Sharp, pointed ends on the vertical and horizontal portions of each cross.

He held the two black crosses, one in each hand. He'd never noticed the crossbars weren't the same. The crossbar on one was slightly higher than the other. On each was a notch. When he tried to slot them together, the first couple of attempts didn't work. He kept at it, and damn if the crosses didn't slot into one another, forming a new cross that resembled a shape akin to an *H* but with the crossbar extending past the sides with a thicker inner crossbar. The two black crosses formed one black double cross. He did the same with the Brevard crosses—another black double cross.

Simple puzzles, part of their *Game of Twins*.

He looked more carefully at the murder photos. In each of the body positions, a double cross was formed: their arms were out perpendicular from their bodies, and their hands were folded against each other. The Haverford twins on the pool table and the Blount twins on the stone slab, both indoors; the Brevard twins, outdoors. The three body positions were identical.

He yelled at the top of his lungs, "Derbert, you have been such a dumb piece of shit."

The black double cross. He could swear he'd seen a similar shape before. Over the past couple of years, Hinke realized from time to time that he had a hard time remembering things from distant and recent times. The thought that he might become like his mother, who had deteriorated over several years with dementia after she was seventy, frightened him. It seemed the harder he tried to remember something he should know, the further away it got. Then, later, it would pop back into his brain. Maybe he'd remember the unusual black double cross.

He had to find out more about it and its connection to the occult.

It took him the rest of the day to draft a profile of the *Game of Twins* killers:

-The victims are beautiful teenage TWINS ages 13-15; though the unsubs do not hesitate to kill others as collateral damage. No apparent relationship among any of them. *No idea how they were chosen.*

-Murders (likely of the Abercrombies, too, who were killed after being abducted in 1911) are all linked by common threads that only DH could understand.

-The murders require multiple people: probably at least two, maybe three individuals; they likely include a female.

-They are smart, organized, and highly disciplined. Are they taking on more risk with the latest murders? It seems to be escalating.

-They are arrogant beyond imagination, taunting and teasing law enforcement. *Psychopaths? Sociopaths?*

-The killers are persons of means. $ not part of the crimes.

-Killers are a closely knit group, sect, cult, family…? If a family or families, maybe they don't use the same names now?

-Twins murders are ritualistic "sacrifices" to an Evil? *But why?*

-Precise wounds on the girls' bodies required know-how; maybe killers are experts with knives: hunters, fishermen, other outdoors sportsmen, doctors, dentists, veterinarians, butchers, taxidermists, soldiers or military, police, others?

-Black double cross symbol is part of murders; their occult logo? *Where else does it appear?*

-*Games of Twins* is their own nomenclature; everything since the beginning has been about Games and Twins; *but what is their motive(s)?*

-The killers like their games—sick versions of scavenger hunts and hide-and-seek; they leave physical clues intentionally, most specifically for DH—that link all crimes:

Land/Polaroid pictures

Pool balls

Anniston Realty invitation

Dog's collar

Game of Twins announcement

Gold necklaces

-They left Land/Polaroid photos taken before/after twins were murdered in all murders (other than the 1911 kidnappings)—then hid them, usually in or around a nightstand at the murder scene.

-The world of the occult is woven into their Game. *How?*

-In the early 1950s, the killers moved from the New Canaan, CT area—and may now reside in an affluent area of Atlanta (or nearby) *Need Evidence!*

-Their house has an unusual lower-level custom floor and stone table (per the Blount photos*); Need Evidence!*

-They take souvenirs from the murder scenes; photos, clothes, jewelry, etc. are always missing and they likely hoard what they didn't use as breadcrumb clues; *Need Evidence!*

-They killed Matty Elder and may be in the drug trade in Atlanta? *Need Evidence!*

Hinke was formulating a plan to find evidence. He was getting a good picture of the killers but hadn't one solid lead. A lot of questions remained. One, though, he'd never asked, bugged him: *"Why was I chosen to be in their Game of Twins?"*

Hinke had no doubt they would kill again, the crimes occurring in 1911, then 1950, then last year, and now this year. Maybe they were ramping up for others. *Why the time intervals?*

He had to find them to stop more twins murders.

Chapter 48 – The Wiz

J. Edgar Hoover, with his prodigious faults, transformed a small ragtag bunch of men in the 1920s into a huge, professional law enforcement organization with over seven thousand special agents and ten thousand other personnel by 1970. He enabled the establishment of over fifty field offices and the FBI's Quantico training facility. But perhaps Hoover's most impressive legacy was the National Crime Information Center (NCIC) and its central data repository that cobbled together hundreds of information sources from local, state, national, and international levels—along with the reams of highly proprietary data collected daily by the Bureau. In 1967 Hoover hired Duncan Wiseman, AKA "The Wizard" or "Wiz," to set it up and gave him a carte blanche budget. By 1975, the NCIC was a light-year better than any crime database in the U.S. or internationally. The Wiz got dozens of calls daily.

Hinke had never met Duncan Wiseman and wasn't sure what to expect, but Wiseman didn't look like a nerd who spent his days buried deep in the bowels of the new building, surrounded by big computers. He looked more like a drill sergeant, with a thick muscular body and crew cut with a big, friendly smile.

Hinke knew nothing about computers but understood that if the data existed in the computer or wherever it could be sliced and diced to help answer questions and find needles in a haystack. And help solve crimes.

"You must have influential friends, Special Agent Hinke," he grinned, not adding, *to get a same-day appointment with me.*

Hinke smiled and took the wallet out of his back pocket. He hoped he had a couple left. He handed Wiseman one of his old FBI cards that read, "Special Agent Derbert Hinke, J. Edgar Hoover, Special Operations."

"Touché," Wiseman laughed.

"Thanks for seeing me on such short notice. Been working on a cold case for twenty-four years. Long story. I recently got a few new ideas. I now think the people who murdered twin girls back in 1950 lived in New Canaan, Connecticut, or thereabouts and now live in the Atlanta area—and have done more killings and kidnappings. Probably married and multiple family members, maybe multiple names. I believe that they are white and affluent. I think they moved south in the early 1950s. I'd need possible names and addresses, ages and whatever else I can get."

"The twin girls outside Atlanta, I'm guessing you think are related? Didn't I read a Negro man killed them?"

"He got killed in prison, and no, it didn't go down that way," Hinke told him flatly. Then added, "There are the twins who got snatched in Alabama last year as well. I'm sure they're dead. Same perpetrators."

Wiseman said, "1950 is reaching back, but there's a reasonable amount of archived case information in the database."

"I assure you there's none on the Haverford murders—and you won't have any information on the recent crimes, either, other than that the crimes occurred.

Wiseman's eyebrows jumped, and he replied, "I see." He leaned back in his chair. "Should I assume there's a good reason to keep this data in the dark?"

"Multiple good reasons. Call me DH."

"They call me the Wiz, but not sure I deserve it."

The Wiz continued, "The good news is that I can probably get you the aggregated, that is, summary, data of people fitting your description. The bad news is that I can't give you any list that identifies actual names. Director Hoover got me in a heap of trouble when he told me to use US Census data to help on what he called his Official and Confidential files; many, I'm sure, were used for blackmail purposes—or worse. The Director of the Bureau of Census got wind of it, and I was the one who got dressed down. It's verboten per Title 13 US Code for even the FBI to access personal-level census data. Aggregated, no problem, but that's not what you want."

Hinke didn't know about Title 13 restrictions, but that made some sense.

"Hypothetically, though, such a list could be created?"

"Yes, but it's time-consuming— even with the Census Bureau being the most sophisticated user of computers in the government. You see the stacks of punch cards around my office?"

The Wiz tossed him a six-inch stack wrapped with rubber bands. That's data for a small piece of one FBI file case."

This time, Hinke raised his eyebrows.

"But we're moving to digital storage on magnetic tape, which will help the computer storage issue immensely."

Hinke hadn't a clue what the Wiz was talking about. He asked, "Maybe the aggregated numbers could help me get an idea of how many people I might be looking at?"

"Let me see what I can do. I have a new intern who I think would love to tackle this. It could mean looking at four census years: 1940, 1950, and possibly both 1960 and 1970. Could take a couple weeks, assuming I can convince Census that we're not doing anything nefarious with their sacred data. Of course, my intern could misinterpret my request, and Hoover is no longer around." The Wiz gave Hinke a wink and smiled at him.

He told Hinke, "In the not-too-distant future, you'll have a small computer and monitor, like a TV screen, on your desk and be able to pull up an answer like that yourself in seconds."

Hinke frowned. "No way."

"You might be surprised."

"Thanks, Wiz. What's your alcohol of choice?"

"Scotch, single malt, preferably Glen Fohdry."

Chapter 49 – Black Double Crosses

Back in his office, Hinke called the Theology Department at Georgetown and identified himself. In turn, he was immediately directed to Dr. Lincoln Radcliffe, a historian with a longtime interest in Christian and religious symbolism.

If these black "double crosses" were as unusual as he thought, he hoped they would point him toward the murderers. He no longer doubted that the world of the occult was woven into these murders—a place he'd balked at investigating for twenty-four years. It creeped him out, and he would fess up to that. He'd had supernatural encounters with the Haverford twins' apparitions in the Big Cottage, then the Blount twins in the basement of the rental house in Anniston. The Brevard girls he'd seen floating above the outdoor stone table in Woodstock.

Had he truly come to grips with the world of the unseen? Encounters that impinged on his once-solid worldview? Encounters he certainly couldn't admit to anyone at the FBI. Or was he a pussy who didn't want to enter the fray between Good and Evil?

He had to put on his big boy panties.

It was a hot, muggy May day in the District of Columbia. Barely halfway there, Hinke had pitted out his dress shirt; he covered that up with his blue, pinstriped, seersucker suit coat. The walk over to Georgetown University was less than a half mile from his modest third-floor flat.

As a George Washington University undergrad and Law School grad, he'd always been a bit jealous of Georgetown and its hoity-toity reputation and beautiful campus. Regardless, he'd always loved walking up the Hilltop, with its distinctive neo-medieval style architecture and incredible views looking down on the Potomac and Northern Virginia suburbs and the District. The campus was quiet; school was out for the summer. He asked a young woman if she could direct him to the Department of History. She politely told him to go straight up toward Healy Hall and hang a left. He'd see the sign.

With a patrician name like Lincoln Radcliffe, the professor wasn't what he'd envisioned. He was barely five feet, with long white locks combed back into a ponytail, big tortoise shell glasses, and a generous potbelly. To say that his small office was cluttered would be an understatement. Made Hinke feel better about his basement office disaster. Several file cabinets, bookcases, and stacks of papers surrounded him. There was one rickety side chair in addition to Radcliff's ancient office chair. The professor didn't apologize for the mess.

"Have a seat, Agent Hinke. Cup of coffee?"

"Sure, if you're having one, and call me DH."

The little man scurried out saying, "Back in a jiff."

As promised, the professor was back in a few minutes with two steaming cups of coffee. "New pot," he said with gusto, sitting behind his big desk, not a square inch uncovered. Hinke could barely see him via the tunnel formed by papers and books in the middle of his desk.

The professor tapped a healthy pinch of tobacco into his cherrywood pipe and re-lit it with a huge gold lighter. "DH, cross symbols is a big topic going back more than a couple thousand years. How much time do you have?" he asked with a chuckle.

Hinke cut to the chase. He opened his small briefcase and pulled out the two black crosses from the Haverford murders and handed them both to the professor.

"These aren't any old crosses, Professor. I'm on Social Security, and the FBI is going to put me out to pasture sooner than later. In my spare time, off and on, I take another look at cold cases, especially those I didn't solve. This case was assigned to me twenty-four years ago by J. Edgar Hoover himself."

Radcliffe's eyes lit up. "How fascinating!"

"Crosses like these were part of at least three sets of horrific murders. Are you squeamish, Professor?"

"Hate snakes and Dobermans, but no."

Hinke wouldn't be surprised if a viper were crawling around in this office mess; no one would know. He handed him an enlarged photo of the Haverford girls on the pool table, the final photo. Professor Radcliffe was transfixed for several moments and then put the photo down.

Hinke gave him the short version of the Haverford murders in New Canaan. "By the way, that photograph was taken by the murderers. They left us early Land Polaroids. Nasty people did this and are yanking my chain. I saw six cross symbols at the crime scene: the two individual wooden black crosses, the crosses carved into each of their bodies, and their individual body positions themselves. But clearly, there are two more."

There was barely enough room on the professor's cluttered desk. He fit the two crosses together and put the result in front of the professor.

"Here's another."

Then he pointed toward the death photo: their bodies lengthwise, and a single crossbar formed by their arms, thicker in the interior joined together, mimicking the black double cross.

"No idea why it took me twenty-four years to put the crosses together. Other than I'm a dumbass, and I've always been frightened by the crosses."

The professor couldn't help but chuckle. "DH, I'm thinking you're not a dumbass. This unusual double cross is frightening."

"Have you ever seen anything like it?"

The little man popped out of his chair and rolled a footstool in front of a tall, overpacked bookcase. He pulled out a book, then moved his stool and retrieved a couple more. Back behind his desk, the professor thumbed through the three books. Then he talked a mile a minute—not as fast as Hoover used to, but at a serious clip. He spoke and gesticulated while Hinke tried to listen and understand.

"Ah, here's what I was looking for!" Radcliffe exclaimed.

 "In simplest terms, your cross is two cojoined Passion crosses. Also called the Cross of Suffering, with the four sharp points, the three nails in Christ, and the spear impaled in His side. A crucifix without a likeness of Christ."

He turned the book around to show Hinke and pointed out several shapes and sizes of the Passion cross.

Hinke told him, "I did a little of my own research into that shape years ago, but it meant nothing to me then."

"Then there's the Obelisk from the days of ancient Egypt, which became incorporated into several symbols, including the present-day Candara font punctuation marks used in liturgical and non-liturgical texts. A specific use: if put immediately before or after the name of a deceased person, it means everlasting life. Double crosses, dual crosses, shown side by side are not uncommon in religious architecture."

Hinke nodded. "Close Very close."

The professor picked up another book and thumbed to the page he wanted. "Here's another similar shape to your black double cross."

"It's on the ceiling of Serres Church, a thousand-year-old church in Rennes-le-Chateau, France, which hundreds of years ago was connected to the Knights of Templar. The Templars used dozens of their own symbols besides their signature red cross going back to the eleventh century. But there's much mystery when, and if they disappeared after being tossed out by the Pope.

"Your black-double-cross symbol, from what I can see, is unique but is likely a cousin or amalgam of others. Twins are held in high regard in most cultures and religions, indicating additional power or strength of parents and the twins themselves. My best guess: the twins were part of a sexual ritual, a type of sacrifice, with the thicker inner crossbar indicating they are honored and will be cojoined together through eternity. In this case, maybe Hell as paradise."

The professor picked up the black-double-cross and stared at it. "Yes, it's a strong symbol of Evil. Maybe making sport of what they see as inferior Christianity. In a sick way, it's Evil's own twins. Anyway, that's my two cents."

Hinke pondered, and the professor continued, "This happened, again, didn't it, DH? Murders of twins? I remember hearing about the twins murdered outside Atlanta. I don't remember reading how it happened. I thought the suspected murderer was a black man who got killed in jail?"

Hinke told him directly, "His name was Orville Johnston, but no, he didn't kill the twins, who were found in the exact same position—with black crosses."

The professor nodded without asking a question.

"Professor, do you believe in the supernatural—you know, ghosts and witches and other occult shit?"

Radcliffe chuckled. With his hands, the professor re-combed his white hair several times. "I believe in a good God and that He's supernatural. And, I guess, yes, there's an Evil constantly battling against Him, hopefully on our behalf. But I can't say I've had a close encounter with a spirit or seen voodoo magic or watched a witch cast spells. But supernatural things on either side of the ledger or especially if caught in the middle, they're more likely than not. Other dimensions of the supernatural? How about you, DH? Do you believe in the supernatural?"

Hinke smiled. "Most of my life I thought it was malarkey, but's that's all changed." He told him about his encounters with the twins and added, "Yeah, being a Catholic I always believed in God—sort of, at least. The Devil I wasn't too sure of. Seemed like God was kicking plenty of tail already without needing a Devil. That would be piling on."

The professor laughed heartily.

But Hinke's brow furrowed. "I do believe whoever did these murders is pure Evil. My journey to find that Evil started for me in New Canaan, Connecticut, a long time ago."

The professor said, "I've got a friend at Yale who's written books about the history of witchcraft in New England. He's the go-to-guy. I'll give him a call to introduce you."

"Thanks, Professor. I was thinking about a visit to Connecticut."

"Be careful, Agent Hinke—of the black-double-cross symbol. Like you, I believe it came straight from Hell."

Walking back with his coat off and his necktie in his briefcase, his shirt sleeves rolled up, Hinke was steamy and frustrated about the black-double-cross. He'd seen it before. Where? It was driving him batty.

He wasn't positive but believed the killers lived in an expensive Atlanta home with an unusual red and black stone floor and stone table that were put in after they arrived in the 1950s. An existing or new home with a basement floor—a house they still lived in today. They might own multiple homes, but only one had the unique stone floor.

He was on his third or fourth cup of coffee. He'd lost track. He paced his basement office. He'd looked at the crime scene photos dozens of times. Trying to divine what he'd missed.

He kept coming back to the three small Polaroids of Cherry and Merry Blount found in Orville Johnston's bible. One while the twins were standing partially clothed in front of the massive stone slab and the other two while they lay naked on the shiny rock deathbed. One when they were obviously alive and one after they'd been murdered with the black crosses impaled into their sex. Each photo was taken at a slightly different angle. But he wasn't interested in the twins. He was interested in the floor with its intricate patterns of red and black squares. He tried to use his readers with a magnifying glass. He needed help.

He needed the FBI Crime Lab to discretely blow up the photos and take the bodies out of the enlargements. He'd been around a long time but didn't have a heavy hitter contact who'd be willing to do that, off the record. He called Helen, whom he thought was in her Florida condo. No answer. He left a short message.

An hour later, she called him back.

"How's your tan?" he quipped.

"Derby, this old lady doesn't need to get leatherier. I like the sun, but I'm usually covered up—and always with my cute fishing cap."

"Helen, you always look cute. Caught anything today?"

"Went out in the deep water this morning with a few others. Hooked a nice Cobia, about twenty pounds. Should be good eat'n as the Floridians say. "What's up in your world?"

"I'm getting closer, but no persons-of-interest. I think they live in a ritzy section of Atlanta—and have an unusual black and red stone basement floor and stone altar where they killed the girls from Anniston. Checking out a couple other things, too. I need a favor, though. I need to get the Polaroids from those murders enlarged—confidentially, without them getting into the system."

"Let me make a call, and I'll get back to you by 5:00 p.m."

"Helen, you're best, and you always have been. Thank you. You coming back to DC anytime soon?"

"Maybe—I'll let you know. Goodbye, Derby."

Chapter 50 – The Enlargements

The following day, Jacob Knabb, the assistant director of the FBI's Crime Lab, welcomed Hinke into his office. Knabb was forty-ish, well-groomed with slicked-back, jet-black hair. He wore glasses with black rims and had an intelligent glimmer in his eyes, not unlike the Wiz.

With a smirk, he said, "You must have friends in high places, Special Agent Hinke. What can I do for you?"

"Call me DH. I need enlargements of these three Polaroids," which he spread out on his desk. "Horrific, I know; they're part of a murder investigation. The pictures, I can't risk seeing the light of day, at least not yet. I think whoever murdered these girls has murdered other sets of twins over several decades. I had no leads for twenty-three years—until last year. If this were to become a full-fledged FBI investigation of multiple murders, I'd never catch up with them. No one would. The Bureau, I'm sorry to say, would fuck it up."

Knabb smiled knowingly. He picked up each and looked at them carefully. "Okay, I can do that and, yes, they are grisly."

"I'd like a couple color sets of each—then a couple more sets with the bodies blocked out if you could do that so that I can show only the floor to others."

As he nodded affirmatively, Hinke said, "I don't know my rocks real well. Do you have any idea what type of stone that might be?"

Knabb picked up one of the photos and walked over to a scope that was on his sofa credenza. He peered down at one color Polaroid. As Knabb looked at the Polaroid, Hinke commented, "The people who I think had the table and floor made have unlimited money, if that's any help."

Knabb concentrated on the Polaroid. "Maybe granite, but I'll look at the enlargements. Granite floors are unusual since, besides being pricey, granite can get slippery."

Out of his briefcase, Hinke pulled two black crosses, fit them together, and put them on Knabb's desk. "If you could get a handle on the repeating black and red pattern. Is this double-cross part of the design? God knows, my eyes aren't good enough to tell."

Knabb nodded yes and added sardonically, "This was no ordinary home renovation, and it took a serious stonemason. Let me check who might be in a couple of our databases. Give me a few days, and I'll let you know what I find."

Hinke stood and shook hands. "Can't thank you enough."

Knabb smiled. "You will let me know when you catch the bad guys?"

"I promise."

Hinke spent a week in the office on pins and needles, but no word yet from the Crime Lab or the data guys. Knabb finally gave him a call. The Crime Lab director told him, "Ninety percent sure that the floor and table are granite; honestly, I've never heard of a basement floor made of granite, but that's what it looks like. A bit unclear because there are only pieces of the floor in the photos, but, yes, I think the black cross designs are consistent with the photograph you gave me."

Hinke asked, "How many other basement floors in Atlanta do you think are constructed of granite and with such a design?"

"My best guess? Zero."

Hinke concurred. "I need to find where that floor is. Or find who built it."

Knabb was a step ahead and handed Hinke a short list of businesses, wholesale and retail, that had done granite work around Atlanta over the last couple of decades.

Hinke thanked him. "I'll take it from here."

It was a high-end granite floor and table with the black double cross pattern. He almost whistled on the way out. Tracing the floorwork back to a specific company or stonemason—he knew that was a longshot. But it was worth a try. If he could find the house, he was confident there'd be more evidence of the crimes.

Chapter 51 – Caroline

Hinke needed help and needed a person whom he could trust implicitly, which he'd never been good at. Caroline Knopfler, besides being a tall blonde beauty, was smart and eager to learn how to get ahead in the Bureau. It had been several months since their chance encounter when she'd helped him find info on Matty Elder. A couple months later he called her to have drinks in Georgetown. He asked how she liked the Bureau.

"Interesting place but more chauvinistic than I could have imagined."

Hinke laughed. "Hard to argue with that."

It was clear she hated her supervisor. *Maybe if she could be elsewhere in the Bureau?*

Hinke decided to ask him straight up and walked into his second-floor office unannounced. Her supervisor was Special Agent Karl Trask, a sour-faced doughboy—of indeterminant age.

"Karl, I do Special Operations work, and a colleague mentioned that Caroline Knopfler might be a good fit to do legwork for me on a couple field cases."

Trask couldn't help his sneering smile. "Ah, Miss Knopfler. Nice legs and a nice piece of ass. I once asked her if she'd polish my knob, but the bimbo refused. Female agents are a joke. You want her; you got her. Maybe you'll be luckier than me getting a blowjob..."

Hinke thought, *What a dipshit. Why would anyone want to work for you?*

He got her transferred. Caroline worked solely for him.

She hadn't planned on a relationship with an older guy, but it happened. Breaking many rules, she knew her new boss could care less about; one of the many things she liked about him.

How she came to be involved with a man thirty-five years her senior, Caroline couldn't explain to her friends and certainly no one at the FBI—much less attempt telling her parents, both younger than Derbert Hinke. She was a big girl, no Pollyanna. She'd made the mistake of dating a few special agents since she joined the Bureau six years ago—though it was against the rules. After those short-lived forays, she'd decided to become a nun for a year until Derbert Hinke bought her a drink in Georgetown. Her vow went out the window that night. It wasn't like she was looking for a guy, much less an older guy, but she fell head over heels for an agent who was getting Social Security. He was unmarried and unattached, handsome, gentle, kind, funny, intelligent, and sexually skilled beyond anything she'd ever experienced. At this point in her life, he was the perfect boyfriend— and the perfect guy to mentor her as an agent.

Helen had called him to say hi after the Brevard cases. He gave her a quick update and then told her he was seeing a woman at the Bureau. Long ago, Helen had told him that he could have any private life he wanted except marriage. She knew her powers over Derby only went so far, especially when she wasn't seeing him often. Helen kidded him good-naturedly and said, "I'll bet she's younger than me." Hinke didn't have the heart to say, *Yep, nearly a half-century*. Helen gave him one warning. "The people you're after, Derby, they sound dangerous. You need to be careful what she knows about your investigations, lest she become part of this game you talk about."

Hinke told her, "I will." He knew that he had to be careful with Hollis Delacroix as well.

Chapter 52 - The Stonemason Search

June 7, 1974

Canton, Georgia

Hinke had given Caroline the best two enlargements and the list of stonemasons around Atlanta to see what she could find out. After a couple days driving around in sweltering pre-summer heat, she'd come up with nothing—until she reached the second to last name on the list: Stoney's Stonecraft in Canton, Georgia, thirty miles north of Atlanta. She was melting in her suit coat, and so she took it off and tossed it on the seat. She grabbed her briefcase. She looked through the window and didn't see anyone, but the door handle worked. In the small, dusty office, she heard loud banging in the back. She opened the door to the adjoining room. An elderly black man had a chisel and hammer in hand. He was working on a long piece of rock.

He saw her out of the corner of his eye, flipped off his goggles, and turned toward her. Surprised, an understatement.

She walked up and stuck out her hand. "Hi, I'm Special Agent Knopfler of the FBI." The thick older guy, dressed in jeans and a dusty long-sleeved shirt, put down his tools.

"I'm Stoney. I ain't done nut'n."

"I'm not looking for you, Stoney; I'm looking for a stone floor."

"Ma'am?"

"I'm trying to find out who crafted this floor. It's important." She pulled two photographs (the ones with the bodies cut out) from her briefcase and put them on a nearby worktable strewn with tools.

"We're thinking this floor, and the table are granite. What do you think?"

He refocused on the photos.

"Yeah, It's granite. Nice stone from overseas. Impressive work; a lot of panels needed cutt'n to get a pattern like that for the floor and table, if that's what it is."

"We think this floor got put in an Atlanta house in the 1950s."

"It was 1951."

Caroline's eyes popped wide open. "And you know that how?"

"I knew the guy who made it."

She couldn't stop herself from exclaiming, "Really?"

"Lyle Brown. We did a few jobs together, but not that one. He showed me a picture of it once before it was done. Big job down in one of the rich parts of Atlanta."

"Do you know where Lyle is these days?"

"He was murdered in an alley in Buckhead around the holidays in 1951. Throat cut. Never found the killers. Lyle carried around a lot of cash. Cops said it was a robbery-murder."

Caroline immediately doubted that. "We think that murders happened on the granite table over the years; likely, the people who own the house are the killers."

He nodded.

"Did Lyle have any family?"

"Maybe, never talked about any; he did a lot of work here but lived in Asheville and often went back on weekends. Photography, his hobby."

"North Carolina?"

"Yes, ma'am."

"Anything else you can tell me about him that might be helpful?"

"He was strictly cash and carry."

She said, "I was afraid of that."

She handed him her card. "Will you call me if you remember anything else about Lyle?"

"Sure will. Hope you get whoever killed him and the others. ma'am, I sure didn't know the FBI had agents like you."

She grinned. "You mean female? There aren't a whole lot of us in the field yet. There aren't a whole of blacks either. But one day, there will be a lot more of us. Well, Stoney, you have the perfect name, and I appreciate your help." She shook his hand and left.

Back at her Atlanta hotel, Caroline took a quick shower and then called DH, who was in the office. Trying not to sound too excited, she told him, "The granite floor was put in an expensive house in Atlanta in 1951. That's confirmed by a stonemason in Canton who knew him."

"That's great! A name or address?"

"Not yet." Then she took a leap. "I think the killers murdered the guy who made the floor. His name was Lyle Brown. He was from Asheville but did stonemasonry work in Atlanta back in the day. He got killed in an alley in Buckhead in November 1951. Throat cut. I dooubt coincidental. I'm guessing he figured out what the table was for."

Hinke smiled. "Interesting hypothesis. You are pretty amazing, Miss Knopfler."

"I need to get to Ashville tomorrow and get on it."

"Ever been there?"

"Nope. Isn't that where F. Scott Fitzgerald hung out?"

"It is. I'll have a reservation made for you at the Grove Park Inn. You'll love it. Oh, and if the room is available, I'll make sure you get it.

"What?"

"You'll see. Have a good trip."

Hinke put a call into the Wiz, who said, "It's still in progress."

"That's fine. I wanted to let you know that I've confirmed these people moved into a big house in Atlanta, proper, in 1951. Does that help?"

"It does. I'll keep you posted."

The following day, June 8, 1974

Asheville

It was pleasantly cool in the mountains of North Carolina when she arrived by plane, got a rental car, and headed to the Grove Park Inn. The majestic stone hotel was stunning; she'd never seen anything like it. Inside, the mammoth fireplaces facing each other across the huge lobby were astounding. When she checked in, the friendly hotel clerk told her, "Ah, you're staying in the Pink Lady Room, 545. Enjoy!"

After checking in, she sat down at the huge wood bar backed by twenty yards of mirror and dark polished wood. She asked the studly bartender, "What's up with the Pink Lady Room?"

His smile widened. "Ah, I'll give you the Cliffs Notes version, but first, let me make you a Pink Lady."

She looked at her watch. Too late to get started on her mission today. He came back with a pink cocktail in a martini glass.

She took a sip. "Oh my, that's yummy. What's in it?"

"Maybe after you drink another one, I'll tell you."

"Make me another."

Now, with two drinks in front of her, the bartender asked, "Do you believe in ghosts?"

"No."

He smiled. "Well, the story of the Pink Lady is fanciful, but it's said she was a beautiful young woman in the 1920s who, shortly after the inn opened, plunged to her death from the balcony of Room 545— before all construction was finished. Perhaps she was meeting an older married man who told her their affair was over and made a leap? Or she a debutante who drunkenly walked out onto the roof and slipped? Or, who knows? Regardless, she's a benevolent ghost seen by many as a mist or apparition but apparently enjoys playing pranks like opening all the windows on a winter night or rearranging items in the room.

Caroline said, "Wow, that's cool."

"You're here by yourself?"

"On business."

"What kind?"

"Interior designer. Came to explore…"

"Well, you're in the right place. I'll have your second Pink Lady sent to your table."

She replied, "That would be quite lovely," those words strung together by her for the first time. She wondered if Fitzgerald's ghost also still roamed the halls. Dinner was better than tasty. She had a nightcap outdoors where the air was chilly, and thought to herself, *"This place is marvelous. I need to come here with DH."* She slept like a baby in Room 545.

The next morning, after a sumptuous breakfast that included a bacon and cheddar omelet, fresh fruit, Danish, and coffee, her game plan was to check out local businesses that did stonework and then hit the phone book for all the "Browns." Both longshots, she knew. The idea of cold-calling the forty-three Browns was mind-numbing. She debated role-playing versus being an FBI agent but nixed that—in case she did find a lead. She'd give the minimal information and take it from there: she was investigating an old murder case of Lyle Brown, a stonemason who had made his home in Ashville and died in 1951 in Atlanta. She was trying to contact any business acquaintances or family who might have known Lyle or know where any of his business records or possessions might be.

There were more than a dozen businesses in town that did granite custom countertops, backsplashes, counters, shower walls, and other household stuff—primarily for kitchens and bathrooms. Only a few were open on Sunday. Those she talked to were friendly and apologetic but didn't know Lyle Brown. Discouraged and tired at the end of the afternoon, she wondered why she hadn't thought about granite headstones and burial slabs. She stopped at the next gas station, which had an outdoor phone booth and phone book. On a lark, without even calling, she headed for Zion's Headstones on the outskirts of town. An unimpressive business front but a cute white country house adjacent.

He was out back with his chisel and mallet, working on a beautiful flat piece of granite.

"Are you Zion?"

A spindly, grey-bearded black guy turned, took off his safety glasses, and asked, "Who wants to know?"

Caroline introduced herself and began her introductory schpiel.

He stopped her. In a slow southern accent, he told her, "Name's Zion Koubek. Lyle was my uncle on my mom's side."

He offered her a seat at a small table. On his wall, she noticed a framed Purple Heart and asked, "Army?"

He nodded, and she said, "My dad has one of those, too, but he'll never talk about it."

"I won't either."

She figured what the heck and put the photos (without the bodies) in front of him on the table. "Your uncle we know built this stone floor and table in a house in Atlanta twenty-three years ago. We believe the same people who own the house killed two girls—and maybe more— on the granite slab. And likely killed Lyle. Did you or anyone in your family keep anything of your uncle's personal or financial records, tax returns, bank statements, client information, diary, photos…anything?"

"Ma'am, Uncle Lyle sure loved his granite. I remember his shop got sold after he passed. I don't know if there's anything of Lyle's left. He hesitated. "There's one person who might know, but it might be better if I ask her. Lyle had a daughter—my cousin, Maybelle. She's a strange woman who always carries a gun."

"Good to know. Any help would be appreciated."

"Why don't you give me until tomorrow morning to see what I can find?"

"That would be great." She gave him her card and said, "You can reach me at the Grove Park Inn."

He chided, "My tax dollars at work," and she winked at him.

Back at the hotel, she kicked off her dreadful heels and collapsed on her bed. Maybe she could catch DH before he left work.

"Hi, from Asheville."

"How's the Grove Park?"

"Better than spectacular."

"See the Pink Lady yet?"

"Not yet. Fun story."

She was sure he'd say no but asked him, "DH, do you believe in ghosts?"

"Absolutely."

She wasn't sure if he was pulling her leg or not and replied, "Okay, I'll keep my eyes peeled. I may be onto a good lead. I found Lyle Brown's uncle, the stonemason who built the floor…"

"And…?"

"He's going to check with a relative and get back to me, hopefully by midday tomorrow, to see if anyone kept any of Lyle's stuff."

"Maybe we'll get lucky. Sleep well."

"I will unless the Pink Lady visits."

He chuckled and said, "Oh, by the way, I'll be in Connecticut tomorrow morning. Probably back by noon the next day. If you can get back by the day after tomorrow, let's rendezvous at my place for an early dinner. I'll pick up food I know you'll like. We can compare notes."

Caroline giggled. "Oh, I expect more than just dinner."

"Yes, ma'am." He felt his cock twinge as he hung up.

Caroline slept great and hadn't bothered to set an alarm. She debated going on a run around the beautiful hilly property and golf course below the hotel. Instead, she got up and took a long, hot shower and pondered what wonderful breakfast she would eat this morning.

She toweled off and walked out of the bathroom naked to fetch a clean pair of undies. She was taken aback seeing her standing, gazing out the window. The Pink Lady turned and smiled.

"Such a glorious morning," she said.

"That it is."

The comely apparition in a long pink dress grinned. "I'm sorry to have startled you."

"It's okay; I'm pleased to meet you. I could have breakfast brought up."

"Ah, thank you. I never stay long."

"You don't always come at night?"

"Not always. And the view this morning is spectacular. You are beautiful."

Caroline blushed and turned to her bed to pick up the towel and wrap herself.

When she turned back, the Pink Lady was gone.

"Damn," exclaimed Caroline, and told herself, "DH will never believe it."

The next day, she met Zion at noon in the lobby. All he'd told her on the phone was, "I found a few photos that you might want to see."

She was pacing when he arrived in his work clothes. She asked, "Could I order you a drink? Or we could eat lunch."

"Thanks, but I need to get back to work."

He handed her a manilla folder. "I hope you find out who killed Lyle."

He walked out, and she went to the bar before opening the envelope. The same bartender was at his post. She said, "The usual."

He grinned and turned to mix her drink.

She took a deep breath and opened the envelope. There were five crystal-clear eight-by-ten color photographs of Lyle Brown's work: the killers' basement floor taken from different angles at different stages of construction, including one when it looked finished and one looking down on the granite table. Ten times better than either the Polaroids or the enlargements DH showed her. He was going to go apeshit.

She was looking out at one of the mammoth fireplaces when the bartender put a napkin and Pink Lady cocktail in front of her.

For grins, she asked the bartender, "Shall I tell you about my extraordinary encounter with the Pink Lady this morning?"

He did a double-take and smiled.

"If you will, I'll join you for the next Pink Lady round."

319

Chapter 53 – Connecticut Witchery

June 10, 1974

New Haven, Connecticut

Things were looking up. The following day, Hinke flew from National to New Haven to see if Radcliffe's professor friend at Yale could shed more light on the crosses—and the occult angle—that he'd pussied out on for years. Then he'd drive the Gold Coast of Connecticut back to LaGuardia with a stop in New Canaan and maybe stay the night. What was it about the town that both compelled and repelled him?

Thaddeus Cornwall was associate director of the School of Divinity at Yale University. Witchcraft in its heyday during the last half of the seventeenth century was his expertise; he'd written three books on the subject as it related to Christian doctrine of the day.

Dr. Cornwall looked the part. Tall, thin, and angular. Ichabod Crane-ish. His dark-paneled office was as immaculate as Radcliffe's was messy. Hinke expected a dreary theologian, but that wasn't what he got.

Cornwall gave him a friendly handshake and offered a chair at his large conference table, where they both sat. "How is Lincoln these days?"

"I only spent a couple hours with him; he's a jovial, intelligent man who loves his symbols."

"That he does. So, an FBI agent wants to know more about witchcraft and the occult? Seems a bit incongruous."

Hinke showed a slight grin. "A practicing Catholic growing up, I'd never given the possibility of supernatural presences much thought—ghosts, witches, angels, and the like. Then that all changed…"

"Few people have had a supernatural encounter, but I'm guessing you did."

"Yes, my first was when I started investigating the murder case of the Haverford twin girls in New Canaan in 1950."

"I remember; a schoolteacher murdered them."

"I'm positive he didn't. A couple weeks after their deaths, I saw their ghosts in the cottage where they were murdered. And then other supernatural occurrences in the cottage as well. I'll abbreviate the story. I saw twins who disappeared—and I know are dead—in the basement of a house in Anniston, Alabama. Then a few weeks ago when investigating the murders of the Brevard twins outside Atlanta, I saw ghosts of those girls hovering above the big stone slab where they were murdered outdoors. In the distance I also saw three dark-hooded figures looking down at me from a bluff. I don't believe they were ghosts, but I do believe they were pure Evil. I also believe they killed the twins."

"Agent Hinke, you are indeed a fortunate man to have had multiple encounters. I'm jealous."

"You've not experienced a supernatural happening?"

"Regretfully, not to date."

"I shied away from believing that the occult could be part of these murders, and you can imagine what would happen to me if I were to bring this up in the hallowed halls of the FBI. Once I brought up the subject in the presence of Hoover and nearly got fired. Professor, what was it about Colonial America—for witchcraft to be such a big deal?"

After a moment he said, "Do you know what the most virulent witchery area was in the late seventeenth century?"

Hinke grinned. "Trick question. It's here and not Salem."

"Correct. It was a time when people, particularly in the northeast colonies, believed scripture, literally, according to how elite leaders of the day wanted them to believe it—as a matter of social control. The idea of truth and the little science of the day were held in disrepute. In fact, seen as Evil itself. Too unmooring for the ignorant masses. Fear, the Christian leaders believed, was the best way to keep the minions under their thumb.

"The idea of witchcraft and witchery had been around for centuries in Europe. Versions were imported from across the pond, and at that point in early American history, the powers-that-be used it to stoke fear while professing they would protect citizens from these boogeymen—and eliminate them whenever advantageous. As the colonies grew and became, shall we say, more cosmopolitan, witch hysteria faded and eventually died out."

"You don't think witches and the supernatural were there back then—or now?"

"I do but perhaps in forms few of us recognize or understand."

"Like they are biding their time?" Hinke asked. He got no answer, then out of his briefcase he pulled the two black crosses used in the recent Brevard murders.

The professor's eyes opened wide.

"These two black crosses were used in the recent murders of twins, Mareissa and Matilde Brevard, in Woodstock, Georgia."

Hinke slotted them together and held them up.

"Professor, have you ever seen a black double cross, a symbol, like this? Your friend at Georgetown showed me a few old cross symbols but none exactly matched these."

He took his time. "No, I don't think so. Unusual, to say the least."

Hinke told him, "Since 1950, at least three sets of female twins have been murdered: their bodies laid out as crosses and crosses carved into their bodies. I believe there was another set in 1911. The worst of it—these crosses were impaled in their vaginas as sacrificial exclamation points."

The professor's eyebrows lifted again, and then Cornwall told his story.

"Many years ago, I ran across a diary from around 1690. The woman who wrote it, Clarice Willis, begged her father to tell her what he knew about the infamous witch executions in New Haven. She wrote down a story that I was never able to verify about a beautiful New Haven woman who was burned at the stake after being acquitted of witchery. I was interested because it has been widely accepted that convicted witches were only executed by hangings. But she was acquitted. Her case was dismissed by a judge who was said to have relations with her.

"That night after the trial, a mob formed outside her house—demanding her to come out. She did, then waved her hand, extinguishing all torches and frightening the mob. She told them to leave or suffer the consequences but was shot in the arm and then dragged to a field outside town. Her teenage twins escaped through an underground pantry in their house. They watched from afar as their mother was crucified and burned. A black cross was part of the execution. With dogs, the mob caught up with the girls, who were assumed to be witches themselves. One was killed, but the other was rescued by an Indian brave who helped her murder the mob's leader. She escaped into the woods and disappeared."

The story was jarring.

The professor gave him a moment.

"The end of the story in the diary was that a few months later, other twin girls were kidnapped from a nearby town in an Indian raid. Found dead the next morning half eaten by animals."

"What were their names, the New Haven women?"

"The mother was Abigail, the twin who got away, I think, Pamela. I can't recall the other. Maybe Priscilla? No last name in the diary story, which remains unverified.

Hinke was silent for a minute, then said: "Revenge. It's about revenge. At least that's how it started."

Driving the Merritt Parkway from New Haven back down the Gold Coast, Hinke was finally finding his bearings in the Game of Twins—twenty-four damn years after the Haverford twins were murdered. He took 123 and headed toward New Canaan. But wasn't sure it was the best way.

No gas stations to be seen; he turned into Pauline's Antiques' small gravel parking lot. There was an "Open" sign on the door. He entered but saw no one. It was bigger than it looked from the outside but not overly packed with old, dusty stuff. More like a large room in a well-decorated old home. And lots of windows, unlike other dark, dingy antique stores he'd been in.

An attractive, petite woman, maybe fifties, with short brown hair, appeared from the back of the shop. She extended her hand and gave him a feminine handshake. "I'm Pauline Chaussee, the proprietor."

A sucker for accents, hers most assuredly French, he used his real name, Derbert Hinke.

"Can I help you, Monsieur Hinke?" she cooed.

"Umm, maybe I'm looking for small gifts I could get for two female coworkers.

Pauline said knowingly, "Ah, let me point out a few things, s'il vous plait."

There were a lot of items to choose from. Many, she said, from Colonial America and the eighteenth century: China plates and cups, colorful figurines, pewter bowls and teapots, a miniature skillet, a small American sampler, books of Jonathan Swift, engravings, and more. After about ten minutes, the adorable brunette said, "Monsieur, I will let you look alone for a bit. I'll be in the back room. If you need me, ring the bell on the counter."

"Merci, Mademoiselle Chaussee," he said.

Within ten minutes, Hinke was bored to tears with the antiques but wanted to know the proprietor better. He wandered around her shop and was intrigued by the beautiful stained-glass windows hung from the ceiling rafters. He guessed most were from old churches or monasteries.

One stained glass piece in the corner caught his eye. It was rectangular, maybe one foot by two feet. It was burning crimson—the light from the shop window, setting it ablaze— with the same black double cross in the middle that was starting to dominate his life. Maybe the shape was more common than he believed?

"A fascinating piece, don't you think, Mr. Hinke?" Pauline Chaussee said, walking up from behind him.

"It's beautiful but ominous. I've not seen a cross shaped like that," he fibbed.

"Unique, one of a kind."

"It would be the perfect gift for one of them."

"I am sorry, monsieur, it is not for sale."

"What if I offered you $200?" He took out his wallet.

"No, monsieur."

"Okay, name your price."

Again, she shook her head.

"Do you mind if I photograph it?"

"Mais oui, monsieur."

He walked out to his Cadillac rental and got the Nikon from his bag. Back inside, he snapped a few photos of the striking stained-glass.

"Madame, may I ask where you found this?"

"Certainement. A good friend who was headmistress at Greenwich Academy—I was a student of hers—gave it to me many years ago before she moved to Atlanta. An extra window she had made in case the one in her kitchen was ever broken. But she gave it to me on one condition. I keep it for my own."

It hit Hinke like a ton of bricks. He remembered the black double cross necklace swinging from her neck as she bucked up and down on his dick. Twenty-four years ago. Priscilla Loncart. Now in Atlanta. The case was accelerating his paranoia. He must think quickly. He decided not to ask anything further about the stained-glass piece.

"Monsieur Hinke, are you all right?"

"Fine—my mind was elsewhere."

His heart was pounding. He looked at his watch and told her, "Thanks so much, Miss Chaussee, but I must be going. Next time I promise to buy a gift in your shop, and I'd love to take you to dinner."

Pauline Chaussee blushed and smiled. "I'd like that, Monsieur Hinke."

Chapter 54 - Priscilla

Pauline hadn't talked to Priscilla in over twenty years. The woman who had extracted more from her, sexually, than any man or woman. Incroyable! It was as if Priscilla could read her mind, delve into her innermost being—and always know exactly what she wanted. She thought back fondly to all the times they'd rendezvoused here in the shop, the shop that she'd bought for her, and off and on in her mansion.

She flipped the sign on her door to "Closed." Standing in her shop, she focused on the gift she'd been given long ago. She conjured up Priscilla and couldn't keep her hands from reaching under her skirt. She called her.

Priscilla was pleasantly surprised. The two old friends traded stories like they'd never been apart.

"Priscilla, you remember what you gave me before you left for Atlanta?"

"Certainly. You still have it?"

"Yes, but today, a nice-looking older man wanted to buy it and told me to name my price."

Priscilla stood up in her bedroom and asked, "Did you catch his name by any chance?"

"Funny name. Hinke? Yes, Derbert Hinke."

Rarely was Priscilla surprised. This time, she was. But she smiled; she always had a Plan B.

"Pauline, my love, please come and visit me in Atlanta whenever you'd like."

Pauline smiled and told her old lover, "I'll do that, mon cher."

After visiting Pauline's shop, Hinke decided not to stop in New Canaan but instead drive back to New York and take the redeye back to DC. There he had a home phone message from Caroline. She told him she should be back from Ashville and in the office by noon—and that she had a big surprise for him. He was too tired to wonder what that might be and hit the sack.

The following day, June 12, 1974

Washington, DC

His night was anything but restful. He got up early and was at FBI headquarters by 7:00 a.m. He grabbed a cup of coffee and trudged down to his dungeon office. Hinke had to remember everything he could about Pamela Loncart, formerly the headmistress at the Greenwich School, attended by the Haverford twins. As he read his notes from 1950 he conjured up an image of her. She was a truly beautiful woman with a long auburn mane, dark eyes, and a killer body. In her late thirties, she was confident, articulate, and sexy without effort. He wondered what she looked like now?

He'd asked her the standard questions. Where she'd been that night the twins were murdered. *She was home with her husband and newborn twin girls.*

Did she know anything that might be going on between the Haverford girls and their teacher, Tommy Muldoon? *She told him no, and that if she'd heard anything of that sort, he would have been disciplined and likely fired on the spot.*

Tommy had never had any other liaisons with students or teachers? *No.*

Did she know anyone who might want to hurt Nellie or Natalie? *No, she couldn't imagine.*

Looking back, he wasn't sure why he hadn't considered the possibility of Priscilla being jealous of Tommy and his sexual attention directed at them—instead of her. But that still didn't explain the complexity of the murders.

Who else knew the twins and Tommy and knew how interoffice mail worked well enough to use it nefariously? Priscilla, whom he never seriously suspected. *Sloppy work, DH*, he scolded himself, seeing it in retrospect. Then she seduced him, and he got no additional information. What had she gotten? He remembered his files being out of place in his briefcase. In retrospect, she did that on purpose. He was now sure that she read them. She'd been taunting him, playing with him.

He got another coffee and took the elevator to the fourth floor to see if any calls came in and ponder the part Tommy Muldoon had played in the Haverford murders. Tommy gnawed on him as he tried to piece together more details from twenty-four years ago. The note had been on the bed next to Tommy. What happened to it? He raced back downstairs. Maybe it was stuck in one of the Haverford files. It took him a half hour to find it. A typewritten note with no signatures, only the names of the twins. Easily could have been created by Priscilla. He took the note back upstairs and flipped a rolling board, where he wrote: "If Priscilla knew the twins' vacation plans and could plant a note at Tommy's apartment after the twins were dead, why include Tommy Muldoon at all?"

He paced for ten minutes. Then the obvious hit him: *Because she could. Theirs was a daredevil game. Tommy was a diversion, a slight-of-hand. It was their Game of Twins.*

He got close in 1950, and that's why he got shut down. That wasn't going to happen this time.

Back in his office, the Wiz called. "DH, I'm doing this on the phone and not putting it in writing."

After a pause, Hinke told him, "Okay, what's the scoop? I'm going to jot down notes."

"I focused on the most granular information I could glean from our conversation. Households who moved from New Canaan to Atlanta 1950 to 1955 and are now in Atlanta."

"How many?"

"Two…well, four. It appears they share two addresses. Last names are Sutterland, Hawthorne, Tillie, and Loncart."

"I thought you couldn't provide names?"

"My intern screwed up."

Hinke chuckled. "Addresses?"

"Hawthorne and Tillie on West Paces; Loncart and Sutterland on Rilman, off West Paces."

"My lips are sealed. That's a huge help. Your Scotch will be on your desk soon."

Chapter 55 – The Granite Floor

The world got brighter when Caroline, entered his office with a manilla envelope.

He told her, "Lock the door and come here." In front of his desk he kissed her passionately.

After a minute, she broke the long embrace and smiled. "That could get you in big trouble, mister. But a nice surprise. Now I'll show you mine."

They sat down at the conference table, and she laid the photos out on the table. "Apparently, Lyle Brown was a photographer too."

The photos made the double cross design on the granite floor and the table perfectly clear.

Hinke said, "These are amazing."

"Sorry, though, nothing on the backs to indicate the address or client or date."

Hinke thought to himself, *"That, I can deal with."*

She asked, "What do you make of the vertical things?"

There was one clear photo of three of them, several feet from the granite table. Hexagonal, vertical cases maybe eight feet tall—with a granite base and glass halfway up.

Hinke told her, "I'd bet every cent I have they were built to display items from the dead twins: jewelry, clothing, and whatever else from the crime scenes. I'd wager they're full now—and will provide the best evidence linking the killers to their victims."

"That's disgusting, but I think you're right."

"Caroline, you've done yeoman's work finding these photos. We are almost there. I can feel it."

He told her about his trip to Connecticut: his meeting the professor at Yale and the stop at the gift shop. Finally, an answer to the question mark about black double crosses. Without mentioning his one-nighter, he told her that at least one of the murderers was Priscilla Loncart, former headmistress of the Greenwich School, whom he'd first interviewed in 1950. He added, "Plus, I'm certain others in her family or extended family were involved."

He gave her the list he'd jotted down after talking to the Wiz. "That's 1970 census data, who knows what may have changed in four years, but I want you to find out anything you can about Priscilla Loncart and the others who live with her and near her. I'm hoping those are the only residences. Regardless, try to find driver's license, property ownership, legal records, taxes, phone numbers, and whatever else you can dig up. I'm guessing she and others have long been members of Atlanta high society. Tell me what you can about that neighborhood. And anything else that may be germane. By the end of tomorrow. Thanks."

"Jeez, DH, you are a demanding old fart."

He grinned. "What if I cook you dinner tonight, babe? Say 7:00?"

"Umm, that sounds nice. I assume that means you're picking up Chinese?" she chided.

"You know me too well."

Caroline said, "Tell you what, I'll bring dessert. Your favorite dessert."

"Blackberry pie?"

"Oh, no. Much better than that. Me"

"Yummy. See you later."

Luckily, he got a hold of Hollis Delacroix and asked if they could meet for dinner on Thursday night. "Maybe the Colonnade. As much as I hate to miss dining with your gorgeous wife again, we need to talk alone. Sorry for the short notice."

Hollis said he'd get a reservation for 7:00 p.m. "DH, what's so important?"

"Let's talk about it tomorrow at the Colonnade. Thanks, Hollis."

Hinke hung up. Hollis was sure it involved his murder and Hinke's murders and maybe how they intersected. Hollis couldn't wait for dinner on Thursday.

Jim Laidlaw was Federal Judge for the United States District Court for the Northern District of Georgia. Hinke had gone to law school with him at George Washington, though they hadn't talked in years. He hoped the judge would remember his name.

He called late afternoon maybe the judge wouldn't be in court. His assistant answered. He wondered if the judge would have a few minutes on the phone and gave his title and name, Special Agent Derbert Hinke, saying he was an old classmate from GW.

She put him through.

"DH, how the heck are you?"

"I'm good, Jim."

"You're in DC? You got a family?"

"With the Bureau for nearly three decades. Never married, no family. How about you?"

"Thirty-year anniversary in a couple of weeks. My daughter is a lawyer in LA. My son, he was killed in Viet Nam four years ago."

"Jim, I can't even imagine…"

The judge got right to the point. "DH, what can I do for you?"

"Jim, I need your help. Could I run a hypothetical by you and get your wisdom on how to best proceed?"

"Shoot."

Hinke took a deep breath and tried to be as brief as he could.

"There's this agent who's been investigating a series of teenage female twins murders that he believes are connected going back at least to 1950 and maybe further."

"You mean like the murders of the girls in Woodstock?"

"Yes."

"Wasn't a black man arrested, then he died in prison?"

"Yes, but this agent is one hundred percent sure he wasn't the killer."

"I see."

"He believes that the same people are behind his murder and the girls in Woodstock, plus the kidnappings and murders of twins in Anniston, Alabama, last year. Plus others going back decades. He's positive where the twins from Anniston were killed, including photographs of the crime scene. The best proof is photographs of a unique granite floor from years ago when the floor was put in—and Polaroids of the twins lying dead on a big granite slab in the same room. Only recently has more photographic evidence come to light—and the address."

"Where?"

"High-rent area of Atlanta; the home of a rich powerful family."

"Who?"

"Judge, let's leave it that for now. This agent assumes a search warrant would be needed to view the floor and slab at that address—and believes there are likely souvenirs from several murders; that is a hypothesis. I'm truncating, and there's more to the story. This FBI agent has been working these cases for a long time, but no one at the Bureau knows what evidence he has—or how these murders are all connected."

"I assume this agent knows the world of shit he could be in with the Bureau—much less our legal system?"

"Yes, but he's an older guy who is more concerned with catching the murderers – than any possible fallout. They've been egging him on and providing several clues that only the agent could interpret. They call it *Game of Twins*. He knows they could kill him at any point if they think he's too close. Make no mistake, these are dangerous people, and probably know how close the agent is getting."

"Motive for these murders?"

"Revenge is a big part of it; the rest, I'm not sure. Over the years, as sick as it sounds, I think it's mainly for thrills while they play their *Game*. Judge, I've taken enough of your time today. I've planned a trip to Atlanta and will be in town on Thursday and Friday. I was wondering if we could meet for lunch or dinner on Friday?"

"DH, I'll transfer you to my assistant, Jill; she'll get your information and contact you about a lunch meeting on Friday. I'm working a short day. We'll get a nice private table at 1789, say around 1:00?"

"That would be great, Judge. Look forward to seeing you."

"DH, I don't pretend to know all that's going on with these investigations, but it sounds like the agent needs to be careful."

"He will."

Priscilla and crew, he was sure, lived in two palatial houses in the most expensive part of Atlanta. One of those houses had a granite floor, granite table, and granite and glass display cases. The original Polaroids, their enlargements, and Lyle Brown's photos of his custom work back in 1951—he hoped would be powerful enough evidence to get a warrant to search both homes

No evidence directly connected Brown's photographs to the other murder scene photos. No date, name, or address. He was surprised Brown hadn't cataloged his pictures. But he smiled and told himself, *"With Priscilla's address verified, I can add the year and address. A little evidence tampering, no problem. In for a dime, in for a dollar."*

That was Plan A; there was no Plan B.

Hinke had grown to enjoy the solitude of being a bachelor—not in the mold of Hoover or Tolson—yet realized both men had rubbed off on him more than he wished to admit. His complicity in the death of Orville Johnston was indirect but real; his not giving the Blount family any closure about their daughters, inexcusable; his lies throughout the investigation, he'd lost count. Hoover had ruined thousands of lives over the decades, but Hinke was guilty, too. His quest for justice, he hoped, would help him atone for some of his sins.

Chapter 56 – The Families

Until recently, he'd done his work without enlisting much FBI help, but that had changed. Caroline Knopfler was a Godsend—investigating the granite floors and the Game names and addresses. He needed to tell her that he couldn't have done it without her—which was true—but there would be plenty of time for that. Then, a bizarre thought crossed his mind. He had thirty-five years on her, but he wanted her not simply as a girlfriend. Hell, unless he was shooting blanks, he could be a dad. She might laugh, and he could handle that, but he was going to ask her. Regardless, when this was over, he would quit the Bureau. He knew her well enough to know she wouldn't; she wanted to make her mark. He understood and was okay with that.

Hinke popped out of his daydream and told himself, *"You're out of your fucking mind."*

Hinke had picked up Chinese and a blackberry pie. He had a bottle of Zin open when she arrived in a tight blouse, slacks, and heels. He kissed her. "You look fantastic."

"Thanks. I'm famished."

She wasn't kidding and wolfed down more than her fair share of the Chinese and a big piece of pie. He cleaned up after dinner. They both sat at his kitchen table. She gave him an update:

"I feel like I'm only scratching the surface. Okay, the houses on Rilman and West Paces are close and in the most upscale neighborhood in Atlanta proper. The land of the old money. "For grins, I called a real estate agent and asked if there was anything available in the West Paces area. Price, no object. She laughed and said, "Good luck finding anything for sale.""

"DH, there's weird shit going on here that I'm sorting through. It took me most of the afternoon to get Georgia DMV info with the last names you gave me. Here's the DMV license info attached to the two houses."

She put the driver's license copies in front of him.

"Eight people have one of the two addresses. Those eight people all have one of the last names you gave me: Loncart, Sutterland, Tillie, or Hawthorne. No Priscilla Loncart, but there is a Priscilla Sutterland, and a few have middle names that are one of the last names. A strange sorta of mix and match."

Hinke said, "Priscilla could have changed her name."

"That's what I was thinking. I'll try to put together a family tree for you before you leave tomorrow. First names include Priscilla, Pamela, Patricia, Phoebe, Nigel Jr. and Sr., Reginald, Franklin, and Maddie."

He looked at the grainy driver's license copy for Priscilla Sutterland. "That's her, no question."

"Nigel Hawthorne Sr. and Raymond Sutterland jointly own both houses. They run Hawthorne Industries, a big multinational company. Haven't had time yet to find out more about it.

"Great work. Keep at it and get me what you have tomorrow afternoon, but enough work for today. How about a nightcap and early bedtime?"

Great idea." She stood and slipped off her top and slacks; no foundations. She let her clothes drop on the dining room floor.

He could take a hint and brought in two cognacs.

In bed, after she'd worn his old ass out for the first time, Hinke said, "I forgot to ask you about the Pink Lady at the Grove Park Inn. You get a chance to meet her?"

"I did."

"You did not."

"Yes, I did. And if you fuck me again, I may tell you the details."

"Yes, ma'am, I will. And I may tell you about the several supernatural encounters I've had investigating these murders. Much better than the Pink Lady."

"You're kidding."

"Nope."

Naked, she straddled him on the bed and threw her long blonde hair back. "Let's get to it, big boy."

Chapter 57 – Helen

June 12, 1974

Washington, DC

Hinke got to his fourth-floor office early, gulped down a cup of coffee, and read the profile he had written. His *Game of Twins* killers profile fit them to a T. He was impressed. But rarely with himself.

He flipped through the facsimiles of the DMV records for the eight people Caroline had identified. Then exclaimed, "Holy shit!"

He was looking at the birthdates of the women:

Priscilla and Patricia were born on June 28, 1911.

Phoebe and Maddie were born on January 4, 1950.

Sets of twins born during the years of the Abercrombie and Haverford murders. He had to smile. That explained the gaps in murders. Twin girls were sacrificed after one of the families had birthed twins, identical twins being much less common than fraternal twins.

There had to be two more sets of twins born this year and last year.

Phoebe and Maddie were in their twenties. He'd bet his bank account both had sets of twins born in 1973 and 1974.

He called Caroline and knew he sounded manic after yet another cup of coffee. You've got to find out if Maddie and Phoebe birthed twins in 1973 or 1974."

"Easy, DH, I'm going to find out a lot of other stuff about the families."

"This is now the priority. If you can't verify that today, call me at the Omni tomorrow."

"DH, I'm not sure how to find that information in a hurry."

"A couple suggestions: whatever agency in Georgia handles birth certificates, high-society birth notices in the *Atlanta Constitution*, maybe elsewhere."

"But…"

"You'll figure it out."

"But why?"

"It's important."

"Okay, I'll do my best. Do you want company tonight?"

"Thanks, but not tonight. I'm too wound up. Assuming things go well in Atlanta, you and I are going to take a vacation."

"We are? To where?"

"Anywhere in the world you want to go. I love you."

She hesitated, but only for a moment. "I love you, too. Good luck in Atlanta."

Hinke left the office early. In his flat, he packed and paced. He doubted he'd get much sleep tonight. He wished it were already 9:00 a.m. when his fight would leave National tomorrow. He double-checked the two AMT auto-mag Vs with a few dozen clips. He'd been to the new FBI range in the J. Edgar Hoover building several times in the last month. It was a light-year better than the old one, spacious and with room for twenty shooters. He was surprised he'd not lost his touch, though he knew his eyesight had deteriorated. No worse than a couple of 7s. He hoped the guns wouldn't be necessary.

Last week, Helen had called and left a message to say she'd be in town for a couple of weeks. His mind elsewhere, he hadn't called her back. He wanted to share the good news. She'd been his biggest supporter for over two decades. Hinke called her DC flat. There was no answer; he left a short message.

"Helen, sorry not to get back to you. Been a wild week, and likely to get wilder. Wish me luck. I've got the bastards in my gun sights. I finally know who killed the twins, and I think I can prove it. Going to Atlanta in the a.m. Let's get together when I'm back."

He opened his safe and put an envelope on top of his other personal documents—his updated will. Then shut it. He poured himself a bourbon and sat down in his favorite easy chair and tried to relax. A half-hour later, on the edge of dozing off, he heard a knock on his door. Strange, he wasn't expecting anyone.

There stood Helen, a figure from his past, as enigmatic as ever. It had been twenty-four years since he first met her, and she was as attractive a woman in her eighth decade as he'd ever seen, looking ten or fifteen years younger than her age. She was dressed in a stylish beach outfit of loose pants, a diaphanous blouse, and sandals, a stark contrast to the serious business at hand. Her hair past her shoulders was a scintillating silver gray, a testament to the years they had both lived.

"Helen, you look as beautiful as the first time I saw you," he said, his voice filled with a mixture of nostalgia and longing.

She stepped in and gave him a big kiss.

"Thought I'd stop by with your favorite bourbon. I won't stay long. I know you've got a lot on your mind."

From the sack she was carrying, she pulled the bottle and handed it to him. "I'll have a drink with you."

He got two tumblers from the kitchen, then poured them each a couple fingers as they stood near her dining room table.

Hinke held his glass up and toasted. "All evenings with you, Helen, are special. Here's to finally bringing the killers to justice."

She clinked glasses.

"You've finally cracked these cases?"

"Helen, it's a long story. Suffice it to say that I was an idiot in 1950."

"Why would you say that?"

"She played me then, and I think she is playing me now."

"Derby, you look like the cat that ate the proverbial canary. Pray tell, who?"

His grin widened. "Priscilla Loncart and relatives killed the Haverfords and were involved in all the other murders."

Her eyes bore into his, and he thought, *And to think I fucked her and never caught her.*

"Derby, I knew that when you got back from New Canaan in 1950."

Hinke was perplexed. "Knew what?"

"That you fucked Priscilla." Her face now inscrutable.

Hinke told Helen, "I'm sorry that ever happened. Back then I never took it seriously that a woman would be involved in the murders. Along with several relatives, she migrated in 1950 to Atlanta, where they bought two huge homes in the West Paces area. In one, they had an ornate granite floor and table built in. A sacrificial table. And a few tall vertical cases that I'm sure now include souvenirs from the murder scenes. It's where they murdered the Blounts. I have photos of the custom granite floor when it was laid in 1951. Plus Polaroids of the Blount murders from last year. It's the house where Priscilla lives on Rilman. The family tree is confusing, but the last names include Loncart, Sutterland, Hawthorne, and Tillie."

"Oh, my Lord," Helen exclaimed.

"I'd forgotten the striking necklace she wore with their insignia black double cross, a symbol used in all the murders—a symbol I only recently came to understand. They are deep into the occult, which I'd never wanted to believe until I had multiple encounters myself with the twins' ghosts. Never admitted that to anyone, including you. Hopefully, I have enough evidence. A federal judge acquaintance of mine could issue a warrant to search Priscilla's house—or convince a lower court judge or prosecutor. There will be plenty of evidence there, or they can take me to jail."

"You've told the judge who you think the murderers are?"

"No, and none of the specifics yet, but I'll see him for lunch the day after tomorrow. Tomorrow evening, I'm eating dinner with Atlanta Detective Hollis Delacroix. I haven't decided yet how much I'll tell him other than his murder case is going to be solved, and he'll get the credit. I've felt guilty keeping him in the dark since I met him in Anniston."

"Your young lady friend knows who the killers are?"

"Caroline is plenty smart enough to deduce it."

Helen said, "Seriously, Derby, these people sound ruthless. Your life and hers could be in jeopardy."

"She's got a gun and knows how to use it. Once you leave, I'll call and remind her to be extra careful. I'm only taking my notes and photographs to Atlanta; the other critical files are in my safe—and more in my downstairs FBI office. You have the combination to my safe and file cabinet in case anything were to happen to me. My will is in there, too. I know you'd do the right thing with the files."

Helen listened in on the panoply of thoughts pinging around Hinke's brain: *What if I can't get a search warrant issued? I don't have a Plan B. Maybe I'll go in and blow them all away. What should I tell Hollis? Should I have put a man guarding Caroline? If I fail, what will happen to me?*

He started to sit down on the sofa, but Helen said, "Derby, why don't you relax in your favorite chair? My old back is acting up, and it feels better when I stand. I'll give you a neck and shoulder rub. Your burden has been great. You need it."

"Excellent idea. Helen, you're the best."

Drink in hand, he lowered his butt into his favorite chair in the center of his living room. She stood behind him. He groaned with pleasure as her hands kneaded his neck and shoulders. After a few minutes, he thought he might nod off and said, "That feels so great."

Then, he felt a prick on the back of his neck.

She moved in front of him and pulled her necklace from under her blouse. He saw it: the exact black double cross necklace that Priscilla had worn.

His body started twitching, his eyes in disbelief. He stuttered, "I'll be damned, you were in it all along. What was that?"

"A deadly frog poison."

He wanted to strangle her but was already losing control of his limbs and gasping for air.

"Derby, listen. You're being paralyzed, then you will be dead in less than a couple minutes."

Hinke was in too much shock to do or say anything except, "Why?"

"I've been part of their family for nearly seventy years after I helped them kidnap the Abercrombie twins back in 1911. My lot was determined long ago by the family and our Dark Lord. My principal job was to create a monster like Hoover. When Priscilla's twins were born, they wanted a new player in the *Game*. Selfishly, I chose you to enjoy and join the *Game*. You played magnificently, but, yes, you've flown too near to the sun. Derby, with you, I rarely used my own powers. I concentrated on Hoover. I thought about moving to the side of the persons-of-light, where you are, but they would have killed you and then me in the worst ways imaginable. When another set of twins is born, and the *Game* starts up again, whoever investigates -- I assure you that the *Game* will be less rigged in our favor. Some of your clues will live on, I promise."

Hinke's eyes fluttered. His arms and legs spasmed. His drink tumbled to the floor. Then he was still.

She kissed his forehead and said, "I did love you, Derby. I am so sorry."

She propped him up the best she could and looked at the tiny injection prick, hidden a bit above his neck hairline—where no one would notice. She opened his luggage to retrieve the nitroglycerin tablets from his dopp kit. She unscrewed the top, took one out, and placed it under his tongue. She let the open bottle of nitro fall to the floor and join the booze that had been in his drink. How convenient that Derby had a suspect ticker.

From the same piece of luggage he'd packed for Atlanta, she collected his notes and photos, then zipped it back up. From his safe, she pulled the rest of the critical evidence that wasn't in either of his offices. She'd brought the booze in an oversized bag, and that's where she put it all. She rinsed out her glass and put it inside a kitchen cabinet. His ticket to Atlanta lay on his kitchen table. She put his luggage next to the table. Then she left with the bag of Derbert Hinke's most valuable crime information.

The same evening

Capitol Hill, Washington, DC

Caroline worked late into the muggy evening. Once or twice a week, she walked home from FBI headquarters to her place on Capitol Hill, but tonight, she took the last DC Transit bus at 8:00 p.m. to the Hill from FBI headquarters. Of course, the AC on the bus wasn't working, and by the time she got to her front door, she was sweating like a pig. *"I should have walked."* She told herself

Two years earlier, she'd gotten a steal; her own two-story renovation-in-progress brownstone only two blocks from the Capitol. That was the good news. The bad news: it was in one of DC's most crime-ridden neighborhoods in. Gunshots at night were the norm and not the exception. But she never felt like she was in danger. Friends and family were shocked she'd live in the "slums" by herself, but she'd grown up tough with three brothers—and, besides, she always carried her gun outdoors and had one on her nightstand.

She popped a beer and cooled off—jazzed knowing she could help DH on the case that she knew had tormented him for years. Hopefully tomorrow she could answer his questions about the births; still mystified by his request. The hot shower revived her. Out of the shower, she was toweling off when she heard her doorbell ring.

She wrapped a towel around her, walked to the door, and looked through her peephole. If it had been a black guy or an unkempt dirtball with long hair, she would've gotten her gun or not responded. The well-groomed white guy said, "Package for you from a Derbert Hinke. Just need your signature, ma'am."

As she opened the door, he slammed it back hard, hitting her square in the face, throwing her to the floor, and knocking the wind out of her and the towel off her. Then, he was on top of her. *"I've been trained for this,* she thought. But then she felt a syringe pop into her shoulder. Her assailant stuffed a cloth into her mouth.

"Might as well have a little fun first—right, cutie pie?"

She felt him dive inside her. *"This can't be happening,"* a faint voice inside her moaned. *"Lord Jesus Christ, help me!"*

Thankfully, it all went black.

The next day

Capitol Hill, Washington, DC

The weather was supposed to be nice, but it was in the low eighties. Caroline had planned to walk to work the next morning with her friend Carla, a secretary at the Bureau who rented a nearby flat. Carla got no response after she knocked several times. Maybe Caroline had forgotten and already left for work? Or she was with the secret boyfriend she refused to talk about. Still, it wasn't like her. At FBI headquarters, Carla walked up to the third floor. No one in Caroline's cubicle. She returned to her second-floor cubicle, waiting for her boss to arrive. She begged him to send an agent to Caroline's place. He balked. She told him, "If you don't, I'm quitting on the spot."

Twenty minutes later, an FBI special agent knocked several times on Caroline Knopfler's door. Hearing nothing, he picked the lock and, gun raised, entered. She was naked on the floor in her living room, her neck slashed, likely raped first. Her place was in disarray.. Her purse and empty wallet were strewn next to her on the floor. Violent crimes were all too common in the nation's capital, which had the highest per-capita crime rate in the United States. FBI agents weren't immune.

Four days later, friends and family gathered at a quiet cemetery outside of Alexandria, Virginia—more than a few judging her. How could she have been so foolish to live in such a violent neighborhood? If she'd only listened.

Helen was an old pro at winnowing through a lot of files in a hurry. She'd had fifty-two years of practice with the Boss. Hinke had already done a lot of it for her. The best was in his safe. By noon the following day, before Hinke's body was discovered in his flat, Helen had rifled through the contents of his fourth-floor and basement office files and cherry-picked the best—the rest she shipped to an incinerator in northeast DC.

She carefully culled through the remaining content—putting a portion in a banker's box—which she accompanied to an FBI archive in Rockville, Maryland. She had explicitly indexed and shelved the box in the cavernous warehouse. She was leaving a loaf of breadcrumbs for other investigators down the road—if they were clever enough. She had a box of Hoover's ultrasensitive P files in her own flat; she hadn't yet decided what to do with those.

Chapter 58 – Dinner with Hollis

The same day

Buckhead, Atlanta

Hollis Delacroix was five minutes late and upon entering, asked the pretty hostess, "Has my guest, Mr. Hinke, arrived?" Derbert Hinke was the most punctual person, male or female, he'd ever met.

"No, not yet. I'll be looking out for him. I'll seat you and bring him back when he arrives."

It'd been a hard day in the salt mines, and that was the Atlanta Police Department. He'd been assigned a new homicide yesterday. A wife was shot several times, likely by the husband, who had disappeared to who knew where. Plus, he had two other cases that were complete mysteries thus far. But he was anxious to hear what DH had to say.

At 7:20 p.m., Hollis was halfway through his drink. The Colonnade was filling up. Only a couple other black people in the restaurant, which wasn't terribly unusual.

By 7:45, no Hinke, and Hollis had finished his second Jack. He shook his head. He knew Hinke didn't have a family. He'd at least try to call him at home but was thinking this could take a few more calls. He signaled the young waiter and told him he needed to see Frank. The kid's eyes got as wide as saucers.

"Hey, chill out. I need to use his phone for a few minutes. Tell him it's Hollis."

A year ago, he was having dinner with Mei at the Colonnade when two masked guys charged into the restaurant and yelled, "Everyone put your cash and jewelry on your table. Now!" Hollis told Mei to get under their table. From the back of the restaurant, Hollis yelled at them, "Hey, assholes, get out now or you're dead."

Bad decision that they both moved in the direction of the sound, back in the far corner. With his .357, Hollis blew away the guy on the right. The other hightailed it out, and Hollis followed. He aimed for the guy's legs and put him on the asphalt with one shot. Later, the Colonnade's manager, Frank Lorenzo, told him, "Whatever you need whenever you need it, Detective."

Frank appeared in less than a minute. "Hollis, how you doing, man? Need another drink? Dinner? On me."

"Thanks, Frank, I'm good, but can I use your office phone? I was supposed to meet a colleague here at 7:00, and he's never late. I may need to make a few calls."

"Sure, no problem."

Frank led him to a small, dark-paneled office on the second floor, which was fine other than the stench of cigarette smoke.

He called Hinke's home number first. After several rings, he left a message on his answering machine.

Next, he called the Omni, where he was sure Hinke would be staying, and identified himself. No Derbert Hinke had checked in that day.

Having no idea who to call next, he dialed the Federal Bureau of Investigation in DC. After identifying himself as an Atlanta detective, he said, "I need help locating one of your agents who was supposed to meet me tonight in Atlanta. Derbert Hinke."

He got put on hold for several minutes. His call went up two levels until he finally reached Zach Martini, special agent in charge of the DC office, after hours. Hollis explained the situation as quickly as possible.

Agent Martini said, "Detective Delacroix, I've known Special Agent Hinke for twenty years. I'm sorry to tell you DH was found dead in his apartment this afternoon. You may know he had heart issues. Apparently, he died last night from a heart attack."

It wasn't like DH was his best buddy, but the news hit him like a hammer in the solar plexus. He didn't know what to say.

"I'm sorry. We're all sad to lose him. Can I get your number and have an agent call you back about the funeral services?"

Hollis gave him the number, said thank you, and hung up.

He sat in Frank's office chair, unable to move. He was certain Hinke wanted to talk to him about his murder case and the other cases Hinke had been unable to solve.

Frank knocked on the door and opened it to check on the detective. He saw the look in Hollis Delacroix's eyes. "Frank, he didn't make it because he's dead."

The Next Day

Georgetown, Washington, DC

The following afternoon Judge Jim Laidlaw walked into the 1789 restaurant in Georgetown at 1:00 p.m., and the hostess immediately escorted him to a table in the corner. It had been a brutal week; a good lunch and a couple drinks and a free afternoon sounded wonderful.

"Thanks, Missy, I'll take my usual single malt. Please be on a lookout for Mr. Hinke."

"Yes, sir."

By 1:45 the judge had finished his second Scotch and was miffed. He put two twenties on the table, stomped out, and decided to take his anger out hitting the golf ball around Congressional.

Before he teed off, the federal judge called and yapped at his secretary, "Jill, find out why the hell FBI Special Agent Derbert Hinke stood me up for lunch."

When he finished his round of golf at 7:00 p.m. there was a message for him at the bar.

It simply said, "Derbert Hinke died in his apartment two nights ago; apparently a heart attack."

"Oh my Lord," the judge said out loud.

Chapter 59 – The Funeral

The following week

Arlington Cemetery, Arlington, VA

Helen knew Hinke was a WWII Army vet who'd received several medals, including two Purple Hearts. He had no close family and was a loner. She didn't know if he had any good friends outside the Bureau. She had enough pull to schedule an Arlington National military funeral with honors, which included pallbearers, a rifle salute, and a bugler. Only thing missing was the full marching band. Then a family member or friend needed to accept the flag after it was folded, ceremoniously.

After the short service on the way to his resting spot among the thousands of white crosses, Helen introduced herself to Hollis Delacroix. She'd made sure his visit to DC was paid for anonymously.

You must be Detective Delacroix. I'm Helen Gandy. I worked with Derbert for many years. I was Hoover's executive assistant until he passed two years ago. He was such a good man and a great agent.

"Derby, not Hoover."

"You paid for my trip. Thank you."

"Least the government could do."

"I didn't know him well, but he seemed like a great guy. I was supposed to eat dinner in Atlanta with him the night after he died. Not sure what he was going to tell me. I know he was investigating the kidnappings of twin girls from Anniston, Alabama, which he told me might be related to other twins murders. I was investigating the murder of an Atlanta drug dealer who strangely was found murdered about the same time in Anniston. That's where I met DH. Don't know if he ever established any tie to the crimes. My case is cold, and if I were a betting man, it will stay that way."

"Detective, I'd like to ask a favor. Derbert thought of you like a son. Would you accept the flag?"

"There's no one else?"

"No."

Hollis got pensive. "Well, okay, it would be an honor."

"Thank you, Detective."

Now she was sure that Hinke had kept Detective Hollis Delacroix mostly in the dark. She didn't want him to meet the same fate as Hinke's girlfriend.

Maybe she was getting soft in her old age by not mentioning Delacroix to her coven. She didn't give a damn.

Chapter 60 – Louis Giles

A month later

Lake Lanier, Georgia

When the phone rang at the Woodstock Police Department, Deputy Louis Giles picked up. "Hey, Louis, it's Hollis Delacroix."

"How you doing, Detective?"

"I'm good. Family's good. Listen, Louis, sorry I haven't called earlier. In case you haven't heard, Derbert Hinke is dead."

"What? How?"

"Found in his place in Georgetown; they say a heart attack. Thought you should know."

"Sorry to hear that. Real sorry. Hinke was a stand-up guy." He didn't add, "especially for an FBI agent who'd break any rule to solve a case"—if that was the right thing to do."

"That he was."

"Hey, Hollis, why don't you come up to Lanier and fish with me? You're a fisherman, aren't you?"

"Yeah, that would be great."

"Maybe next weekend?"

"Lemme check with the wife. I'll get back to you. Oh, Louis, forgot to mention he died in DC the night before he was coming down to eat dinner with me in Atlanta. Sounded important, but I don't know what it was. You ever talk to him after the Woodstock murders?"

"Can't say I did," Louis lied.

"You wouldn't know what was that important, would you?"

"Uum, no."

Neither admitted it, but both men had more than a vague idea what was important.

After hanging up, Louis Giles admired the beautiful sapphire and diamond ring on his right hand and twisted it off like he'd done hundreds of times to check and make sure it was there. J. Edgar Hoover's name was engraved on the inside. He'd gotten a couple more appraisals of the ring itself, which indicated it was worth in the mid-five figures. But then, out of the blue one day, an English-accent-speaking guy called him. Said he worked for Christie's, an auction house in London with offices all over the world. He'd heard about the ring and its former owner's name engraved inside. He told Louis that assuming the ring and engraving were authenticated, it could bring an opening bid of at least a couple hundred thousand dollars. He emphasized, "An opening bid." Louis was polite and got the guy's information and thought that was unfuckingbelievable.

Nobody in the office, thank God. He needed a drink. He kept a pint of bourbon in his top desk drawer. He poured out the remnants of his coffee in the waste can, then sat back down and poured the cup a third full.

It all flooded back at Louis Giles.

The only person in the world whom he could've talked to about the murders in Woodstock and Baron Brevard's suicide—that person was now dead. *Heart attack? My ass.* He knew Orville Johnston was innocent. Dead, thanks to him and others. He knew the Blount twins were dead, and no one else knew that.

These were bad motherfuckers who'd done all this shit. Could he be a loose end too?

Giles poured himself another bourbon and tossed it down in two gulps. He figured, if they were going to get rid of him, they could do it anytime they wanted. But he hoped he was small potatoes, not worth the trouble. Now that Hinke was gone, he tried to convince himself it was over. Or was he deluding himself?

He intended to do a little early evening fishing but got waylaid by a couple high school buddies who wanted to drink a few beers before he left Woodstock for Lanier. It was almost dark when he got to his tiny lake house near Chestatee on the north side of the lake. No way to find his place at night unless you'd been there in daylight. He flipped on the outside porch light.

He planned to sell his little lake house and buy a much bigger place now that he could afford it. The only separate room was the dinky john with a mini-shower. He was starving but didn't have much other than eggs, bacon, and a half loaf of bread in the fridge. No TV in the lake house; he'd pay for Southern Bell phone service when he got his new place. He wolfed down the food and washed it down with a Bud.

If he was going to get up at 5:30 a.m. and be out on the water, he needed sleep. After a hot shower, he collapsed in bed but was restless. He sat up and felt compelled to open the nightstand drawer. Immediate déjà vu. He didn't own a bible. The last time he'd seen one was at Orville Johnston's. A bible from his nightstand with horrible Polaroid photos of the Brevard and Blount twins. With trepidation, he picked up the bible and opened it in the middle.

Then screamed, "Holy Shit!" "Holy Shit!" "Holy Fucking Shit!"

Photos in a cut-out in the middle, same as in Orville Johnston's bible. He hesitated, then flipped them right side up.

He turned the first. The two beautiful Brevard twins are in short shorts and midriff tops with their German Shepherd, Thor.

The second was Thor standing in a barn.

The next was the shocker. The dog's decapitated head on a huge bed.

It would haunt him forever. He now understood why Barron Brevard had blown his brains to smithereens.

Louis Giles had been truly frightened only one time in his life. When his pop went at him with a belt, he took the belt beatings twice, but not the third. His father took it instead. Giles left the photos on the bed, grabbed a beer for the road, locked the door as if that mattered, and gunned back to his rental on the outskirts of Canton.

There, Giles went directly to the bottle of bourbon above his fridge and poured a man's glass. He sat down at his kitchen table with his two handguns in front of him. All he could do was shake his head and say, "I am so fucked."

Epilogue

Fourteen years later, June 1988

Jacksonville Beach, Florida

Usually, she only went to the beach in the morning before it got too steamy. But this early afternoon the temperature wasn't ghastly, the skies were more cloudy than sunny, and there was a nice breeze. It was a process for her to get to the beach from her beachfront condo, but her daytime helper, Joey, a nice young man earning his way through Jacksonville State, would politely do whatever she asked. She could walk a few steps alone, but they had it down to a science. He'd push her in the wheelchair from her unit down the elevator and outdoors to the end of the little boardwalk near her ten-story high-rise, then gently carry her to the yellow Adirondack chair with its pillow, which was as much a fixture on the beach as the white lifeguard stands that typically emptied out by 4:00 p.m.

In her beach bag she had the essentials for a ninety-one-year-old: a big floppy beach hat, a tube of zinc oxide to smear a bit more on her nose and cheeks (with the gloves she wore, the only skin that was exposed on her wrinkly body), pain pills for her arthritis, and of course a small jug of Bloody Mary's and a plastic cup. Also, the walkie-talkie so she could let Joey know when she wanted to go back to the condo. He always positioned the chair close enough to the water where she could touch her toes on the wet sand when high tide rolled in.

He poured her a stout Bloody Mary—half vodka, half spiced tomato juice—and put it in the cupholder.

"Call me if you need anything, Miss Helen."

"Thank you, Joey."

With gnarled, aching fingers, she groped for the cup and sucked down a little Bloody Mary with a straw. Hanging on with both hands shaking, she managed to put her drink back in the cupholder. A chore, but she was glad she had her sight and hearing. Her brain, she was sure, was as good or better than others in their nineties. On the other hand, she often couldn't remember what she'd been served for lunch that day. Sometimes, though, the distant past was like she was living it again, especially when she was outdoors in her favorite spot on the beach looking out at the majestic Atlantic. She let her mind drift back to the day, nearly eight decades ago, when the beautiful woman climbed off her yacht at the wharf, invited her to sail away, and changed her life forever.

Her walkie-talkie spoke after she'd nodded off. "Ma'am, there are three women who say they're here to visit you."

She fumbled for the walkie-talkie in the other cupholder. "Who the hell are they?"

"They say it's a surprise; one says you were like an older sister to her a long time ago."

Helen smiled.

"Bring chairs for them and whip up another batch of Bloodies."

"Roger that."

A few minutes later they arrived, women from three generations, all beautiful, including Priscilla, who was only ten years younger.

They walked in front of her chair.

Priscilla said, "Helen, this is Maddie, my daughter, and my grandniece Pamela."

Maddie said, "It is my honor."

"Mine, too," said the teenager.

Each leaned down to give her a hug. Joey arrived with three folding chairs and placed them around Helen's chair. He left a cooler with ice-cold vodka, tomato juice, and a couple of Cokes—and quickly disappeared.

"I remember how much you liked the water," said Priscilla.

Helen smiled. "Yes, since I first sailed with your mother, Penelope."

Priscilla said, "We owe you debts of gratitude. I've told Maddie and Pamela about what you did to save the Tribe. Special Agent Hinke was on the verge of winning the Game and perhaps destroying us. We may have gotten a bit ahead of our skis in the last two sacrifices, but Maddie and Franklin and Nigel performed admirably."

Helen noticed that Maddie did not seem pleased with her mother's comments. Helen intervened and added, "The sacrifices of the Blounts and Brevards were brilliantly conceived and will surely go down in the annals. Maddie, you should be proud."

Priscilla smiled and continued, "Helen didn't only eliminate Hinke. Arguably, for five decades as Hoover's executive assistant and the keeper of all his files, she was the most powerful woman in government and did much to create the monster that he became—destroying the lives of thousands of persons-of-light without herself lifting a finger to harm anyone. Except for Hinke, whom she poisoned."

Maddie rolled her eyes as her mom pontificated.

"Ours is a game of revenge and tradition…and of a future where the Dark Lord reigns supreme…and where persons-of-light are slaves. Each of us has our own role to play. Not all of us can bring twins into the world like Maddie and me and Pamela's mother; her plane crash with Nigel was tragic. There were no twins for thirty-nine years. Perhaps if Pamela is fortunate enough to bear twins one day, there will be more sacrifices."

The teen bet that wouldn't happen but said nothing.

"Not all of us can make riches to fill the coffers of the Atlanta Tribe like Raymond and Nigel. Maddie and Franklin's businesses are generating millions—and one day, billions. Outside our Atlanta Tribe others are incented to contribute. We are making progress.

"Penelope's vision started with revenge that was initiated by your namesakes centuries ago. But my mother had a grander vision. The sacrifices have helped honor our Dark Lord, glue us together, and provide you rewards on earth and in the afterlife. All of us are on the path to the day the Dark Lord prevails over the Lord of Light, a formidable foe. We will chip away until what they call the scale of justice falls permanently in our favor.

"You've seen the plaques in my *Game of Twins* room. The Rules and the Players. There is a growing list of names starting with Penelope. Maddie and I are on the list with several others. Helen, your name is honored as well. The fine player he was, Derbert Hinke is the only honoree so far who was not a witch."

Maddie said, "Helen, Pamela has a question for you."

"Yes, my dear, what is it?" The more Helen looked at the auburn teen beauty, the more she looked exactly like her great-grandmother, Penelope. And she had her startling black eyes.

Shyly, the teen asked, "Aunt Helen, if you have it, could you give me your black double cross necklace?"

The old woman smiled. "But of course my dear. It needs to be passed on."

Thrilled, Pamela shouted, "Thank you!"

Pamela got up and kissed her on the cheek.

"It's in my jewelry case on my dresser. I'll call Joey on my walkie-talkie to make sure you get it."

Priscilla and Maddie wore their necklaces. The last time she'd worn hers was fourteen years ago in Derby's flat, the night when she killed him. The remembrance sent a shudder through her old body. The terror in his eyes after their friendship of twenty-four years had been unmistakable.

After a minute Priscilla asked, "Helen, are you all right?"

Helen snapped back to the present. "Yes, tell you what, I'm getting tired and will take a nap out here for a bit. Don't worry about the chairs and glasses; Joey will get those."

The three could take a hint and said their goodbyes. After kissing her cheek, Priscilla said, "Helen, thank you for everything. I'm sure you and I will meet in the Dark Paradise a lot sooner than these ladies."

Helen deflected and asked her, "Dear, before you leave, could you hand me the walkie-talkie and my pills—and refill my cup?"

"Certainly. Thank you for seeing us."

As they waved goodbye, she managed, "Thank you all for visiting."

Before she forgot, she got Joey on the walkie-talkie. "Joey, the ladies are coming up. Show them my jewelry case. They are going to take the black necklace. I'm staying out here a bit."

"Miss Gandy, it looks like a storm coming in." She could feel the fresh breeze and see the ominous, dark clouds on the horizon.

With relish she said, "I'll call you if the storm gets close."

He knew better than to argue. "Yes, ma'am."

Her old body ached. She washed down three pain pills with a gulp of her Bloody Mary.

But the pills would not make her heart ache less.

Her mind drifted back again to the twins and the black double crosses. She remembered the name of Penelope Loncart's yacht: *Twins*—with the two black anchors, the shape of the family's black double cross. She had always loved the sea, but more after her ride that included the Abercrombie twins. None of them returned to Port Norris. When her life veered off and she became a servant of the Dark Lord. She tried to reach back and remember the files her lawyer in DC would not open until 2025 but couldn't. Maybe too many Bloodies or her increasingly feeble mind.

The incoming thunder crashed, and lightning bolts lit up the black sky as the storm hurtled toward her. The lifeguards were long gone. She sat alone on the beach.

Helen Gandy had loved Special Agent Derbert Hinke, more than the sea and more than her adopted family, now called the Atlanta Tribe—and more than the Dark Lord. Her head in her lap, she cried, then kicked off her sandals. Wobbly, she braced herself up using both armrests of the hefty Adirondack chair. The pain was immense, but as she looked out on the Atlantic, the beach now at high tide, lapping her feet—it didn't matter. Not one iota. Bent over like the hunchback of Notre Dame, her steps into the water were slow but resolute. She smiled at the beauty of the ebony sky and water converging. The force of the waves made it harder and harder to walk forward. Now waist-high in the water, her strength was sapped.

"Derby, please forgive me."

She put her hands above her head and dove into the next wave as she'd done hundreds of times since she was a child.

Another Note from the Author

This book is a fiction noir that may be too much to bear for readers always expecting a happy ending. But if you haven't yet read the other *Game of Twins* books, do not despair. Read on. There are better days to come in this battle between Good and Evil.

In *Game of Twins*, Forty years after the death of Special Agent Derbert Hinke, Hollis Delacroix's daughter, Suzanne, is the top homicide cop in Atlanta—and is pursuing the murderers of another set of twins in Atlanta— and other cold case murders now spanning a century. Louis Giles is the wealthy sheriff of ultra-prosperous Woodstock, Georgia. Kip Davies, Ted Davies' son, is a top criminal attorney in Atlanta like his dad and is a longtime friend of Suzanne's. Strangely, though, the story only takes off when Kip's nephew, David, is unjustly kicked off his middle school lacrosse team by Pamela Loncart: lacrosse mom, crooked DEA agent, girlfriend of the most powerful drug lord on the planet, and member of the Atlanta Tribe occult coven. Then it's Suzanne Delacroix battling Pamela Loncart— and much more.

Enough of a tease.

Hey, you can enjoy reading the books as standalone – and read them in any order you want, but, regardless, I hope you enjoy the total story. And who knows, the story may continue…

Tom Ranseen September 2024

PS. The story was written with a TV series in mind. Hope you will tune in when that happens. For more information, please go to www.gameoftwins.com.

eBook ISBN: 978-1-7324120-4-0

paperback ISBN 978-1-7324120-9-5

Author bio

Tom Ranseen is a longtime Nashville, TN business guy who now writes crime thrillers. His *Game of Twins* series includes *Game of Twins*, *Game of Twins – Kidnapped*, *Golden Frog Poison – Game of Twins*, and *Game of Twins – The Secret Agent* – and he's working on the 5th in his series. He loves that his two grown kids live in the Nashville area, and he spends a lot of time with his Airedale Terrier, Keri. As a Duke graduate, he's a fanatic college basketball fan.

The books are all available online at your favorite online bookseller as eBooks and paperbacks. The "anchor" book, Game of Twins is also available as an audiobook. Go to www.gameoftwins.com for more information.